THE STATION SERGEANT

BY
JOHN MCALLISTER

ₚ

Portnoy
PUBLISHING

First published in 2013 by Portnoy Publishing

1

Copyright © John McAllister 2013

ISBN: 978-1-909255-00-5

Printed and bound by CPI Group (UK) Ltd, Croydon, CR0 4YY

Cover design: David Rudnick

Typset in: Adobe Garamond by Sheer Design and Typesetting

Portnoy Publishing
PO Box 12093, Dublin 6, Ireland.

www.portnoypublishing.com :: Twitter: @portnoypub

CHAPTER 1

ALONG THE RIVER WERE ONLY farm dogs and evasive answers. They were the least of RUC Sergeant Barlow's problems. The BBC weatherman had forecast a dry morning with rain in the afternoon. Barlow glanced up at the sky. *If they'd mentioned a frigging downpour, I'd have sent someone else.* His police-issue cape was good at keeping the water out, but rubberised Cortex provided no comfort for a man on a chill December day. The bicycle ploughed through a puddle, spraying water onto his socks.

Barlow was feeling very frustrated. The farmers he was obliged to visit wouldn't give him a straight answer if their lives depended on it. He glowered at the sky through the battering rain. The clouds had the tone of old bread gone fusty, all pink and grey. The new moon lay on its back, so they could expect a month of this weather. A dead man's moon, he knew from hard-won experience. The constant rain and driving sleet at the turn of the year soured tempers and scoured old wounds.

Rolling hills caught the wind and the rain, and funnelled it at him. His cheeks reddened from cold. The spray from the puddle had soaked into his boots. Nearby a horse whinnied. It sounded miserable. *I know how you feel, son.* He pedalled harder to get some heat back into his toes.

Above his head an insulator exploded. A telephone wire whipped into the sky. The sound of gunfire came an instant later. He hurled himself off the bike and rolled into a ditch, his bulk setting up a tidal wave of icy rainwater that soaked through his shirt and ran up his sleeves. His heart started to pound.

A rifle, he thought, and drew his revolver. A touch of the catch and the barrel hinged forward. *Bloody hell!* The gun wasn't loaded. Searched his pouch for bullets and found a couple thick with grease and dotted with fluff. Thumbed them in, muttering, 'Hit the bugger with these and he's more likely to die of blood poisoning.'

His hands were shaking so much he nearly dropped one of the bullets into the ditch. 'Brass monkey weather,' he told himself to excuse the fumble. All the time, his eyes remained fixed on the hedge, half expecting a volley of bullets to tear through the sparse winter foliage. If he had a clear view of the farm buildings on the Denton Demesne, did that mean the gunman had a clear view of him?

More shots cracked out. From how far away was hard to judge in the blustering wind. He crouched even lower in the freezing water although no further shots were aimed in his direction. No bullets tore through the hedgerow. *Something light. A .22.*

He heard the thundering hooves of cattle, interspersed with bellows of pain. The sound of their panic came from behind him, across the road from the Denton Demesne. The ground-shaking rumble of the stampede quickly faded into the distance. The bellowing stopped, except for the plaintive lowing of a calf left behind. A blackbird began to sing. He sat back and looked at the hedge. Twelve foot high at that point, so the gunman probably hadn't seen him coming. *Some youngster acting the maggot.*

Barlow clambered to his feet, his gaze riveted on the farm buildings. The slightest movement from there and he'd jump right back into the freezing ditch. Water poured out of his cape. He yanked it off. The wind turned his policeman's uniform ice cold. It clung to his body and he began to shiver. Wished he still had his old uniform jacket. It buttoned tight to the neck. Trust Headquarters to go all modern with collars and ties right at the start of winter. *A man could catch his death.*

Having established that he was still alive and in no immediate danger, he let his temper build to a point where it might just overcome the fear he felt. 'Wait 'til I get my hands on that wee so and so. I'll wring his frigging neck.'

He kept his left arm tight across his chest, to protect his heart. If those bullets had hit someone there would be hell to pay. *As if I haven't enough problems at the minute.*

A kick-back in diving into the ditch had sent his bike wobbling over to the opposite side of the road. Keeping his revolver trained on the hedge, he backed over to the bike, hauled it upright and tried to work out what to do next. The stampeding cattle had been in a field across from the Denton Demesne and therefore not their problem so far as the injured livestock were concerned. But the shots had come from the Demesne. He checked his watch. *Nearly one o'clock.* The Demesne workers would be up at the Big House getting their lunch. So, they weren't in any danger. *Jammy bastards.* At the same time, most of them were former soldiers. At the very least they could have helped him spot the gunman.

Pitching himself with a pistol and only two bullets against a more than competent marksman with a rifle was a lonely thought. At that distance, with a revolver, he'd never hit the marksman, but he reckoned he could at least make the bugger duck. *If I have to?* The very thought of that eventuality made him shiver even harder.

Around the corner, a metal gate clanged against its retaining post.

Someone's making a run for it. He crouched, revolver at the ready. *What if they come this way?*

Waited a long minute. Then another. Sucked on an imaginary sweet to delay things further. No one came around the corner. The gunman had gone in the opposite direction. Barlow sighed in relief as he mounted his bike and rode on, keeping the front wheel close to the edge of the ditch. No harm being ready to dive for cover, just in case. No one was waiting to ambush him around the curve in the road, although twenty trees seemed to be aiming their branches at him.

He wondered what people would think if they saw him cycling up the road, gun at the ready. *Like a nervous virgin on his wedding night.* He holstered the revolver and approached the laneway leading to the farm buildings with extreme caution. Eyes watching everywhere at once, poised on his toes for flight, if necessary.

The gate continued to rattle in the wind. Fresh tyre tracks streaked out of the gateway onto the road. *A racing bike?* He leaned over for a closer look at the tyre tracks. *Definitely a narrow tread.* Nearly half that of his own bike. *Some young gobshite, with even dafter parents.*

Even as he watched, the pounding rain beat at the tyre tracks, blurring their outline. He balanced himself – one foot on the road, the other on a pedal – and sucked on an imaginary peppermint while he thought things through. No way could he catch someone on a racing bike. Sighed in feigned disappointment.

Another gust of wind reminded him that he was soaked to the skin. From memory, the stockmen on the Denton Demesne kept spare clothes in the grain store in case they got caught out in bad weather. He had to get out of his own clothes before he foundered and he was sure the stockmen wouldn't mind if he borrowed some of theirs. *It's an emergency after all.* Anyway, if they did mind, they wouldn't dare say.

A long forty yards of poured concrete laneway led from the gate to the farm buildings. When widening the original laneway Captain Denton had removed the flanking hawthorn hedges. Barlow warily eyed the wooden posts and strained barbed wire that now kept Denton's prize herd of Aberdeen Angus cattle from straying. *That fencing wouldn't provide enough cover for a flea.*

Any potential gunman still up there had to be hiding in the farm buildings, all of which were single-storey structures, with the exception of the combined byre and the hayshed. Barlow looked down at the mud again. The bicycle tracks were gone. Obliterated. He hawked phlegm, spat and pushed the gate open.

His head told him he was no longer in danger. His heart hammered away to catch up on the years it might never see. The walk along the forty yards to the first building seemed to go on forever. He'd forgotten the loneliness of those wartime walks. Stepping out from the nearest trench or wall of sandbags, in some now-forgotten street in London or Liverpool or Salford. Flies circling the trickle of cold sweat, collar damp-glued to his neck. Hearing cars in the distance, the odd horn blowing. *Holy Mary, Mother of God.* Standing over the bomb, listening for the tick, tick, tick. The last sound he'd ever hear.

Up ahead, something moved.

CHAPTER 2

Barlow stiffened, ready to run. *The way I came? Over the fence?* The revolver was back in his hand once again. He didn't remember drawing it. He spotted the movement the second time: the hayloft door swinging in the wind. But no sign of anyone moving it. Nothing. He couldn't watch everywhere at once. He needed flankers. Some of his old squad, guns at the ready. *Guns!* He laughed at himself. The only time his lot had carried guns was on the rifle range.

He began to breathe again and pushed on.

The farmyard was spotlessly clean. *Probably hosed down daily.* No chance of picking up footprints or tyre tracks in the odd corner. The cold from the wind and the rain bit further into him. Deep-down, bone-shivering cold, which made thinking difficult. Right now, he'd give anything to be back in his own house. Toes tight against the range and the rich aroma of stew simmering away on the side.

Maybe he should search the place? He started with the grain store and found the door locked. Gave it a good rattle and a shove, to be sure. Noticed a gap in the stonework. Stuck a finger in and found a key. *Thank God for fools.*

Inside, with the door closed behind him, the room seemed almost warm. Wooden feed bins lined the walls. The air held the musky smell of animal feed and pipe tobacco. A selection of work clothes hung from hooks.

Grateful for small mercies, he stripped to the skin. Towelled himself dry with a rag. Picked through the spare clothes and put on a heavy cotton shirt and overalls. The work clothes gave off a humid smell of cattle manure. He wrinkled his nose in disgust, but thought things could be worse: at least the Dentons didn't keep pigs.

He folded his uniform and underwear, and shoved them into an empty animal feed sack. Tied the sack to the back of his bike. Heat returned to his body, or rather the chill left it. Rubbed at his arms and legs to speed the heating process. Kept one eye trained on the window and the rain pelting down outside. Heading out into the rain again held no attraction, but it had to be done.

Maybe a cigarette first? He felt the packet, but it was wet, the tobacco soggy. 'Balls.' He flung the ruined cigarettes into a corner and swung the cape over his shoulders. Placed his police cap on his head. In a way, the cap was a comfort, a symbol of his authority. People stepped aside to let *Sergeant* Barlow pass.

He tried the remaining single-storey buildings one by one. Found all of them locked, the keys in place. The byre door opened with a slight push. The cow byre ran long and narrow straight ahead of him. His boots scrunched the grit on the smooth concrete, creating little echoes as he worked his way from stall to stall, revolver in hand. The stall dividers, made of thick planking, would stop a .22 rifle shot, but not a bullet from his Webley.

Two bullets? Frig!

He found nobody in the byre. Barely a wisp of straw on the ground, the open stalls providing no hiding place for man or gun. At the end of the building he stopped and caught his breath. Somebody had been here. Could still be here. Every instinct borne out of a lifetime of policing told him that. At least, with a bomb, he usually knew where it was lying.

Walked back to the middle of the building, looked up at the hatch leading to the hayloft. The hatch door hung down, open. No stockman would have left it like that. He cocked his revolver, cleared his throat noisily and spat.

'This is Sergeant Barlow,' he thundered. 'You up there, show yourself.'

Up above, he could hear the sound of straw rustling. His heart pounded. The straw rustled again and a blast of air came down the hatch. He remembered being outside and watching the hayloft door swinging in the breeze. It had to be that. Tried not to be too relieved. At least he hoped it was the wind, or a mouse, or a rat moving the straw.

'Last chance,' he called. 'If I have to go up there, I'll kick your arse into the middle of next week.'

Two planks, with a series of foot-holes cut out of them, served as a makeshift ladder leading to the hayloft. He climbed slowly. Made plenty of noise with his feet. Wanted anyone up there to know he was coming and not to startle them with his sudden appearance. Went through the hatch, revolver first. Crouched, checking for an ambush.

The loft had no windows. High-stacked bales of hay and straw stretched deep into dark recesses. The wind pushed loose straw around, making a crackling sound. All seemingly innocent, and yet…

He positioned himself for a quick getaway down the hatch and roared, 'Come out before I put a bullet up your arse.'

After a slow count to fifty and a longish hesitation, he relaxed and holstered his gun. A gleam caught his eye. Three spent shell cases lay close to the open hayloft door. He examined them carefully, but didn't touch them. As he thought: .22s. His knees creaked as he knelt over them and sniffed. The tart smell of fresh-fired gunpowder made him sneeze.

Rose to his feet again and stood in the hayloft doorway. Held tight against a blustering wind that threatened to suck him out. He could see the telegraph pole with the damaged insulator. The snapped wire lay entangled in the dead stalks of last summer's ragweed. The gunman had gone. Run. That he was sure of. In spite of the rain and the wind, the fields and hedgerows, the relief at being alive made the very clouds themselves seem fresh and new.

Remembering the stampede of panicked cattle a few minutes earlier, he looked away to the right. A herd of cattle stood huddled together against a distant hedge. Not one of them was grazing. A calf tried to work its way free of the group and got shoved back.

He growled. 'No countryman would panic animals that way. Yon bastard's away back into town by the tin bridge.'

His eyes followed a long strip of churned-up earth. The cattle had run from a nearby field, through an open gate into the corner where they now huddled. On the ground right beside the gate he could make out an unusual-looking lump. At first, he thought it was a calf that had fallen and been trampled into the mud. Slowly, as his eyes adjusted, the form took shape.

He was looking at the body of a man.

CHAPTER 3

BARLOW CAUGHT HIS BREATH. CARELESS shooting was one thing. A man lying dead or injured as a result of that shooting was something else. He jumped through the hatch, down into the byre. The man could still be alive.

He ran the length of the byre. Crashed the door shut in his wake. Grabbed his bike and pedalled furiously down the laneway and up the road to the field where the man lay. Found the gate secured by a complicated twist of barbed wire, and climbed over rather than waste time trying to undo the barbed wire. The gate groaned under his solid form and the gatepost swayed sickeningly, but held firm. He charged up the field. The rain-sodden ground slurped underfoot. With each step he had to fight his boots free of mud and fresh cow dung. Air rasped into his lungs from the effort. He slowed his run rather than risk a heart attack.

The gateway between the two fields was a mud bath. The man lay face down, half buried in a glár of dung and rain-soaked soil. Cattle hooves had churned the ground all around the body. Barlow stopped at the edge of the glár. *He's definitely dead.* A hoof had gone through the back of the man's head, compressing bone and scalp deep into the skull. Grey brain matter and gouts of blood formed a halo around the head and shoulders. What he could see of the coat – a fawn stockman's clothes-saver: worn into holes and tied at the waist by a length of baler twine – confirmed it for him. It was the owner of the land. Stoop Taylor: farmer, former soldier and part-time dealer in second-hand machinery.

Seeing Stoop lying like this caught Barlow in the throat. The older World War Two soldiers were beginning to die off. Stoop had been lucky to get home alive. Despite his injuries, or perhaps because of them, he'd returned with a German wife and a son.

Stoop's wife would have to be told. The news broken to her. The rain continued to teem down. It seemed wrong to leave Stoop's dead body just lying there. The man deserved to have someone standing honour guard. *What if the wife comes looking for him?* Yet he had no choice but to abandon the body in order to alert his people in the police station.

He stepped into the glár, took off his cape and covered Stoop's head and shoulders. Then he backed away. This was a suspicious death. He didn't want Detective Sergeant bloody Leary moaning about a contaminated crime scene.

He needed access to a phone. The Big House on the Denton Demesne? *Too far away.* Was that smoke coming from Stoop's chimney? Stoop's wife – the German frau – must be in. He examined his clothes: the heavy work shirt and the overalls. The state of me, I can't go in there dressed like this. *It's not respectful.* Then he remembered that Stoop's late brother, William, had owned the adjoining farm. The brother's wife, known locally as the Widow Taylor, still lived there, and she had a phone.

He trudged down the hill, figuring the list of upcoming problems. Stoop's suspicious death, and possible murder, meant big trouble and the recently appointed Acting District Inspector, DI Harvey, seemed just the sort to overreact. Maybe he should phone Captain Denton first. After all, he was a Justice of the Peace, as well as the Chairman of the local Policing Advisory Board, and he could be on the scene in five minutes. Then he remembered. Denton had taken the entire family on a winter cruise. Barlow nodded in approval. Not bad for a man who started life as an under-gardener at Ballymena Castle. *And got fired for cheeking his future wife.* All the same, trust Charlie Denton to be away when he was really needed.

Barlow climbed over the field gate and cycled back the way he'd come. A dog shot out of an old chicken house, snarled and bared its teeth.

'I'll teach you manners,' Barlow roared, taking one foot off a pedal and aiming a kick at the dog. The dog swerved. The bicycle skidded. Barlow straightened it as he swore at the dog. Cattle on the other side of the road craned their necks in curiosity. Even though they had the benefit of shelter in a lean-to, they still looked miserable.

Barlow turned up the laneway beside the chicken house. The dog ran ahead. The bike rattled and banged over ruts ground into the earth by generations of carts. *The Widow Taylor. Stoop might be her brother-in-law, but how will she take the news?* Not too badly, he hoped, thinking he'd enough problems with his own women at home. The wife not well again and the daughter... He couldn't say Vera was slacking at her studies, but boys – one boy in particular – had come into her life ... And ...

Nobody was in the farmyard. He propped the bike up against the wall and strode over to the house. A half-door opened onto a small porch. The porch was in the lee of the wind, and dry apart from a few swirled drops of water on the tiled floor. A holly wreath hung from a peg on the hallstand.

He banged on the main door. 'Police,' he shouted when it failed to open quickly.

The Widow Taylor appeared from the kitchen. She wore an apron over a jumper and a tweed skirt. He'd never seen her dressed up before. She normally wore old work clothes. The blue of the Campbell tartan scarf lifted the colour of her eyes.

Damp air from cooking wafted around her. She appeared anxious, like most people when the police turned up at their door.

'Can I use your phone to contact the station, Missis?'

She nodded. He wished she wouldn't do that. He'd learned over the years, from visits to the farm to do the Tillage Returns, that a nod meant she'd made up her mind: sometimes in agreement, sometimes in disagreement. But always a nod. It confused him no end.

'Come in,' she said. Her voice held no warmth; neither did she express any surprise at his outfit. She nodded again and led the way into the kitchen. Placed the kettle on the range.

He stood, uncertain about what to do next. Stoop's sudden death would give her a shock. He couldn't just blurt it out down the phone, with her listening. Other than the wreath, there were no decorations to be seen. *And it three days before Christmas.*

She pushed a chair away from the table. 'Sit there while you make your call.'

The deal table was scrubbed white. His cap made a stain of damp on the wood. Took it off and set it on the flagged floor. Settled himself and reached for the phone.

'I've a bit of bad news, Missis. Your brother-in-law …'

'So he's dead.'

He looked at her in surprise. She nodded for a third time and went back to the range. Fussed over soda breads on the griddle, turning them upside down. 'Sergeant Barlow, if he was injured, you'd phone the ambulance people first.'

'You're right. Anyway I'm sorry.'

He'd forgotten she was quick on the uptake. Read *The Times*. Borrowed books from Mr and Mrs Savage's Lending Library rather than use the public one. *Maybe a bit above herself? But no harm in that.*

He picked up the receiver, almost surprised at hearing a dial tone. The broken telephone wire lying in the field must run in the other direction. Sergeant Pierson answered. *What's he doing out of the cell block?* Got put through to the new District Inspector's yes man, Inspector Foxwood.

Foxwood was English. *With a name like Clarence, he has to be.* In Barlow's opinion only two types of Englishmen came to work in Northern Ireland: Englishmen who hadn't succeeded at home and Englishmen who married a Northern Irish girl who wanted home to mummy. On the whole, Barlow thought Foxwood a good officer, in spite of his practice of sucking up to superiors and his disdain for anyone or anything west of Liverpool. Foxwood's wife came from Belfast. When he got his next promotion, Foxwood would head in that direction. *And he's welcome to it.*

Foxwood listened to Barlow's account without interrupting him. Then asked a few succinct questions. *A bit of commonsense there.* The Widow Taylor placed a mug of tea in front of Barlow. He quickly drained the mug and she offered him a refill. 'Easy on the sugar this time, Missis.' He nodded in the direction of the second heaped spoonful – *that bloody nodding is catching* – and she stirred it in.

Foxwood told him to remain where he was. He'd organise roadblocks to catch the gunman, then he'd be straight out.

Barlow sipped his tea slowly, prolonging his enjoyment of the second mugful. The hot liquid seeped through his body. By the time it reached his toes, the chill that had resulted from his earlier drenching was beginning to recede.

The widow stirred a pot of stew for her supper. An even bigger pot held porridge for the pigs. A tart smell of pie emanated from the oven. Apple, he guessed. The waft of fresh food made him hungry. He could have eaten the porridge destined for the pigs. But the widow didn't offer any, and he didn't like to ask.

'You'll be wanting the good room to talk in private?' she said.

'If you don't mind.' Felt he should say something about Stoop. 'Did you see much of your brother-in-law?'

'No. He and my husband fell out. They never spoke after that.'

'Aye,' he said, the memory coming back to him.

When she died – about 1950 or 51, according to Barlow's recollection – the mother of the two Taylor brothers had left most of the land to William, the Widow Taylor's then husband. William and his wife lived well on fifty acres. His brother Stoop and his wife struggled to make ends meet on twenty acres. The uneven division of land in the mother's will had caused a rift between the brothers – a rift that had never healed.

The Widow Taylor kept herself busy at the range. He tried to say something nice about Stoop. Found it hard going. Stoop would take a drink if offered, but seldom bought one back.

By now, the rain had eased to a hard mizzle. Barlow slipped out of the kitchen to his bike and brought in the Tillage Book. Unwrapped it from its oilcloth cover and waved it in her direction. 'The census.'

Her head nodded sharply. 'You're not due. You only come every second year.'

'Aye, Missis.' He didn't need telling. Tillage Books were for pleasant summer afternoons when even the town's hard men and troublemakers put their feet up and watched the world go by.

She nodded again; he thought she looked sympathetic. 'Not a couple of days before Christmas, and in battering rain.'

'The new District Inspector does things differently,' Barlow replied.

He worked ponderously through the ledger. Could have answered the questions himself without bothering to call on her. The Widow Taylor maintained a strict rotation of crops: wheat, root and fallow. The animals remained the same: six cows, six followers and six calves. He kept his eye on the page so that she wouldn't confuse him with her nods.

As he reached the last question, she suddenly observed: 'There must be more to life than your ledger.'

He looked up, startled at the anger in her voice. 'Sometimes I wonder myself, Missis.' Couldn't think what else to say, so he drank his tea. The widow nodded vigorously and they finished the census.

It was always the same with her: never welcoming, but never unfriendly. A kind soul, people said. Her only son dead in the Korean War and her husband the year before that of pneumonia. With fifty acres to her name, she could have got herself another husband, but she met every approach with a steady rebuff.

'Funny woman,' he said to himself as he went to greet the police reinforcements.

CHAPTER 4

ACTING DISTRICT INSPECTOR HARVEY BRUSHED past Barlow and stood in the cramped porch, head jerking to and fro, working out where to go next. Harvey barely achieved minimum height for a policeman, and even the smallest size uniform managed to look loose on him. Barlow reckoned Harvey was too mean to spend money on food. Whatever Harvey did manage to eat got burned off by his quick, nervous ways.

'Barlow, you're out of uniform. Foxwood, make a note.'

Barlow blocked the doorway, thereby keeping Foxwood out in the rain. 'I got soaked, sir.'

'You're on report.'

'Very good, sir.' He registered Harvey's flicker of annoyance. The man had expected an argument, which would mean that Barlow could be charged with insubordination as well. *I'm not that easily caught.*

Barlow led them into the parlour that doubled as a dining room for guests. Even with the light on, the room was dark and gloomy. The cream chintz settee looked out of place among the heavy Victorian furniture. The sideboard featured a permanent shrine to the widow's dead son. Pictures, mainly of him as a child; hair cropped to a heavy fringe. A last photograph before he went off to Korea. His medals and badges set out on a purple cushion. The smell of Mansion House polish hung heavy in the air. Barlow touched the boy's identity discs, remembering a lanky youth with a screwed-up nose and lips that couldn't keep from smiling.

'When you're quite ready, Sergeant,' said District Inspector Harvey. He'd taken up position at the top of the table. Back straight, head held high. Inspector Foxwood sat to the side, fountain pen unscrewed, ready to take notes.

Barlow made his report. Harvey remained silent until Barlow described the gunman escaping by bike. 'You didn't pursue?'

'No, sir.'

'You let a killer get away?'

He remained silent. Harvey had his own opinions and nothing would change them. Personally, he preferred the old District Inspector's standing instructions when it came to dealing with trouble: "Don't get your fool head stove in. Think of the paperwork."

Inspector Foxwood skimmed the pen down his notes. 'This suspicious death ... 'He hesitated, clearly uneasy at correcting District Inspector Harvey. 'Suspicious death coincidental with a gunman being in the area.'

Barlow noted that Foxwood didn't say murder and abbreviated the rest of his report, anxious to get out of the room. Harvey ordered Barlow to change back into his uniform, wet or not, and proceed to the deceased's house. He could tell deceased's wife that her husband was dead, if it hadn't already been done.

Harvey said, 'Final point, Barlow. Don't forget you're on report. My office tomorrow morning, nine o'clock sharp.'

On his way out of the house, Barlow put his head round the kitchen door, wanting to thank the widow for her hospitality. She wasn't there. Instead, Constable Gillespie was sitting at the kitchen table, looking very comfortable, a slice of soda bread in one hand and a second waiting on a plate. Barlow was dying to nag at Gillespie for malingering, but Harvey's attitude had got him annoyed. The way he felt, a couple of sharp remarks between himself and Gillespie could turn into a real argument.

Gillespie had a doctor's chitty for everything, other than driving his beloved squad car: bad feet, bad back, damaged knee cartilage and weak chest. Despite these disabilities, he managed to frequently stand for days on end in icy water trying to land a salmon, or tramp across bogs on a rough shoot. If a couple of fish didn't appear on a certain sergeant's doorstep soon, Gillespie would find himself doing a lot of foot patrols.

'You've to run me around to Stoop's place,' he said, as if the order had come directly from Harvey.

Gillespie gave a pathetic cough and tapped his chest.

'Unless you want me to take the squad car myself.'

Gillespie instantly grabbed his cap. 'I'm with you, Sarge.'

'Aye.'

He went on ahead of Gillespie. Retrieved his uniform from the sack, slipped into an open shed in the yard, and changed behind bales of straw. His skin recoiled as the ice-cold underwear slid over his body. The uniform hung heavy with wet. 'Life's a bugger,' he said, and got into the car.

In two minutes they were at Stoop's house. Gillespie complained the whole way there. That wet uniform would destroy the leather seats. The stain would never come out.

Barlow instructed Gillespie to wait in the car. Then, standing in Stoop's yard, he looked up. Between the roof of the house and the sky lay the disputed thirty acres of land that had been willed to Stoop's brother, William, and thereafter to his wife, Alexandra. That had to rankle with Stoop, especially every time he saw the Widow Taylor bringing in her cows for milking. Barlow realised that from now on he needed to refer to William's wife as the Widow Taylor, the name she was known by locally. Stoop's widow he'd refer to as Frau Taylor. Otherwise he'd get the two of them totally muddled up in his head.

He could see the Widow Taylor up on the hill now. The dog ran with her, nipping at the heels of the milk cows to move them on. An old pony limped beside her. He checked his watch. *It's a bit earlier than normal,* he thought. *On the other hand it's a bad day and the cattle are better in out of the rain.*

On the road a car pulled up and a woman got out holding a brown bag carefully in front of her. The first neighbour arriving with food for the wake. *How in the name of God do they find out these things?* But it was always the same in the country. The first sign of trouble and neighbours you hadn't spoken to in years were suddenly there to lend a hand. Anyway, the neighbouring woman was a bit premature. Frau Taylor would want time to compose herself before she'd be fit to receive visitors.

He said to one of the constables at the gate. 'Keep her back for a few minutes,' and stepped carefully across Stoop's yard.

Stoop's home was a cotter house: four rooms in all, with an extension at the back for a bathroom. The paintwork had blistered with age. The roofs of the outbuildings canted inwards and second-hand machinery choked the yard. He stared in surprise at the number of horse-drawn harrows and ploughs lying there. *What was Stoop doing with that lot? They'll never sell.* Not when even the most tight-fisted farmers were digging deep to buy Ferguson tractors.

Barlow got the smell of damp before he even entered the house. But at least – *Thank the Good Lord* – it wasn't up to him to break the bad news. Inside, he could see the Frau and her son sitting in the small living room with WPC Day and Trainee Constable Jackson. The air hung thick with fug from the coal fire burning in the grate. In the corner, blue mould stained the wallpaper. WPC Day was doing the talking. *She's a good one for showing sympathy.* He also liked the fact that Day thrived on difficult tasks. *Now if I could only get her to take her head out of wedding books and do those sergeant exams.*

The Frau looked shocked and upset as she absorbed the news of her husband's death. She wore a washed-out cardigan over a long, shapeless dress. The boy chewed his lip, and huddled into himself.

Stoop and the Frau, if he remembered right, had met on the Elbe in 1945, so the boy had to be about fourteen. He seemed older. *Stoop and his mean ways would age anybody.*

All four were staring at a glimmer of a fire. They looked up as he entered. He frowned. No talk from the Taylors, a bad sign, and no tea either. A cup of tea settled shock and got people chatting. "Milk, sugar? You'll take a sandwich? A bun?"

Behind the bare stair treads he saw a shelf with the family's food set out: a bit of butter on a saucer, a batch loaf with the heel cut off. In the corner sat a sack of potatoes. *Maybe the Frau doesn't have anything to offer visitors?*

From upstairs came a sound. *Mice?* That wouldn't surprise him. 'I'm sorry for your trouble, Missis,' he said.

'Thank you.' It sounded like 'Zank you.'

The sound from upstairs came again. 'Is there anybody else in the house?'

'Nein,' said the Frau.

'No,' said the boy.

Both spoke too quickly.

'Who else would there be?' asked WPC Day.

Barlow glared. Jackson was fresh out of training college, and knew as much about real life as a baby in a pram. WPC Day should have known better.

He stepped into the kitchen and looked up the stairs. A shadow moved against the back wall; the shadow of a man with his arm sticking out. A long arm, with something bulkier than fingers at the end of it.

CHAPTER 5

BARLOW HOPED THE SHADOW WOULD go away, that it was his imagination. He flicked up the flap of his holster and checked to his left. All four people in the living room were staring at him, the Frau and the boy stiff with fear. The Frau looked close to tears. WPC Day and Jackson appeared mildly curious. He longed to throttle them for their lack of caution in the house of a victim, when a shooting had occurred and the gunman was still at large.

Barlow said, casually, 'Constable Day, Gillespie's in the yard, fussing over the car. Would you tell him I said to lock and load.'

'What?' she asked.

'Now,' he said. They could all be dead and those two would still be wondering what it was all about.

WPC Day stood up, stiff with indignation. 'Yes, Station Sergeant.' She took her time walking past him and out of the house. He itched to put a toe up her backside to hurry her on.

The shadow upstairs hadn't moved. *Maybe it's the light bouncing off the outline of a wardrobe or something?* A false alarm like that would take some living down with Gillespie.

The Frau came to her feet.

'Please sit down,' Barlow said, still sounding relaxed.

The sound of running footsteps could be heard coming from the yard. The door opened and Gillespie tiptoed in. 'Lock and load, are you serious?'

Barlow nodded and drew his own revolver. Had the shadow changed shape? *Someone leaning forward in order to hear better?* Wardrobes didn't do that. His heart fluttered in fear. 'Is your revolver loaded?' he asked Gillespie.

'What for?'

He pointed at the shadow.

'Bloody hell,' said Gillespie, and stepped to the other side of the stairs. Barlow nodded his approval. Bunched-up forces made easy targets. He kept the shadow covered while Gillespie loaded his revolver. Gillespie had six bullets. He didn't dare ask if Gillespie had any spares to go with the two that remained in his own revolver. Barlow knew he had become careless. But, against that, in twenty-five years of policing, his fists and his truncheon were all that he'd ever needed.

At long last, Trainee Constable Jackson realised something was wrong, and jumped to his feet. The Frau screamed. The boy shouted a warning in German and dived at Jackson's knees. The two of them tumbled to the ground and thrashed about among the fire irons.

'Bullshit!' Barlow said as the shadow disappeared. Used his revolver to track the sound of running footsteps from the room up above, but he didn't fire. A window screeched open. He and Gillespie formed a plug in the doorway as a man dived through the upper window.

The man did a back flip in mid-air and rolled, parachutist style. His hip caught the edge of an old plough and he came to an abrupt stop at WPC Day's feet. She squealed and kicked. A pistol went flying. The man tried to stand up. Barlow took a running jump from the kitchen doorway and crashed onto his back. The air whooped out of them both.

Barlow rolled clear. Mouth open, nothing going in or coming out. Wondered if he'd ever breathe again. Lay helpless as Gillespie slapped handcuffs on the man. WPC Day burst into tears. Jackson appeared in the doorway, limping, holding the boy firmly by the scruff of the neck.

Dung now covered almost every inch of Barlow's uniform, *bloody shit in hell*, because Stoop kept a dirty farmyard. He sucked in one deep, delicious breath, then another. Clambered to his feet and stood looking down at the man. *First a rifle, and now a pistol? What's wrong with these people?*

The man they'd captured was long and thin. So thin, in fact, his cheeks appeared to be sucked in. He had cropped blond hair and the wartime eyes of someone who had seen too much. What they called the thousand-yard stare.

Barlow didn't want to look at those eyes. He had hoped never to see eyes like that ever again. He'd seen a battalion of them, or what was left of it, after the Royal Ulster Rifles came back from Korea. Buying the boys drinks and turning a blind eye when things got out of hand never seemed enough.

The Frau knelt in the muck beside the man. She crooned to him in words he couldn't understand.

'Missis, come away from the prisoner,' said Gillespie.

'He is my husband,' she said.

Barlow closed his eyes. This had turned into one hell of a day.

The rain had started again. That, and only that, made sense.

CHAPTER 6

DUSK HAD FALLEN BY THE time Barlow cycled into the station yard. Every push on the pedals had resulted in water pumping through the eyelets of his boots. He'd given up contemplating which was worse: his hunger headache or the smell of fresh manure that enveloped him. Gillespie had refused to give him a lift in the squad car. *You'd think he owned the bloody thing.* And District Inspector Harvey had told him that the local members of the Masonic Order were right when they referred to Barlow as a clown and an imbecile.

'That would be the Mayor, Mr Fetherton,' Barlow had responded.

'I'm told you've hounded the Mayor and many of the local Masons, for years. Well that is going to stop.'

'Sir, the Masons do a lot of charity work and they do it quietly. But a clique of them is using the power of the Masonic Order to line their own pockets.' Barlow couldn't keep the anger out of his voice. 'They've cost this town a fortune in rigged contracts and sweetheart deals, and I intend to jail the pack of them, starting with our Mayor.'

Harvey had looked indignant. 'My office, nine o'clock tomorrow morning. Let's see if you're so smart then.'

Barlow dumped his bike against the yard wall. Gillespie had the squad car parked well clear and the hosepipe ready. A jet of water hit Barlow before he could undo the first button of his jacket. 'What the bloody hell do you think you're doing?'

'You want the shite off the clothes, don't you?'

Barlow's fingers were thick with cold. The chill water made it almost impossible to undress. 'You'll be the death of me.'

Gillespie said, 'What about me and my chest, out in this weather?

Two soap-downs and a rinse later Barlow made a run for the back door. The jet of water pursued him to the last step. The rain continued to fall steadily. He stopped on the doorstep for a moment and looked up at the rain falling out of the dark sky into the lights of the yard. With a bit of luck it would continue for a few days. He'd make sure Gillespie got his feet wet. Hopefully, his alleged *chest* would carry him off.

Inside the police station a change of clothes awaited him. Someone had taken them out of his locker. And that someone – WPC Day, he guessed – had gone to the trouble of airing them over the stove. He towelled down quickly, dressed and went into the kitchen. His legs hung heavy, every step a deliberate effort.

WPC Day was waiting there for him. She handed him a mug of tea cool enough to down in one go. 'Are you all right, Papa Bear?'

'Oh, I'm "Papa Bear" now?' But he was too miserably cold to feel satisfaction at her looking remorseful.

He took his time over a second mugful. His body warmed up to the point where he was now shaking with cold. WPC Day served him leftover brown stew and a slice of bread thickly spread with butter. The knife and fork wouldn't coordinate in his hands. He used a spoon on the brown stew, and gulped the cool tea every time his mouth burnt.

She sat across the table from him. He nodded, approvingly. She'd done well at the farm. Instinct and training had kicked in when it mattered. But he didn't like the pucker between her eyes. She was twenty-four and anxious in case she missed out on a husband and a family. Most of her friends were married with children.

Twenty-four? He could nearly double that.

'If your boyfriend doesn't pop the question soon, I'll marry you myself.'

'Your wife and daughter wouldn't like it.'

'There's that to it,' he said, pushing the mug over for another refill.

Sergeant Pierson bustled in, all business. Barlow made his face expressionless. He kept Pierson in charge of cells and detainees, and any other dead-end job going. Pierson aspired to making inspector grade and didn't mind who he walked on. The District Inspector before Harvey had seen through Pierson, but now he was Harvey's blue-eyed boy. Pierson wore Old Spice aftershave, which irritated Barlow's sinuses.

'The only man in custody is the German, Kurt Adenauer,' announced Pierson. 'The doctor noted some fresh bruising, presumably caused while attempting to escape. All other injuries date back several years and are not relevant to this case.'

Pierson's voice hurt Barlow's aching head. Pierson could have been a town crier, the way he was bawling in Barlow's ear.

'What's he charged with?'

'Possession of an offensive weapon, with intent. Other charges may follow.'

He'd rather choke than give Pierson the satisfaction of asking, 'What other charges?'

WPC Day said, 'We searched Stoop's house and found a .22 rifle. The German is probably the gunman who shot at you.'

'That'll give DS Leary something to do.'

'It means a lot of paperwork. He'll lose his Christmas leave.'

'Shame about that.' All the same, he thought, catching the German was handy. It stopped District Inspector Harvey from instigating a witch hunt for the gunman. Pulling in all known troublemakers. Stirring up all kinds of bother over Christmas.

Pierson said, with contrived casualness, 'The DI had a word with me. I'm being reassigned tomorrow.'

He knew the job Pierson was hoping to get. Rather than stay quiet, he said, 'I wouldn't allocate you "Paper clips and stationery".'

Pierson gave a derisive laugh and left the room.

WPC Day's grip tightened on his arm. 'Papa Bear, Harvey has been on to Headquarters. He wants you transferred.'

He'd been expecting this. Nonetheless, he felt sucker punched. He stuttered. 'I was born in Ballymena and I've been stationed here since before the war.'

'First or Second?' she asked, trying to be light-hearted for him.

'The Boer War,' he said.

The awful way he was feeling now, it could easily have been the Crimean War.

CHAPTER 7

BARLOW THOUGHT HE'D DO A tour of the station and then head home. In every department heads were down, conversation strictly business. Word had got around that Barlow was in trouble with the higher-ups. No one wanted to add to his problems.

Long before he reached the Enquiry Office, he heard the row, and Constable Jackson's voice rise in temper. 'This isn't a hotel, you know. And leave that fire alone.'

He heard someone give the coal fire a final poke, then a beautifully modulated voice said, 'It's Christmas and no man should be alone at Christmas. Please inform Mr Barlow that Edward would appreciate the usual room.'

'Cells. They're cells. And you can't just book in.'

'But, my dear chap, I always do.'

Barlow came around the corner and into the Enquiry Office. The office had a wood plank floor and a high counter to protect the duty officers from the drafts created by the arriving and departing public. The room also held a few rickety wooden chairs; the coal fire was designed to give the room the illusion of heat. Jackson was leaning over the counter, threatening the visitor with a pencil. 'If you don't leave right now I'll do you for wasting police time.'

Mr Edward Adair, gentleman and tramp by profession, smiled at Jackson's youthful enthusiasm. He continued to warm his hands at the flames. The heat caught his breath and he coughed.

Sergeant Pierson stood behind the counter. Pierson looked guilty. Barlow was sure he'd heard confidential books – the Station Sergeant's books to be precise – being put away as he walked down the corridor. 'Shouldn't you be mopping out the cells or something?' he said, looking directly at Pierson.

'Sergeant, this man won't go,' said Constable Jackson. He sounded like a schoolboy caught out not doing his homework.

'Changed times, Edward,' Barlow said to the tramp, feeling sorry for the man because he looked so damp and miserable A wisp of steam curled up from his shabby greatcoat.

'And my accommodation for the festive season?' asked Edward.

'New inspector, new rules.' Barlow held his hands high in a gesture of despair. 'There's more than you getting their marching orders.

Edward vibrated with indignation. 'So it's like that, Mr Barlow. And after all these years?' He coughed again.

'Aye.'

Edward pointedly buttoned his coat as he prepared to leave. 'And a happy Christmas to you.'

'Would you move out of that hut before you catch your death of cold?' Barlow called after him.

Edward stuck his nose in the air. The front door closed behind him.

Jackson scratched at himself to remove imagined fleas. 'Sarge, who is that old drunk?'

Barlow shot behind the counter and prodded Jackson hard in the chest. 'That old drunk, as you call him, is *Mister* Edward Adair.' He prodded a second time.

Jackson retreated. 'Easy, Sarge.'

'*Mister* Edward Adair is a friend of Captain Denton. And –.' The finger pushed gently against Jackson's cringing breastbone. 'Call me "Sarge" once more, and you'll be on nights 'til kingdom come.'

They heard Harvey's tiptoe footsteps in the corridor. Jackson made himself busy straightening the Incident Book. Barlow raised his voice. 'Are you looking for something sir?'

Harvey stepped into view. 'Sergeant Pierson, new Orders of the Day.' He slapped a sheet of paper on the counter and marched off.

Barlow picked up the paper:

DAILY ORDERS

Ballymena is now a 'no crime' area. No contravention of the law will be tolerated.

ALL crimes will be reported, with a view to prosecution.

Harvey came tiptoeing back. 'Pierson, tell Gillespie I won't need him tonight. I'll take my own car to the Round Table Ball. And, Jackson, I need another packet of cigarillos.'

Barlow snorted in disgust. The old District Inspector had always got his own cigarettes. And his own vodka to hide in his bottom drawer. And while he might have cursed like a trooper, he never insulted a man by ignoring them the way Harvey had just ignored him.

He signed himself out. Went home to do a lot of hard thinking.

CHAPTER 8

THAT NIGHT BARLOW COULDN'T SLEEP. He got up, pulled on an old overcoat for warmth and went down to the kitchen. He didn't poke up the fire in the range, fearing the rattle of metal on metal would disturb his daughter, Vera. With all that schoolwork and studying over the past few months she needed all the sleep she could get.

Without having to get out of the chair, he reached up to the overhead clothesline and rubbed his fingers against his uniform. The trousers were still saturated but, with the exception of the shoulders and collar, the jacket was almost wearable. Vera's school uniform hung on the clothesline beside his uniform. He wondered what she really thought of the cramped house they lived in, and the area generally. The millrace across the way was choked with broken furniture and pram wheels. The houses in Mill Row where they lived, barely habitable. Vera never brought anybody home. Heart and soul, he himself hated the house, *but needs must.*

He made a pot of tea and sat back to think. So far, he had let Harvey make all the running. His only possible ally was Captain Denton, the Justice of the Peace, and he was out of the country. Maybe somebody at Headquarters could lose the paperwork? Delay his transfer until Captain Denton got back.

A long night spent in front of the range yielded no obvious solution. How Maggie, Barlow's wife, would cope with a change of town, God alone knew. Then there was Vera's schooling to think of. He tried to ignore his own feelings on the move.

He roused himself at the sound of the mill horn blowing to rouse their workers. He stripped the clothes from his body and threw them in a corner. Shaved and did a whole-body wash, standing at the sink in the scullery. Wrapped the roller-towel around his waist and went looking for his best uniform. Vera stumbled downstairs just as he was finishing his morning porridge.

She was wearing a pink dressing gown that had moulded comfortably into her body shape with the passing of the years. Vera had inherited his bulky build and was tall for a girl. He could hardly believe that she was seventeen. Nearly eighteen, as she kept pointing out. *Where have the years gone?*

His cooking began and ended with the frying pan, which didn't help Vera's figure. Recently, however, Maggie's old cookbooks had begun to appear on the kitchen table. Vera had taken up cooking and hadn't managed to poison them all yet.

'Aren't you for school?' he asked her.

'It's the Christmas holidays, Da.'

'What about Woolworths then?' He checked his watch. 'You don't want to be late.'

'They want me again on Boxing Day.' She poured herself a cup of tea. 'You go on. I'll take Ma up her breakfast.'

He remained seated. 'So, how are you going to spend your day?'

'This and that, see some of the girls. Maybe go to Caufields for a coffee.'

He nodded as if he agreed with her. *For girls substitute boys, and one boy in particular.* He wasn't supposed to know about Kenny Cameron and their budding romance.

He said, 'As soon as my back's turned you'll put on those tight American jean things you wear.'

She gasped. 'How do you know…?'

'I know,' he said levelly. Every policeman in the town had instructions to report back where they had seen her, with whom and what they were up to. The policewomen were particularly good at it, especially when it came to details about clothes.

She said, 'It was my own money, I saved it up.'

He spooned the last mouthful of porridge, but held it on the plate while he stared at her. She forced a smile, obviously unsure of his reaction. His stare turned to a nod as he reached a decision. 'I'd have bought them for you for Christmas if you'd said.'

She shook her head as if not hearing him right. 'What?'

Now that he'd made the decision, he had to bite down a smile. 'They couldn't be any more indecent than the way you roll up your skirt before you get to the school gates.'

'Frig, you never miss a bar.' After a while she got up.

'Where are you going?'

'To take Ma up a cup.'

'I'll do it.'

She moved to the scullery. 'It's no bother. You have your breakfast in peace.'

'I'll do it,' he said, and couldn't keep a rumble of impatience out of his voice.

He waited in the living room until she had poured the tea and buttered some bread, then he took them from her and carried them up the tight stairs. Maggie lay in the middle of an iron-frame bed. Her eyes were open yet she didn't see him come in. With a double bed, a chest of drawers and a wardrobe, there was barely enough room for him to reach across to the one and only window in the room and pull the curtains open.

'Maggie.'

Eyes focused on him from a face sunk with exhaustion.

'Your breakfast, love.'

'I don't want any.'

'Ah now, love, you have to eat. And didn't Vera buy the mug for you herself.'

He put the plate holding the thin slices of bread on the bed. She struck at the plate, knocking it to the floor.

'Later,' she said in a tired voice.

Everything was "later" when he could do with her talking to Vera about the facts of life. Now. Not in six months' time or a year's time, when it would be too late.

He retrieved the plate and the bread. Sat on the edge of the bed and touched her arm. It lay rigid with tension. He cajoled and gently bullied her – 'Eat up now or you won't get better' – until, finally, she drank the tea and nibbled at the bread. He fetched her metal comb and hand mirror. She showed no interest in tidying her hair, so he went downstairs again and put the mug and plate on the kitchen table. The red poppies on the mug blazed like a posy of flowers in the otherwise colourless room.

'How is she?' asked Vera.

'Not a good day.' He couldn't hold back a sigh. 'Not a good day at all.'

Vera gave him a warmer of tea and he nodded his thanks. She busied herself making a show of unpacking her leather schoolbag to do a bit of studying. Gave the bag an impatient thump. 'I don't know why I bother. I'll never get a decent job.'

'Maybe Woolworths will give you more than Saturday work?'

She dumped the bag on the floor and sat down again. 'I don't want to be a shop girl all my life.'

She became flushed and upset and he didn't know what to do. He fought down the temptation to remind her that, before the Second World War, people with degrees dug ditches and many a good family starved.

He compromised with. 'A decent job is one where you wash before you go to work, not when you get back.'

'You know what I mean, Da.'

'I do.'

He did and he didn't. As a young man, he'd thumped a drunk getting the better of a policeman. As well as thanking him, the police inspector had produced the application form to join the RUC, and had insisted that Barlow sign it.

Barlow got up and carried his mug and plate to the scullery. Placed them in the sink, went back to the living room, pulled up his braces and slipped on his jacket. Vera made a fuss of helping him, using a clothes brush on his shoulders to knock off some dandruff.

At the door he turned. She still looked upset. The high colour clashed with the natural red of her cheeks. She was still his child, but her eyes had already seen too much. It pained him to acknowledge that his wee girl was growing up and learning about life. He nodded to her and went out the door.

His bike lay where he'd left it against the house wall. It sat there unsecured every night. Dare anyone touch it. They and their family would regret it for a long time.

He checked the tyres with his thumb, *still hard enough*, mounted it, rang the bell and looked up at the bedroom window. On a good day he got a wave. That day nothing.

'Happy Christmas,' he said to himself – it was the day before Christmas Eve – and he set off for the police station.

CHAPTER 9

Barlow arrived for work earlier than usual. He found Sergeant Pierson in the Enquiry Office, surveying the world that he fervently hoped would soon be his. Barlow sniffed and got the smell of Old Spice and of the great unwashed.

Sniffed again. The great unwashed became the odour of a farmstead. Someone had trekked fresh manure across the wooden floor. 'You've had a farmer in?'

Pierson condescended to say, 'Tommy Abernathy reported four cattle missing.'

'Knowing Abernathy, they've probably strayed.' Other than that, he ignored Pierson and checked the Incident Book. *A quiet night.* A couple of the young Dunlops arrested for being drunk and disorderly. A verbal warning issued to another lout. No doubt accompanied by a boot up the backside.

The front door opened. Edward Adair progressed in. His eyes were red-rimmed and the greatcoat he wore thinned by use until it was a mere fragment of its formal glory. In contrast, his hair was oiled and brushed to a shine and his regimental tie done up in a neat Windsor knot.

Edward announced 'I am here to confirm my accommodation for the festive season.'

Pierson twitched as if attacked by fleas but didn't dare scratch himself.

'Go away,' said Barlow.

Edward ignored him and beamed at Pierson. 'Young man, having failed to secure my accommodation on a voluntary basis, I now wish to place myself in police custody.'

Barlow said, 'Not now, Edward, not now.'

Edward put his hand on his heart and intoned as if swearing a great oath: 'I, Edward Charles George Adair confess that I did wilfully and deliberately, and with malice aforethought, cause or compel, by means of threats or other illegal means, the payment to me of monies by way of blackmail or extortion. And that in addition ... '

Pierson's mouth opened wider and wider. Showed off his metallic fillings. Barlow grabbed Edward by the collar. Dragged him to the fire and out of earshot. Before he could speak, the front door opened again. This time impelled by a kick. An ageing man, Geordie Dunlop, bulled in. In spite of the driving sleet outside, he was wearing just an open-necked shirt over his trousers. His bulging biceps and stomach showed clearly through the wet cotton fabric.

A hand the size of a shovel grabbed at Barlow's throat. 'I've a bone to pick with you.'

Barlow deflected the hand. 'Piss off, Geordie.'

'Arresting my grandsons, and them sweet innocent boys.'

'They're a pack of ne'er-do-wells, like the rest of you.'

Geordie positioned himself for a killer blow to the face. 'The pride of their mother's heart.'

'Then she's easily pleased.'

Barlow rose up on his toes, positioned his fists ready to block the threatened punch. Geordie reeked of whiskey, and it always made him aggressive. The first blow was only seconds away. Pierson didn't rush to help his superior, Barlow noted.

Geordie's face had gone florid with fury. 'You've a down on the Dunlops. I'm not putting up with it no more.'

Edward put a crooked finger to his mouth and gave a gentle cough. 'Rifleman Dunlop, it's "*anymore*". "Not putting up with it *anymore*".'

Geordie looked around and spotted Edward. The fist dropped down. He backed off and touched a finger to his forehead. 'Major Adair, sir, I didn't see you there.' He gave what passed for a smirk. 'You finish sorting out the Sergeant Major. I'll take anything that's left.'

Barlow got between them and turned his back on Geordie. Felt safer that way, knowing that Geordie never attacked a man from the rear. Much as he ached to release his frustrations, he didn't want a fight. Harvey was bound to add "Unseemly Conduct" to the charge of being improperly dressed while on duty the day before.

'Edward, what the hell are you talking about?'

'Grammar and construct.'

'For heaven's sake!' If he shook some sense into Edward, Geordie would go for him. And if he didn't, he'd probably burst with frustration.

Edward relented. 'Blackmail. Blackmail and being a Peeping Tom.'

'Have you finally gone mad?'

Edward smiled. 'As you are aware, my habitual abode is situated under Curles Bridge. After each Round Table Ball, a number of the participants retire to the adjoins and surrounds of the bridge. There they engage in social intercourse of a highly intimate nature.'

'You mean shagging? You dirty old man.'

'Shagging yes, dirty no.' Edward looked offended.

Geordie said, 'Major Adair, sir, do you want me to thump the bugger for you?'

'Thank you, Rifleman Dunlop, but I'm quite capable of taking care of myself.'

Barlow didn't know which neck to wring first. He concentrated on Edward. 'So you watch?'

'One ascertains, one identifies. A nod here, a wink there, everything perfectly civil, and my comfort is secured, my edification enhanced.' Edward pulled a piece of paper from his pocket. 'Proof of my culpability: last night's participants.'

He grabbed the "proof". Edward's copperplate hand had recorded cars: models and registration numbers. The number of vehicles involved surprised him. 'By the holy heavens, you had a busy night.'

Edward said, 'One vehicle had a group session. The springs need oiling.'

'Bloody hell!' He looked at the list again, *which one?*

A crash of metal and a choked cry caused Barlow to forget the list. Other sounds followed. He couldn't identify them. *From the cells.* He headed towards the back of the building at a brisk pace.

Edward trotted after him.

'Go away.'

'My dear chap.'

Behind Edward, came Geordie. He ignored Geordie. *The devil takes care of his own.*

The cry arose again: high-pitched and frightened. A number of policemen appeared out of hidey-holes and cubby-holes. *They should be on foot patrol,* he thought, as they formed rank behind him.

He pushed through a heavy metal door into the cellblock. Noticed how tatty the place had become. The grey paint chipped and tired, the linoleum worn down to colourless. Adenauer's cell door hung open.

Barlow found himself staring into the muzzle of a revolver.

CHAPTER 10

THE MUZZLE BORED INTO BARLOW's forehead. Kurt Adenauer held the revolver, his free arm wrapped around Jackson's throat. A good shrug and the young constable's neck would snap. *Jackson's personal weapon*, Barlow supposed. Things had to stay calm, very calm or he and Jackson would both die.

'Dickhead,' he told the young officer, surprised that his voice stayed normal. His mind seemed to be set in treacle. He'd no idea how to deal with the situation. Other than run and hope for the best.

Jackson had gone red from choking. Adenauer's face was colourless. His lips compressed until pure white, the eyes staring, unfocused.

He said to Adenauer. 'Son, I don't know where you spent your war. The only thing we fight about around here is football.' Adenauer, he remembered, didn't speak English. Or at least he claimed he didn't. The Frau had to translate for him out at Stoop's farm.

The revolver still bored into his head, trying to force him backwards out of the cellblock. He had to lean into the muzzle to keep his balance. It hurt, but if Adenauer managed to get out that door, there would be shooting. He sensed the other officers edging out of sight. Ached to go with them.

Too frightened to stare into Adenauer's eyes, he looked at Jackson. 'Tell me son, is that revolver loaded?'

Jackson managed to choke out. 'Regulations.'

Of course, loaded. Jackson was still at the Cowboys and Indians stage. Even so, the more they talked, the better chance they had of calming Adenauer down. Get him back into that cell. *Take the initiative*, and keep your voice steady.

He focused on Jackson. 'So you walked into a cell wearing a loaded weapon. Your hands busy holding a tray, and no back-up. Would you care to quote that regulation at me?'

Adenauer snarled something in German. The muzzle bored deeper into Barlow's skull. He tried to hold his heartbeat down. He didn't want to die because at that moment he couldn't think of one thing he'd succeeded at in life.

He heard a distant creak as a heavy door swung on its hinges. The armoury. Someone had authorised the issue of rifles. Then came the metallic click-click of rounds being worked into the breach.

Lock and load, he thought, and didn't want it to happen. Once Adenauer saw those Lee Enfields, the trouble would start. What could he say to this man without making things worse? If only the bugger spoke English. He became aware of Edward peering around his elbow. Edward spoke in German. He'd forgotten about him and Geordie. They shouldn't be here; this was police work. 'Clear off,' he said.

Edward ignored him and continued to speak in hesitant German. The armlock on Jackson's neck eased and Jackson went a more normal colour. The muzzle didn't press quite as hard. Barlow found it easier to keep his balance and some of the madness had gone out of Adenauer's eyes. Edward, with his clothes worn down to frayed cloth, had the German puzzled.

Somebody kicked a cell door. Adenauer's finger went white on the trigger. One of the young Dunlops shouted. 'Where's our breakfast?' They kicked the door again.

The revolver didn't fire. Barlow closed his eyes for a moment and mixed a prayer of thanks with mental threats of what he'd do to the Dunlops. He reopened his eyes and said to Adenauer. 'Look, son, Ireland. Nein Germany, Nein Hitler.'

Behind him came a scurry of feet and the hiss of cloth brushing along walls as people eased into doorways. He raised his voice a notch. 'Hold your position. Everyone keep calm.'

The finger on the trigger stayed white. One of the Dunlops kicked the door again and shouted. First chance, Barlow promised himself, he'd wring their bloody necks.

Geordie growled in a voice that carried. 'You two in there. Shut your beaks!'

They did.

Geordie shouldn't be there either. He dreaded the paperwork if either civilian ended up getting hurt.

Edward kept talking in German. The words came out uncertain after many years of non-use. At long last, Adenauer replied to a question. The finger eased on the trigger. Edward laughed; *he always was a mad bugger.* 'Mr Adenauer says you remind him of his grandfather.'

'Well I hope he liked him.'

Edward translated. Adenauer nodded. That nod released more of the tension in the German. He released his arm from around Jackson's neck. Jackson gulped air and stumbled away.

Now it was just himself and Adenauer.

Again uniforms hissed along walls as armed officers took up new positions. He hoped Gillespie was among them. Gillespie would stop them trying anything inventive. Adenauer lowered the revolver to heart height. *That's something anyway.* The dent in his forehead still hurt because of the blood rushing back. He gulped breath. Less air seemed to come in than go out.

'Tell Mr Adenauer to go back into his cell. We'll bring him a fresh breakfast.'

Edward translated.

'We can arrange a family visit if he wants. His Frau Taylor or whatever she's called.'

Again, Edward spoke the words. The mad look faded from Adenauer's eyes. Barlow put out his hand, palm upwards. Ever so slowly, the revolver came into his hand, muzzle first. He hoped that Adenauer wouldn't change his mind and pull the trigger.

Finally, the revolver was his.

Adenauer snapped to attention, did an about-turn. Marched down the corridor, and back into his cell.

Armed men, led by Gillespie, pushed past Barlow and secured the cell door.

CHAPTER 11

BARLOW FELT LIKE HE'D BEEN dragged six ways through a hawthorn hedge. Even so, the day's duties still had to go on.

On the way to the front desk he passed the detectives' office. The door lay open. He had a feeling that this was deliberate. Detective Sergeant Leary sat at the back of the room, ostentatiously reading the *Daily Mirror*. Leary was small and fat, and inclined to be lazy, and there was nothing Barlow could do about it. The detectives were a law unto themselves. Ninety percent of local crime rated a thick ear. The uniform branch dealt with the rest. The detectives spent most of their time making cups of tea and running to Matthews Bakery for buns.

Leary called out. 'Barlow, on your rounds yesterday, did you by any chance sample some of the local brew?'

'What do you mean?'

'Those empty shells you *alleged* you saw in the hayloft. They weren't there.'

'They were.'

Come to think of it, the shells had been lying in a bad place. The wind could have caught them. Maybe they rolled out the open door or down the hatch into the byre? Barlow thought not. Leary might be lazy, but he seldom missed the obvious. 'You should have tried looking for them with your eyes open', Barlow said. He looked back as he turned to go. 'While you're at it, somebody's nicked four of Tommy Abernathy's cattle.'

Leary scowled. 'That's the third lot.'

'Much more of this and you won't have time to study the buxom women in *The Mirror*.'

The missing shells puzzled Barlow. Could the "escaping gunman" have been one of the farm workers heading home for lunch? If so, then the gunman had been in the hayloft all along. *Or two gunmen?* The very thought gave him the shivers.

He found Edward and Jackson sitting in front of the coal fire. Jackson huddled into himself, shivering. Geordie had gone home. It saved Barlow having to thank the man for rearing two good-for-nothings.

Jackson jumped to his feet. 'Sergeant… I don't know how… I can't thank you enough.'

Barlow said, 'You pull another stunt like that and I'll post you to the Copelands.'

'But the Copelands don't have a police station, sergeant. They're all rock and puffins.'

'You annoy my head once more and they will have.'

Jackson seemed to appreciate a normal bollocking, and looked better. Rushed off and made himself busy behind the counter.

Barlow took Jackson's chair. His jellified knees wanted to crash into it. Turning to Edward, he asked: 'Did you know what you were saying back there, all that Deutschy talk?'

Edward looked indignant. 'One read *Mein Kampf* in the original German in one's earlier days.'

'There's been a lot of whiskey down your throat since then.'

They nodded at each other. Just another bomb that the two of them had managed to walk away from.

Barlow said, 'Christmas. I wish I could help.'

Edward held out his hand. 'One requires the return of one's list of last night's participants.'

Proof of a felony? Not the sort of thing he should hand over. *Where's the blessed thing got to anyway?* He rummaged through his jacket and trousers. Found the list in his hip pocket.

Edward leaned forward and touched the page. 'Some of the participants, particularly the lady in that car, tend to be exhibitionists by nature.'

'What do you mean "exhibitionist"?'

'They find that an appreciative audience enhances their enjoyment.'

The phone rang. Jackson grabbed it. 'Yes, sir. Right away, sir.' He said to Barlow. 'District Inspector Harvey wants to know what's keeping you.'

CHAPTER 12

DISTRICT INSPECTOR HARVEY SAT BEHIND his pedestal desk, lights arranged so that the focus stayed on him. Behind him, on the wall, hung a large photograph of the young Queen, the symbol of his authority. Even with all of that, in Barlow's eyes he still lacked his predecessor's hovering presence. A turkey cock, where there should have been a hawk.

'What kept you, Barlow? I said nine o'clock, sharp.'

Barlow became enthusiastic. 'This "no crime" thing of yours, sir. You're right, we had got slack and complacent.' He placed a file in front of Harvey. 'I think we should start with this one. It's ready to go to the DPP.'

'What is?'

'The papers on the Ezekiel Fetherton case. I was just doing a final tidy-up when the old DI died.'

Harvey almost rose to his feet in indignation. 'I told you before. I have no intention of prosecuting the Mayor.'

He nodded as if in agreement. 'You must have come well recommended to the Masons.'

'What do you mean by that?'

The mixture of indignation and embarrassment on Harvey's face intrigued him. If he managed to hang on in Ballymena, he'd be guaranteed to give Harvey an ulcer. 'A safe pair of hands, sir.' Phrased in that way, it could be a compliment. Or an insult that Harvey couldn't prove.

He put the file back under his arm – no way must Harvey get a chance to destroy it. Stood to attention and stared at the portrait of the Queen. He, his old boss, and the King took up their appointments on the same day. Now the other two were gone, and Harvey had the King's portrait removed and Elizabeth's hung on the wall within hours of taking over his new role as District Inspector in Ballymena. Not that Barlow had anything against the Queen. *But it's a rum do, Missis, when you let people like Harvey run the show.*

Harvey squared off the files on his desk while he recovered his composure. 'Sergeant Pierson informs me that he briefed you on the prisoners last night. Specifically on this Kurt Adenauer.'

'You could call it that, sir,' he said, remembering the way Pierson had bellowed in his ear while he was trying to shiver the chill out of his bones.

'Then you must be aware of the police doctor's report. The doctor recommended that Adenauer be sectioned under the Mental Health Act.'

Pierson hadn't mentioned that part. But no point denying it, Harvey wouldn't believe him anyway. He'd deal with Pierson in his own good time; make him look bad for a change. Anyway, he should have known that a sectioning was likely. He'd seen Adenauer's eyes.

Harvey said, 'You should have made appropriate arrange-ments. Constable Jackson could have been killed and an armed and dangerous man let loose on the countryside.' Harvey was by now vibrating with righteous indignation. 'What would Headquarters have thought of that?'

'Not a lot, sir.'

Harvey shuffled through the files on his desk. Pointedly opened one. 'This morning's incident with Adenauer was the last straw. You're being transferred. Demoted if I can manage it.' Looked up briefly. 'Final point, I want things tidied up for your successor. You'd do better concentrating on that instead of worrying about other people's business.'

Barlow wandered to the door instead of striding purposefully. That sort of slackness annoyed Harvey. He paused, resting his hand on the handle. 'These indecency charges. You'll want me back to testify of course?'

'What indecency charges?'

'It's a fair scandal, sir, what goes on around Curles Bridge after the Round Table Ball. Last night, I thought it time we did something about it.' He pulled out his notebook and thumbed through the pages. 'I couldn't see their faces, but we'll get the men through their cars.' He found the page he wanted and tapped a particular line. 'That one. A spanking new Triumph, just like yours, sir.'

'What?'

He showed Harvey the car registration numbers copied from Edward's list. All of the cars, bar one. Saw no need to embarrass WPC Day. 'I've no head for numbers, that's why I wrote them down, careful like.' He pointed to the Triumph. 'Both those parties, I could swear – totally not dressed.'

Harvey looked like he would deny this. Sweat sheeted his face. 'Sergeant ... I ... '

'The lady was an exhibitionist,' he said, encouraging him.

Harvey wiped sweat from his forehead. Gritted his teeth and tried to sound pleasant. 'We've had a bad start. Perhaps when we get to know each other better?' Poked through his drawers and produced a notebook. 'A new notebook, a new year, a fresh beginning?'

Barlow allowed the exchange of notebooks to take place. 'Fine by me, sir.'

CHAPTER 13

THE REST OF THE MORNING passed quite pleasantly. Harvey stayed in his office and out of the way, while Barlow manned the counter. The war with Harvey had just begun, but from here on in he could pick his own fights. WPC Day brought him regular refills of tea. Barlow wished he had a wife like her.

In the afternoon, Sergeant Pierson arrived back from court full of news. Kurt Adenauer had been remanded in custody and was on his way to the Crumlin Road Prison in Belfast. The Dunlops had been given bail of ten pounds each. They had the money in their hands before the magistrate finished speaking.

More fool them, thought Barlow. You rile a magistrate at your own peril. 'Where did they get the cash?' he asked Pierson.

'Money they had on them.'

'Then what?'

'Things in the courthouse were *all regular*, so I came back to the station.'

Barlow kept his voice down. A serious cock-up merited quiet words of scorn. 'More than a week's wages left after a night's drinking, and you never thought to ask yourself where they got it.'

Pierson looked guilty.

'So much for your "*all regular*". If you did less arse-licking, you might find time for the job you're paid to do.'

Pierson slunk off to guard the cells' only occupant, Edward. Hopefully, Pierson would have the sense to leave him in peace. Allowing Edward to bed down in the cells over

Christmas was the least Barlow could do for the man. After all, he'd given him the goods on Harvey. At the same time, he prayed that Edward would stay in his "accommodation" until Harvey left for Belfast and his Christmas holidays. Wished Harvey's family all the joys of the season with a man like that in the house.

Jackson produced the Incident Book and dared ask what Edward was to be charged with.

'Same as you. Annoying my bloody head.'

Gillespie came limping in for an early lunch break. 'It's raining again.'

'I've seen healthier drowned rats,' Barlow agreed, for once inclined to be pleasant to Gillespie. Blamed it on Christmas.

Gillespie rubbed at his neck. 'The rain's getting into the joints. It'll give me arthritis.'

Barlow took an incoming call while he tried to come up with a put-down to Gillespie's latest complaint. *He might be right about the arthritis.* In the army they'd nicknamed Gillespie *Tea Leaf* because, like many stolen items, he'd fallen off a lorry. A .88 shell going off under the rear wheels had speeded his journey.

The call came from the local pathologist. 'This autopsy on Andrew Taylor, also known as Stoop Taylor ... '

'Doctor, I think you should speak to DS Leary, who is handling the case.'

'Barlow, if I don't tell you, you'll die of curiosity and I'm busy enough as it is.'

The pathologist had a cultured voice that could be quietly insistent. He'd done his early medical training in a Japanese prison where boots and rifle butts taught him the value of the softly spoken word. Nothing worried the man except incompetence and complacency. Even now, fourteen years after the war had ended, he remained scrawny thin.

'Right, Barlow, in English for your benefit. You discovered the deceased, Stoop Taylor, lying face down in liquid mud, yet I found no contaminants in his lungs or air passages. One must assume, therefore, that he was dead before he hit the ground.'

'Heart attack?' He crossed his toes for luck.

'That, Sergeant, is presupposing he had a heart. The straightest thing about Stoop Taylor was the curvature of his spine.'

The pathologist, he knew, intended that remark to be dry humour, but a bite of annoyance echoed in the words. Stoop, he remembered, was an angry little man, and the pathologist had a short way with fools and time-wasters. Somewhere, sometime, the pathologist and Stoop had crossed swords.

He remained silent, hoping to hear more details of the fall-out. Noticed Gillespie and Jackson listening to every word. Gillespie he could do nothing about, the man refused to be shamed, but Jackson...

'Those flapping ears of yours are causing a draft.'

Jackson's face burned. 'Yes, Sergeant. Sorry, Sergeant.' He made himself busy tidying the pencil mug.

Not a bad youngster. Hadn't the street sense of a newt, but willing to learn.

Beyond Jackson and through the window he could see the roof of the sweetshop across the way. Lumps of moss had gathered between the slates, causing the rain to split into dozens of rivulets. Oil from the decaying vegetation set up dull rainbow patterns in the flowing water. And beyond the sweetshop were the straggling chestnut trees in the People's Park. He'd looked out that window and seen that roof and those trees a hundred thousand times. This time something in his psyche made him shiver.

The pathologist was still talking. Barlow's brain did a quick reprise, trying to register what the man had said.

'You are listening, Barlow?'

'I am, Doctor, but I had to deal with a problem here.' He glared at Gillespie and Jackson. *Dare they distract me again.*

'For the second time,' said the pathologist, with emphasis on the "second". 'Taylor may have suffered a heart attack, or died of natural causes, or of shock.' The doctor paused, then gave an emphatic, 'However.'

That "however" and the casual mention of shock gave him a sinking feeling. The last thing he needed over Christmas was complications, causing a lot of extra work for everybody.

'However,' repeated the pathologist, 'the herd of cattle trampled over the body, causing severe trauma. You undoubtedly noticed that the brain had been eviscerated. In addition, the spine was broken in two places and the left shoulder blade shattered.'

'Arms, legs?' he asked, wishing the pathologist would get to the bad news.

'You don't want to know,' said the pathologist, with an air of satisfaction at an old adversary getting his comeuppance.

'And?'

'And in the middle of the reduced bone mass and excoriated flesh I discovered some foreign objects.' The pathologist's voice changed as if he was holding up something to the light. 'I am no expert, of course, but I think it's a bullet that disintegrated on impact.'

Barlow had been planning an easy afternoon coupled with some shopping in McHenry's grocery store on the way home. 'Thanks, Doc,' he said with heavy emphasis.

'Doctor,' said the pathologist, and waited to be put through to Leary.

The cars and the police vans were Gillespie's responsibility. 'What about my lunch break?' he moaned when told to get the vehicles started and warmed up.

Jackson tried to slip away.

'Where are you going?'

'To fetch my wet weather gear, Sergeant. I always get the dirty jobs.'

He began to think that some day Jackson might become a real policeman. An inspector, even. The lad had a couple of brain cells that occasionally sparked intelligence.

CHAPTER 14

Barlow was reaching for his cap when Vera burst in the Enquiry Office door, breathless from running. She struggled to get the question out. 'Da, are you all right?'

'I'm fine,' he said, and sighed. Police wives thrived on bad news, and constables who carried stories home from work were ten times worse than their wives. He found it interesting that Vera's boyfriend, Kenny Cameron, had come with her. Kenny was lanky and had a face pockmarked with acne. Right then he hung nervously in the doorway, letting in a blast of cold air.

The news of the attempted breakout had to be around the town. He wondered what the young couple were up to when they heard the news.

'Look at your head, Da, it's all bruised.'

He touched his forehead. It had swollen and probably gone purple. Much as he tried to steady his hands, they still shook when he signed off reports. 'I'm fine,' he repeated.

She started to cry, standing in the middle of the floor, her face gone mottled red. He lifted the counter flap and went out and put an arm around her.

'The man's not well. He didn't mean any harm.'

'But he could have. The gun…'

He'd have loved to say, 'the gun wasn't loaded,' but he never told her lies. At least, not ones he'd be caught out on. 'Crying makes your face blotchy.'

'Da!'

'And there's young Cameron thinking what a beautiful daughter I have?' Kenny looked ready to run at the mention of his name.

Vera covered her cheeks with her hands. 'Da, you can't say things like that.'

At least she'd stopped crying. He gave her a handkerchief and told her to blow her nose, adding, 'A bit of make-up would tone down that colour.'

'What make-up? You don't allow…'

He looked her in the eye. She stared him straight back: half cheeky, half rabbit. He realised how much he missed that in her mother.

She grinned. 'You really are in a funny mood.'

'Christmas does things to a man.' And nearly dying and knowing his daughter would have to cope on her own. He didn't want her to end up like him, an orphan. In his case, he was eight when his mother died; he never knew his father. The man had said, "We'll not see each other for a year at least, and you know I'll be back for you." His mother believed him. The next day the man left to start a new life in America. The promised passage money never came; neither did the hoped-for letters. No one ever heard from him again. At least that's what his good- living, Bible-thumping Christian family claimed, though for years afterwards they continued to receive letters with American stamps.

He undid the top button of his jacket and pulled out his wallet. The wallet was new when he'd been new to the job. It had darkened with age, the leather worn to soft sandpaper in places. *A bit like myself.* Took his time leafing through receipted invoices, many with pencilled notes scribbled on the back. When Vera's eyebrows had gone high enough with curiosity, he extracted a note and gave both it and her a shove towards the door. 'I'm busy today. Do your own Christmas shopping.'

Her eyes widened. 'A fiver, Da?' Again he got the cheeky grin. 'You're not expecting four pounds change, are you?'

'Five pounds?' he roared. 'I thought it was a ten shilling note.'

She hustled Kenny in front of her and fled. The door banged shut, cutting off the chill draft.

It opened again. Only her head appeared. 'Have you any ideas, Da?'

'A sensible pair of shoes out of John Suiters, not those fancy high-heel things you get in Fyffes.'

She laughed. 'I was thinking of something you'd like.'

The head disappeared and the door banged shut one final time.

'Liquorice Allsorts or wine gums,' he shouted after her and went off to destroy Detective Sergeant Leary's dreams of a liquid Christmas Eve lunch. Somehow managing to keep his face straight in the process. Leary muttered about half-done autopsies and full test results not in. But, bullet or not, pieces of metal found in a body needed investigating.

They told Inspector Foxwood of the development. Foxwood fled from his mounting paperwork with a sigh of relief. Harvey looked pleased. A murder with the suspect already on remand would go down well with Headquarters.

The Deputy Chief Constable that Harvey reported to asked if the murder scene had been secured. 'Of course, sir,' smarmed Harvey. He smarmed some more, then hung up. 'Barlow, you did secure the murder scene?'

'It wasn't a murder scene then.' Decided to skip the "sir" and went on. 'Anyway, I assumed…'

Harvey tapped the desk sharply with a knuckle. 'You assumed. You must never assume.'

He finished stubbornly. 'With all those inspectors and detectives present, they'd have ordered the area secured, if needs be.'

"All those inspectors" included Harvey himself. Barlow thought it best not to remind him of that. Foxwood blanched as Harvey's glare turned on him. 'I warned you. Barlow is lazy and incompetent. He has to be watched at all times.'

Foxwood's expression worked between indignation and guilt, but no words came out. Foxwood finally stuttered. 'I'm sorry, sir.'

'And so you should be.'

Barlow stood at easy attention. Kept a derisive eye on the portrait of the young Queen while Harvey barked his orders. Barlow and Foxwood must secure the murder scene without further delay, supervise the collection of data for forensic testing and take witness statements. Nobody knew where Stoop had actually been killed so the "murder scene" comprised the entire farm, including the farmhouse.

'What about a search warrant?' Barlow asked.

Harvey looked disgusted. 'And give them more time to destroy evidence.'

'Proper procedures should be followed at all times.'

He enjoyed watching the colour in Harvey's cheeks change to a shade of purple.

'We'll get one later if we have to,' compromised Foxwood.

Harvey indicated they should leave immediately for the farm. Obviously, searching cow-clabbered fields in the pouring rain was best left to underlings.

Once in the corridor Foxwood pulled Barlow aside into a window recess for a confab. They saw Gillespie in the yard below them, going from squad car to police van, gunning the engines to warm up the vehicles. Gillespie looked suitably miserable with the rain streaming off his cap.

Foxwood said, 'Searching the site where you found the body is strictly for Forensics.'

'Detective Sergeant Leary and his team?'

'Naturally,' said Foxwood, with the uniformed officers' disdain of the over-rated detective branch.

They settled on the number of uniformed officers they needed to search the house and outbuildings. Foxwood nodded in agreement when Barlow suggested the officers most suitable for the job.

Foxwood, he realised, was open to suggestions.

I'll make use of that some day.

CHAPTER 15

BARLOW HAD NEVER BEEN IN mainland Europe, or further afield, in his life. Even during the Second World War, his travels hadn't extended further than Dover in the south of England. He'd only heard second-hand about the results of the Allied carpet-bombing of cities in Germany. Only in London had he walked across the remains of buildings to get from the beginning of a street to the other end. But he had been to the cinema. Had watched *Pathé News* showing the walking skeletons of Dachau and Bergen-Belsen concentration camps. The eyes he saw then on the screen were like those of Frau Taylor when he called to see her that afternoon. Eyes gone way beyond despair.

The house would be torn apart by the searchers: floorboards ripped up, things broken. He didn't know which was worse for the Frau: people arriving to destroy her possessions, or them seeing how little she had to break in the first place. He tried to harden his heart, reminding himself that the Frau had attempted to conceal an illegal alien. Was, by her own admission, a bigamist, and faced a possible charge of murder or conspiracy to murder.

The Frau stood in the doorway as the policemen poured into the house, jemmies at the ready. She wore a dark blue dress that hung shapeless in the rain, and pink slippers with the felt pile aged to colourless. She had her hair plaited German housewife-style. *Good for keeping the nits at bay*, he thought, and regretted being unkind.

There were no sympathetic neighbours to usher out. Like all good gossip, the fact that the Frau had been harbouring the murder suspect had got around. In a way he felt sorry for her. *Condemned without a trial.*

He allocated the search of the gutters, downpipes and gullies to Gillespie. 'You're a quare man with water,' he informed him.

Gillespie smirked and rolled up a sleeve. Under his uniform he wore a diver's suit.

'I must be getting old,' Barlow muttered, hating to be bested.

WPC Day popped out of the house to report that finding forensic evidence would be difficult. The house was as clean as elbow grease and hot water could make it. He grunted in reply and dragged Jackson down the yard to give him his orders.

The liquid mud from the dirty yard flowed with them and pooled around rusted machinery. Someone, the boy presumably, had made a start at tidying the place. *What are they trying to hide?* the cynic in him wondered.

Jackson wore chest-high waders and rubber gloves to his shoulder. In spite of the cold, sweat already beaded his forehead.

Barlow said, 'Son, I took note of what you said about me always picking on you.' He pointed to the sheds and scattered outbuildings. 'You stay inside and dry. Poke around, see what you can find.'

'Yes, Sergeant,' said Jackson.

Barlow turned away, heard a mutter and turned back. 'Did you say something?'

'No, Sergeant.'

He walked on again, smiling in pleasure as he passed Gillespie. Gillespie had forgotten that he wore a wet suit, not one of the new dry suits. A downpipe poured water into his sleeve. It would take time for the icy water to heat up in the gap between the wet suit rubber and bare flesh.

The Frau still stood in the doorway, soaked through. The boy stood beside her, his mouth twisted with the intolerance of youth. Even Barlow's teeth grated at the ripping and tearing noises coming from inside the house.

'You'll catch your death, Missis.'

He scratched his head. *Where could the woman go?* Not the house, and she needed something better than a draughty shed. From where he stood he could see the river. A sludge of grey water, with the wind coming off it in slabs of chill air. Walked over to the squad car and looked in. Gillespie had left the keys in the ignition. That made the vehicle improperly secured. He'd look up the law and quote it the next time Gillespie got smart.

He opened the car door and indicated. 'Get in, Missis.'

The boy clenched his fists and stepped between them. 'Where are you taking my mother? She's innocent.'

'Of what?' he asked, and had to think what they called the boy. Most of his own childhood he'd been treated as a nameless drudge. In the workhouse they had addressed the young Barlow as "you" or "you over there". *Peter.* He didn't know what recess in his mind that came from, but *Peter* it was.

'Peter, do you want your mother to end up in hospital?'

The Frau was shaking with the cold. She stood with her head hunched into her shoulders. Arms huddled over her breasts. Gillespie's cape lay over the back seat of the car. He lifted it out and gave it to Peter. Peter put the cape around his mother with an embarrassed gentleness. The Frau pulled him under for shelter.

Their spark of concern for each other pleased him. He kept the car door open. 'Frau Taylor, you're doing no good standing there.'

She hesitated, fear in her face. Peter urged her to get in. Barlow nodded his encouragement, knowing that the boy had no memories of people being taken away in cars and never seen again.

He slipped into the driver's seat and turned on the engine. For a while he let the heater do its job, but sat with one eye on his watch. He didn't like leaving the men unsupervised. Some of them wouldn't see a ton of dynamite unless they tripped over it. But no way could he leave possible suspects in a car with the engine running.

An itch worked in his brain. Something he'd seen, hadn't seen. Missed. He needed to walk around until that something came to him. Waves of panic came off the Frau. They interfered with his thoughts. Back at the police station he'd throw her into a cell and let her panic to her heart's content.

He rolled down the window and shouted for WPC Day to get the Frau a change of clothes. She appeared after a short delay, and got into the front passenger seat. She held a bundle of clothes and had an eyebrow raised in a silent query.

He could see that Gillespie was edgy. His eyes spent more time on the car than searching for clues. He knew the man would never forgive him if he took the car, so he put it in gear and drove out of the yard. Nice and slowly to prolong Gillespie's irritation.

Behind him the Frau whispered, 'Mein Gott,' and hugged Peter to her.

WPC Day dared ask. 'Are we for the station?'

'You like surprises, don't you?'

A handle creaked as the Frau tried the door. 'It doesn't open from the inside, Missis.' Two hundred yards along River Road he turned into the laneway leading to the Widow Taylor's house.

He could guess from the Tillage Book returns that the Widow Taylor had little left over for herself after she paid the bills. But now, coming directly from her late brother-in-law's house, he saw for the first time the difference those top thirty acres had made. Compared with the Frau, the Widow Taylor lived in luxury.

Substantial ditches, topped with white hawthorn to catch the wind, marched the laneway. The Widow Taylor's farmyard was small and neat: a four-cow byre with a hayloft above, a meal house, tool shed and cobblestones that glistened in the rain. Heavy black gloss covered all the doors. The window frames gleamed white and the walls were distempered at least once a year. The Widow Taylor had a stove that never went out, whereas the Frau had no option but to produce meals on Stoop's miserable two-ring cooker which was fuelled by bottled gas. Elsewhere, however, the lack of a man about the Widow Taylor's was evident in the fields, in the unpulled ragweed and the straggling hedges.

The Widow Taylor stepped out of the byre, shovel in hand. She wore a Barbour jacket over a pair of men's trousers and rubber boots. A battered duncher kept her hair dry. She stared at the squad car.

An old pony wandered out of the shadows of a lean-to. Barlow blinked in surprise. The pony had no halter and the shed had no barrier to ensure that the pony stayed inside. The pony snorted its disapproval of the rain and disappeared back into the shadows.

He got out and opened the door for Frau Taylor. WPC Day looked like she expected him to do the same for her. The WPCs had started to nag about feminism and their rights. In his opinion, if they wanted equality with men, they could open their own doors.

WPC Day took the hint. She got out of the car and whispered. 'Papa Bear, you told the men between shifts to make their own tea. That could apply to you as well.'

'Dare you.'

The widow still stood at the byre door. He sensed more than a lack of welcome.

CHAPTER 16

THE WIDOW TAYLOR SEEMED PUT out at their unexpected arrival. Barlow hesitated. *Maybe we should have gone somewhere else?*

'We're doing forensic tests up at Stoop's house,' he said and indicated the Frau. 'Rather than have her stand in the rain...' He let his voice drift to silence, not wanting to state the obvious.

The Widow Taylor's head nodded. She said, 'No one else would take them,' and walked over to the house.

He shivered at her cold charity, and followed the Frau and Peter and WPC Day through the little hallway into the kitchen. They stood, uncertain of their welcome, although a cut Christmas cake and a bottle of Harvey's Bristol Cream sat ready to entertain visitors.

The police capes and Frau Taylor's dress dripped water onto the flagged floor. The widow nodded her head a few more times before telling them to sit down. She fetched a fresh towel for the Frau out of the big press. Opened the fire door on the range to let more heat into the room.

WPC Day stood guard while the Frau changed behind the scullery door. Peter sat at the table and glowered. Barlow sat across from him, pretending not to notice.

Peter said, 'We didn't do anything. The German man, we worked together all day on the tractor.'

'What was wrong with it?' he asked, thinking he could ask Adenauer the same question.

'It wouldn't go,' said Peter.

Hardly a technical explanation, and *was that a hesitation before he spoke?* Barlow chewed on one of his imaginary sweets while he thought about it. Maybe Adenauer had used German terms and the boy didn't know the equivalent words in English. 'Spark plugs? Big End? Distributor brushes?'

Peter looked confused, said nothing.

Barlow had another chew. 'Why weren't you at school?'

The boy's eyes flickered.

'Lying doesn't help, son.'

The boy scowled. 'We work.'

The Frau reappeared. She looked more relaxed, but still cautious as she took her seat at the table. *Take away the worry lines, put on a few pounds and she'd be a good-looking woman.* The Frau caught him looking at her and a first, uncertain smile flickered. WPC Day raised an eyebrow at him and he glared back.

The Widow Taylor brought over the tea things. The tea itself came in a big pot kept for workers at harvest time. Then bread and butter, cake and apple tart still warm from the oven. The widow sat well away from the Frau. The Frau held a cup of tea to her chest and looked miserable. She and Peter talked in German. Peter tried not to eat.

Barlow put a slice of apple tart under the boy's nose and the curling odour proved too much. Cake followed the apple tart, then the widow's soda, soaked in butter and layered with homemade damson jam. For a few minutes Peter became a child again. Politely refusing more, even as his hand stretched for the next slice.

The widow refilled their cups, but didn't rejoin them at the table. Took up station against the drying rail on the range. Her eyes moved from one to the other in a restless circle.

He sensed her eyes rest more on him than on the others. It was horrible how a dispute that started between two brothers, both now dead, could carry on down the family. *Why did I bring the Frau here?* Somehow, behind the widow's lack of communication, he'd always felt a warmth.

He nodded to her, in appreciation of her ingrained country-folk hospitality. The widow dimpled a smile back. Lines in her face, that he'd assumed were caused by hard living, creased deeply. Thought she should smile more often.

As if uneasy at his stare, the widow moved about the room. She searched out a bottle of C&C brown lemonade and poured a glass for the boy. The fizz sparked as he drank, and it lodged in his eyebrows. He laughed at its tickle on his face.

A tear slid down the Frau's cheek. 'My son, I wish him the good things I never have.'

Barlow closed his eyes for a moment. Did he expect too much of Vera? They lived in a house with an outside toilet and a zinc basin for a bath. She seldom complained, but that wasn't the point.

Thinking of home life and its complications, he wondered about the Frau and the two men in her life. Asked, 'What is Adenauer to you?'

Her face closed up again. Peter stopped eating and slapped down the glass of lemonade, half drunk.

She said, 'The solicitor say we not speak to you.'

'We'll see you in court,' said Peter.

'You're watching too much television,' he said, wondering if the boy even knew what television was. He remembered seeing a huge radio on the corner of the sideboard. A pre-war monstrosity that Stoop must have bought in a job lot. Wanted to keep the Frau talking.

'What time did your solicitor say to expect him?'

WPC Day looked startled and stared hard at him.

'He come?' The Frau sounded doubtful, as if the solicitor's own life might be at risk if he tried to help her.

'Of course he'll come.'

'We go to that nice man, Mr Comberton, you tell us to.'

He wished she hadn't mentioned that piece of advice, especially in front of WPC Day. But Adenauer had needed a good solicitor.

WPC Day pretended to wipe her mouth, drawing her thumb over her throat as she did so. Harvey wouldn't want a solicitor complaining about illegal searches. At least, not until the interrogation was finished.

Peter spoke in German and pointed at the widow's telephone.

'Smart kid,' said WPC Day. She repeated the German words, and then said them in English. 'Two, three, zero, two. He knows Comberton's number straight off.'

At least the Frau now knew she could have a solicitor present, and Barlow had more important things to do than sit and play word games. He decided to leave WPC Day and her schoolgirl German to question the Frau. Slapped on his cap and left.

The widow and the dog saw him out. She closed the inner door, muttering something about keeping the heat in.

He nodded his thanks. 'It's good of you, Missis, taking them in.'

'Please call me Alexandra,' said the Widow Taylor.

Alexandra. He knew her name from the Tillage Returns, *but to actually call her that…* ? He took his time swinging on his cape and adjusting his cap in the hallstand mirror, conscious all the time of the soft smell of a woman coming off her. In the confined space their bodies touched. His hand drifted towards her hips, then someone's heel nipped the dog's paw. The dog growled, his foot twitched. The moment had passed.

Unsettled, he got into the car and drove off. The widow Taylor– *Alexandra* – watched from the doorway. He found himself reluctant to leave, and too embarrassed to stay.

CHAPTER 17

BARLOW DIDN'T GO FAR FROM Alexandra Taylor's house. Just down the road to the field where he'd found Stoop's body. The mud clung to his boots, making it a hard slog up the hill to where Leary and his men stood in a weary group, talking amongst themselves. Obviously trying to justify giving up the search.

They'd done a fair amount of work, he noted. The trampled earth had widened outwards as the forensic team circled the murder scene. A satisfactory amount of mud had transferred itself to their faces and hands.

'We've taken six dozen samples of liquid shite,' Leary told him.

He shrugged non-committally. Nothing short of a smoking gun found in Adenauer's hand would please Harvey.

Leary took him down to the police van to show off the only substantial thing they'd found: A .22 bullet.

'Where did you get that?' He'd visions of it circling aimlessly until Leary plucked it out of the air.

Leary pointed to the cattle in the next field. 'One bullock has a flesh wound, the other ... Almost a bull's eye, except at the wrong end.'

'The poor brute.'

'Poor be fecked. 'At least he's nice and dry at the vet's. Look!' Leary pulled at the top of his red pullover. The colour had leached onto his white shirt.

'I didn't know you were a royalist.'

'What?'

'Red pullover, white shirt, blue face.'

'Ha, bloody ha.'

Barlow stood in the doorway of the police van to examine the bullet against the evening sky. 'Perfect. There'll be no trouble making a ballistics match.'

Leary looked down in the mouth. 'Stoop's rifle hasn't been fired in months. We even found a dead spider in the barrel.'

'And the bits of metal in the body?' He phrased it that way to annoy, rather than give the accolade of "bullet fragments".

The reply came with a glare. 'They're not big enough for a ballistics test. We'll have to rely on a metallurgical comparison with the bullets in Adenauer's pistol.'

'Unless you find another beast with a bullet up its backside.'

Leary said, 'I spent my day scooping bits of brain into glass jars. The last thing I need is your smart-ass remarks.'

Barlow looked back up the hill. Night had begun to draw in. The trees marking the boundary between the two farms stood black against the dark sky. Alexandra's land squeezed Stoop's farm on two sides, and looked down on it from the top field. Reason enough for Stoop to turn sour and bitter.

'You've got the killer. All you need now is the proof.'

A constable came out the gate leading into Stoop's farmyard, and shouted. 'Sergeant, Gillespie says they've finished in the house. You're to bring his car and the woman back.'

He roared at the constable. 'Tell Gillespie, those jemmies are designed to knock back any nails they took out. I want the place pristine for the Frau.'

The volume of the shout made Leary jump. The constable seemed less impressed. 'And Gillespie says he wants to see you, private-like, as soon as you get here.'

Barlow nodded and tramped back to the squad car. Before he got in, he stopped and checked his uniform. Glutinous mud caked his feet and legs. Gillespie was going to go spare at the mess in the car, and Leary had a lousy Christmas coming up, analysing liquid shite.

All in all, not a bad day.

He drove back to Alexandra's farm. It was heavy dusk by then and the headlights swept the buildings as he turned into the yard. He beeped the car horn rather than risk meeting Alexandra again and thanked God for the dog getting under their feet in the hallway. *Lord alone knows what would have happened otherwise.* He liked the name Alexandra. There was something brisk and determined about it. He tried to ignore the ache for her in his body. Couldn't stop his mind from working out the last time he and Maggie... *A hell of a long time.*

The Frau and her son got into the back of the car. WPC Day took the front passenger seat. It gave her the chance to whisper, 'Mr Comberton's in Belfast, at the High Court. He'll be here as soon as he can.'

The drive to Stoop's farm took one minute. The policemen were just exiting the farmhouse. Frau pushed past them, demanding, 'What you do? What break?'

Constable Gillespie motioned for Barlow to come with him down the yard. Barlow held up a hand to indicate "wait", and stood on until Peter had followed the Frau into the farmhouse. As soon as they were out of sight he pointed down the line of the car headlights into the manure pit. At a piece of dull metal that gleamed in the light. Right at the back, barely showing under a scoop of manure, lay an empty rifle shell.

He nodded in satisfaction. 'I knew I'd seen something the first time.'

If one showed, then the other two were likely to be there as well. He sent Jackson to tell Leary that his team were needed.

And to bring their little glass jars. All the uniformed officers crowded into the farmyard. Everyone wanted to see the detectives wade through manure.

While they waited for Leary to arrive, he followed Gillespie into a crumbling grain store. Half-hundredweight hessian bags of meal lay stacked in one corner; plastic bags of lime fertiliser lay in another. The walls were built of lava stone, held together with cow dung and chopped straw. Any distemper ever slapped on had long since leached away.

Gillespie focused his torch beam on one spot. 'Jackson found this,' he said as he moved a fertiliser bag and pulled a loose stone out of the wall. Barlow saw a roll of white five-pound notes. The roll was the thickness of his hand.

Gillespie said, 'They've been there a while. White fivers went out of circulation years ago.'

Barlow counted back in his head. 'Three years, 1957.'

From up the yard he heard a raised voice. English. Foxwood had arrived back from somewhere and was looking for him.

'Quick, put them back,' said Barlow.

CHAPTER 18

MR GREENAWAY OF BALLYMENA'S FIRST and only television shop stood in the doorway of his shop thinking that 1959 hadn't been too bad a year for the television trade. All the same, with most of his stock converted into cash, Australia and the good weather there tempted a man heartily sick of rain and cold.

As soon as he turned the corner, Barlow spotted Mr Greenaway standing outside his shop. All along the street, the shop lights were already dimmed. Barlow increased his pace, weaving past the few remaining shoppers, trudging wearily, heads bent. As he drew closer, he relaxed a bit and slowed his pace. At Mr Greenaway's feet sat a boxed television. The man was building the strength to load it into the back of his old Morris Oxford.

Without being asked to help, Barlow lifted the enormous box and eased it into the car. In the shop window sat the only television left unsold. Overhead a sign read: 'General Electric. 54 guineas delivered'. A sign underneath read: 'Watch both BBC and the new Ulster Television'. Barlow stepped into the shop, picked up the television in the window and put that into the back of the car as well.

'That's not sold,' protested Greenaway, his words of thanks choked by annoyance.

Barlow produced his wallet and counted eleven fivers into Greenaway's hand. 'You'll not be asking me to split a fiver for the odd change?'

Rather than argue, Greenaway put the notes into his wallet.

'And you'll throw in the aerial and the fitting of it before Christmas.'

'It's Christmas Eve,' protested Greenaway.
'Isn't that why I'm buying it?' said Barlow.

CHAPTER 19

TRADITIONALLY, SINGLE, UNATTACHED POLICE OFFICERS got the duty watch on Christmas Day, allowing their married comrades to stay at home with their families. Normally, Barlow took a few days off at that time, but he and the rest of the married officers were back on duty for the New Year, when the single officers headed for the pubs and anything else that took their fancy.

Stoop Taylor was to be buried on the day after Boxing Day. Harvey was still with his family in Belfast and Foxwood had gone to England, so Barlow and Leary were ordered to attend, representing the police.

Stoop hadn't been to church in decades – 'That would have meant putting money on the plate,' muttered Barlow – but the local Presbyterian minister had agreed to conduct the service.

All the poor minister could say was pious hopes. "I'm sure in his own way... Behind that gruff exterior I'm sure there lurked..."

Barlow sat in the church and watched to see who turned up at the service. The stone walls and marble plaques to dead heroes and self-glorifying benefactors oozed cold, making him glad of the extra vest he'd thought to put on. Other than the Frau and Peter sitting on their own in the front row, there were a couple of Stoop's near neighbours and a handful of cousins. Peter wore what looked like a second-hand suit cut down to size. The Frau's black coat could have belonged to her late mother-in-law, and probably did.

The cousins turned to examine everyone as they came into the church. At one point a frost seemed to come off them. His curiosity aroused, Barlow looked behind as well and saw Alexandra

Taylor step into the back row. He nodded. She nodded back, ignored the cousins.

By the time the coffin was being carried out of the church, Alexandra had gone, slipped away in case anyone tried to carry on the family dispute.

Edward Adair waited at the graveside: boots gleaming, beret at regulation angle, the black hackle of the Royal Ulster Rifles standing proud. Edward and Barlow saluted as the coffin was lowered into the grave.

'One felt there should be one representative from the Regiment at the interment,' said Edward to Barlow.

Barlow nodded. Gratitude was like cream left out in the sun. Quickly gone sour. Neither the British Legion nor the Regiment had thought it necessary to send a representative to the funeral of a man who carried the scars of his wartime service to the grave.

After the interment, when rain hung over the cortège but didn't engulf them, the Frau and Peter walked back home. No one accompanied them. The neighbours went home and the cousins took themselves off to Ballymena and the Castle Arms Hotel for a late lunch. Edward Adair hung around the gate of the churchyard, hoping for the offer of a lift back to town in the squad car.

Barlow said to Leary, 'I'd hate people to think so little of me that they didn't bother to come to my funeral.'

Leary replied, 'I wouldn't worry about that. Half the town will be there, celebrating. And, to make sure you don't come back, they'll drive a wooden stake through your heart.'

CHAPTER 20

BARLOW HEADED FOR THE CANTEEN at the back of the courthouse. Suppressed a burp. Christmas and the New Year's feasting had bloated his system and still half a goose remained for that night's supper. At the counter, he restricted himself to a mug of tea and a Kit Kat– *a man can have too much of a good thing* – and took a table at the far corner of the room.

Someone had abandoned a *Daily Mirror*. He swapped the A4 envelope he was carrying for the newspaper and opened it at the racing pages. Reckoned he couldn't pick a winner. Not with his current run of luck. Just to prove it, he decided to do a four-horse accumulator.

Jackson came looking for him. 'Sergeant, the Kurt Adenauer case is on next.'

'Right.'

He tucked the A4 envelope under his arm and followed Jackson's hurried steps. Wet footprints tracked the passageway leading from the front door. Obviously, it was pouring with rain again. Even walking on damp tiles put his teeth on edge.

Never had he seen the front hall so crowded. With the Christmas recess extending into January, the number of cases in court had quadrupled. He didn't recognise half the young criminals up in court that day, but he did know their fathers: men dressed in their Sunday best, who bent and twisted work-thickened hands in and out of each other. And the mothers: decent, God-fearing women in coats and scarves, worn out from anxiety, nervously twisting handkerchiefs in their thin hands.

Jackson had to slam to a stop as the younger Dunlops burst out of the Magistrate's Court, yelling 'yee-haw'. Barlow ignored their noisy delight. That incident in the cell block, where their kicking the cell door had nearly got him killed still rankled. The case against them for causing an affray had been put back, not dismissed. He'd get them some day.

Geordie saw Barlow and shook his fist at him. 'See you, Barlow. See you.'

Harvey and a strange man with him had got caught up in the throng. Harvey went puce with anger. 'Sergeant, control those people. At once.'

'People? I only see scum, sir.' He raised his voice. 'Out, you lot, before I do you for loitering.'

One of the Dunlop grandsons said, 'You'll squeal louder some dark night.'

'Falsetto,' said the smallest of the three, and made a cutting motion with his hand.

'I'll hold him down for you,' said Geordie. He flexed shoulders thick with muscle. 'One finger should be enough.'

Barlow caught Jackson's eye and jerked his head. Jackson squared his shoulders and marched forward. 'You will vacate the premises. Now.'

The young Dunlops lipped back even as they edged towards the door. Barlow ignored them. They wouldn't dare touch young Jackson, not with Geordie around to keep an eye on things. He was more interested in finding out about the stranger with Harvey. A foreigner by the look of him who wore a dark broadcloth suit with wide lapels and carried a fedora in his hand.

Barlow reckoned the suit was at least one size too big, as if the man expected to keep growing into middle age. The man's shoes gleamed a black gloss that reflected every light.

Harvey preened with importance. 'Sergeant, this is Herr Prim. Herr Prim is a secretary in the German Democratic Republic Embassy in London. A very important official, may I tell you.'

Tempted though he was, Barlow resisted clicking his heels together. Herr Prim might introduce himself as a secretary, but under that laughable suit his shoulders were square and his spine straight. The man might pretend to be a civilian but, he guessed, back in East Germany Herr Prim had a wardrobe full of uniforms.

Herr Prim walked on into the courtroom without speaking. Harvey trotted after him. At the doorway, Harvey made way for Solicitor Moncrief and a youth. Moncrief's jaw had a twist and a dent, giving his face a sour look.

Moncrief's smirk almost straightened his lips. 'Harvey, I can't believe the Dunlop case isn't ready to go to trial.' He indicated the youth, a tall, pudgy boy of fourteen. 'I kept Denholm off school especially today. Winning a case looks easy. I wanted him to see me fight one where a favourable outcome is impossible.'

Barlow's mouth dropped open. No sound came out.

Moncrief looked at him and his smirk widened. 'So Barlow's still around?' he said to Harvey.

'You should be grateful I'm still here,' Barlow replied. Look at the money you're making, keeping your Masonic friends out of jail.'

Moncrief ignored the remark, and looking directly at Harvey, he said: 'I warned you he was trouble.'

'Did you now?' said Barlow.

Harvey hastily interjected. 'Herr Prim, Mr Moncrief is the solicitor for Ballymena and District Council.'

Barlow said, 'Where he makes sure the councillors do exactly what they're told to do by their masters – and I don't mean the voters.'

'Really, Barlow! And in front of an important visitor,' spluttered Harvey.

'Don't worry, sir. Coming from East Germany as he does, Herr Prim knows exactly what I mean.' Then, turning to Moncrief, he added: 'But you're becoming overconfident, and I'll get you one of these days. See if I don't.'

'You're delusional, Sergeant,' said Moncrief, and walked on. Denholm followed his father. The tips of Harvey's ears glowed red.

Barlow had this urge to help Moncrief along with a well-placed kick. Instead, he muttered 'Come the revolution,' and took a seat near the front of the courtroom. Well away from everyone else.

Gradually, the tensions in his mind eased. In a town littered with churches, this was Barlow's cathedral. He admired the craftsmanship of the men who had made the benches and the desks. Their matching of grains and the dovetailing of joints, the butter-glow off oak under stark lights and the perfect blending of function and beauty. Sometimes he wished he'd remained a carpenter.

The Frau sat close to the dock. She had her hair done up in a tight bun and wore a dark red woollen coat. He'd seen that coat before in Dunlop & Carson's window. Had thought about buying it for Maggie for Christmas, but – *thank the Good Lord* – the television he'd bought instead was responsible for getting her out of bed for a couple of hours most evenings.

Herr Prim took his seat and, as he did so, the Frau tried to make herself invisible.

Constable Gillespie slid in beside Barlow and handed over a clipboard. All the cases already heard had been struck off. The officers who were no longer needed in court had been sent off about their business.

Barlow nodded in approval. 'Why don't you go for Sergeant?'

'Paperwork gives me migraines.' Gillespie pinched his nose between finger and thumb to indicate he was suffering.

'Maybe you shouldn't be driving, then?'

The look he got back made Herr Prim's cold stare seem friendly.

'Anyway,' said Gillespie. 'You'll never guess who's representing the Dunlops. Moncrief!'

'So I see,' Barlow said through clenched teeth. 'Geordie must have gone mad when he found out. That bastard Moncrief will see them hung.'

CHAPTER 21

THE CLERK OF THE COURT called for silence as the County Court judge, Mr Justice Donaldson, took his seat on the bench. Barlow knew Donaldson of old and didn't like the man. Donaldson had a short fuse and a nasty streak when riled.

He watched as two prison officers brought Adenauer up from the cells, wrists handcuffed in front of him. Barlow knew that he would have secured Adenauer's hands behind his back. Not doing so was a mistake, in his opinion, and he thought the prison officers old enough and experienced enough to know better when dealing with a man who stood taut with tension. Even so, Adenauer looked better than he had before Christmas, had put on weight, his face less gaunt.

Slowly, as if against her will, Barlow saw the Frau's red-sleeved arms reach up and stretch out, as if the couple could touch at that distance. Adenauer turned and stared at her. For a moment, he became a husband and a lover, then Donaldson gave a sharp cough and Adenauer looked away with a soundless snarl. Barlow eased his truncheon loose and nudged at Gillespie to do the same.

Detective Sergeant Leary took the stand. At an earlier hearing the court had remanded the defendant, Kurt Adenauer, in custody over the New Year, he intoned. The police now requested that he be remanded for a further month as enquiries were still ongoing.

'Merely a month?' snapped Donaldson. 'If the Dunlop case is anything to go by, ten years would seem reasonable.'

Leary spluttered excuses about workload and the inordinate amount of time devoted to the Adenauer case at the expense of other ongoing prosecutions.

Barlow frowned, not in the least concerned about Leary's blood pressure heading into the stratosphere, but he *did mind* Donaldson belittling the police in open court. Leary continued to give evidence, and Barlow sensed evasions, omissions rather than actual lies.

Beads of sweat stood on Leary's face when the defence counsel stood up. 'Could the Detective Sergeant say if the murder charge against my client still stands? Surely, in the light of inconclusive forensic tests ... '

Barlow looked at Gillespie, Gillespie looked back. A choking sound came from Harvey's direction. It seemed that it was news to him as well.

The prosecuting counsel popped up and said with surprising smoothness, 'We expect to bring additional charges against the accused.' Counsel indicated Herr Prim. 'This gentleman is an accredited diplomat from the German Democratic Republic.'

The defence counsel feigned outrage. He looked accusingly at the prosecuting counsel. How dare this be sprung on him? Leary disappeared off the stand with evident relief. Herr Prim took his place and identified himself as a secretary in the German Democratic Republic Embassy in London. He swore on the Bible to tell the truth, the whole truth and nothing but the truth.

Barlow chewed on an imaginary sweet while he tried to make sense of this. Communist East Germans didn't believe in God, let alone the Bible. Herr Prim wanted to be seen as a credible witness. *Why? What's the man up to?*

Yes, Herr Prim could identify the pistol.

The score on the butt made it unmistakeable. The pistol belonged to the captain of the motor vessel *Peenestrom* out of Rostock. That pistol, together with a considerable sum of money, had gone missing from the ship's safe. The same night crewman Adenauer disappeared.

The Frau jumped to her feet and screamed abuse at Herr Prim. Adenauer shouted as well and tried to go to her. The prison officers tackled him and he fought back. The Frau now mixed tears with her fury.

Donaldson hammered at the bench with a paperweight. 'Silence! One more word, woman, and I'll hold you in contempt of court.'

Barlow walked forward and took the Frau's arm. Got the smell of *Camay* soap and a cheap perfume. A Woolworth's special that Vera used to favour. 'Hush there, Missis, or you'll get into all sorts of bother.'

He saw Adenauer twist clear of the prison officers' restraining arms. Slash at the throat of one with his cuffed hands and headbutt the other. They fell away. One prison officer banged and bounced down the wooden stairs into the holding cells.

Barlow had no sympathy for them; they'd been too lax. He let go of the Frau's arm and blocked Adenauer's charge as Adenauer came bursting out over the dock. Found himself being pushed back, and fought for balance. Adenauer gripped Barlow's windpipe and the room started to darken. Gillespie hammered at the German's head with his truncheon. A jab in the face from Adenauer's elbow sent Gillespie spinning.

Desperate to breathe again, Barlow rammed his hands between Adenauer's arms, breaking the German's grip on his throat. A gulp of air wasted time and Adenauer's joined fists caught him way below the belt. Barlow fought to stay upright. If he went down, a boot would do for him.

Donaldson ordered the prisoner to be controlled. Gathered his robes around him and stalked out of the courtroom. Barlow wished the judge had done something practical and used his paperweight on Adenauer's head instead of on the bench.

Jackson appeared out of nowhere. Gillespie rejoined the fight. Two truncheons hammered the maniacal German. Herr Prim appeared at the edge of the brawl, but stayed well clear. Adenauer again grabbed Barlow by the throat and swung him around in a circle, creating space for himself. Then Adenauer let go, lunged forward and grabbed Jackson's revolver out of its holster. In one swift move he had it cocked and aimed.

It didn't seem fair. Two men battering Adenauer, and Adenauer had gone for Barlow. *What's he got against me?* He held up his hands using the peace sign.

Herr Prim's hand appeared from under his coat, holding a miniature pistol. Hoping he was doing the right thing Barlow dived for Herr Prim. He caught Herr Prim's wrist and forced his arm up. Behind him, Adenauer's revolver went *click, click, click*. Herr Prim's pistol fired.

The flash burned past Barlow's forehead. His ears hurt from the explosion. The bullet buried itself in the ceiling. Plaster cascaded down, paint flakes and dust drifted after. Herr Prim struggled to get in a second shot. Barlow pasted him on the nose and twisted the pistol out of his grip. Heard a finger snap.

At long, long last Adenauer went down. A blow from Gillespie knocked the revolver out of his hand. Leary bounced up to sit on Adenauer's legs.

Gillespie struggled for air. 'Sarge, it's a bloody good thing Jackson's revolver wasn't loaded.'

He felt himself all over. Somehow, he was still alive and uninjured. Normally, if he didn't have bad luck he'd have none at all. 'Give Jackson his due, he never makes the same mistake twice.'

Gillespie looked at Barlow like he had two heads. 'You didn't know for sure that the gun .... ?'

Harvey was dancing a jig of fury over Herr Prim's dangling finger. The Frau was shaking so hard that the chain on her silver bracelet began to rattle.

Barlow double-checked that Adenauer was well secured, hands behind his back this time. Rather than have the Frau see Adenauer being dragged back to the cells, he led her from the courtroom. They went outside and sat together on the front steps of the courthouse in the rain.

CHAPTER 22

A COIN TAPPED GENTLY ON the window. Dah – dah – dah – dahhh. Barlow opened the door to find Gillespie standing on the doorstep. He'd been half expecting him to call but was surprised at the lateness of the hour, near bedtime. Gillespie was still in his uniform. Had the *Belfast Telegraph* tucked under one arm and was holding two bottles of Tennents by the neck.

'I was passing,' Gillespie said with some embarrassment.

Barlow nodded in appreciation at the constable for not using the doorknocker. Gillespie never knocked, knowing that Maggie would be in bed and, hopefully, asleep. Never asked after her, but on the way out always said, 'Give Maggie my regards.'

Gillespie stooped in through the low doorway, nodded at Vera and inquired how she was finding the schoolwork. 'Fifth year at the Academy,' he said and grimaced in mock disgust. 'My lot are only good for digging ditches.'

'You've got one at Queen's, studying medicine.'

'A degenerate throwback,' said Gillespie.

Vera hung his jacket behind the scullery door. Fetched them glasses and brought one for herself. Both men gave her a dollop out of their bottle.

Gillespie sighed. 'That's a bad habit you taught her, Sergeant.'

'Me? You started it.'

Vera went back to her books and pretended to like her beer. After the first sip her nose screwed up. The two men sat and watched the fire while they drank.

'You're late tonight,' said Barlow, aiming his remark partly at Vera. School hadn't yet started after the Christmas break. The only thing stopping her from watching television was her own stubborn nature. Somehow, she'd got into a tangle over irregular French verbs and refused to stop until she had them sorted out.

He found it eerie, seeing images of himself in her. The not letting go.

Gillespie said, 'Harvey made me run Herr Prim to the boat. He's still… ' His eyes flickered in Vera's direction. 'Still having diarrhoea over you thumping a diplomat.'

'Herr Prim was going to murder Adenauer.'

'He claimed he panicked. He thought Adenauer would kill us.'

'The bastard's in the Stasi. The only time he'll panic is when they put the gun to the nape of his own neck.'

They finished their beers and sat on. Their toes toasted nicely in the heat from the fire.

Barlow's eyes were drawn to the only display items on the wall: a photograph of a primary school class and a second photograph of men wearing the uniform of the Royal Ulster Rifles, the feather hackles standing proud on their green berets. Gillespie stood in the centre row of the second photograph, displaying the chubby cheeks of youth that he'd never lost.

After a while Gillespie said, 'Anyway, this Kurt Adenauer case has got me worried.'

Vera's head stayed down but his daughter was listening; that he could tell. 'In what way?'

'Today. The money found during the search of Stoop's farm, and that pistol.'

'Aye, I've been thinking about that.' He stood up and fetched his jacket from the scullery. Took a notebook out of the pocket and put it in front of Vera. 'Who does this belong to?'

He bit down a smile when she pretended to come out of her studies. 'You, Da.'

'How do you know that?'

He got a look only a daughter could give. 'Because you've just taken it out of your pocket.'

He threw the notebook to Gillespie.

'Who does it belong to?'

'You.' Gillespie took another look. 'Hell, it's mine.'

'How do you know that?'

Gillespie took a look inside. 'That's my writing.'

'What does that tell you about Herr Prim and the pistol he says was stolen from the ship's captain?'

Gillespie said, 'You produced a notebook from your jacket pocket and I...' He smirked over at Vera to include her in the mistake. 'We assumed it was yours.' He held up a finger as if to silence himself, and continued after a pause. 'We found a German pistol in Stoop's house, so we assumed it belonged to Adenauer.'

Barlow added. 'Herr Prim didn't produce any documents giving the registration number of the missing pistol. Therefore, I'm betting Herr Prim didn't have a number to start with.' The more he vocalised his worries the more they made sense. 'The chances are that if Herr Prim didn't have the registration number of the pistol allegedly stolen from the captain, then no pistol was stolen in the first place.'

'And the money he said was taken?' asked Gillespie.

'One hundred and twenty pounds.'

Gillespie sighed in relief. 'There had to be ten times that.. .'

'Ten times what?' asked Vera.

'Mind your own business,' said Barlow.

'I'm practising to be nosey. Isn't that what policemen do?'

Before he could tell her to shut up, she smiled sweetly and offered to make them tea. She had an apple tart fresh out of Matthews Bakery that day. Would they like it heated?

When she had their hands entangled with cups and plates, she asked, 'Da, why would this Herr Prim lie under oath?'

'The East Germans don't like deserters among their sailors. It creates bad publicity. They want him back so they can jail him as a warning to others.'

'And the money?' persisted Vera.

They told her about Jackson finding Stoop's hidden hoard. And of them handing it over to the Frau. Gillespie wanted Vera to do a Scout's Honour first, not to blab. Barlow shrugged and said not to bother. If she could hold out against his interrogations, nobody would get anything out of her that she didn't want to tell.

He enjoyed the way Vera nodded sagely as they recounted the story. Then she stood over them, playing the prosecutor. 'You're sure it was one hundred and twenty pounds they say he took from the ship?'

'According to one of the detective constables, and that's about all he'd tell me.' That holding back of information annoyed Barlow. *You'd think we were on opposite sides.* It had taken a lot of flannel and the price of a cup of tea to get even that amount of information out of the detective constable.

Gillespie said, 'Harvey's ordered Leary to keep the investigation strictly confidential.'

Barlow kicked at Gillespie's booted foot. 'You're Harvey's blue-eyed boy. You run him everywhere, and you've no problem about claiming overtime.'

'It's my flat feet, he's sympathetic.' Gillespie stretched himself out of the chair. 'I should be off.'

On the doorstep he said, 'Give Maggie my regards,' and was gone.

CHAPTER 23

VERA LOCKED UP FOR THE night. She came back and curled up on the rug in front of the stove. 'You're worrying about this Adenauer case, Da.'

'What makes you think that?'

'You've been like an angel since you found Stoop Taylor lying dead.'

He kinked his head and looked at her, puzzled. 'What do you mean?'

She gave a smirk that he recognised as part nervousness. 'When you worry about something, you get into a bad temper. And when you're in a bad temper you go quiet rather than take it out on people.'

The Adenauer case *was* worrying him. He was also worried about Harvey. The man was doing his best to get rid of him. He could leave on a reduced pension. Maybe he should jump before Harvey pushed? And that would create another set of problems. The pension would keep him in bread and butter and the odd pint, but what about the medical bills for Maggie going private?

Vera would make a good policewoman, he decided, dragging his thoughts back to the present. She had an instinct for trouble. All the same, he didn't want to hint about their own precarious financial position. Maggie gave her enough anxious hours without landing any more worries on her young shoulders.

'Kurt Adenauer,' he said. 'An open and shut case of premeditated murder if I ever saw one. And yet … '

She slid over to rest her head on his knee. 'What?'

He stroked the black silk of her hair. 'Adenauer's ship, *The Peenestrom*, got into London Docks late on the Wednesday before Stoop Taylor was killed.'

Her head lifted. 'Are you sure of that?'

He pressed it back again. She hadn't sat curled into his legs like this since Kenny Cameron and his hormones had come into her life. It implied a loss of innocence that made him uneasy.

'I got a friend in Customs and Excise to check the dates.'

'Hearsay, but acceptable in the circumstances.'

He gave her a loving clip on the ear. 'According to Herr Prim, Adenauer stole the pistol and the money when the captain was off the ship.'

Her head came up again. 'How did he get into the safe?'

A good question, and trust his daughter to think of it. The answer was so neat it grated his teeth. 'According to Herr Prim, the captain needed papers out of the safe for the Agent. That's the man who arranges cargos for the ship. The ship arrived late in the Wednesday afternoon, near closing time. The captain, in his rush, forgot to lock up.'

'Very convenient.'

'Anyway, Adenauer caught the boat train to Liverpool and the ferry that evening to Belfast. He arrived to stay with Stoop and the Frau some time on the Thursday. The next day he shot Stoop in the back.' He stopped.

'And?' she demanded.

'The next bit's gory.'

'I like gory,' she said and flexed her fingers in a mock threat. She still played with chicken legs. Pulling the tendons to make the claws go in and out. She only had to point them at him and he got the shivers. Not that he dared let on.

'Adenauer thought the whole bullet had gone through the chest. He left the body in the gateway and used a .22 to terrify the cattle, get them to stampede over the body. If it hadn't been for the bullet fragments, we might have assumed death by misadventure.'

Vera pulled away from him. She went to the table and started to tidy her books. She seemed unsettled by what he'd told her. Hopefully, she wouldn't have nightmares. You never knew with kids.

Thumping the books to make them fit into her bag, she asked. 'It seems funny, him shooting at the cattle from the hayloft. Why not from the roadside?'

He touched his throat, remembering the expert way Adenauer's fingers had locked around his neck during the fight in Stoop's yard. 'A German that age, he's an ex-soldier.' He puzzled over the events in the hayloft. 'I heard the shots fired by the .22. Let's assume the first one was a ranging shot at the insulator holding the telephone wire. Which makes Adenauer either very lucky or a marksman. And of course, once in the hayloft, there's less chance of being spotted by a casual passer-by.'

He wanted to move about the room to quell the restlessness in himself. He couldn't because Vera blocked his way. 'Our case against Adenauer is all assumptions: he did this, he did that. Harvey and Leary are very reticent about what proof they've got. By this stage, they should have set a date for the hanging.'

She swung round. 'Not if he's a nutcase. They wouldn't be that mean.'

'It's not that.' He pressurised her into a seat and out of the way, and took a turn around the room himself. 'If I could be sure of things: the dates and times of Adenauer's movements. Where that pistol really came from.'

'What if the gunman in the hayloft wasn't Adenauer?'

He wanted to shout at her not to be stupid, because that was the one piece of hard evidence they had got that didn't make sense. The gunman in the hayloft had escaped on a racing bike. The only bike they'd found on Stoop's farm was a rickety bone-shaker that the Frau used to go shopping.

He said, 'It has to be Adenauer. There couldn't be two homicidal maniacs out there.'

Vera's pen rolled onto the floor. She ducked down after it. Looked at from that angle she needed to lose weight around the hips. His little girl was turning into a woman before his eyes. He felt both pleased and sad.

Her voice echoed back at him from under the table. 'But why would Adenauer want to shoot Stoop in the first place?'

He stopped pacing and stretched upwards. Only so far, or he'd thump the ceiling and waken Maggie. 'You tell me. Young Peter is probably his natural son. The Frau said he was her husband, and yet she married Stoop and lived with him in that God-forsaken hole.'

The more he allowed himself to think about the case, the less it made sense.

'Nearly fifteen years later, Adenauer follows to seek revenge on the man who now possesses his woman. Maybe he wants to take her back with him? Maybe she refused to go and he exploded in a blind rage? Who knows?'

'But why wait fifteen years?'

That puzzled him as well. It seemed a ridiculous amount of time to wait before coming after your woman or taking revenge. He scraped his knuckles over the plaster ceiling, needing a physical hurt to distract his thoughts from all the unknowns.

Lime stuck to the back of his hand and he brushed it off. 'If what they say about Germany immediately after the war is half true, then the Frau coming to live with the meanest man in Christendom makes sense. At least she'd a roof over her head and food on the table.'

One thing puzzled the reluctant paper-pusher in him. 'To get into the country she needed documentation: passport, marriage certificate and immigration papers. They'd tell us a lot. Yet we searched that house from top to bottom and I'm guessing that we didn't find any of them. Not one.'

'What do you mean, you're guessing?'

He was annoyed with himself for letting slip that he was having problems with Harvey. Now she'd picked up on it, maybe he should tell her something of his troubles at work. Give her fair warning that he could be transferred to another town in the near future.

'This is Harvey's first big case and he doesn't want me involved. The detectives are sworn to secrecy. Any man who speaks out of turn gets transferred to the back end of nowhere.'

'He's an idiot,' she said.

'Well, we know that.'

He checked the clock, *bedtime*, reached past her and lifted the kettle onto the range for a final cup of tea.

He picked up Gillespie's copy of the *Belfast Telegraph*, opened the results section and pulled the list of horses from his hip pocket. 'Frig and bust,' he roared.

Vera jerked erect. 'What, Da?'

'My four horses: six doubles, four trebles and an accumulator. They all came up.'

She jumped to her feet and hugged him. 'Fantastic! How much did you win?'

He untangled her from his neck. 'Nothing. What with one thing and another, I never got to the bookies.'

CHAPTER 24

THE NEXT DAY, BARLOW WAS on the afternoon shift, two until eight. Even before he got to the station he could smell trouble. He stood for a moment beside the Memorial Garden – a railed-in area of shrubs and flowers, and signs proclaiming "Keep off the grass".

Now what's Harvey up to?

Harvey's personal squad car sat at the front of the building instead of being parked safely in the yard. *Gillespie will go mad if he sees that.* And two civilian cars sat in police bays. Cars he didn't recognise even though they had local number plates. All the same, something about them seemed familiar ... He checked his watch. Too close to start time to take a stroll up the town and casually run into a foot patrol, to hear what was going on.

He shrugged, gave his jacket a tweak, checked that his cap was positioned at the right angle and marched into the station.

Only Jackson manned the Enquiry Office and, for once, the young officer looked relieved to see him.

'*All regular?*' asked Barlow.

Instead of replying, Jackson swung the Incident Book around to let him read the entries.

'Bloody hell!'

Edward was back in the cell, and this time he wasn't a *guest* looking for *accommodation* over Christmas.

'What has that fool man done now?'

Jackson didn't know. Edward had arrived in and asked to speak to Harvey on a personal matter. WPC Day escorted Edward to Harvey's office. Soon afterwards Harvey had exploded in a fit of temper. 'You should have seen him, sergeant. I thought he was going to have a heart attack.'

'Pity,' said Barlow, wanting to be callous, in order to cover an eerie feeling in the pit of his stomach.

Those cars, their registration numbers? Wished he had his old notebook so that he could check and be sure.

'What else?' he asked, feigning disinterest by flicking through his "IN" tray.

'Then Sergeant Pierson was sent to Belfast. The Vehicle Registration Office, and I only heard that last bit accidentally.'

At this bit of news, Barlow had grounds to be interested. He looked up. 'Belfast, the Vehicle Registration Office, you say? Now what would take that man there?' He pointed. 'Shouldn't you have something recorded in the Incident Book?'

'I was told to mind my own business.' Jackson sounded anxious, verging on panic for having let Barlow down.

Barlow made sure the young constable saw his solid nod of approval. 'Son, you asked the right questions. It wasn't up to you to supply the answers.'

Jackson whooshed out air in relief. 'Later on people started to call here to see DI Harvey. Again, they asked for him personally.' He glanced around anxiously, in case someone had crept up on them and was listening in on their conversation. His voice dropped to a whisper. 'I kept a list of their names.' The whisper became so faint Barlow could barely make out what the young lad was saying. 'I was told not to, 'Jackson finished, as he dug out the list from the deep recesses of an inner pocket and handed it over.

Six names, Barlow noted. He knew the men: who they were and what they did for a living. But what had that got to do with Harvey? And, presumably Edward, if things had started to happen after Edward spoke to Harvey.

First things first. See what Edward has got to say for himself. On the way to the cells Barlow had to pass the interview rooms. He could hear Harvey's high-pitched voice coming from one of them.

Pierson stood guard at the door. 'Walk on, Barlow.'

Barlow went toe to toe with him. 'Try that again.'

'Station Sergeant Barlow.'

'That's better.'

Barlow flicked a hand at Pierson to stand aside, and walked on. At the door of the next interview room he put a hand out as if to turn the handle. Heard Pierson's feet shuffle on the linoleum as he tried to build the nerve to stop him from looking in.

Barlow walked on, kept the smirk to himself. Was aware of Pierson following him on tip-toe. *Bloody Harvey clone.*

Gillespie stood guard at the door leading into the cells. He blocked Barlow's path.

'Sorry, Sarge,' he said.

So, he wasn't allowed to speak to Edward either? From thrown shadows Barlow knew that Pierson was close behind him, listening in.

Barlow told Gillespie, 'Your car's out front, and there are a lot of kids around it on bikes.'

'If they scrape it...'

'Aye.'

He turned to go. Gillespie whispered into his back. 'Sarge, lock and load.'

Barlow told Pierson, 'I'll go and sign in for the shift. Be a good little messenger boy, and tell District Inspector Harvey I'll be waiting for him in his office.'

No way was he going to be escorted there.

CHAPTER 25

ON HIS WAY TO HARVEY'S office, Barlow again made a point of passing the interview rooms. This time he heard two people speaking. Harvey for one. The second voice puzzled him for a minute, then he recognised it.

Moncrief! Bloody Moncrief.

Moncrief with the twisted jaw and the twisted mind and the twisted hate. The Moncriefs had tried to keep him out of the police force when he first applied. Even put it around the town that his mother had been a whore riddled with the pox. Put it around that she'd infected many a decent man with the disease, and wouldn't cease her immoral ways. Put it around that the only way the workhouse authorities could stop her was to suffocate her between two mattresses. Moncrief had even carried that tale with him into the army. Spread it around, until he got a warning that not even Moncrief had dared ignore.

Barlow stepped into Harvey's office. The lights were on, although no one was there. *Dare anyone else be caught wasting electricity in the station.* The snide thought was to try and convince himself that everything was normal, that things would work out. With Moncrief involved, the end result had to be brutal.

A used police notebook sat on Harvey's desk among the other papers. It was only a guess, but it had to be Barlow's own notebook, the one he'd stupidly let Harvey take off him at Christmas. *I should have stolen it back.* He wished he dared crosscheck the car registration numbers in the notebook with the numbers of the two strange cars parked at the front door.

Footsteps sounded in the corridor outside. Harvey's quick, tip-toe steps and Moncrief's more measured stride. Everything Moncrief did was measured, everything geared for his own benefit.

The door opened, the two of them came in. Barlow snapped to attention, honouring the picture of the Queen.

'What have you touched? What have you been at?' demanded Moncrief.

'Nothing, of course, sir,' said Barlow, getting in a good response in case Harvey or Moncrief recorded what the defendant has said in response to the charge.

Harvey was in uniform. *Still looks like a bantam cock,* thought Barlow, *and a ruffled one at that.* Moncrief could have stepped straight out of a bespoke tailor's window. *Bet you his pyjamas are starched.*

'Barlow,' snapped Harvey, ready to begin.

But Moncrief placed a steadying hand on his arm. 'District Inspector, seeing that I am not personally ... '

'Yes, yes. Of course.'

Harvey walked across the room and sat at his desk. Fiddled with files. Stacked them neatly. Repositioned them again.

Moncrief's smile twisted his jaw even further to the side. 'Barlow, District Inspector Harvey had an unexpected visitor this morning, your former Company Commander, Major Edward Adair. Edward Adair, or the town drunk as he is better known as, attempted to blackmail District Inspector Harvey.' Moncrief went across to Harvey's desk and extracted a folder thick with papers. 'Edward Adair alleged that on the night of the Round Table Ball he had observed Mr Harvey and an unnamed female copulating in a public place.'

Moncrief turned to Harvey who had gone an unhealthy creamy-purple. 'Have I got my facts right so far, District Inspector?'

'Yes.' Harvey couldn't have got another word out if his life had depended on it.

Barlow could only hope for Divine intervention. He glanced up at the ceiling. *Lightning never strikes when you need it.*

'Edward Adair,' continued Moncrief, 'admitted that he has already approached seven other men whom, he alleged, had committed obscene acts in public, and on the same night. That...' Moncrief referred to a page in the folder. 'That to secure his comfort and to enhance his edification, each of those men had given him a sum of money.' He closed the file again. 'After a formal caution issued by District Inspector Harvey personally, Edward Adair further admitted that this was an annual – shall we say, extortion – of money by him.'

In all his years, Barlow had never laid a hand on a prisoner, other than to apply a necessary restraint. Right then, he'd have wrung Edward's neck like a diseased chicken.

Things were happening that he didn't know about, quiet deals done. Still, he fought back stubbornly. 'No man would dare testify to that in court. Their mothers would kill them for letting the family down in front of her neighbours.

'Oh but we have two men, Barlow. Two upright citizens willing to testify in open court.'

'And when they get their names spread over the local newspapers?'

Moncrief laughed. 'Funnily enough, I've already spoken to the proprietors of both papers. Neither man thinks the case newsworthy.' If it weren't for the fact that Moncrief was already holding a huge manila folder, he would have rubbed his two hands together with glee. 'Barlow, how many years do you think Edward Adair will get, and how long do you think he'll last in prison?'

Not long, Barlow had to admit to himself. At that moment, Edward was sitting in a narrow cell, the door locked behind him. *He must already be twitchy.* "Years," Moncrief said. And, yes, Edward deserved to get years, but Moncrief and his cronies would make sure he got five years at least.

Moncrief referred to the folder again and extracted a page. He held it up for Barlow to scrutinise. 'If you sign this form, all charges against your former Company Commander will be dropped.'

Barlow stared at the form. It had already been filled in: dates, times and details correct.

No they couldn't ask that of me. Not that.

Moncrief held the form even closer. Harvey uncapped his fountain pen and brought it across.

'Surely,' purred Moncrief. 'Surely, when you've spent so much time and gone to so much trouble for your old Company Commander: keeping him alive and trying to stop him from drinking himself to death. Surely you'll not fail your old comrade now?'

Barlow thought fast. 'Of course Edward's solicitor will want to know why the District Inspector's name was on the list.'

'Only by error, Barlow, a simple typographical error.' Moncrief's voice had resumed its gloat. 'That drunken fool Edward Adair misread a two for a five. The Triumph in question belongs to a certain Mr O'Connor. Mr O'Connor plays a saxophone in a dance band and was playing at a venue that night. He claims that afterwards he went drinking with friends, but is unable to provide a witness to corroborate his story.'

Harvey found his voice at last. 'A one-time offer, Barlow. Instant decision: yes or no.'

The form was Barlow's application to resign from the Royal Ulster Constabulary. With immediate effect.

CHAPTER 26

THE CLOCK TICKED IN HARVEY'S office. Outside in the station yard someone cleared their throat. It had started raining again, darkening the room. Raindrops rattled noisily off the window. This was one of Barlow's old wartime walks, except that now *he* was the target. He needed someone else to do the long walk to save him.

Barlow pushed past the two men and walked over to Harvey's desk. Picked up the phone with a steady hand and dialled.

A woman answered. 'Ballymena Brewery Company.'

Of all people, Mrs Anderson. Thank God.

'Sergeant Barlow here. May I speak to Captain Denton?'

'I'm afraid he's in a meeting right now, and can't be disturbed.'

At least he's there.

Barlow said, 'It's about Edward. It's really urgent.'

'Oh, my God, he's not hurt? Is he all right?'

Mrs Anderson's husband, Arthur, had come home from the war with terminal tuberculosis. Corporal Arthur Anderson had been Edward's Company Clerk and Edward had used his own post-war bounty to buy the Andersons a house. Mrs Anderson had never forgotten Edward's kindness and had set aside a bedroom for him, which he was welcome to use anytime. Edward visited regularly for a meal and a hot bath and, more recently, a shared bed. But he never stayed long because the Anderson house was "dry". No alcohol allowed.

Barlow assured Mrs Anderson that other than being in jail, Edward was unharmed. She put Barlow on hold while she buzzed through to Denton.

Harvey said, 'Barlow, you're wasting your time. This is a police procedural matter and outside the scope of the remit of a Chairman of the Policing Advisory Board.'

The receiver rattled at the other end.

'Barlow?'

'Sir.'

'Speak.'

Using words like "alleged" and "perhaps" Barlow told of Edward's method of raising money to fund his Christmas drinking. That Edward had only now, allegedly, got around to asking Harvey for his contribution. Denton interrupted occasionally with a terse question. That worried Barlow because Denton liked to talk things through in detail.

When Barlow began to tell how he had identified one of the cars as belonging to Harvey, Harvey snatched the receiver from his hand and gave his version of events. This time Denton listened without any interruptions.

And that really worried Barlow. When Denton went totally quiet, his temper was up and the man was likely to explode in any direction. Finally, Harvey ran out of anything to say other than to remind Denton that a civilian Chairman of the Policing Advisory Board had no powers to interfere in the day-to-day running of the police force. And, in particular, the prosecuting of offenders or the disciplining of officers whose behaviour had fallen well short of the required standard.

Denton said, 'Put the phone on the loudspeaker.'

Harvey did as he was told.

'Now, who's there?'

'Myself, Solicitor Moncrief and Barlow.'

'Harvey, your rank is still that of Acting District Inspector and your record in Ballymena has not been one of unqualified success. However, I will personally guarantee your promotion if the charges against Edward and Barlow are dropped.'

Harvey started to argue, but Denton interrupted him, saying, 'Your choice,' and told him to put Barlow back on.

Barlow took the receiver and cut off the loudspeaker function.

Denton said, 'I depend on you to take care of that drunken idiot. You've let me down and it could cost me big time.'

He hung up. Barlow stood on with the receiver still held to his ear. He needed to stand that way for several seconds so that Harvey and Moncrief wouldn't see the shock on his face. Denton had known about the Harvey all along. Worse, the only way he could have known about it was because he had engineered the entire situation in the first place.

What was it that Edward had said about one of the ladies, the one with Harvey? That she was an exhibitionist and liked an audience. Witnesses, in fact, to Harvey's adultery. Knowledge was power, and Barlow had cost the Chairman the ability of having Harvey react to his suggestions as if they were commands.

He hung up, feeling sorry for the lady involved. A Mrs Carberry who had made some bad choices in her life: Married a waster who spent her inheritance. Then divorced him just before he was killed in action, costing herself a War Widow's Pension. *The things that poor woman has to do in order to make ends meet.*

He turned around. The other two men stood, watching him. Harvey hadn't yet said yes or no to Denton's offer.

Barlow said, 'I'll release Edward.'

He stepped around them and walked out the door. Harvey still hadn't spoken.

Sometime later Harvey marched into the Enquiry Office and snapped to a halt on the public side of the counter.

Barlow glanced up from the case files he was processing, assessed Harvey's mood and came to a respectful attention. 'Can I help you, sir?'

Harvey snapped, 'Jackson, get lost.'

Barlow jerked his head. Jackson grabbed a bundle of files – the wrong ones, not the ones waiting to be distributed – and ran down the corridor, out of sight.

Harvey said, 'Barlow, I will never forgive you for the embarrassment you caused me today. He held up a finger as he detailed each point. 'You blackmailed me. You concealed Edward Adair's crimes. Crimes you had knowledge of after the fact. And finally, you made me look an utter fool in front of some important people.'

Harvey's voice shook, from temper, not fear. 'Don't worry about being posted. I have no intention of posting you. But you are unable to work by the rules and you totally ignore them when it comes to protecting your friends.' He leaned on the counter and stood on tiptoe to get somewhere near Barlow's height. 'I will not rest content until you are charged, arraigned, tried and convicted. I plan to personally escort you from the Ballymena courthouse, in handcuffs.'

CHAPTER 27

JANUARY PASSED WITH THE USUAL downpours of chill rain and driving sleet. February wasn't too bad, although cattle still disappeared off farms and the Dunlops had plenty of money to throw around them in the pubs. Barlow recorded one and noted the other, and longed for enough proof to tie them together.

At the beginning of March Barlow parked his bike in the yard and went into the police station to start the afternoon shift. The Incident Book held little of interest. Only the usual thumps and bumps. However, Detective Sergeant Leary had asked Jackson to pass on a message. "Would Sergeant Barlow please call with him, at his convenience?"

Meanwhile, a farmer waited to see him. The farmer had made his complaint earlier in the morning, but wanted to speak to him personally. He appeared anxious, and had taken time to dress in his town clothes of jacket and mustard-coloured waistcoat before coming to the police station. Two mature bullocks were missing. Eight hundredweight each, prime animals, both ready for the mart. A commotion started among his cattle at dawn. He thought a pack of dogs were in worrying the calves and he ran to investigate. Saw a lorry drive off, but was too far away to read the number plate.

The man became breathless with annoyance.

Barlow made a note to make sure details of the lorry would be passed on to the patrols. With no great confidence of getting any cooperation from that department, he requested that a detective speak to the farmer.

JOHN MCALLISTER

The farmer seemed highly impressed. A *detective* on his case? Went into the interview room confident that his cattle would soon be on their way home, safe and sound. Barlow didn't disillusion him. A seventh theft of cattle, and a lorry to haul them away in, made it a case of organised crime. Those bullocks would be prime sirloin steaks before the day was out.

To Barlow's surprise, a detective constable appeared, pen and pad in hand. On his way into the interview room the detective threw a smile and a nod in the direction of the desk.

Barlow turned to Jackson. 'DS Leary did say "please"? You're sure of that?'

'Yes, Sergeant.'

Leary had *asked* to see him and with a *please*. Things had to be bad. He headed for the detectives' room where he found Detective Sergeant Leary making a play at being busy, reviewing a case with a junior colleague. That day's *Mirror* lay unopened and the files on the desk had been worked on. Somebody had put every loose paper in their files and the files into cupboards, and he sniffed polish in the air. That hadn't happened since Methuselah was a boy.

Leary looked up and smiled when he came in the doorway. Leary even half-rose in his seat and motioned for him to sit opposite. The detective constable slipped out of the room. The door closed with a solid click, ensuring they wouldn't be overheard.

That made Barlow determined. Whatever the problem, it stayed in this room. No way would he, Barlow, get involved.

Leary started, 'Barlow,' and stopped again.

'Out with it.'

'The court this morning.'

Leary looked like he hadn't slept in days. Might even have lost weight. Barlow put that down to wishful thinking on his part and gave a noncommittal, 'Aye.'

'The Dunlops?'

'Aye.'

Leary's fingers played with a file. 'We weren't ready to go ahead.'

'Again?' He restricted himself to a breathy whistle. The Dunlop case meant a pleasant morning's paperwork for someone, a doss day at most. A month's adjournment seemed reasonable. A three-month delay, even allowing for Christmas, was stretching things.

Leary, he realised, was using the Dunlops as a throat-clearer. Whatever Leary wanted to see him about had to be serious. He wouldn't have minded a cup of tea.

'So we went for another adjournment,' said Leary. 'They'll go to trial next month, if I'm still here.'

He pretended to be pleased. 'You lucky man: the city or maybe even the border with Donegal. Didn't your family come from way up there originally?

Leary scowled, doubly annoyed with Barlow. First, Bally-mena was a sought-after posting. No great crime and the wives loved the town. They'd a choice of good schools and were less than an hour from Belfast city centre and the shops. Secondly, Leary's family hadn't been near Donegal in well over a hundred years. Not since his ancestors had swapped their Catholic reli-gion for soup during the Great Famine in 1845.

'It's not funny,' snapped Leary and went quiet until the irri-tation drained out of his face. 'Stoop's murder. The case is going nowhere fast.'

'That's a shame. Especially with Mr Harvey telling Head-quarters that it's a clear case of premeditated murder. And that he's got his man.'

He could see the murder files on Leary's desk and itched to read through them. 'So tell me,' he said, feigning sympathy as Leary sat sweating with fear. The sweat ignited the Old Spice Leary favoured and the smell twitched his nose. *You'd think he wore it to annoy me.*

A detective constable came back with a cup of tea for both of them. Then, obviously under orders, slipped out again, leaving Leary to crawl without any witnesses present.

Barlow normally never took a cup of tea from the detectives. Always felt that one of them would spit in it. This time he drank with confidence.

With a bit of humming and hawing, Leary came out with the problem. Stoop was dead before the cattle trampled the body. Dead before he hit the ground because the pathologist had found no trace of mud in his lungs or airways. Barlow knew that already, but Leary could be a bit pedantic at times.

The only evidence of violence on the body was the bullet fragments. The bullet shattered on impact with the shoulder blade. More than that it was impossible to say because the panicked cattle had made a mess of the torso.

'Those damn hooves slice like scalpels,' complained Leary.

'Good at scooping out brains too,' Barlow said, remembering the void where Stoop used to keep his meanness and spite.

He wouldn't have minded a biscuit. Leary kept a drawerful, but the drawer stayed closed. That made Barlow even more determined not to get involved.

'You've always got ballistics,' Barlow prompted.

They had and they hadn't. The bullet fragments were too small, making it impossible to say for certain that they'd come from Adenauer's pistol. Everything had been sent to Fort Halstead in Kent to see what they could do. So far, nothing, and the British Army, who ran the laboratories there, refused to be rushed. They'd more important things to do, like build atom bombs.

'What did Stoop's wife, or whatever she is, say?'

Leary handed him the Frau's statement to read. 'According to the statement her cousin…'

'Cousin?'

'She blames her poor English. She meant to say cousin, but her head gave the wrong word.'

'Aye.'

He continued to read. Her cousin had arrived unexpectedly the day before. The cousin was tired and unwell and hadn't left the house all day. After breakfast, Stoop went out to repair a lean-to in the far field. Peter went to school soon afterwards.

He sucked on a sweet. Peter at school? Now why did the boy lie about working on the tractor with Adenauer? *Hardly bad English on his part.* He read on.

According to the statement, the Frau began to worry when Stoop didn't come home for lunch. She'd just put on her coat to go looking for him when the police came.

He returned the Frau's statement to Leary. 'According to this, the man's as innocent as snow.'

'Driven snow, more like. Adenauer's prints were all over the hayloft. And yours and a couple of hundred other people's.'

He sipped at his tea while he thought things through. *Not bad, warm anyway.* The Frau was lying about Adenauer not leaving the house. Then he had another thought. Adenauer was an old soldier. Maybe he spied on Stoop's farm for a while before calling.

A biscuit would have helped him figure things out. He'd remember Leary's meanness the next time he wanted a favour done. Asked, 'What sort of bike does the boy ride?'

'None,' said Leary. 'He walks two miles to school every day and two miles back. And he was at school the day of the murder. All day. I checked with the headmaster.'

'You've still got enough to hold Adenauer.'

'What?'

'The assault on young Jackson? The attempted escape?'

Leary said, '*Diminished Capacity.* In Queen's English: not guilty because the man is of unsound mind.'

Barlow enjoyed watching the fat detective squirm. 'Illegal alien?'

'For God's sake, he wants to stay in the country, not disappear over the border.' Leary shivered, as if Harvey's breath of disapproval had run down his back. 'All we have is the theft of money and pistol from his ship.'

'What about the shenanigans in the courtroom, him trying to shoot me?'

'In my book, justifiable homicide.'

He raised his eyebrows at the spite in the words. 'Not Stoop's murder?'

'No.'

'Does Harvey know all of this?'

Leary's whole body sagged. 'No.'

Barlow drained his cup. 'Harvey will go spare.'

He left.

CHAPTER 28

DISTRICT INSPECTOR HARVEY STOOD AT the front desk, all a-jangle. 'Barlow, where have you been?'

'DS Leary wanted a word, sir.'

'Not about Kurt Adenauer, I hope. I don't want you anywhere near that case, and that's an order.'

He thought he might get involved just to spite his superior. There again, he'd better things to do than Leary's work. 'If you say so, sir.'

Harvey looked put out, as if he'd been expecting an argument. 'Yes, right. Come with me.'

He rushed off. Barlow paced after him to find Captain Denton, the Chairman of the local Policing Advisory Board, waiting for them in Harvey's office. Denton stood to the right of the portrait of the Queen, flexing his legs. Something he did after sitting for long periods. Throughout his working life, including his stint as junior manager in the brewery that he now owned, he had hated deskwork. It cramped him. Wherever it was he'd taken his wife and children over Christmas and the New Year, he'd managed to catch the sun. Rumour had it, a world cruise – impossible in a period of just three weeks – which Vera had debunked saying "only as far as the Norwegian Fjords", like Captain Denton was some sort of cheapskate.

Barlow touched his forehead in a casual salute. 'Welcome back, sir. You were missed.'

In his opinion Denton spent too much time in the police station. Although he had to admit that the old District Inspector, Andy Thornton, sometimes needed encouragement in order to make decisions. Harvey had no problem in that respect. It was just that in Barlow's opinion, making the right decisions tended to be beyond Harvey.

Denton said, 'Shooting that diplomat dead would have caused less fuss. At least Herr Prim wouldn't be around to claim police brutality.'

'I'll remember that for the next time, sir.'

Harvey spluttered. 'Barlow, remember who you're talking to.'

'I'm well used to him,' said Denton, furrowing his eyebrows at Barlow in a way that meant "Watch your tongue".

'Either way,' said Harvey, 'A Board of Enquiry will have to be convened.'

He looked at Denton, who continued. 'The East Germans have again raised the question of one of their diplomats being assaulted by a member of this force. You Barlow. For diplomatic reasons, we must be seen to take Herr Prim's allegations of an unprovoked assault seriously.'

Denton hesitated, giving him time to worry about what was coming next.

'After some discussion with the Chief Constable, we have decided that it would be unfair to suspend you from duty. However, someone else will have to act as Station Sergeant until the matter is resolved.'

If Harvey had won Littlewoods Pools, he couldn't have looked more pleased. Harvey would do his damnedest, Barlow reckoned, to have the enquiry find him guilty.

Harvey phoned for Inspector Foxwood, who appeared promptly. Harvey sat even more upright in his chair and said with all formality: 'Inspector Foxwood, Sergeant Barlow is no longer Station Sergeant. Sergeant Pierson will take over that post.'

Foxwood didn't look surprised. Something concocted between them, Barlow realised.

Foxwood asked, 'From what date, sir?'

'With immediate effect.' Harvey's nose pinched in disdain. 'You are dismissed.'

Barlow kept his face blank of emotion, sick that people hated him that much. He turned away.

Denton said, 'Barlow, I'll chair the enquiry myself.'

'Thank you, sir.'

Denton looked annoyed as his mind switched to a new track. 'You've had no success in tracing the cattle stolen from local farms.'

All of a sudden the stolen cattle became Barlow's fault, not Leary's. *Will that come up in the enquiry as well?* Harvey was likely to include all sorts of allegations.

'We're following various leads, sir,' he said and noticed Harvey's look of surprise at this bluff. They hadn't a single lead to follow. *If only the old farmer had managed to take a note of the number plate.*

Denton gave him a look that could have cut corn. 'Don't give me that old flannel.'

'It's the Dunlops, sir.'

'Of course it's the bloody Dunlops.'

Barlow sucked on an imaginary Mint Imperial. 'What they do with them is the problem. Most of the local butchers wouldn't sell three beasts a month.'

Denton growled. 'I'm more concerned about my Aberdeen Angus.' He nodded to Harvey. 'You tell him.'

Harvey plainly enjoyed the telling. It meant long cold nights for him. A lot of cattle had been stolen recently, he said, and Captain Denton was concerned that someone would try to steal his prize cattle. Particularly on Saturday nights when the stockmen liked to spend time with their families.

The pub more like, Barlow thought, but didn't say.

In a way he wasn't surprised at Denton misusing his position as Chairman of the local Policing Advisory Board. Denton never did anything for nothing. Even in primary school, Denton had kept the younger boys safe from bullies, but it cost them a penny a week for the privilege. If they hadn't the penny the younger boys paid in other ways: cleaning his boots or carrying his school bag. Denton could never understand why Barlow would thump a bully free of charge. He'd say. 'You're a fool to work for nothing. My grandfather did, and it put us all on the street. The bailiffs took everything, even my baby sister's tricycle.'

A stakeout was more a job for detectives than the uniform branch, let alone a senior sergeant. Barlow didn't say that either. Instead, he looked at Denton, who may or may not have agreed with him. But Barlow already *owed* Denton for saving Edward from jail and for being able to keep his own job. There'd be no more favours until that debt was paid.

Harvey's instructions were detailed and took nearly five minutes to deliver. Finished, he asked, 'Any questions?'

Barlow shook his head and wrote in his notebook. *From eight at night to six in the morning. Every Saturday until further notice...* He put his pencil away. Put his notebook away. Brushed a fleck of dust off his uniform.

Harvey sat back in his chair, arms folded over an incipient paunch. 'Fair warning, Barlow.' He held up a finger to focus Foxwood's attention. 'And Inspector, you bear witness to this.

'Sergea....' Harvey smirked. 'Barlow.' He let the word roll off his tongue as he treated him like a felon awaiting his just desserts. 'Final point, Barlow, my "zero tolerance" approach to crime is to be applied in every case. Any exception will be taken as a deliberate refusal by you to obey a legitimate order.'

Barlow aimed his snap to attention at the Queen rather than Harvey, and headed for the door.

CHAPTER 29

BARLOW STAMPED HIS FEET TO keep them warm. The door of the old chicken house on Alexandra Taylor's land had long since disappeared. Schoolboy stones had shattered the glass in the rooflight. *If I ever get my hands on the wee skitters…* A north wind mixed sleet with rain and came at him from both the side and the top.

The dog, a Jack Russell with a tear in its ear and a white muzzle, lay curled into fresh straw in one of the old nesting boxes. The dog's eye never left him and its teeth showed.

'Bugger off,' he said for the twentieth time, and the dog growled back.

When the light went out of the day, Denton's Aberdeen Angus had taken shelter in the stead across the way. He hoped they were still there. Had no intention of going looking for them. He was wet from his feet to well above the hang of his cape, and from the collar down. The two damps met at the seat of his pants.

A car came along the road. Its lights picked out the shafts of rain angling into his face. He muttered to himself when the car stopped at the bottom of the laneway. The dog barked. He told it to shut up. Stepped through the remains of the chicken wire fence at the edge of the field.

The car's interior light came on and the window rolled down a crack. 'Report,' said Harvey.

'Nothing to report, sir.'

'Stay alert, I might be back later.'

'And goodnight to you too,' Barlow said and watched Harvey drive off. Looked at the dog straggling back to its bed. 'You could at least have piddled on the wheels.'

Alexandra appeared, lantern in hand, an old coat thrown over her clothes for protection.

He touched a finger to his cap. 'Missis, this old laying-house is a quare windbreak.'

If she didn't mind, he planned to improve things by putting plywood over the broken windows. Maybe buy an old door in the market to block the entrance. 'This could be a grand chicken house again.' He wouldn't mind either. A houseful of hens would create a bit of heat and he'd experienced worse smells in the course of his job.

Confusingly, she nodded her head even as her tone indicated disagreement. 'The foxes destroyed us.'

She stood on and he began to wonder if Harvey had asked her to check up on him as well.

She nodded again. 'Come up to the house.'

He was glad to follow her. If only to melt the blocks of ice where his feet should have been. The heat in the kitchen enveloped him. The kettle steamed on the stove as she put supper on the table: the remains of a stew, and homemade wheaten bread. She pushed a chair out for him and he dared loosen his jacket by a button.

She nodded. 'Take it off.'

His cold-thickened fingers struggled with the buttons. She mixed her fingers with his helping. He struggled to keep his breathing steady when her heat and her scent enfolded him as she slid the jacket down his arms. She hung it in front of the range while he sat down again and ladled stew onto the wheaten bread. His hand remained steady; he thought it should be shaking.

'Boots, too.'

He gulped a mouthful of food down and begrudged unlacing his boots when he could be eating. *If this is leftovers, what would a real meal taste like?*

'I'm supposed to be on guard duty, Missis,' he said, as she slid the boots from his feet.

'Alexandra,' she reminded him, and added. 'The dog will bark if anyone comes.' She nodded again. 'How many Saturday nights will you be here?'

'Until the weather improves.' He said it with some bitterness.

The family silver and cleaning cloths covered half the table. One picture in a silver frame showed her and her husband on their wedding day, she standing taller than him. She looked out of place in white beside a man old enough to be her father.

He said, 'You're still a fine-looking woman.'

'Was,' she said, and carried on cleaning the silver while he ate. Finished, she took a last look at her wedding photograph. 'All these years, a lifetime of back-breaking work, and only bits of silver to show for it.'

She went to the range and fussed with the kettle. 'I come from a big family. I never had a bed to myself until after William died.'

He took a mouthful of food and chewed slowly, rather than commit himself with words. She put a drink down before him: a hot whiskey with cloves, a strong one. Then she sat back at the table with her own whiskey and they drank in silence.

'Go ahead and smoke. I know you do,' she said.

He lit a Woodbine and puffed slowly while she cleared the table.

He offered her one.

She nodded and said, 'No.'

He kept the pack held out. She hesitated, nodded and took one. Didn't object when he steadied her hand while she lit her cigarette from his. Nodded again and drew the smoke into her lungs. Exhaled with a sigh of pleasure.

He felt his heartbeat speed up, slow, speed again. It had been a long time. He didn't… *What harm would it do?* Maggie…. He tried not to think of Maggie and of the lonely nights spent lying by her side.

With the cigarette butts stubbed out on the edge of his plate, Alexandra got up and stood over him. 'I'll go up.' She pointed to the ceiling above his head. 'If you keep the bedroom window open you'll hear the dog.'

He had another Woodbine. Watched its swirls of smoke along the ceiling and listened to her footsteps as she got ready for bed.

When the house was silent again, he stripped off his shirt and socks and hung them on the towel rail on the stove. After mulling over his options, he removed his trousers and stretched them over a chair. Hopefully, the heat would take the dampness out of them for the morning. Wrinkled his nose in distaste when he looked down at his combinations. Their whiteness had faded with age. He wished he'd thought to buy a new pair.

The stairwell was unlit and the linoleum cold under his feet. A cracked stair groaned underfoot. He moved carefully through the unknown house, seeking the bedroom above the kitchen.

The door creaked open at his touch. In the near dark, he got the impression of little knickknacks: of glass perfume bottles and fine china ornaments. His fingers touched a dressing table and brushed the soft roughness of an antimacassar. He'd almost forgotten the perfumes in a woman's bedroom. These reminded him of Curles Wood on a spring day. Of a zephyr wind curling the scents of the flowers into the fresh sunlight.

He got into the double bed and pushed the hot water bottle away with his feet.

Alexandra lay still. He eased a hand out to the side until his knuckles touched thigh. Felt only the smoothness of naked flesh. Her body quivered at the cold off his hand. He ran his palm down her thigh and furrowed her skin with his fingers on the way up. She made no protest, gave no encouragement. After the third furrowing he turned onto his side and cupped a hand round her far hip.

He could see her outline against the grey darkness of the window. She lay staring at the ceiling, not looking his way. He might not have been there for all the attention she paid him.

Did she want him or not? He couldn't say and began to fear he'd misread the signs. It had been a long time since…anything. Maybe Alexandra was terrified of saying no?

He slid his hand free and rolled onto his back. Alexandra's head turned his way. Had he got it wrong? What would he do if she protested at him coming into her bed? *She did say the front room.*

What if she complained? Harvey would take the greatest pleasure in jailing him for attempted rape.

Alexandra asked, 'Why did you stop?'

Her hand searched for his arm. The hand was work-roughened, calloused and ridged with old hacks. It rasped over his skin in the most delicious way. He wanted her to do it again, this time over his whole body. He tried to hold her, but she pushed his hands away and rolled onto her knees. The rising bedclothes sucked in cold air and he shivered.

Relief at not facing a rape charge let him surrender totally to her as her hands worked at him. Now the old combinations became handy because the buttons slid free at her touch. Her fingers scoured the hairs on his chest, clawed at his nipples. He'd be sore in the morning, but didn't care.

He could only see a vague outline of her head against the white of the ceiling. The rest of her body stayed hidden under the bedclothes. Strands of her hair crossed to and fro over his face. Her hot breath quickened as she worked her hands over his shoulders and down into the sleeves.

He sank his head in the pillow and arched his back. The combinations slid from his waist. Then hips, knees, ankles. Gone.

She and the bedclothes closed over him. He wanted to cry from pleasure.

CHAPTER 30

MARCH SLIPPED VERY PLEASANTLY INTO an April morning. The dawn chorus woke Barlow. He loved to snuggle into the candle-wick bedspread and listen to the birds' celebration of life. The dawn chorus outside his own house consisted of men with mill lungs spitting their way to work.

He dozed off and came awake again in early daylight. The curtains flapped sunlight into his eyes. *Something else as well?*

He looked at Alexandra. She lay with her hands behind her head. She often did that when she wanted to surrender to him. *Is she in the mood?* He slid a hand onto her leg.

'It's Easter Sunday,' she said.

'You'd need to look at the calendar to know, Missis.' There'd been hardly a glimmer of sun in months.

She raised herself up on an elbow. The blanket fell away from her breasts. They sagged on her bony frame. He tried to turn her under him. She covered herself up again and held out against his pull. 'You'll be getting me a cup of tea first?'

The dog barked. He tried to ignore it. The dog barked again. *Noisy git!* He got out of bed and looked out the window. Could Harvey be doing an early morning check? *It would be just like the bastard.* A vehicle of some sort was parked near the bottom of the lane. *That's what woke me.*

'I'll be back,' he told Alexandra and reached for his uniform.

He dressed quickly and left the house. Reached the end of the lane before he heard the echoing thud of cattle hooves on wood.

'Begod!' he said, and drew his truncheon.

The dog came out to meet him. 'Bugger off.'

The dog ignored the order and stayed at his heels as he took a look up the county road. Someone had reversed a cattle lorry into the gateway of Denton's land. Could see the shapes of two men driving cattle into the lorry with sticks and whispered shouts. Four animals were in already.

He kept the bulk of the lorry between him and the two men as he slipped down the road. A fifth animal twisted and sidled and tried to turn back. Anything other than join its companions. The bullock kept the men too busy to look around. Finally, the beast stumbled up the ramp and they closed the gate.

The two men drew breath. One asked the other. 'What's the difference between Sergeant Barlow and one of these bullocks?'

It's the Dunlops. That young lot, the grandsons.

The young Dunlop answered his own question. 'The bullock's eyes are wider apart.' They roared with laughter.

That gave him a chance to consider his options. The young Dunlops were tough men. One he could take on single-handed. Two didn't worry him, not with the truncheon as back-up.

He stepped out into the open. 'You're under arrest.'

The young Dunlops' mouths opened in surprise. He jumped forward and hit the comedian on the shoulder, then backhanded him across the face with the truncheon. Not a clean blow. The truncheon scraped along the side of the lorry on the way in. The man staggered back, but didn't go down.

'Damn,' he said and knew he was in trouble when a third Dunlop appeared round the side of the lorry.

The two uninjured Dunlops came at him. They hefted sticks they used for loading cattle. He hadn't thought of that. They stayed back and prodded at his chest. He grabbed one stick. The second stick cracked his knuckles and he lost hold.

The injured comedian threw a stone that hit off his cap. He shook his head to clear a sudden dizziness and charged. A stick caught his elbow as he swung. His own blow missed. He tried a backhander at the new attacker, and got lucky. The edge of the truncheon caught the attacker's nose. Blood spurted.

The man on the left grabbed at the truncheon. The dog came scrambling between their legs and bit the man. The man let go of the truncheon and Barlow staggered back, caught off balance.

Before he could recover, the comedian ran in and rabbit-punched him in the kidneys. He felt his knees buckle. A fist caught him in the pit of the stomach. He needed to be hinged in two directions: backwards and forwards to hump over both blows. *And I thought Geordie was trouble.*

A kick to the back of the legs took him to his knees. The Dunlops brought the sticks down on his back and ribs. *That's nice. They don't want a murder charge against them.* If he could just get to his feet, he'd happily swing for the lot of them.

He couldn't put even one leg under him. He felt humiliated because he was older than any two of those boys put together. Softening down into old age. That realisation hurt nearly more than the blows.

He heard the dog. It snarled, and then yelped as a stick caught it. Snarled again. One of the Dunlops yelled when its teeth made contact with his ankle.

He started to fall forward. Put his hand on the ground for balance. *I'm beat.* Someone trod on his fingers. A boot slammed into his ribs, knocking him sideways.

A loud crack sounded.

It could be his head splitting open, but he didn't think so. *Maybe I'm dying.*

The blows stopped and Alexandra's voice carried strong. 'The next man touches him, I shoot to kill.'

He opened his eyes. The dog stood right in front of him. It licked his face.

'Piss off,' he said and found enough strength to give it a pat. The dog backed off.

Now he could see Alexandra, the shotgun held at waist level. At that range she could hardly miss. Him as well if she didn't aim higher.

She called, 'Are you all right, Mr Barlow?'

'Aye,' he said, feeling a silly question deserved an equally daft reply. He wasn't "all right"; he hurt everywhere.

A Dunlop knee stood within range and the truncheon still hung on his wrist by its loop. He gripped it with his injured fingers. They all closed over the wooden stock, so nothing broken.

A good swipe with the truncheon made the owner of the knee yell and stagger back. Two-handed, he stabbed the truncheon into the comedian's groin. He rose to his feet among them. Even injured, the Dunlops were dangerous. He went over them three times: elbow, knee and shoulder, to make sure they knew their manners for the next time. *Nobody messes with Barlow.* With every blow more strength poured into his body.

He prodded the Dunlops with the truncheon and the dog nipped at their ankles, until they clambered into the lorry among the cattle. Alexandra helped him swing the lorry ramp up and clip it into place. Then he stood back satisfied. The Dunlops couldn't be more secure if they were in Crumlin Road Prison itself.

He tried to pat the dog again. It snarled at him so he threatened it with his boot. It growled and retreated into the chicken house. He leaned against the lorry and breathed a sigh of relief. But not too deep because his ribs hurt.

Alexandra nodded to herself. 'I'll call the station and ask them to send some help.'

She wore a pink silken dressing gown and wellingtons. He liked the dressing gown on her, the way it hissed against her flesh. She'd bought it after the first Saturday. Before that, she'd used an old coat.

He forced the lingering fuzziness out of his head. Needed to stay focused on the present. He didn't want the Duty Officer to send carloads of men to help. He needed Harvey to see him come in with the goods, single-handed. Had to prove to himself that he could still do the job on his own.

'Just put on the kettle,' he said.

She nodded again. In agreement or not, he didn't know which. She went back to the house.

The keys were in the ignition. He drove the lorry into the farmyard and parked it with the tailgate hard against the midden wall. Not even the Dunlops could get out of that. Not without first making a lot of noise.

He went back into the house. Alexandra waited for him in the kitchen. The tea already wet and ready to pour. He subsided into a chair and supped the hot liquid. Started to feel good.

Three to one? He'd never stood a chance on his own. How many times had a willing passer-by helped him with an awkward drunk?

Alexandra nodded. 'You'll want a bite of breakfast before you go?'

He pulled her away from the stove and put the pot of morning porridge on the side. He took her back upstairs. He felt daring because she liked to start things. They undressed. She wore only knickers under the dressing gown. They were new as well.

They got into bed, entwined their bodies and made love. Gently. Sadly. There would be no more Saturday nights before the fire with a drink and a smoke. Sometimes on those nights they talked farming and cattle and prices. Sometimes they listened to the BBC Light Programme.

CHAPTER 31

BARLOW AND ALEXANDRA LAY ON long after milking time and smoked cigarettes.

'You're quite a woman with a shotgun,' he told her, and raised an eyebrow.

'Mr Barlow!'

She sounded outraged, but she smiled and flexed her leg against his.

He stretched out with his hands above his head, enjoying her touch. 'The RUC owes you something for your help. Maybe they'd fix up that henhouse for you?'

He could feel her mind drift to the cows lowing their discomfort in the field. He should never have brought up business.

She said, 'I told you; the foxes destroyed us. What they didn't eat, they killed.'

He wanted to do something for her. Needed an excuse to come back. 'They made money at a time.'

'That was during the war. The American soldiers staked out the chicken runs in exchange for a hot meal.'

He remembered seeing them when home on leave. American Rangers. They trained in the area before the landings in Dunkirk. When they drew bead on a fox they weren't thinking of a free meal. They saw an enemy soldier.

He needed her talking, if only to keep her mind off the cows. 'You must have found it difficult to feed them, what with all the rationing.'

She laughed, a pleasant sound with a tinkle of youthfulness that always surprised him. 'They brought jeep-loads of food.

Chocolate, nylons, lipstick, anything they thought we needed.' Her voice became dreamy. 'All they wanted was a warm welcome and plenty of home cooking.'

He could hardly imagine this house full of laughter and young men. *Maybe some of those GIs got more than a meal?* He didn't blame her for that even if, illogically, he felt jealous. Her husband was decades older than her and had the Taylors' grouchy attitude.

His wandering attention focused when she ran a hand down his leg. 'Mr Barlow, you're not doing your duty.'

Before he left, he rang the station to report the arrest of the Dunlops. As an afterthought he asked, 'Is Gillespie on this morning? Good. Tell him to get the hosepipe out. I'll be with him in twenty minutes.'

'What about Captain Denton's cattle?' asked Alexandra. She was dressed now, ready for milking, the old trousers smelling faintly of the byre.

He smiled. 'Technically they're evidence. Though how we're going to keep them in the evidence room is beyond me.'

He drove slowly, easing the lorry over rough sections of road. No need to have the Dunlops killed by panicked cattle. The gates into the station yard lay open. Gillespie held the hosepipe ready. A phalanx of men drew truncheons and waited.

Edward stood among them. Somehow in his dawn wanderings he'd seen the officers gather in the station yard and stayed to watch. Harvey waited as well, and Captain Denton. Denton's Rolls Royce took up enough space to make the turn into the yard awkward.

Gillespie indicated with the hosepipe where to park. The turn brought the lorry close to Harvey. He had to jump clear as its wheels threatened to nip his toes. Gillespie gave a thumbs-up, and then held up a hand.

Barlow parked up and got out, stretched and yawned.

Harvey came storming up. 'Barlow, where are the culprits? Why did you let them go again?'

Rather than answer, he went around to the back of the lorry and lowered the ramp. The Dunlops hobbled out. The cattle tried to follow. He drove them back with a roar and enjoyed seeing Denton's face go beetroot when he recognised the Dunlops under their coating of manure, and his own animals.

Barlow played up his injuries, rubbing his sore back and flexing stiffened shoulders. But he stopped and sniffed as he limped past Edward. 'You're sober and you smell of bubble bath.'

'So?' said Edward.

'So, did you spend last night at Mrs Anderson's?' He raised an eyebrow. 'Did she scrub your back for you?'

Edward coloured. 'There are some questions a gentleman never asks.'

He gave him a friendly pat on the shoulder. 'She's good for you, Edward. Why don't you move in with her?'

'I have my reasons.'

'Aye, the house is dry.'

He watched as the three Dunlops bunched together. Not in fear, but in a tight triangle of fists. The policemen held their noses as they closed in on them. Nobody went too close or got too funny. The Dunlops had long memories.

Gillespie turned on the hosepipe. The Dunlops' injuries meant they could only move slowly as they tried to avoid the ice-cold jet of water. Harvey pretended outrage. 'These men are injured.'

A thousand years of nobility went into the cold stare Edward gave Harvey. 'One against three, a *prima facie* case of police brutality.'

A shout of laughter went up from the watching policemen.

CHAPTER 32

An hour later everything about Barlow hurt. Even picking up a pencil required concentrated effort to make sinews and tissues work. The police doctor called and examined him in the near privacy of the kitchen. But first he saw to the prisoners and sent two off to hospital: one with a broken elbow and the comedian with a severe reduction in his hopes of procreating.

The doctor became almost sympathetic as he prodded Barlow. 'Assessing the damage for my report,' he claimed.

'Your car tax has lapsed.' The next prod went deep and he sucked air. 'I'm just saying.'

'You're lucky,' said the doctor. 'Nothing broken.' He made it sound the worst of bad luck. 'Take aspirin and a couple of days off. You'll be all right.'

Harvey came in, vibrating with indignation. 'Why did you arrest the Dunlops? Why didn't you pursue the lorry to see where they went to?'

'I thought about doing that, sir, but the old bike's not what it used to be.'

Harvey flushed. 'Are you being insolent?'

'Never.'

WPC Day had followed Harvey in, notebook in hand, ready to record his orders. She gasped when she saw the bruising on Barlow's chest and ribs.

He quickly pulled on his vest. 'You should see the other half.'

He meant his back but her look travelled below waist level. He caught her eye. She showed no sign of embarrassment. As he'd suspected, she'd given her body to the boyfriend and still no ring. Next thing, she'd be pregnant and the bastard would do like his own father and disappear off somewhere.

He had to admit to himself that Harvey had a point. He should have used Alexandra's car and seen where they took the cattle to. But he'd never really believed the Dunlops would rob the Denton Demesne, because Geordie never played a dirty trick on a friend or on an old soldier. Obviously, the grandsons had stopped listening to Geordie. And they might be under arrest, but no way did he figure them as the brains behind the operation. The stolen cattle had to go somewhere local for processing, and from there to the shops.

Again he asked himself: Who could dispose of all that meat without anyone noticing? The answer sat at the back of his mind. *If I could just jog it loose.*

Harvey wanted the Dunlops in court immediately after the Easter break. That meant Barlow couldn't go home. He had to stay on and write reports about the arrests and the injuries suffered by the Dunlops. About Alexandra discharging a shotgun with intent. His own bruises. The use of a truncheon on suspects. Every report to be done in triplicate to show the culpability of the individual Dunlops.

Pierson *suggested* that he man the front desk while he wrote up all these reports. He smiled and agreed. At least Pierson hadn't made it a legitimate order. He eased his bruises onto a high stool while Pierson disappeared into the back with a yard-high bundle of files.

Hand strain soon added to his list of woes. Who did what and when, he found hard to remember. His head had been spinning at the time. Should he mention the dog biting the Dunlops? He thought not. Harvey might order it put down for attacking people.

At least the morning stayed quiet. Jackson dealt with the few callers and, in between, made fair copies of his scribbles.

They took a break. He pulled up a chair to the fire while Jackson made him a cup of tea. The doctor had told him, "Plenty of liquids for a few days, and no alcohol." Jackson made him a second cup. What he really needed was a pint of draught beer.

The door crashed open. Geordie burst in, ploughed through Jackson, grabbed Barlow and slammed him against the wall. Agonies of pain played along his ribs.

Geordie hauled him off the wall then slammed him back again. 'Murdering swine. Pig trotter from hell.'

He turned a gasp of pain into speech. 'Go away.' At least Geordie was sober this time. Christmas and Easter Sunday he always accompanied his wife to church. The rest of the year he devoted to drink and trouble.

Geordie drew a fist back. 'You've crippled my grandsons. Their mother's distraught.'

Jackson had been knocked to the floor in the charge. Geordie let go and went to help the young constable up. He dusted down Jackson's uniform with rough hands. 'No offence intended, son. I didn't see you there.'

'None taken,' said Jackson.

'It's this other gobshite I want to sort out.'

Jackson looked for guidance. Barlow shrugged. Then Geordie was on him again, bashing him against the wall with every word. 'Would you fight like a man?'

'Would you piss off.' One more bruise and he thought he'd be in bed for a month. He felt drained, his head hurt. *Could I have a touch of concussion?*

He asked. 'Who do they sell the cattle to?'

Geordie's fist threatened for a second time. 'What cattle? We never took nothing.'

It had been one a hell of a day and, with Harvey around, the year no better. He ached to get some of his own back. Get involved in a good milling. Even as his fist clenched, his body said, *hold on, not today.* Unclenched the fist. 'Geordie, go away.'

Jackson said, 'Mr Dunlop, Sergeant Barlow merely defended himself.' He flapped a piece of paper in front of Geordie. 'Would you like to see the medical report on the contusions and abrasions suffered by the Sergeant?'

'You pulled a gun on them,' shouted Geordie.

A complete lie, but obviously the grandsons had been too embarrassed to admit that a woman had bettered them. Nor did Barlow dare tell Geordie about Alexandra and the shotgun. He might go looking for revenge on her. Steal her cattle.

'They pulled three sticks on me.'

Geordie looked pleased. 'Fair enough. They're only lumps of lads against the likes of you.'

'Big lumps, but like the rest of the breed, they went down easy.'

Geordie brought the fist close to his nose. 'If you were any sort of man, you'd take the first swing.'

'I do and you'll need a stand-in to take the second swing for you.'

At long last, Geordie realised that he wouldn't oblige him with a fight. He shook him off his hands and stumped out the door. His voice carried back. 'If there was half a man in that uniform.'

More like half the age. Half a lifetime ago, he'd have thumped back to get a good row going. *Then again, maybe not.* If Vera, God forbid, ever got injured he'd want to take a swing at the person responsible. Realised she now was at the age where she had to make her own mistakes.

Four times in one day he'd been reminded of ageing.

Reports or no reports, he went home.

CHAPTER 33

THE FOLLOWING MONDAY HARVEY ARRIVED for work early. So early he nearly beat Barlow in the door. Barlow made a point of yawning as he said, 'Good morning, sir,' and looked at Harvey's cheeks with interest. Their colour was reassuringly high.

Harvey ignored his greeting. 'That diplomat you hit. They're still on about it. The Chief Constable wants to see me first thing this afternoon.'

Barlow wondered if a nick on one of Harvey's cheeks would cause it to jet blood. 'I stopped a murder, sir.'

'I wish to God you hadn't.'

Harvey steamed on. Seconds later his voice could be heard from the detectives' room. Loud and clear, and taking no excuses. He wanted enough evidence to hang Kurt Adenauer three times over. And he wanted it now.

Barlow went back to leaning on the counter. Pierson was Duty Sergeant and Acting Station Sergeant. Let him get on with the job. It felt sort of funny having all the coming Saturday nights free. Home with Vera and Maggie, watching television until the white dot, held no attraction.

Alexandra. The name echoed in his head like a hurting loss. *And why not?* She was as good as dead to him, and not just for the sex. Having her snuggle in and being made to feel appreciated, the press of her breasts on his back. *There must be some way to get out there again.* Maybe help out, do odd jobs around the farm. He'd like that anyway. Never got enough exercise.

Pierson, he noticed, had got into the habit of working all sorts of crazy hours in the station, and then taking work home.

Too good for the gobshite. He checked out the window. The day looked hazy but dry. Maybe he'd walk down the street. Hassle one or two not-so-innocent citizens.

The row in the detectives' room stopped. The internal phone rang. *Harvey or about Harvey,* so he let Pierson take the call. Could feel trouble in his bones.

Pierson said, 'Yes, sir. Two cars with drivers, two officers and two WPCs. I'll go myself, sir.'

If he'd overheard right, Harvey had ordered the Frau brought in for questioning. Two cars. That meant the boy, young Peter, as well. He seethed in anger. In a way he agreed with Harvey. A lot of points about Stoop's last day needed clearing up. But terrifying a woman and her child half to death was not the way to go about it.

His own attitude puzzled him. It didn't make sense, him being sympathetic towards a German: a former enemy, a woman who may have colluded in the death of her husband. But the Frau was trying to make the best of a tough life. He admired her for that.

The cars set off with every flourish Pierson could manufacture. They'd be away a while. Meantime he moved restlessly through the building. Handed paper-pushers their caps by way of a hint to be out walking the streets, not dossing in odd corners.

Just to be sure, he demanded that certain files be in front of him by a certain time. Wanted to pass them up the chain of command as soon as possible. Increase Pierson's stack of work by the end of the day rather than let it reduce. Happy now that everyone knew what to do, he took his ease in the Enquiry Office and awaited Pierson's return.

The cars arrived back and pulled up ostentatiously at the front door. Officers crowded the Frau and Peter. Hurried them into the police station. Both handcuffed. Peter had wet himself. From the puff of Pierson's chest he'd just cracked an international conspiracy and rolled up a communist cell.

WPC Day caught Barlow's eye and raised hers to heaven. They could only stand by, helpless, while the Frau and Peter were fingerprinted in a forceful manner and in public. No sympathy or charity shown. The Frau looked to him for help. He didn't dare shake his head back.

WPC Day put an arm around Peter and took him down to an interview room. Peter tried to shake her arm off. The Frau's face developed a frozen, haunted look when they put her in a different room.

The escort dismissed, Pierson swaggered into the Enquiry Office and started in shock at the extra files that had been gathered for him. Barlow only wished there was a hundred more, and he hung back when officers came seeking guidance on obscure points of law or police procedure.

Pierson preened himself when they bypassed Barlow and came straight to him. He didn't see Barlow catch the officers' eyes and pass them on with a jerk of the head. Pierson took his time answering the questions. Meanwhile, officers heading out on patrol added more files to his pile.

The front door opened and an older man and a youth edged in. The youth looked shaken. The man said, 'I've got to report a crime.'

'Have you now?'

'Mr Fetherton says I must.' The man gulped nervously. 'I wouldn't do it myself.'

'And you are?'

'Wilson, Jimmy Wilson. I run Mr Fetherton's newsagents and stationers on Market Street.'

Anything about the Mayor was of interest. He nodded at Wilson to continue.

'Simon Whithead here stole a rubber.'

'A rubber you say. Are you sure?'

Wilson dug into his pocket and produced a tuppenny rubber. 'This one here. He's a nice young fellow, always pleasant, but Mr Fetherton insists.'

'See your man there,' he said, pointing at Pierson, and checked his watch.

The Frau and Peter had been in the interview room for almost an hour. Guessed Harvey was up to his dirty tricks again because their solicitor, Mr Comberton, hadn't appeared.

In front of Pierson, he picked up the receiver and rang Mr Comberton's office.

CHAPTER 34

THE INTERVIEW ROOMS IN BALLYMENA police station erred on the side of small and pokey. Old wooden kitchen tables and creaky chairs sourced by Barlow at McKinneys' auctions made do as furnishings.

Leary sat at one side of the table, Peter at the other. WPC Day sat to the side with a hand gripping the boy's. She let go when Barlow entered the room in time to hear Leary try the soft-soap approach. 'Now, son, you've got to tell us. How else can we sort things out and let your mother go?'

Peter looked at Barlow. 'I wish to see my solicitor, Mr Comberton. Telephone number two three zero two.' He kept the quiver in his voice under control.

'He's on his way.'

Peter showed anger. 'You said that before.'

'I didn't say anything, but he is on his way.' He threw a hard look at Leary. 'Now.'

Leary scowled back. 'Mr Harvey …'

'I don't care about Mr Harvey and his shortcuts.' He threw in a sop for Leary. 'Keep your rubber truncheon for the likes of the Dunlops.'

The boy shuddered at that. 'I was at school,' he blurted out.

Both Leary and WPC Day's mouths tightened. They must have heard that a hundred times.

He leaned over the table at Peter. 'If Kurt Adenauer loved your mother, really loved her, he'd have come long before this.'

'He couldn't, he was a prisoner,' said Peter. He clamped his hand over his mouth in horror.

Barlow said to Leary. 'How often must I tell you? Rattle them first, then hit them with the unexpected question.' He left the room. Now Leary had his opening he could pick away until the whole story came out.

Kurt Adenauer in prison for fifteen years? Fifteen years took them back to the war and an awful lot of atrocities. A man like that, killing a crippled old soldier like Stoop wouldn't cost him a moment's thought.

Barlow had never killed a man. Never drawn his gun, even as a threat. But he had sent men to their death, and those deaths still haunted his dreams. They obviously haunted Adenauer as well.

The next interview room held the Frau, Harvey and Fox-wood. The Frau and Foxwood barely glanced at him as he slipped into the room. Harvey jerked his head for him to leave. He pretended to misunderstand and stood with his back to the door.

The Frau's face was bloated with crying. 'He a cousin. We no leave house all day.'

Harvey screamed at her. 'Prove it.'

'We no leave.'

'You're a liar. You helped this alleged cousin of yours kill your husband.'

'No.'

Harvey thumped the table. 'Your fingerprints were all over the hayloft and on the rifle. Maybe you're the one who fired the shots?' His fists drummed the table hard. 'Premeditated mur-der? We still hang people like you.'

She seemed to shrink into nothing. 'No no no. Kurt not like that.'

'Like what then?'

They'd found the Frau's fingerprints in the hayloft? It had to be true or Harvey wouldn't have said it. Then the Frau had helped Adenauer to kill Stoop. He felt disappointed. Had thought better of her.

'Mrs Taylor, I'm sure you've got a good explanation,' said Foxwood in a gentle, soothing voice. 'Maybe Adenauer forced you to help?'

'No,' she whispered.

'So a team effort,' said Harvey, jumping back in. 'Maybe you came up with the idea in the first place?'

Her mouth quivered. No words came out.

'Right,' said Harvey. 'Your fingerprints were all over the rifle.'

'I no touch.' She made a helpless, rubbing motion in the air. 'I lift to clean. No more.'

That, in Barlow's eyes, made a good defence. The house might be a hovel, but the old flagstone floors had been scrubbed until the original pink showed. He wished he could hire the woman to clean for him. He and Vera did their best, but he didn't have the energy and Vera spent the evenings studying.

'Was the late Mr Taylor your husband?' asked Harvey.

She nodded.

'Where are all the papers to prove it? Your marriage certificate, for instance?'

'I'm sure the papers can be got,' murmured Foxwood. He smiled over at the Frau. 'They can, can't they?'

'There aren't any papers,' said Harvey. He thumped the table. 'I'll tell you what you are. You're a German whore. You don't know the real father of your son, do you? He could be any one of a thousand soldiers.' He thumped the table again.

Too much, thought Barlow.

'Somehow you convinced Stoop that the child was his.'

'No.'

'Or used a lonely old man to help you and your son escape post-war Germany, in exchange for unlimited sex?'

Barlow saw the Frau stiffen as that brutal remark struck home. *So there's something in that.* Why else would she live in the bog-end of nowhere with a man who begrudged potato skins to laying hens?

Either Harvey didn't see the Frau's reaction or he misinterpreted it. He carried on being nasty. 'Do you know what we do with whores in this country?'

She stayed silent.

He spat his words into her face. 'We take their children. That's what we do. And they never see them again. Not ever. *Kaput!*'

She shook so hard the chair creaked under her.

Foxwood said, 'Now, Mrs Taylor, we don't want that to happen.'

'My solicitor?' she asked in a faint voice.

Harvey said, 'Unless you cooperate fully, I will seize your son under the *Children and Young Persons Act, 1950*. He rolled the final words out and seemed to enjoy them. 'He'll be gone forever.'

The Frau's face went pure white.

Pierson opened the door and threw Barlow a gloating look. 'Sir, Sergeant Barlow personally rang Frau Taylor's solicitor. He's here now.' Right behind him, treading on his heels, came Mr Comberton.

The Frau's eyes rolled into the back of her head. Barlow didn't manage to get to her in time because Foxwood was in the way. She slumped sideways. Her head hit the floor. Blood seeped along the linoleum.

CHAPTER 35

Mr Comberton was a slight man who kept his mind alert with regular games of tennis and, according to rumour, had funded his drinking through Queen's University by playing billiards. He brought the same keen eye for an angled shot to the defence of clients.

The Frau lay settled in the foetal position, her arms wrapped around a leg of the table. Barlow thought her as safe there as anywhere. Nobody else had moved to help.

Mr Comberton said, 'Barlow, you'd better have a good explanation for this.'

'Aye,' he said, wondering why he was held to account for everything that happened in the station. He shoved Pierson to the door. 'Call an ambulance. And one of the WPCs.'

That got Pierson offside for a while. *Now for Foxwood.* He wanted the man to get into the habit of doing what he suggested. 'Sir, a blanket to cover the lady?'

'Right,' said Foxwood and made a fast exit.

Barlow stooped over the Frau. At least she was breathing. Colour came back into her face. She muttered in German. He caught the word "Peter".

'Take it easy, love.' Slipped her hand into his. Her ice-cold fingers gripped back.

Mr Comberton hunkered down beside them. He gave Barlow a pocket handkerchief to hold against the cut on her forehead. 'I'm here, Mrs Taylor.'

'Barlow, I told you not to interfere,' said Harvey.

Mr Comberton looked up. 'Harvey, how dare you strike a defenceless woman in custody?'

'She fell,' said Harvey, well on the defensive. 'She fainted.'

Mr Comberton looked at Barlow, who gave the ghost of a nod.

'A fine story. A defenceless widow bullied by three hulking policemen. A woman left almost destitute, struggling to make ends meet. Is that the sort of thing you want to read in the papers, sir?'

The Frau's eyes opened. She seemed shocked that a civilian would dare speak to uniformed officers in that tone.

Barlow admired Mr Comberton and his way with words. He had aimed them to reassure the Frau. In the Germany she remembered, people were shot for less.

A WPC came bustling in to take over.

'My son – Peter,' whispered the Frau.

'He's safe,' whispered Barlow. The Frau pressed his hand to her cheek and started to cry. *Oh Hell!*

Mr Comberton said, 'I will not leave these premises until Peter has been released. I give you my word on that.'

The WPC looked meaningfully at the door. 'Gentlemen?'

Barlow slipped his hand free and they all left.

Outside in the corridor, Harvey became more assertive. 'I can assure you, Mr Comberton, that no one harmed the lady in any way.'

'Would you care to explain then how I found my client on the floor with blood pouring out of her head?'

Harvey spluttered an explanation. This gave Barlow the chance to push the door open into the first interview room. 'Leary, Mr Comberton is here. You say one more word to that boy without him present and you're for the high jump.'

Leary growled back. 'All of a sudden the wee git only speaks German.'

Barlow nodded at the boy in approval. Right then Barlow would have sided with George Smith of the "Brides in the Bath" murders. The heated discussion adjourned to the privacy of Harvey's office.

'You too, Barlow,' said Mr Comberton.

He followed them quite happily and took position beside the Queen's portrait. Thought she wouldn't like the way this case was being handled in her name. Mr Comberton talked at length about shortcuts in procedures since Harvey had taken over. 'As for you, Barlow, you used to have certain standards.'

Eventually, Harvey snarled back. 'I had every right to bring the woman and her son in for questioning. She is withholding information about Stoop Taylor's murder.'

'For instance?' asked Mr Comberton.

'Her fingerprints are all over the hayloft where the shooting took place.'

Mr Comberton raised an eyebrow. 'Please be more precise, Mr Harvey. Which incident are you referring to?'

'The gunman. The rifle.'

'Not the pistol that allegedly was used to kill Mr Taylor?'

Harvey hesitated before he said. 'Not that we can prove.'

'What else concerns you about Mrs Taylor's involvement in this case?' asked Mr Comberton.

Barlow just loved the way Mr Comberton spoke. The way the words rolled smoothly from his lips. He wished he spoke with the same gentle inflexion. It cut more deeply than his own growled irritations.

Sweat popped onto Harvey's brow. Information had been improperly withheld from the defence. Mr Comberton was determined to find out precisely what. Leary got called in. From the look on Harvey's face, a lot of things had been kept from him as well.

Adenauer's pistol used the same calibre of bullet as the one that killed Stoop. However, the bullet was too fragmented to prove that it came from the same gun. Samples of the fragments and the unexpended bullets had been sent to Fort Halstead. A metallic comparison might prove that they came from the same batch. However, the British Army were still proving unhelpful. The results were not yet through and Stoop's army file hadn't yet arrived.

And then there was the problem of the pistol. The captain of Adenauer's ship couldn't supply the registration number of the pistol, or the relevant paperwork to go with it.

Barlow listened with a quiet satisfaction to Leary's dilemma. If Adenauer hadn't stolen the pistol from the ship, where had he got it? And how did Stoop's fingerprints get all over the bullets still in the clip.

Mr Comberton continued with pointed remarks about information being withheld. Barlow listened with half a mind. An open and shut case had become more and more confusing. Had Adenauer produced the pistol on some excuse, let Stoop handle it, and then shot him in the back? And where had all this happened? Not the house. Not the outbuildings. No blood spatter, no bits of bullets to be dug out of walls. Had Adenauer killed Stoop out in the open?

Even that didn't make sense. The .22 rifle used to panic the cattle was not the one found in Stoop's house, and the gunman made his getaway on a racing bike.

The appearance of a second rifle worried Barlow. Even .22s weren't easy to come by: legally or illegally. None had been reported stolen in the time frame between Adenauer jumping ship and Stoop's death.

The whole case stood or fell on motive and opportunity. Why had Adenauer come looking for the Frau after all these years? What was their relationship? Cousin? Or husband, as she blurted out that first day? At the very least, the police needed sight of the marriage certificate and related documents. The woman could be a bigamist.

As if reading his thoughts, Mr Comberton said, 'I have all the relevant documents in my possession.'

Harvey said aggressively. 'Then you, as an officer of the court, are in breach of all the rules of procedure.'

'In what way?' asked Mr Comberton.

'Withholding vital information from the police.'

'Oh?'

Harvey held out his hand as if Comberton could magic the papers there and then. 'I demand all relevant documentation be given to me immediately. Failure to comply may cost you your practising certificate.'

Mr Comberton looked unworried at the threat of professional censure. 'First, Harvey, I did not volunteer this documentation because of your attitude. In my opinion, the police are trying to twist the facts to suit the case against my client.' He gave a sweet smile that Barlow had learned to dread. 'Secondly, you have not yet made available to the defence the search warrant authorising your search of the premises of the late Mr Taylor.'

Harvey looked at Foxwood who had slipped in to join them. Foxwood stood at the door with his hand on the handle as if ready to run. 'Has that not been done yet?' said Harvey.

Foxwood spluttered an excuse about paperwork. Barlow kept his face straight. None of the magistrates were willing to pre-date the search warrant. Perhaps with any other solicitor, yes, but not Mr Comberton. Failure to produce a search warrant could result in some very nasty headlines in the newspapers. Maybe even legal action against Harvey himself.

The chances were Mr Comberton knew this. Everything got talked about in the Masonic Hall. He often wished he could put a listening device in the Billiards Room. Listen in on the illegal acts plotted around the table. All for the good of the town, of course, and money in the members' own pockets.

Mr Comberton jumped focus, another trick Barlow admired. This time, Comberton directed his attention to Foxwood. 'And what is the condition of Mrs Taylor?'

'She has concussion. The ambulance men insisted on taking her to hospital for observation.'

It would be all around the town that the police had battered the poor woman.

'And the boy?'

Harvey said, 'He'll be released into the care of Social Services. I'll see to it myself.'

'Over my dead body,' snapped Mr Comberton.

Barlow blinked. The quiet-speaking solicitor had gone in an instant, from professional cut-and-thrust to blazing passion.

Mr Comberton towered over Harvey. 'That woman is distressed because you threatened her with the *Children and Young Persons Act*. You said she'd never see her son again. This isn't Hitler's Germany, Harvey, but right now you'll never convince her otherwise.'

Harvey said, 'Laid-down procedures for a minor … '

Mr Comberton looked angry enough to go over the table at Harvey. Barlow coughed to remind him that Harvey had witnesses if things got violent.

Mr Comberton's spittle sparked over Harvey's face as he said, 'Laid-down procedures are the last thing that were followed in this case. I am seriously tempted to make a formal complaint to the Chief Constable.'

Harvey didn't dare shrug. Barlow did it for him. Formal complaints meant paperwork, and paperwork at Headquarters went round and round in circles until it disappeared into a void.

Mr Comberton seemed to realise this and changed tack. 'Harvey, let me rephrase my last statement. You're up for membership of the Masonic Order. Social Services walk through that door, and I will take the greatest pleasure in blackballing you.'

CHAPTER 36

Mr Comberton demanded that Barlow accompany him when he went to speak to Peter, and did it with a wink that only he could see. He listened in while Mr Comberton told the boy that the Frau had hurt herself and had been taken to hospital. That it had been an accident. Peter appeared more shocked than frightened and WPC Day gasped, *very unprofessional.* In the distance, Harvey's voice echoed round the building as he took out his temper on Leary and Foxwood.

What to do with the boy was obviously Barlow's problem. A guesthouse wasn't right for an unaccompanied youth. WPC Day didn't have room, not with her parents, two siblings and a grandparent in the house.

'It's a pity you didn't bring that man of yours up to the mark at Christmas. You'd have your own home by this time', Barlow said.

WPC Day looked wistful. Barlow hoped he never saw that look on Vera's face.

'He can stay with us,' offered Gillespie. He hovered nearby, obviously enjoying a row not affecting him personally.

'You've no room either.' Even so, he thought that the best solution. Gillespie had two boys and two girls still at home, a couple of them about Peter's age. One of them could sleep on the floor. They did it often enough when they overnighted with friends.

'Mind you,' said Gillespie. 'I'm down for foot patrol this afternoon.' He gave a pathetic cough. 'Rain's forecast and my chest is acting up again.'

'So?'

'So I'm likely to cough all night. Nobody in the house'll get a wink of sleep.' He coughed again. This time he thumped his chest to loosen phlegm.

Barlow pretended to think things over. Technically, he'd no right to change orders. *However...* He growled at Gillespie. 'You'll need a chitty next for your brain. Didn't I tell you this morning to stay around the Town Hall? You can stand in the porch and salute all the nobs as they come and go.'

'Thank you, Sergeant.'

'Final point,' he said, mocking Harvey's mannerism. 'The District Inspector's back on this "no compliance, no second chance" campaign. Anybody for anything, and no exceptions.' And added to himself, 'Especially around the Town Hall.'

WPC Day and Gillespie took Peter off to the hospital to see his mother. 'Then I must go home,' said Peter, anxious about the family's cattle. They needed to be watered and fed before dark. Barlow said he'd take care of them. Anything to get away before Harvey came shouting. He went home and changed into old clothes.

Forty minutes later he was on the River Road. He got off his bike at the entrance to Widow Taylor's farm and stretched the ache out of his hips. The old dog lay deep in the shadows of the abandoned chicken house. It growled.

'Go on, you cur.'

He pushed his bike up the lane, collecting an armful of ragweed on the way. Threw it onto the midden. The dog followed at his heel.

Alexandra appeared from the byre, fork in hand, and stood looking at him. She wore a shirt with the sleeves rolled up. The trousers tucked into the top of her wellington boots.

She said, 'At least you're not embarrassing me with all those cars.'

'What are you talking about?'

She jerked her head in the direction of Stoop's farm. 'Stoop's woman and her son. Half the countryside has her all but hung for the murder.'

He gritted his teeth, Pierson and his ham-fisted arrest of the Frau. *I'll swing for that man one of these days.* Rather than criticise a colleague he said, 'It's a good day. Maybe I could pull that ragweed in the top field.'

She stared at him for a long time. Her head never moved. He realised she was annoyed at him for trying to change the subject. If he was in her place he'd want to know. At the same time he couldn't just blab confidential information.

'Your sister-in-law, the other Mrs Taylor, we never got a proper statement from her. Then she fainted and bumped her head. We sent her to hospital, to be on the safe side.'

'You'll be keeping her then, her and that German cousin of hers?'

'I doubt it.'

'You'll be wanting me in next then.' She sounded anxious.

He didn't blame her. To the public, police stations were scary places. 'Now why would we be doing that?'

She stared a bit more, then nodded her head slowly. 'I'd no time last year.'

'What?'

'The ragweed. It never got pulled.'

He sighed in relief at getting back to the reason for his visit. 'Maybe, but it's the law.'

'I'd better things to do than pull weeds.'

He stopped his head from bobbing in time to hers. 'The new District Inspector is reading up on these regulations.'

She flexed her shoulder. 'And the rheumatics are a bother.' Her voice still lacked warmth.

'I'm here to do it.'

Her head nodded one final time. 'You're a good man to have around.'

He took that as a yes and wheeled his bike into the tool shed. She harnessed the pony into a small cart and threw a tarpaulin over its back and withers.

The pony had no bit in the head-collar, and no reins, but when Alexandra said, 'Come on,' it followed them out of the yard. The pony limped on its left foreleg and favoured the leg any time they stopped to open a gate.

He said, 'That pony must be twenty, if it's a day.'

'Twenty-one.'

'And hardly fit to pull the cart.'

'It likes to be useful.'

'Has it got a name?'

'Pony,' she said and opened the gate into the top field.

The top field was thick with ragweed. It grew in clumps, with yellow flowers on high stems. They worked about ten foot apart, grabbing the stems a third of the way up. A good pull tore the shallow roots out of the ground. The pony chewed grass and waited beside each pile of pulled weed. Every so often Alexandra forked the weed into the cart. After a couple of hours, she went off with the pony to empty the ragweed into the midden.

He watched them go. Heavy cloud covered the sky. He got a daft notion that the golden heap in the cart was the sun itself. 'I'll be reciting poetry next,' he said and sat downwind of the fairy thorn. A breeze he hadn't noticed before chilled the shirt on his back. The dog waited with him. It lay out in the field, crouched as if ready to run. Never took its eye off him.

'Please yourself,' he told the dog. Decided not to spoil the day with a cigarette.

Alexandra came back with a can of tea and slices of cake. They took the tarpaulin off the pony and spread it on the ground for them to sit on. They ate and drank in silence. He shared an edge of his cake with the dog. It snapped it out of the air and growled.

They sat in a slight dip near the crest of the hill. He stretched out and lit a cigarette and passed it to Alexandra to take a draw. He wanted the taste of her in his mouth. They shared the cigarette in contented silence. Watched the finches play among the grass stalks.

Alexandra kicked off her wellington boots, unbuttoned her shirt and slipped it off. Her breasts hung free behind a vest. A couple of wriggles and her trousers were gone. They looked into each other's eyes.

'I didn't come for this,' he said.

'I know.'

She blew on the remains of her tea to cool it and arced her body over his. He slipped his hands under the vest. Lifted it over her head and down her arms. She leaned further. He slid her knickers down round her feet. She hooked them off with her toes. He'd never seen her properly naked before. Felt privileged.

She poured the tea around the base of the fairy thorn.

'What are you doing?'

'They're my only friends.'

'Now that's a daft thing to say.'

'My brothers think the farm is coming to them. It isn't.'

He began to undress as well. She unlaced his boots and stroked the socks off his feet. He bundled their clothes to make a pillow. It was cold in the spring air. Goosebumps stippled her breasts. She lay down beside him.

He sat up and checked for people on the near hills. Scanned the treetops for boys out looking for eggs. Saw no one. Ran the back of his fingers along her ribs. 'You're a grand woman.'

He felt freedom, a complete break from other people and their problems. All it took was lying naked with a woman in the fresh air, the sap of youth coming back into his bones. Frightening too in case somebody saw them.

He tried to please her the way she had him that first night. When she shivered with cold he covered her with his body. The ground had to be hard, but she didn't complain of his weight. A glow replaced the goose bumps.

As he entered her she whispered, 'My son was conceived here in love.'

All that pouring? She's not trying to get pregnant again?

He prayed to all the saints that it wasn't her fertile period.

CHAPTER 37

They went back to work.

Late afternoon the wind scurried through the long grass, and dark clouds thickened overhead. Alexandra tucked the tarpaulin in around the pony's collar to keep it in place. 'We'd better go in,' she said.

He used the palms of his hands to lever his back straight. His arms felt heavy from effort, his fingers raw from pulling. Looked around him. Felt proud of an enjoyable afternoon's work and the field almost clear of weed. 'We haven't done too badly.'

'You're a grand worker for a townie,' she said.

'You're not too bad yourself,' he said back, and shivered as the wind again cut through the sweat on his shirt.

From where they stood he could see down into Stoop's farmyard. He pointed. 'Maybe I'll hop the fence here.'

The atmosphere became icy. 'What takes you down there?'

He wondered what the problem was. 'The Frau's in hospital. I promised to check on their cattle.'

'I swore no man would take that shortcut again.'

'Oh?'

'Stoop had William's heart broke from pushing cattle through the hedge onto our grazing. They'd words about it more than once.'

He nodded. Half the disputes in the countryside arose over wills and rights of way. Especially after the pubs opened on mart day. He could see Stoop, angry and bitter at the best of times, determined to get his fair use of the land. William equally determined to retain what was legally his.

Alexandra pointed to the boundary hedge. 'In the end we ran three lines of barbed wire to stop him.' Her arm trembled against his as she led him to a particular point. 'Look, he even cut the wire to let them through.'

He took a close look at the damage. The three strands of barbed wire had been cut at one of the posts. Alexandra had found enough slack to nail them back in position.

Her voice sounded nearly as taut as the strained wire. 'I told him, if he ever did it again I'd get the police on him.'

'You did a good job there.' *Best not get involved in a family dispute.* Looked around instead for a change of subject. Saw the old pony head for its loose box at a fair lick. 'That brute's worse than Gillespie when it comes to malingering.'

'He hates the rain.' She seemed glad to change the subject as well.

He walked down with her to the farmyard and collected his bike from the tool shed. Sensed her upset at him having anything to do with the other family. All the same, a question needed to be asked. 'What we did up there ... Is there any chance ... ?

His anxiety almost raised a smile. 'Unfortunately no, Mr Barlow. Not now.'

'It's just –.'

'I understand.' Not completely believing her.

She went into the house and stood with the half-door closed against him. She nodded her head then made it shake. 'I'm due another call soon about crop returns.'

'You are.'

'When the time comes, Mr Barlow, I'd be grateful if you'd send another constable.'

'Now why would I do that?'

'Because it must stop. My family wouldn't like it.'

'Nor my wife.' He said that deliberately.

Her nod came slow and thoughtful. 'I was aware of that too.'

They stared at each other. Her lower lip trembled. 'Please.'

He sought for a word of comfort to give her and found none. He was a married man with obligations. She had neighbours, and the gossiping tongues of neighbours cut deeper than a flensing knife.

'I'm obliged for everything.'

He rode off.

CHAPTER 38

BARLOW SWUNG OFF HIS BIKE in Stoop's farmyard and went to check the cattle in the field. The cattle looked comfortable and content. He threw a bucket of grain along the feeding trough and shook open a couple of hay bales. Checked that the automatic water feeders were working properly and scooped floating chaff off the surface.

The ride back into town was cold and lonely. Once in town, he followed the river's meandering curve to Curles Bridge and to Edward's tar-and-paper hut under the dry arch.

'Or not so dry,' he said, as he put his toe to the bottom of the door and forced it open.

Edward was out so he took a good look around. The hut was tidy and clean. The bed made, army style, with the blankets pulled taut and tucked in tight. He sniffed and got the smell of stale clothes and rising damp. Had to watch his balance in the corner where the riverbank had crumbled underneath the hut.

The cupboard held only milk and bread. The gas stove suspiciously pristine. He left things as they were, forced the door shut behind him and returned to the police station.

Jackson beamed in relief as he walked in the door. 'Sergeant, the shop across the way is shut. Where can I get cigarillos at this hour?'

'Try McGroggans in William Street.'

Jackson disappeared out the door as Pierson came storming over. 'You told that bollocks Gillespie to patrol around the Town Hall. Damn if he didn't book Judge Donaldson for parking on a yellow line.'

'No compliance, no second chance,' he intoned piously.

'Stuff "no compliance".' Pierson looked ready to spit chips. 'The judge gave me hell down the phone. Now he's in, dancing a jig on the DI's head.'

He tut-tutted sympathetically and signed himself off duty. Ran his eye over the "Orders of the Day" for that night. They ran to a page and a half of mainly "don'ts".

'And to think the Good Lord did it in ten lines.'

Pierson preened himself. 'This is the new order. Back-of-the-envelope briefings are out.'

Down the corridor, a door slammed and heavy footsteps echoed on the linoleum. Judge Donaldson appeared; his manner that of a man who has delivered a message, and delivered it well.

His eyes lit on Barlow. 'It's your fault.'

'Your Honour, I'm no longer Station Sergeant. Gillespie is Pierson's man.'

Behind him Pierson choked in indignation.

Donaldson gave a dry laugh. 'I know you too well. I parked on that spot for a lifetime without a word being said. But the moment I criticise the police for delays in bringing prosecutions...' Donaldson moved closer. He had the height to match him eye for eye. 'I'm alleging conspiracy to intimidate the judiciary. If this happens again, I will take it further and much higher.'

'I'm sure it won't.'

'Bloody right,' whispered Pierson.

Donaldson strode on and gave the front door a good bang behind him.

Pierson went back to his paperwork. Barlow smirked. Harvey's blitz of reforms included an aged stack of Procurement and Requisition dockets. Everything had to be written up and all items accounted for, down to the last box of Her Majesty's Stationery Office paperclips.

He headed for the Bridge Bar, favouring a pint before tea and, hopefully, finding Edward sober enough to talk. On the way, he passed a two-man foot patrol. The men nodded and walked on. Normal practice was for them to stop and give him a verbal report. He made a mental note. Those two would be on nights until they'd learned who still ran things.

The Bridge Bar had a fire leaping in the grate and a pint being pulled for him before he managed to get the door shut. Heads turned his way and nodded a greeting. Nearly every regular, including Geordie Dunlop, had served with him in the Royal Ulster Rifles. It was the only pub in the town where he could sit and drink a pint and feel welcome.

Geordie leaned against the bar counter. They hadn't met since Easter Sunday when Geordie tried to start a fight in the Enquiry Office. Currently, the grandsons were serving eighteen months in Crumlin Road Prison for attempting to steal Denton's cattle. According to the medical reports produced at the trial, the Comedian Dunlop's ability to procreate remained unimpaired. Which did nothing for the advancement of civilisation.

'Look what the cat's dragged in,' said Geordie.

'Evening, Geordie,' he said, relieved that Geordie had got over his temper.

He looked around the bar and saw the usual crowd slumped over the usual pints. A foursome were playing a quiet game of poker in the corner. Strictly illegal, of course, but the bets never got out of hand and the current winner always paid for the drinks.

The Guinness mirror on one wall and the Tennents mirror on the other reflected an infinity of Edwards. In front of Edward appeared an equal number of pints and chasers. Cigarette smoke curled into the air above his head.

Edward pretended to hunt in his pockets for change. 'Is it my shout or yours, Sergeant?'

He frowned. With that slurred voice Edward could be on anything from his first to his fourth pint. After four pints, he became incapable of stringing a sentence together. Barlow bought two pints of draught beer and joined Edward at his table. Edward reached for the glass. He held it back. 'The hut is like you, bucked.'

'It suffices one.'

'It doesn't, but that's not what I'm here about.'

Edward's hand made a gracious, welcoming gesture. 'Speak on, dear friend.'

'Stoop Taylor.'

'The late unlamented.'

He smiled. Stoop never bought Edward a drink. Stoop would hardly buy one for himself. 'We need his army file, but it's not forthcoming.'

Edward shook his head in despair. 'Sergeant Major, when will you ever learn? The only thing forthcoming in the army is the blame and bull.'

'You've got contacts. The Colonel-in-Chief is a cousin of yours.'

'We don't speak. I find him a disappointment.'

'I wonder what he thinks of you,' and immediately regretted the unkind words. By way of apology he pushed the pint into Edward's hand and sipped at his own. After a day spent in the fields it tasted like nectar.

Edward accepted the pint and the apology with a gracious inclination of the head. 'Why has one need of Rifleman Taylor's army file?

Why, he found impossible to say, but he had to touch physical objects to make sense of things: in this case, Stoop's file. At the very least it would contain details of his marriage to the Frau, if one had ever taken place. Not just the certificates, but the background reports into the Frau's character and background.

While he waited for Edward to mull things over he thought through the paper trail he needed. No foreign national, particularly a German, could marry a British soldier without first being interrogated by the military police, the local police, the padre and the Commanding Officer. Fitness reports prepared, a committee meeting would be convened to make the final decision. All that paperwork had to contain the Frau's life history and details of her extended family tree. If Adenauer were, in fact, a cousin, as she had claimed, it would show up in the reports.

Edward finally said, 'As the recipient of the George Cross, one does have a certain degree of influence with the right people. Perhaps one might have a word with the Regimental Secretary.'

'I would appreciate it,' Barlow said in a way that implied haste.

Because haste was something that Barlow felt was very badly needed in this case. According to the psychiatrists, Kurt Adenauer had responded well to treatment. The hospital expected to discharge him by early summer. By that time, Leary would need enough evidence to hang the man, or the courts would have to release him. Release a man ruthless enough to shoot someone in the back. A man like that had to be kept in jail, if only for the safety of others. And if that meant Barlow ignoring orders and getting involved in the case, then so be it.

CHAPTER 39

VERA HAD THE TEA COOKED and ready when Barlow arrived home: frying steak, onions and boiled potatoes. All kept warm in the town gas oven. She served up, and splashed on a generous helping of gravy. They took the plates into the living room and sat at the table with Maggie.

Of all days Maggie was up and full of chat about the goings on in *Emergency Ward 10*, the weekly ITV hospital serial. Maybe she knew the hospital staff weren't real people doing real things. He couldn't be sure, but it got her out of bed for a couple of hours.

The new doctor on the ward, Doctor Moone, had Maggie worried. The man reminded her of a telegraph pole. According to her, he never ate enough.

He wondered if she ever examined herself in the mirror. *Probably not.* He looked at the drawn face and the black-rimmed eyes. Tried to see a trace of the bright young girl he had married. If she didn't watch herself she'd be back in the psychiatric hospital.

'So what happened today?' he asked, making his voice sound chatty.

Although Maggie was still wearing her dressing gown, at least her hair was combed. A good sign. She needed a visit to the hairdresser to have the grey roots coloured, although he wouldn't dare suggest such a thing.

'One of the patients, a big, bossy woman, convinced herself she had gangrene. The fuss she created. Her with her nose always stuck in a medical book.'

'And did she?'

'Of course not. Nurse Carole put her in her box. She's not one to put up with any nonsense.'

He could have fallen off the chair in shock. He'd got more out of Maggie in less than five seconds than he had in the previous five months.

Vera put down her knife and fork.

'Da, after the final exams, a few of us … We're thinking of going to Portrush for the weekend.' Her voice quickened and her face burned red. 'Kenny's family have a house there. They said we could borrow it.'

'No,' he said.

'That's not fair. Everyone's going.'

'You're not,' he said, and struggled to remain firm, despite her obvious upset.

'Why not?'

'Things go on at weekends away.'

Vera grabbed her plate and stormed off into the scullery.

Maggie started to shake. Rows upset her, he knew, and he needed a way to calm things.

He followed Vera into the scullery and closed the door to stop any angry words from reaching Maggie. With all his heart he wished Maggie were fit to talk to Vera about the birds and the bees. About young men and drink and convenient beds.

'Look, Vera, when boys and girls get together unsupervised. They don't mean to, but … '

She said, 'You're one to be talking.'

'What do you mean by that?'

'You think I don't know about you and the Widow Taylor?'

'Wash out your mouth with soap,' he said. The shock of her knowing turned guilt to anger. 'You're maligning a good woman.'

The tears started. 'That's not what the police wives say.'

He wished she wouldn't cry. Tears didn't suit her. Her face mottled red, and he didn't like to see Vera hurt in any way.

'Alexandra allowed me to use an old hut while I was guarding Denton's cattle. That's all.'

'You weren't there the night Kenny and I called. We brought a flask of tea to keep you warm.'

'What time?' he asked, thinking he could say Alexandra had him up for supper.

'Late. We looked. The lights were out in the house. Just a bloody dog that nearly bit Kenny.'

'Mind your language.'

'Da, how many other tarts have you gone with over the years?'

He slapped her face.

She didn't touch the cheek. He could see the marks of his fingers on her skin. She walked out of the scullery.

'Vera!'

He heard her steps on the stairs as she headed for her bedroom.

The control of her emotions got to him, the adult way she carried herself.

He'd have given his life's blood to draw back that blow. Stood on in the scullery, but Vera didn't come down again. Damned if he'd go up and apologise and find himself trying to justify Alexandra to his daughter. While he waited, he washed the dishes and tidied things away. Wet the tea.

'Tea's made,' he shouted up the stairs as he carried mugs and milk into the living room. Shouted again that it was going cold. He and Maggie drank their tea in silence. Above them gentle snores started. Vera had fallen asleep.

'You spoil that girl,' said Maggie unexpectedly.

'I do?'

'Always giving in to her.' Maggie glared at the television he'd bought at Christmas. 'Getting her nice things when she pleases you. Giving her money.'

He wasn't in the mood for an argument. 'You could be right.' Wished Maggie was back in her bed. He needed peace to think about the day, to dream of life on a farm and a woman with a quick mind to share it with. Tried not to feel relieved when Maggie started to nod off in front of the television.

Long after he'd wished her out of the room she stood up. 'I'll go to bed now.'

'Good night,' he said, trying to sound pleasant, not relieved.

She stood on. 'Do you want to come with me?'

He looked at the clock. Ten o'clock had still to strike. 'I'll be up soon.'

A hand rested uncertainly on his shoulder, and then was snatched away. 'It's been a long time… and I know you have your needs.'

Maggie blushed as if they'd been caught in the very act. She fled – first to the scullery and the outside toilet, then up the stairs.

He watched her go, confused at his own feelings. He couldn't make love to Maggie. Not with Alexandra's sweat still on his body. Felt guilty about betraying Alexandra, but not about betraying his wife.

CHAPTER 40

BARLOW MOVED AROUND THE LIVING room tidying. Straightened the chairs at the table. Set the newspaper with the kindling for the morning. In the end, he faced the stairs. Maggie was his wife. That gave her rights over his body – and his loyalties.

He put a hand on the banisters. Maybe she'd settle for a cuddle? If he went slowly enough she might even doze off.

Maggie appeared at the turn in the stairs. She wore a nightdress, no dressing gown, and had let her hair down. 'Are you coming?'

Her voice sounded strong, confident. He thought she'd put on a fresh nightdress. Got the smell of perfume. 'I'm on my way.' The word "love" caught in his throat.

He switched off the living room light. Stood in darkness rather than let her see his face. Her illness had made her very astute. She often read more into his expressions than he wanted her to know. He still could see her, a black shape in the diffused glow from the street lighting. Started up the stairs, taking slow step after slow step. *How do I get out of this?*

Maggie raised her arms above her head. The movement pulled her nightdress up, bared her thighs. He felt himself harden. Hated himself for this first act of disloyalty. Alexandra had told him never to come back. He tried to build anger against her for that.

When their faces came level Maggie brought her arms down. Something metal, her comb he thought, gleamed in her hands. Whatever it was, it thudded against his upper arm.

It had happened to him before, with a bomb. He could only stand and watch the last ticks. Then the second hand froze on the mark before the twelve and … His hands didn't even shake as he cut the wire and neutralised the bomb. This time, the metal something slammed into him for a second time and he felt himself fall.

Maggie started to scream. That didn't make sense. He was the one hurt. She came bounding down the stairs. The streetlight coming in the window caught the gleam. He recognised his own carving knife. *I'm stabbed!*

Maggie stabbed at him again. He fended off the blow and struggled to keep the blade from his throat. 'Maggie, it's me,' he shouted, trying to bring her to her senses.

After years of not eating properly all that remained of her was skin and bone. Yet he couldn't throw her off and jump to his feet. Pain had him glued to the floor.

He heard Vera's voice. 'Ma, Da, what's wrong?'

'Stay back,' he called, but she came down the stairs and clicked on the light.

The point of the blade rested against his throat. Blood stained Maggie's hands and the top of her nightdress. *Did I hurt her? I didn't intend to.* She continued screaming. His ears hurt from the noise. Her face had gone purple from the effort of trying to kill him.

Maggie's loose hair kept getting in his eyes. He could see Vera hesitate, not knowing what to do. Hear her say. 'Ma, Ma,' in a panicked voice.

'Gillespie,' he said. 'Get Gillespie.'

Gillespie would arrive too late, but it got Vera out of the house. Maggie might turn on her. *Who'll take care of Vera?* He remembered Maggie's sister, Daisy, a sensible woman. Vera thought the world of her. *There that's sorted, I can die now.*

Instead of leaving, Vera leaned forward and touched Maggie's shoulder. 'Ma, do you fancy a cup of tea?'

The screaming stopped. The pressure on the knife stayed.

'What do you think, Ma? A nice cup of tea and maybe a biscuit.'

Maggie seemed to think about it. At least the downward pressure eased. The point of the blade tickled the hairs at his throat.

Vera put a comforting arm around her mother's shoulders. 'Come on, Ma.'

Barlow tried to hold the knife to his throat, but Maggie lifted it away. He closed his eyes, unable to watch his child being murdered.

'I'll take it in bed,' said Maggie.

He opened his eyes again. Maggie was still holding the knife, but wasn't threatening anybody with it. She looked puzzled, the way she did when trying to work her way through the fog of madness.

'What about toast?' he asked. *My last words. What a daft thing to say.*

'I'd need the knife to cut the bread,' said Vera.

'You would,' said Maggie.

All of a sudden the pressure eased. Maggie sat back and held the knife out to Vera, blade first. Barlow's arms slumped, unbidden to his sides. He wanted Vera to run and not step forward and take the knife. What if Maggie sensed a trick? He closed his eyes, unable to watch his daughter get hurt and him not able to do anything about it.

'What sort of jam do you want, Ma?'

He opened his eyes again. Saw Maggie run a weary hand over her face as she tried to decide. 'Marmalade, the thin cut jar.' *The lifeblood's pumping out of me, and they're talking about marmalade?*

At least Vera had the knife. Now she'd blood on her hands. The blood dripped from the blade onto her school skirt. Even as he watched, she wiped her hand against the skirt, transferring more blood. She'd expect the skirt to be miraculously clean in the morning for school. Maggie went up the stairs. Pulling herself from step to step, the way she did on a bad day. Vera put two cushions on his chest, then a tray from the kitchen. *I'd make a grand coffee table.* Her mouth moved, but he heard only the rush of blood in his ears. Vera disappeared and came back and piled schoolbooks onto the tray. 'I'll not float off,' he tried to tell her.

Vera's mouth went up and down again as she tried to explain something. Then she disappeared. For some reason he heard her shoes clatter along the pavement. At least she was safe. For April, the night felt bitter. He wished she'd thought to throw a rug over his feet.

The light bulb glared down on him and hurt his eyes. He closed them and listened to a drip of water. No, not water. Blood. The bomb that got him was the one ticking in his wife's head.

In spite of the tray and the books he floated. He opened his eyes and saw the door lintel go past. He drifted under the night sky. Cloudy. No stars, just when he planned to head their way. *Not planned exactly.* He hoped the blood came off the schoolbooks.

A voice said, 'He's conscious.'

Gillespie's face drifted beside him. Gillespie wore a striped pyjama top. A man should wear long johns on a cold night. Trust Gillespie to go grand. A wool blanket scratched his chin. You'd think they'd give him two blankets. He was still cold. The tray and the books had done a better job.

'Sarge, are you okay?'

'What do you think?'

They loaded him into a vehicle. An ambulance, he supposed. What about the stars? He closed his eyes again.

CHAPTER 41

BARLOW DIDN'T WANT TO COME awake. Large chunks of him hurt and nausea swished around his insides. Something clogged his breathing. Released. Clogged again. He got an eye open.

A nurse stood over him, holding a facecloth. A pretty nurse, with a curl of fair hair along her cheek. Only darkness showed outside the windows, which made it some awful hour of the morning.

'I get one chance of a lie-in.'

She said, 'We want to be neat and tidy for Matron's inspection, don't we?'

Worse things threatened than Matron's inspection. His eyes drifted to the bedside locker.

She smiled and picked up the urine bottle. Pulled the bedclothes back and put the bottle between his legs.

'I'll do the rest,' he said hastily. He wore only a hospital gown. They'd cut away his long-johns on the operating table. Good ones too, ones he'd bought recently. Three women in the room at the time, and him with no blood left to blush.

Only one arm worked, which didn't help the current manoeuvre. His left arm lay strapped across his chest.

Finished and the bottle removed by the nurse he relaxed and developed an ache for a cigarette. She gave him a drink with a straw. *Water, and not a drop of the hard stuff to fortify a man.* You didn't have to be an alcoholic to gasp for the occasional drink.

Even stretched out flat, his head still swam. He worried about Vera, and what they'd done with Maggie. They'd given him a private ward. There'd be more craic in the public ward. But who wants a policeman earwigging on some of the things people got up to.

What the hell had got into Maggie? Not him and Alexandra. No way could she know about that. Vera must be out of her head with worry.

His eyes closed. Just for a moment, he promised himself, but when he opened them again, daylight flooded in the windows. Even lying down, he could see the tops of the trees in the People's Park down the road. What was it he used to get the drunks to say? "The tops of the trees on top of the hill touching the tree trunks and the teals." *Something like that.*

Experienced hands tweaked the bedclothes to make him more comfortable. He looked and saw the Frau. She wore a hospital dressing gown.

'Herr Barlow, you are awake. This is good.'

He watched her check a plastic bag of liquid suspended above his bed. A drip. He hadn't noticed that the first time. She seemed to know what she was doing.

'I think you live.'

'You too, apparently.'

She had a bald spot where they'd cut away her hair, and a line of stitches. Probably imagining things, but he thought the woman had put on weight.

She eased him forward and adjusted the pillows in order to leave him half-sitting, half-lying. Now he could see the top of the hill itself. Another floor up and he'd be able to see the roof of the police station. *Surely to God, Maggie's not there in a cell?*

The Frau said, 'I come say thank you for yesterday. Be sure you okay. Peter say you friend again.'

'You're a great nurse. Is that how you met Stoo … your husband?'

'Yes. All the war I am nurse in Metz. The British come. Herr Taylor he always in hospital. You know, poor boys going home, they want a … memory.'

'Memento.'

'What you say. Herr Taylor, he sell them.'

She placed a hand on his forehead to check his temperature. Unimaginable with all the farm chores she did, but the skin had stayed soft.

'Herr Taylor and I, we fall in love, then war take him away. When war is over I go Lengerich. Then Herr Taylor in hospital, very ill. He see I carry his child and ask marry. We have Peter.'

'That's very romantic.' His brain started to unclog itself of drifting thoughts. 'All that paperwork, just to be with the man you love. You kept it of course?'

'Ja.' She touched her breasts. 'The day you come to house, it here.'

The German thing. Money and papers handy, ready to run if needs be. Safely hidden in her bra. WPC Day, he'd bloody kill her. She'd supervised the Frau changing out of her wet clothes in Alexandra's house. *Typical Irish.* She hadn't watched in case she'd see naked flesh.

The Frau said, 'Mr Comberton and me, we talk. We agree we give Herr Harvey papers. Today maybe.'

Of course, first chance the Frau had slipped the papers to her solicitor. *Quite a woman.* Which made her worth watching. 'Will you get home today?

She nodded. The nod reminded him of Alexandra. 'Once I see doctor.'

'And your husband?'

The freshness of youth ghosted her cheeks. 'Soon I think.'
She went white. 'He cousin.'

'Sorry, I meant cousin,' he lied.

'I am glad him to see.'

That at least was the truth. Her face glowed again with happiness.

'He ask stay until he get papers. We talk and talk old memories. Many sad. Most family, they are dead.'

'Give me a shout before you go. I might be able to arrange a lift for you and Peter.'

He lay back and watched life in the ward as doctors and nurses came and went. He was alive and expected to recover. More than that they couldn't say until the consultant appeared. In the meantime, Sergeant Barlow must rest.

'It's no good grouching,' the Matron informed him when he grumped about not getting home.

Apparently, Gillespie had saved his life. Had stuck a thumb into the severed artery in his arm to stem the bleeding.

'I hope he washed his bloody hands first,' he said, and enjoyed Matron pretending to be shocked at his language.

Matron, he knew, had won a Military Cross for her work during the carnage on the Dunkirk invasion beaches, so she'd heard a lot worse. These days, after a couple of whiskeys, she used language strong enough to turn the blue-rinse brigade's hair white.

The general anaesthetic was the cause of the queasiness he was now experiencing. The Matron believed in kill or cure, so they gave him tea and toast. Everything stayed down. At his request, she also rang the police station and asked for Constable Gillespie to call by.

Gillespie wandered in just before lunch, with Vera in tow.

Vera was still wearing yesterday's clothes. Mrs Gillespie had hand washed the blood out of the uniform skirt and ironed it dry. Vera took one look at Barlow and burst into tears.

'She's been great up to now,' said Gillespie.

Barlow used his good arm to drag Vera onto the bed and give her a hug.

'I'm so silly. I'm being selfish,' she blubbered.

'You were very brave when it mattered.' He felt his own tears start.

Gillespie, with unexpected tact, left the room.

'What's going to happen to Ma, to us?'

She was seventeen years old, a child still, and both her parents were in hospital. His mother had died when he was eight and he'd had no close relatives to take him in. That nightmare still haunted the edges of his dreams. God forbid that Vera would ever go through the same trauma. Last night, if it hadn't been for her cool head... 'Where did they take your ma?'

'To the asylum.'

She made it sound the way it felt: a lingering death sentence. How had Maggie turned into the hollow-eyed, stringy creature she now was? He'd teased the shyness out of this waif of a girl, wanting her to look him in the eye and give him one genuine smile. And a man needed something of himself to leave behind in wartime. Post-natal depression had triggered Maggie's schizophrenia. If Vera ever found that out she'd blame herself forever.

But what had made her violent last night? That had never happened before; never a hint that she might do anyone harm.

All the same, he should have known better. Crushing lows always followed her extreme highs. His row with Vera had upset her. Maybe she'd heard the blow when he struck Vera and had later lashed out in order to protect her daughter? *God alone knows what goes on in Maggie's head.*

'What?' asked Vera.

Had he said that out loud?

The weight of Vera's head on his chest hurt. The stabs had been downwards so, thankfully, the blade bounced off ribs instead of invading his chest cavity. Pain or not, he wanted Vera to stay there forever and be safe. 'Nothing,' he said, yet changes in their day-to-day lives were now inevitable.

Half a lifetime's wages spent on private care for Maggie, up until now. And all just to have a say in her treatment. No way did he trust this electric shock therapy that the psychiatrists swore by. A thing like that was bound to addle the brain. Anyway, the State had now taken over. They'd section Maggie. If she ever got out of hospital again, she'd be a much older woman.

He nudged at Vera until she got off the bed. 'Get Gillespie back in here. I've got a job for the two of you.'

192

CHAPTER 42

VERA AND GILLESPIE RETURNED, TOOK their orders and left. Their visit was only one of many intrusions into Barlow's morning. Peace he found hard to come by in hospital. Hourly checks were made on his temperature and blood pressure. A nurse came to enquire if his bowels had worked that day, and if not, did he need a laxative? One took away the drip. Another wanted blood.

'I've none to spare.'

In uniform he might be *Sergeant Barlow*, the man people crossed the street to avoid. As a patient in Surgical he was someone to humour. He rather liked the change. The nurses were pleasant and worth looking at, dedicated and competent. Not like the twisted old bags he remembered from his childhood. The nurses' home had a reputation for *goings on*, especially after their monthly dance.

Ballymena, he knew, had never really recovered from the Yanks with their nylons and their candy.

Things quietened down after the lunch tray had come and gone.

His boots were under the bed. A hospital dressing gown hung from a hook near the sink. Outside, cloud covered the sky but sunlight blinked through in the occasional gap. Just the sort of day a convalescent might take advantage of and amble down to the front door to catch a breath of fresh air.

Sitting up unsupported he felt fine. Doing the same on the edge of the bed put his head in a gyro spin. When he stood up, he gripped the bed frame and willed himself not to black out. After a few dodgy seconds, lightness took over his head. Kept it floating towards the ceiling while his feet moved across the floor.

The dressing gown nearly defeated him. The right arm went in. But how to swing it over the shoulders, one-armed? Either the dressing gown went on or he'd have to face the world with a backless operating gown.

Eventually, the answer came to him. He blamed the anaesthetic for his sluggish brain. He used his right arm to sling the dressing gown over both shoulders, and then threaded his right hand down the sleeve and tied everything off. Tight. Stuck his feet in the boots. What if the laces tripped him? *Too bad.*

The corridor was clear. Female voices wafted from nearby; that and the noise of the scraping of knives over plates. The first nurse he'd seen that morning, the one with the curl of fair hair along her cheek, appeared out of the sluice room. 'Sergeant Barlow, what are you doing out of bed?'

He held his lower stomach. 'Big one. I can't wait.'

She pointed. 'In there.'

'Great.' He shuffled through the door into the toilet.

Exhaustion made him gasp for a drink of water. Even the thought of drinking out of the tap seemed unhygienic. Not with all those diseases that brought people into hospital.

At the count of ten he peeked out. The nurse had disappeared. Laughter floated up from the nurses' room. He shuffled down the ward at his best speed. Pushed through the swing doors into the main corridor.

A lift door stood open. He got in and pressed G for the ground. The jerk of the lift as it started hurt every muscle. He leaned against the side and tried to get his breath back. The force of the lift stopping hurt. The lift doors opened. Ahead he could see the front door and freedom. The fresh air helped revive him for the worst part. A two-hundred-yard walk to a wartime Nissen hut grandly titled Pathology Laboratory.

The cinder path was uneven. He stumbled into a hedge and stood gulping air. His sweat had saturated the hospital gown. A cold wind turned it to ice. He moved on before some interfering do-gooder insisted on summoning help.

CHAPTER 43

RECEPTION AT THE PATHOLOGY LABORATORY was unmanned. *Lunchtime of course.* Barlow took the left corridor and all but fell into the pathologist's office.

'Don't worry about knocking,' said the pathologist. He sat at his desk, peeling an apple onto that day's *Irish Times*. He indicated for him to sit down. 'Are you here to book your autopsy?'

Never had a chair come so welcome. 'No.'

'Well you're going the right way about it.'

He sat and drew breath and looked around him while the pathologist poured a glass of water from a jug. The room had a single window that jutted out through the curving side of the hut. A desk, a few chairs and a bookcase cramped the small room.

He took the glass and slopped most of the water onto his dressing gown. Shook off what he could and drank the rest.

The pathologist reached for the phone. 'This may sound ridiculous, but you need an ambulance to get you back to the ward.'

'A few questions first, doc.'

'Doctor.'

'Doctor,' he agreed. The pathologist had had the unique experience of assessing the walking dead in a Japanese prison. He'd banked on that knowledge to be allowed time for a private consultation. The pathologist, he also knew, had no patience for time-wasting chitchat so he asked, bluntly, 'Stoop Taylor's autopsy. What was unusual about it?'

'Who said there was?'

Did I see the doc give a nervous start?

'I'm asking.'

'I told you everything the time of the first phone call.'

'You did.'

'In words of one syllable.'

'Easily understood, even by the likes of me.'

'Followed up by a detailed and comprehensive report.'

'That as well,' he said. No way would he admit he'd never seen the report.

'So what?' asked the doctor.

Barlow chewed on his imaginary sweet. His head still floated well above his body. He needed a lie down. One of the slabs next door would do fine. 'I'm looking for the funny bits. The little snippets that don't get into a report.'

Instead of being outraged at the accusation of holding back information, the pathologist smiled. 'Barlow, you only pretend to be stupid.'

'I'm just a plodder, Doc. People like you join up all the dots.'

'Mmm,' said the pathologist. He cut the apple in two and gave him half. They chewed in silence. The doctor stared, first at the ceiling then towards the room where he carried out the autopsies. Barlow knew the man was gifted with almost total recall. He only had to visualise the body back on the table.

The doctor started slowly. 'Stoop Taylor: age sixty-one, weight ten stone three. Height: five-eight. Liver spots on the skin caused by excessive alcohol intake. Advanced liver damage. Early stages of pancreatitis. Time of death somewhere between 8.45am and 12.30pm.'

'That's quite a range of times.'

The doctor said, 'It was a cold day and person or persons unknown moved the body after death. That makes temperature a major factor.'

'Okay, doctor, 12.30pm, that's about the time I found the body. Why 8.45am?'

The doctor looked smug. 'The postman reported handing Stoop a demand for overdue income tax about that time. Stoop was not amused, to put it politely.'

'So time of death is dependent, not on the autopsy but on a couple of watches being right,' said Barlow, dryly.

The doctor ignored the sarcasm and continued to speak even as he poured them both another glass of water. 'Multiple compound fractures of the body. Brain eviscerated. Body discovered face down yet no mud in the airways. Foreign objects found in the chest cavity: metal splinters, speculatively from a bullet. Time of death: probably mid to late morning.'

The pathologist savoured a mouthful of water before continuing. 'In addition, the autopsy uncovered multi-focal calcification in the pelvis, left scapula and left posterior ribcage. All in keeping with a previous history of trauma to those areas.'

Barlow struggled to keep his eyes open. The window kept blurring out. 'Queen's English, Doc.'

The doctor raised an eyebrow. 'Because I'm in the company of an alleged fool.'

'Big words are beyond me at the minute.'

The doctor nodded. He hesitated before he said, 'When Maggie gets out … '

'If.'

The doctor didn't disagree. 'A house with a garden might lift her mind.'

'I'll think about it,' he said, not wanting to discuss Maggie with anyone.

The doctor again looked towards the autopsy room. 'The damage to the skull was traumatic.' He tapped a tune on his desk, a trait Barlow had never noticed before. 'There's not much left, hardly enough brain tissue left to do more than guess.'

'Go on,' he encouraged. This made the trek from the hospital ward worth every grunt of effort.

The doctor appeared to think more than actually speak. 'Stoop didn't suffer a heart attack. There is no evidence of a seizure of any kind. The toxicology report is negative, so poison is not a factor. Yet he was dead before he hit the ground.'

Barlow stayed silent rather than break the man's chain of thought.

The doctor nodded sharply to himself. He'd come to a definite conclusion. Barlow wished he wouldn't. He found nodding addictive.

The doctor said, 'Bear in mind I had to work on an incomplete cadaver. With bits of brain and tissue scooped up out of the mud. On examining these I came to the conclusion... ' Clearly, he hated voicing instinct without scientific proof. 'Not a conclusion, an indication... No, less than that. An intuitive feeling that there is... or may be bruising on the brain mass to the right side of the head.'

His voice dragged as he finally put words to his reluctant thoughts. 'There is a possibility – and I emphasise possibility – that Stoop Taylor sustained a blow to the head prior to death. If that proves to be the case, then that blow is the actual cause of death.'

'There's another problem Doctor. Two actually, and I think they might be related.'

'Go on.' The doctor looked miffed at his revelation being taken so calmly. He picked up the phone and dialled a number. 'Sister, have you lost a patient? Well he's here with me and I've got healthier-looking corpses in the chill room.'

In Barlow's opinion that was the doctor's best idea of the day. Cold sweat stood on his whole body and he ached to be back in bed.

Before people arrived to collect him he needed a few more questions answered. 'Doctor, I knew from the first day that you didn't like Stoop Taylor. May I ask why?'

'Professional confidentiality,' said the doctor in a tight voice.

'Had it anything to do with verifying the paternity of his son, Peter Taylor?'

'I can't say.'

Barlow waited. Let the problem work questions in the doctor's mind. Tweak his interest. 'Then we'll get a court order authorising us to take blood samples for a paternity test. Unless...'

The doctor raised an eyebrow.

'Well, Doctor, everybody's blood ends up here for one test or another. A bit of searching through your files could tell us everything we want to know.' A thought occurred to him. 'Is that what you and Stoop fought about? You refused to do it for him?'

He wished he were in uniform to make the request seem more official. He let out a breath of relief when the doctor scribbled on a pad. "Taylor, River Road. Blood types."

The doctor threw down his pen. 'There's an easier way than that, Barlow.'

'Is there?'

The doctor laughed.

'You need testicles to manufacture sperm for procreation. Stoop didn't have any.'

CHAPTER 44

THE WINDOWS WERE CLOSED AND the blinds drawn. The drip reattached and hung from a wheel-less stand. The door was propped open and every nurse passing checked to make sure the patient hadn't done another runner. Sergeant Barlow was going nowhere.

Sergeant Barlow didn't care. Sergeant Barlow slept, his snores rattling around the building.

Foxwood came to get a statement and in the end scribbled a note: "Come to the station at your earliest convenience" – and left.

God in the form of the consultant appeared with his acolytes in tow. Sister ran ahead to make clear his path. God and Barlow had met before: a small matter of driving while under the influence. Courtesy of the right connections, the case hadn't gone to court, but Barlow's words of caution still seared the consultant's mind.

The snores, the consultant decided from the safety of the doorway, were either caused by terminal brain damage or the body healing itself. Let time decide. He put off his examination until the morrow.

At visiting time, Vera peeked in.

He came instantly awake. 'Hi, love.'

She came in giggling. 'What did you do to the nurses?'

Having her laughing and happy again did wonders for him. 'Why?' he asked.

'I brought you clothes for coming home. The sister said "under no circumstances" and locked them in a cupboard.'

'They're running short of victims to torture.' He reached for a kiss.

Vera was on a high, he noted. She'd had a good day. Off-duty constables had washed the bloodstains off the walls and the floor of the house. Jackson kept being sick. She laughed at that, rather than dwell on what caused the nausea.

'Dad, they must like you to do all that.'

'The devil you know.'

All the same it pleased him. The off-duty officers going in to help had to be spontaneous. No way would Pierson organise a clean-up for him. That's what he liked about the police in Ballymena. They fought and bitched among themselves, but when the chips were down, they were family.

Vera told him that the linoleum had torn when the men tried to lift it to get at the blood. McKinneys had some lovely new patterns. She'd picked one, subject to his approval.

The house and home were important to Vera. He let her talk herself out before asking the question that really interested him. What happened when she and Gillespie took the Frau home?

'A penny for your thoughts,' said Vera.

He realised he'd let his mind drift to the next move against Adenauer. It mustn't happen again. This was Vera's time and she had plenty to talk about.

Lots of people sent their best wishes and promised to pray for his speedy recovery. Edward sent his "felicitations and condolences", and a message that he'd sourced something better than a dusty army file. However, it required the acquisition or hire of a motor vehicle to enable one to participate in verbal repartee with the source.

The words rolled off Vera's tongue nearly as easily as they did off Edward's. That made him proud of his little girl. In his early days in the police, not only could he not pronounce the words, he had to look them up in a dictionary.

Vera probed what Edward's message meant. Barlow wouldn't say.

Edward also sent his apologies. Mr Barlow must not expect a hospital visit. He would be pleased and honoured to stand his former Sergeant-Major a pint at the earliest opportunity.

'Guess who'll have to pay?' Barlow grumped.

Mrs Cameron, Kenny's mother, had offered to put Vera up in the family's spare bedroom until he got out of hospital. 'Imagine, Dad. Four of them living in that house and they still have a spare bedroom.'

'It's up to you,' he said, sensing a hesitation.

Mrs Cameron was friendly, but very formal. You got napkins with every meal. *She's eaten there before?* That made him uneasy. What else had she not told him?

Vera said she'd rather stay with the Gillespies. 'You know what I mean, Dad?'

He did. Vera didn't feel comfortable in the Cameron house. He sensed that Mrs Cameron was hoping the romance wouldn't last. If it did, napkins would be the least of Vera's problems.

CHAPTER 45

FRIDAY, MID MORNING, THEY PUT Barlow's arm in a sling and discharged him. He looked on grimly as the nursing staff gave a sigh of relief when the taxi arrived to take him home. Felt great until he pulled on a sports coat and tried to walk downtown to look at this linoleum Vera fancied.

Before he got halfway, his knees started to knock. He staggered into Caufields and slid into one of their booths. When the waitress came he treated himself to an espresso and a doughnut. McKinneys and the linoleum could wait. Home lay enticingly downhill.

Alexandra hadn't come to see him in hospital. He'd thought she might in the circumstances. He ached for the comfort of her arms. Having a near-death experience had reawakened old nightmares of the dead who came to him in the night. Hughie: the hulking Scotsman from the Gorbals in Glasgow who hated the Irish. They used to get drunk together. All he found of Hughie was a length of greasy thigh bone. Big Willie, who always forgot to duck his head going through a doorway. Alfie from Cheltenham who never talked unless they were on a job; then he told interminable stories.

Edward appeared with the rest, though he had survived the war physically. Edward couldn't accept that those deaths, and the deaths of others, were not his fault. After one horrendous experience, he'd sworn an oath on the Bible. Never again would he visit a man in hospital. He kept the men under his command as hale and hearty as possible. If they got unlucky or careless on a job, the remains fitted into a shoebox.

Throughout all of the war years, Edward never took a drink, never went on leave or took a day off. Edward was there with his men on every difficult assignment, or at the other end of the radio if they needed advice. Edward also had an instinct about unexploded bombs. More than once, he and Barlow defused ticking bombs because Edward said they wouldn't detonate. Another time Barlow put the stethoscope to a bomb and declared it quiet, no ticking. Edward said, 'Run!' Seconds later they were lying in a slit-trench with bricks and wooden beams falling all around them.

Barlow had survived the war because of Edward. All he could do in return was ease Edward's chosen method of death. Drink might kill more slowly than a bomb, but it killed just as surely.

When Barlow finished his coffee he went out onto the street and waited. He flagged down the first car going in the right direction and asked the driver to drop him at the police station. Best get that meeting with Foxwood over and done with.

He arrived as the afternoon shift was reporting for duty. Sergeant Pierson phoned in ill. The station erupted in confusion as everybody angled for the cushy jobs. Inspector Foxwood didn't know whom to agree with.

'You'll bloody do as you're bloody told,' roared Barlow in the end, and looked to Foxwood for confirmation.

'Carry on, Sergeant,' said Foxwood and disappeared down the corridor to the safe haven of his own office.

Sports coat or not, on sick leave or not, he took the parade. He ordered the men to line up, and went down the line. Every man had a uniform defect, every man got bollocked. He read out two pages of Standing Orders in a dutifully dull tone, then told the men their duties for the shift.

'What about us?' asked the WPCs.

'Go and arrange some flowers.'

Their faces dropped. He let their hopes hang a moment. They'd been on office duties since Pierson took over. 'Oh all right, walk the town,' he said, and made it sound like a bother and utter selfishness on their part. 'I don't want to hear one word from you lot about ladders or flat feet.'

They scurried away in case he had second thoughts. He shouted after them. 'And no window shopping.'

One of the office-bound constables protested. 'There's a lot of typing to be done.'

Barlow pointed at him. 'See to it.'

The parade dismissed, the men hastened out the door. A pained voice trailed back. 'Thank God he's in a good mood. Otherwise he'd have given us hell.'

Barlow shouted after him. 'The fact that I owe you lot a drink has got nothing to do with the length of your hair. *GET IT CUT!*

Inspector Foxwood's door lay partly open.

'Barlow.'

He pushed his way into the room. 'Sir?'

Foxwood motioned for him to take a seat. 'Sergeant Pierson will be out for at least a week.'

'It's not like him to be ill.'

'Nervous exhaustion.' Foxwood made it sound like the illness was self-inflicted. 'You coped all these years without any bother?'

'I did what I could, and what I couldn't do, I didn't worry about.' He touched the heaped papers on the inspector's desk. 'It appears to me, Sir, that you're going the same way yourself.'

Foxwood sagged back in his chair. 'I can't remember when I last had a Saturday off, and I take a bag of stuff home every night.'

'The wife's complaining, no doubt.'

'She says when I'm not working, I'm sleeping.'

Barlow rested his hand on the largest pile of files. 'I tell you what. If I check these in detail, all you'll have to do is skim-read and sign.'

Relief brought a glow of pleasure to Foxwood's face. 'Would you? That's great.' His pleasure started to fade. 'I can't ask you to cover for Pierson. I mean, in the circumstances…'

'I won't tell the DI if you don't.'

'And if he asks?'

'Always have an answer ready. Keep him on the back foot. It gives you peace to get on with the job.'

Now that he had Foxwood in the right mood, he let him go ahead with the statement.

Maggie had been schizophrenic for many years. She'd good days and bad days. Mood changes were almost instantaneous. On the night in question, she seemed particularly elated and sat up late. 'For her, that is,' he added to avoid any confusion about times. When bedtime came, she went up first. He stayed behind to tidy things away and bank the fire. He hadn't expected the attack and, no, he had no idea what provoked it.

Foxwood produced the knife and Barlow identified it as one kept normally in the cutlery drawer in the scullery. He signed and dated every page; Foxwood countersigned.

The phone rang. 'Foxwood, is Barlow still there? Send him in.'

Even at that distance he didn't like Harvey's tone. Right then he felt weary beyond words and in no mood for a row.

He sighed and stood and scooped up the bundle of files he'd promised to look at. 'I'll do what I can to help.'

Foxwood opened the door for him. His legs clunked up the corridor. Each step needed a kick forward; the files weighed a ton. A junior sergeant stepped aside to let him past. He dumped the files in the junior sergeant's arms. 'Clear that lot before you go home today.'

'There's no way…'

'Anything that needs to be signed or approved, leave in my in-tray.'

'Aw, Sarge, I'm going out tonight.'

'Son, shit flows downwards, and it's just reached you.'

He walked on.

CHAPTER 46

HARVEY SAT IN HIS CHAIR, all strut; as ready for battle as a fighting cock. Captain Denton sat to the side. Barlow thought Denton's chair had been designed with bow legs, but he couldn't be sure. They might be giving way under the captain's weight. Denton was a muscular man with a heavy frame, and the only boy never to call "quits" against Barlow at a game of hardy-knuckles.

Barlow subsided into a chair.

Harvey said, 'I didn't tell you to sit.'

'Sir, it's either sit down or fall down.' He wiped cold sweat from his forehead and dried it off on his jacket.

Denton canted his head to the side. 'You look terrible.'

'I felt worse the day your beer was off.'

Denton scowled. Harvey snapped. 'That's enough.'

Harvey pulled himself and his papers together. 'Mr Comberton has released the late Stoop Taylor's personal papers.' He stopped as if he expected him to comment. He didn't, so Harvey continued. 'Attached to the papers was a receipt for thirteen hundred and forty-five pounds. Apparently, you found the money in an outhouse and gave it to his widow.'

Again, Harvey seemed to expect a reply. Not getting it, he said,' 'Well?'

'She needed the money then. Not six months down the line.'

Harvey bristled at his casual tone. 'That money could have been evidence. The motive for murder.'

Barlow nodded to himself in approval, and wished he could stop the habit. He liked the fact that the Frau had been honest with Stoop's money. It formed part of his estate. Hopefully, Mr

Comberton allowed her to keep some for herself. Recalling the image of her wearing the new red coat the day of Adenauer's remand hearing, he thought she must have.

'The Frau didn't put the money there. It had been stuck in that hole since kingdom come.'

Captain Denton leaned forward in his chair. 'Are we to assume that that is your line of defence?'

'Against what?'

'Consistent and persistent failure to follow laid-down procedures and guidelines.'

Now, he knew what the meeting was all about: further charges and allegations against him to go with the attack on Herr Prim. At the same time, he sensed an opportunity to get some information. 'Captain Denton, I can hardly respond without first examining the receipt for this alleged money. Obviously, it must be in the context of all papers submitted by Mr Comberton.'

Harvey bristled. 'They are irrelevant.'

'So you say, sir.'

He tried to look innocent and unconcerned. Denton looked at him steadily. After a pause Denton said, 'Better let him see them, Harvey. The last thing this enquiry needs is allegations of failure to disclose.'

Harvey looked like he wanted to argue with the captain, but in the end searched through a surprisingly thick file and handed over a bundle of papers.

All this hidden in a bra? wondered Barlow as he flicked through them.

The marriage of Rifleman Andrew Taylor, bachelor, and Kirstin Reinhardt, widow (Occupation: nurse), had taken place on 23rd September 1945 in Lengerich, in Westphalia.

Embarrassingly, their son Andrew Peter was born on 15th August 1945. Various certificates gave the Frau permission to enter the United Kingdom, with leave to remain, and changed Peter's nationality to that of his admitted father, British. Police reports as to the Frau's good character stated that she'd spent the war years working in a military hospital in Metz, in France.

He handed the file back without a word. If he had the energy he'd walk out. Even sitting, his legs felt wobbly.

Harvey cleared his throat. 'Another aspect of the enquiry will be your mistreatment of the Dunlop brothers.'

He decided on a bit of indignation. 'Who found the men stealing all those cattle? Me. Who arrested the Dunlops single-handed, and three tight men they are? Me. Did I get a word of thanks? No. Or an expression of concern at the injuries I sustained in making the arrests?'

Silence gathered in the room like dust. He missed the room's former unkemptness. Harvey had brushed and polished away the memory of a good man who had crumbled under the pressure of the job.

Harvey opened another file. 'With reference to the Dunlops. You failed to report an assault on your person by Geordie Dunlop, and in this actual building.' Harvey sat in his chair, confident that he now had the upper hand. 'Barlow, the fact that you served with Dunlop during the war is irrelevant. We prosecute all crimes, no exception.'

He didn't blame Jackson; the young officer must have told his mates and the story reached Pierson's ears. With a few embellishments it had made a good tale. But he'd see Pierson in hell for blabbing.

'No blows were exchanged, sir.'

'Not good enough, Barlow.' Harvey flicked through the file. 'According to Jackson's statement, Dunlop pinned you to the wall and issued verbal threats against your person. In addition, he knocked Constable Jackson to the ground, then dragged him back onto his feet.'

He doubted that those were Jackson's words, but it was up to Geordie's solicitor to argue the case. Barlow frowned in surprise when Harvey handed him two statements: Jackson's and a second also written by Jackson. The second statement was supposed to be Barlow's own version of the incident. He read through the pages carefully. *There's hope for that boy yet.* He couldn't have phrased it better or more fairly himself.

'Barlow, you are to sign that statement before you leave this room. I want Geordie Dunlop up in court on Monday. Dunlop's equally guilty of those cattle thefts and I want him in jail as well. ASAP.'

He had a think to himself. He'd taken Geordie to court often enough, but rough words and actual blows had always stayed private. Geordie would be well and truly pissed off, and the only way to calm Geordie was to knock his block off in a good fight. He touched his bad arm. Not him, not this time, but some other poor unfortunate. Then Geordie really would be in trouble.

'It occurred to me, sir. We only got the grandsons for the attempted theft of the captain's cattle. What about a deal? A reduced sentence and immunity from prosecution if they finger the man they sold the cattle to?'

Harvey looked horrified. 'And leave the Dunlops free to thieve again?'

'Or leave the man behind the thefts free to recruit more idiots to do his dirty work.'

Harvey hesitated over his reply, which gave him time to do a bit of wondering. *Three or more cattle stolen at a time? Not that easy to slip into the food chain.* The man had to be someone with connections. Someone who...

Then that little niggle finally jumped from the back of his brain. Where did the hospitals and the army buy their food? He'd never seen a Land Rover parked outside the local butchers. Or an ambulance.

He must have said that last part out loud because Denton asked, 'What?'

'It'll keep, sir.' The last thing he wanted was Harvey making supposedly discreet enquiries around the Masonic Hall.

'Final point,' said Harvey in a tone that made him lean closer. 'Now we come to the money found in Andrew Taylor's shed by Constable Jackson. Jackson didn't actually touch the money, but drew Constable Gillespie's attention to its existence.

Constable Gillespie very properly handed the money over to his immediate superior. Namely you. Unfortunately, both Jackson and Gillespie failed to count it first. Jackson is inexperienced, but Gillespie should have known better. A serious procedural failure for which he will be disciplined.'

Barlow imagined Gillespie's indignant reaction at being formally disciplined. The best way to discipline Gillespie was to buy the man a pint and tell him he was a bollocks. Gillespie doubled as Harvey's driver. The car would hit every pothole.

He started to hate Harvey's mean little heart even as he nodded in apparent agreement. 'I'll tell Gillespie you want to see him tomorrow morning, eight o'clock sharp.'

The next day was Saturday. Harvey seldom got in before nine and never showed up over the weekends. With Denton there he could hardly disagree.

Harvey tightened his lips and looked again at the file in front of him. 'Normally, you would expect a man to hide a round sum of money. Thirteen hundred and forty-five pounds is an unusual figure.'

'Is it?'

Fourteen hundred has a nice ring to it, wouldn't you say?'

'I fail to see your point, sir.'

'The point is, Barlow.' Harvey looked him straight in the eye. 'The point is, thirteen hundred and forty-five pounds is fifty-five pounds short of fourteen hundred.' He stopped again and pulled a copy sales docket from the file. 'And the same night you bought a television for fifty-five pounds – cash.'

CHAPTER 47

HARVEY'S LAST WORD "CASH" HUNG in the air. Denton sat tense in his chair. Barlow had a chew on an imaginary sweet before saying, 'Well aren't you a clever little clogs. You worked that out all by yourself.'

Denton made a choking sound and hastily converted it to a cough.

Barlow swirled the files on Harvey's desk, wanting something in the room to be untidy. 'You're too busy looking at the paperwork to see the bigger picture.'

Harvey indignantly pulled his files back into order. 'What do you mean by that?'

Barlow couldn't see the relevant piece of paper to hold up so he shrugged. 'You've got a report from the German police. According to them, the Frau spent the war years at an army hospital in Metz.'

'So?'

'Metz is in France. Yet she doesn't speak a word of French.'

Sparks of indignation almost flew from Harvey. 'How do you know that? Have you been interfering in this case? I ordered you not to.'

'Sir, for goodwill purposes I asked Gillespie to run the Frau home from hospital. At the bottom of the town he saw a schoolgirl thumbing a lift.'

'A schoolgirl who just happened to be called Vera?' muttered Denton, *sotto voce*.

Barlow kept talking. Didn't want Harvey to interrupt with another outburst. 'Gillespie stopped and told the girl to hop into the back with the Frau. With typical police nosiness Gillespie wanted to know how she was getting on at school. She said she was having trouble with her French grammar and he said the Frau might be able to help.'

He hesitated. It seemed unfair to summarise Vera's excited report in a brief sentence, but he felt he should. 'Mrs Taylor hardly knew a word of French, about enough to order a cup of coffee.'

Which left him with more unknowns to chew over. If the Frau hadn't been in Metz, then she couldn't have met Stoop until March 1945. After the regiment had fought their way into Germany. He decided to keep that to himself.

Denton said, 'It's been fifteen years since the war. She might have forgotten all her French by now.'

'Captain Denton, you were in France for six months in forty-four.' He'd been dying to do this for years, let Denton know he knew. 'If you went out there again, I bet you'd remember enough French to buy a lorry load of vintage champagne and ship it home.'

Denton's face went red as he tried to hold back the laugh. In the end he guffawed out loud. 'I thought I'd got that one past you.'

Barlow turned to Harvey. He pointed at Denton. 'There you are, sir. An admitted smuggler. What are you going to do about that?'

'Time expired,' said Harvey, and smiled ingratiatingly at Denton.

'Customs and Excise might say otherwise,' said Barlow. And now, he thought, was the time to put his own boot in, and give it a good twist. 'Sir, part of my defence will be the fact that your "no crime too small" policy only relates to the kids at the secondary school. You don't mind blighting their lives, but any complaint against a grammar schoolboy never gets beyond Foxwood's desk.'

Harvey looked down his nose at him. 'Of course your daughter goes to the secondary school?'

'The grammar. She got her eleven-plus.'

'I went to the secondary,' said Denton.

Harvey's mouth opened and closed. His jawline bleached white with shock at this major gaffe.

'Final point,' said Barlow, mocking Harvey's way of finishing an interview. 'Before you arrived with your new order, things in this station worked smoothly. Up until then, Leary and I had a good working relationship. He sat on his fat, lazy arse ticking and blotting the procedurals while I went out and solved the cases.' It tore at his stitches but he managed to lean forward into Harvey's face. 'Leary has followed procedures to the letter in the Kurt Adenauer case. And he's got nowhere.' He jabbed a finger as well, and winced. *That bloody hurt.* 'Adenauer's up for remand again next week, and he's going to walk because you've got nothing on him.'

'I'm still right,' said Harvey. 'You keep ignoring procedures and some day innocent people will get hurt.' He blazed anger back. 'When I was a constable I had a sergeant just like you. He always took the easy way out.'

The photograph of the Queen shuddered as Harvey stood, crashing his chair back against the wall. 'We knew the Germans were going to bomb Belfast that night. A crowd of neighbours in a side street didn't want to go to the shelter. They were afraid looters would break in and steal their bits and pieces. The Sergeant overruled me and let them stay.' Harvey's voice developed a shake. 'A stick of incendiaries landed on them.'

He pulled back his sleeve to show the burn mark running up his left arm. 'I saw a man walk back into the flames because he couldn't bear to live without his family. I put what remained of one little girl into an apple box.'

Barlow was shocked to see tears in his eyes.

'Do you want more?' Harvey slumped back into his chair and sat with his head in his hands.

Denton stood up, came across and helped Barlow to his feet. 'I'll take you home.'

He felt weary beyond words. Needed Denton's supporting arm.

He stopped in the doorway and looked back at Harvey. 'Sir, I'll tell you two things. One because I don't want the integrity of any other officer questioned. And the second because it's the right thing to do.'

Harvey kept his head down until he searched for a handkerchief and wiped his face.

Barlow reached into his pocket and produced a bank passbook. 'I have this on me because I'd planned to buy a bit of linoleum.' He lobbed the book across the room onto Harvey's desk. 'If you check you'll see that I withdrew fifty-five pounds on the day I bought the television.'

Harvey looked through the book and nodded, satisfied. He got up and brought the book back to Barlow.

'What else, Barlow?' His voice sounded normal again. There was no apology.

'You're thinking of getting the Frau in again to ask her more questions. Don't. If you want Adenauer hung, leave him to me.'

Harvey said. 'Don't you dare tell me how to run my own station.'

CHAPTER 48

THE ROLLS ROYCE ENGINE PURRED Barlow into near sleep. He got his eyes open again when the car stopped outside his house, one of a row of former mill cottages. Noticed a lorry tyre had been added to the collection of abandoned prams and furniture in the millrace across the street. *If I ever get the bugger who did that...*

Denton was waiting patiently for him to wake up. 'You realise, I have to do my job as the Chairman of the Police Board?'

'Yes, sir.'

'But I won't let Harvey hang you out to dry.'

'I know that.'

'Why don't you sort out a transfer for yourself? Harvey will keep pushing until he has you in jail. Anywhere you want. I'll put in a word.'

They sat on.

Denton picked at his fingernails. 'Maggie is now under the National Health, which frees up your salary.'

'You're well informed,' said Barlow dryly. The Masonic Hall was worse than a mother's convention for gossip. He wished he'd some way of listening in, then he'd hear real crooks at work.

Denton said, 'I could help you find a house with a garden, at a good price.'

Barlow wouldn't mind, as much for himself as for Vera and Maggie, if she ever got out. *A bit of privacy,* instead of hearing the neighbours through the walls.

The only move he wanted was to the River Road. Living with Alexandra. Watching the final flares of sunset from a bench in the yard. *Dream time*, he told himself and said, 'There's a bit of sorting to be done first.'

Denton seemed to be in no rush to leave. A group of children gathered to look at the car. They pushed each other around so as to catch their reflections moving on the car's shiny paintwork.

'I could do with a couple of things', Barlow said finally.

'Isn't that why you and Edward made me quartermaster?'

'You were good at the job.'

'Working with you, I learned to read every line of every requisition.'

'Comforts for the troops.'

Denton gave a disbelieving grunt. 'What do you need?'

'A car.'

'What are you not telling me?'

'Enquiries are proceeding, sir.'

'Okay, I get the message. Ignorance is bliss. Take the wife's shooting-brake for a few days.' He raised an eyebrow, half sarcastic. 'Anything else?'

The thought of the shooting-brake made Barlow's writing hand twitch. The shooting-brake was an up-market estate car with external wood and trim. Mrs Denton treated it like a child, having it washed and waxed weekly and the wood oiled with the change of seasons. Unfortunately, in town, she tended to park wherever the shooting-brake stopped. The last day on the job, he'd book it for obstruction and then run for the hills. Denton's wife had a tongue that could slice beef.

He retrieved the imaginary sweet from where he'd last stored it and had a good suck. He'd an idea who was the brains behind the cattle thefts, but confirmation from an independent source would be better. 'Aye, who supplies the army and the hospitals with all their meat?'

Denton made the connection immediately. 'Why the hell didn't I think of that?'

'You've been honest too long, sir.'

'I resent that.'

'That you're honest?'

'That... ' Denton gave up pretending to be indignant and developed a supercilious tone. 'Tell me, Barlow, you never got a medal, did you?'

'The Colonel didn't like me.'

'Now why doesn't that surprise me?'

They sat in silence after that. The talk of army life triggering the same memories in them. Denton had come back from the war with a commission and a lorry load of smuggled champagne. The champagne bought him a junior share in a failing brewery and, after a year of legendary rows, the hand of the owner's daughter.

Hard banging on Barlow's window made them jump. Jackson stood outside, gasping for air after the long run.

'Sergeant, the German boy, Peter. He's been shot.'

CHAPTER 49

PETER LAY WHERE HE'D FALLEN in the field behind the house. Someone, it had to be the Frau, had turned him onto his back and crossed his arms over his chest. Brought a pillow for his head and tucked an eiderdown quilt around him.

Barlow stood over the Frau where she knelt beside the body. Noted the pucker of puzzlement creasing Peter's forehead, dragging down one eyebrow. He could have been an old man lying there. WPC Day stood awkwardly beside them, a hand on the Frau's shoulder. The Frau had dried blood on her hands and on her forehead where she'd rubbed in her confusion.

Barlow felt utterly spent. If it hadn't been for Denton's discreet help, he'd never have made it up the slope. Jackson came behind with two chairs taken from the kitchen. He nodded to him to put them down, force the legs into the soil to make them balance.

He subsided onto the chair. A wind chilled the already cold sweat on his body. He snuggled into his sports coat and reached out to cover the Frau's joined hands. 'Missis, I'm sorry for your trouble.'

'Thank you.' It came out as "Zank". She seemed very composed.

'Could you tell me what happened?'

'I tell others.'

He understood that the Frau wasn't being awkward. The officialdom she dreaded was waiting to take over her son's body and she would lose him forever. She needed these last few minutes alone with Peter. Barlow had other priorities. The police had to know whom they were pursuing.

'Tell me.' He pushed her hands upwards. WPC Day pulled on her shoulders and they got her into the second chair. Mud caked her knees. She didn't seem to notice.

She looked at him. Fresh tears ran down the tear tracks on her cheeks. 'I hear two shots. M1. I know it not good.'

A shiver ran up his spine. 'The American carbine? Are you sure?'

'Sergeant Barlow, you hear soldiers – boys – killed, you never forget.'

A carbine upped the ante quite a bit. For a pistol to be accurate Adenauer had to be close up. The M1 was deadly up to three hundred yards and worked in any wet or muddy conditions. He imagined a line of policemen attacking a well dug-in Adenauer, and shivered again.

Barlow looked round him. A bucket of cattle nuts lay spilled near the body. Their sour odour helped dampen the smell of blood. Peter, he guessed, had been on his way to feed the cattle when he was shot.

He leaned forward and pulled a corner of the quilt free. Saw two bullet holes on Peter's shirt, both to the left of the sternum. One bullet had sliced through the aorta; the other had shredded his heart. Blood caked Peter's shirt and pooled in the ground around him.

He pushed his good arm against his knees to stop them from shaking. That could have been Vera lying at his feet. By the grace of God, Maggie didn't know that his revolver was now kept loaded. If she had, she might have reached for it instead of the knife.

He looked back over his shoulder. At a guess, the shot had come from Alexandra's land. He eyed the distance from where he stood to the boundary hedge. About one hundred yards uphill. Not a trained sniper, they'd have gone for a headshot, but a marksman nevertheless.

Why?

Nobody liked Stoop well enough to be overly annoyed at his death. There had been no muttering, that he'd heard, against the Frau and her son, blaming them. *Then why the boy?* And why now?

Officials gathered around the body. He sensed their respectful impatience to get on with their job. He jogged the Frau's elbow. 'Come on down to the house, love.'

She nodded and knelt once more before her son. Tidied his hair and rested a hand on his cheek. A wipe at tears with the back of her hand put more blood on her face. She stood again and walked unaided down the field. He struggled after her.

At the door of her house she stopped. He could see her work out the words in her mind before she spoke. 'Sergeant Barlow, I need Adenauer come to me.'

He wanted to be absolutely sure that Adenauer still remained safely locked up in the asylum. Nobody else had a reason to kill the boy.

Mrs Denton's shooting-brake he saw was backed into the yard among the squad cars. Its back door lay open, the boot filled with trays of crockery and sandwiches. Denton's wife and two of her friends were unpacking the boot and carrying the trays into the house. Another woman waited at the gate with a plate of pastries. Cars lined the grass verges.

'I not understand,' said the Frau as people got out of the cars and came towards her. Every woman carried a plate of food.

Barlow said, 'This is the country, love. Your troubles are their troubles.'

'Please, bring Adenauer,' said the Frau before she let Denton's wife take her into the house.

Foxwood stood close. As soon as the Frau was out of hearing he whispered. 'We've got a problem. The hospital let Adenauer loose in the grounds for an hour this morning.'

'By himself?'

'They said he's much better. They said…'

'Break out the Lee Enfields, sir.'

Foxwood nodded towards the squad car. 'I already have. They're in the boot.'

The farmyard swarmed with police. Constables he hardly knew or didn't know at all. Men brought in from outlying stations and from other Districts.

His head was swimming with exhaustion. He let Foxwood get on with organising the lines of beaters and went and sat in the shooting-brake.

Adenauer had managed to find a pistol, even if he hadn't stolen it from the ship. Peter had been killed by an M1, but the only M1 that Barlow knew of in the area was housed in the military museum. It seemed impossible, but Adenauer had an arsenal of weapons stashed somewhere or had access to one. And the racing bike had never turned up, nor had anyone complained about theirs being stolen.

He rubbed his injured arm. A new habit of his while he thought things through. First a pistol, then a .22 automatic rifle, now an M1. What would Adenauer use next, and on whom?

CHAPTER 50

BARLOW HADN'T FALLEN ASLEEP, BUT only became conscious of movement when the shooting-brake rattled over a cattle grid. He forced his eyes open. Captain Denton's wife was driving. That didn't make him feel safer.

'Jackson will take you home. You wanted to borrow the car anyway.'

He glanced around. Jackson sat in the back, too overawed in the presence of Mrs Denton to speak. They were on a private drive running between lines of venerable chestnut trees. He'd climbed every one of them in his day, progging chestnuts. Sold them on: one for a penny, two for a penny if they were small. Iron railings separated the car and the three of them from the cattle in the fields. The cattle were colourless in the twilight. They stood under the trees, chewing their cud. Mrs Denton switched on the headlights full beam.

'Denton's done well for himself', Barlow said.

'It was my family home,' she said.

'In those days this place was all fur coat and no knickers.'

Jackson gasped.

Anger glinted in her eyes. 'I still can't understand why you were our best man.'

'Edward couldn't be trusted to stay sober.'

The car crunched over the gravel forecourt and pulled up at the front door. Before she got out she placed a friendly hand on his arm. 'John, you were always a true friend.'

People called him "Sergeant" or "Mr Barlow" to his face and a lot of uncomplimentary things behind his back. She always called him "John". Right from his first week in town, when they *discussed* her habit of speeding through a built-up area.

'In primary school, when I lived in the workhouse, Captain Denton shared his sandwiches with me.'

He watched her swing out of the car: knees together, the way the Queen did on the Pathé News. This was the one-time hellcat he'd locked in the cells with Denton. She screamed and Denton cursed, but he swore they'd both stay there until they'd set the date. From the blush on their cheeks when he let them out, the engagement had been sealed with more than a kiss.

All the women in my life. How in the name of God did I end up with Maggie?

Jackson got in and familiarised himself with the controls.

Barlow pointed. 'Go around the side of the house and down the back lane. We'll take a look while we're here.'

'Look at what, Sergeant?'

'The night, the stars, a jug of punch.' He glared at Jackson. 'Use your loaf for a change.'

Instinct, nothing more than that, worked at him. The River Road drew Adenauer for whatever reason. He could be hanging around the area. Where else would he go? And why did he shoot the boy, other than out of spite? Why not the Frau as well for giving herself to a man like Stoop?

The back lane had no bordering trees, but was still marched by iron railings. He watched the clumps of trees where the cattle had taken shelter for the night. Didn't stare along the line of the headlights, but in the afterglow of their passing. When people thought it safe to move.

They came to a gate. Made Jackson back up and turn into the field. It wouldn't hurt to do a ten-minute check. Suss out the parkland as far as the river.

The shooting-brake rattled and bounced over the cattle-trod ground. He liked hearing fresh manure squirting from beneath the wheels. Gillespie would have to clean the car before returning it to Mrs Denton.

Cattle congregated under the trees for the night. Their moist eyes could have been giant fireflies. One large clump of trees stood empty of cattle. He pointed and Jackson drove as close to the clump as he could.

The ground between the trees seemed clear. They backed up and tried again from a different angle. Still clear, but something had driven the cattle away. He found a torch in the glove compartment and shone it through the windscreen into the trees.

A solid shape crashed out of the branches, hit the ground and rolled. The shape jumped to its feet and ran for the river.

Adenauer.

CHAPTER 51

JACKSON JUMPED OUT OF THE car and raced off in pursuit of Adenauer. Barlow sat on and cursed his weakness. A hundred-yard sprint would probably kill him. Jackson ran through the trees, his shape flickering in and out of the lights, then he was gone.

'Bollocks.'

He was in Denton's car, so had no way of contacting the police station for backup. His ears strained for the sound of gunfire. The chances of Jackson surviving a gun battle against Adenauer were like him winning the football pools twice over.

He felt helpless. Maybe he wasn't fit to run after Adenauer, but he could run the bugger down. What Mrs Denton would say about blood on her front grille he didn't dare think. He struggled into the driver's seat, his legs scraping over the gearstick. Even that effort made him out of breath.

The engine was still running. He slapped the gear stick into reverse. The car shot back and he stopped it quickly, afraid a cow had come nosing up behind him. Cattle were worse than police wives when it came to curiosity.

Adenauer had broken to the right, away from the Frau's house. Barlow headed downriver after him. He had to reach across with his right hand to change gear. This meant the car was bucking over tree roots, unguided. Ricochet the wrong way and he'd be into a tree. There'd be hell to pay if that happened. The old shooting-brake was like a family pet.

He swept around the grove of trees. The headlights picked up the shapes of two dark figures running along the edge of the riverbank. Younger and fitter, Jackson was gaining on Adenauer.

'Silly bugger,' roared Barlow. If Jackson got too close, the only thing he'd catch was a bullet in the chest.

He struggled with the gears to get them into third, and pressed hard on the accelerator. The engine screamed like a stuck pig. The shooting-brake ate the ground between him and the runners.

Adenauer glanced back.

Is he limping? Barlow thought so.

Jackson glanced back as well. Lost his footing in a sudden dip and fell. Barlow could almost hear the "ooooff" as he hit the ground. His body slipped sideways, hesitated on the edge of the bank, and then disappeared into the river.

'Oh God. Oh bloody hell.'

Adenauer must have heard the splash because he slowed and looked back. Ran on, slowed again.

Stopped.

Well short of the two men, Barlow slammed on the brakes and brought the car to a shuddering halt. He couldn't save Jackson on his own. Not one-armed and him hardly fit to drive the car. Adenauer mustn't feel threatened. Even at that distance, he could sense the tensions vibrating through the man.

Adenauer stood, his head moving between the car and the river. Gradually, he spent more time looking at the river. The river flowed in his direction. Jackson had to be going that way as well.

He struggled out of the car. If Adenauer saw the white sling he might understand that Barlow was no danger. That it was up to him to save the young constable. Even in his sports coat Barlow felt frozen in the bitter wind. Adenauer wore slacks and a shirt. *You'd think a man with an arsenal of weapons would have thought of protective gear as well.*

The car lights picked up a dark shape in the water. It slid out of sight, then appeared again as it came level with Adenauer. Adenauer kicked off his shoes and jumped into the water. Came up. Looked around and jack-knifed back under the surface.

'Good man,' said Barlow, puzzled, because this was the man who had tried to throttle him. Had pulled the trigger intending to kill. Had probably killed Stoop and young Peter, and here he was trying to save Jackson.

He half-fell into the car, crashed the gears into first, and drove up to where he'd last seen the two men. The surface of the water remained placid. *They can't both be drowned.*

Adenauer surfaced and struck out for the bank. Barlow felt guilty for all the roustings he'd given the young officer. *Jackson wasn't a bad lad.* Willing, and he never made the same mistake twice.

He hurt for the loss of the young officer. Then he realised that Adenauer was swimming one-handed, dragging something with him.

He got out of the car and sat at the river's edge, feet in the water. Leaned over and caught hold of Jackson's shoulder strap. Steadied Jackson as Adenauer heaved his inert mass onto the bank. Jackson coughed and spluttered. Vomited a stream of water.

'Dunderhead,' said Barlow and banged Jackson's back to help the water out.

The young officer lay still, didn't respond to questioning or to Barlow's thumb digging in under his ribcage. There had to be a head injury there as well, Barlow decided. Adenauer was on his hands and knees, gulping air. He suddenly snapped upright, with Jackson's pistol in his hand.

Barlow made his sigh loud and put-upon. 'Put that bloody thing away. You're not going to shoot, and you know it.'

At least he hoped Adenauer wasn't. He found it hard to be absolutely positive with the pistol pointed straight at him.

'Your gun,' said Adenauer.

'I'm off duty. Look!' he pointed at his sports coat.

Adenauer hesitated, then he broke Jackson's revolver and tried to shake out the bullets. None came. Adenauer held it up to the headlights to be sure. Barlow could see through the chambers. No bullets. Jackson had picked a hell of a time to stop playing Cowboys and Indians.

'Not Germany,' said Adenauer.

Jackson had pursued a supposedly armed and dangerous man with an unloaded revolver. 'No sense either,' Barlow said.

Adenauer grabbed his shoes and forced his wet feet into them.

Barlow said, 'Give yourself up. You'll do a few years in jail, but you won't hang.' Adenauer scrambled to his feet. 'Son, jail's a hell of a lot better than the cemetery.' Better than hypothermia as well. There was no way he could move the now unconscious Jackson without help.

Adenauer went over to the shooting-brake. Barlow heard a door open. Without that car they were done for. He couldn't even make Captain Denton's house for help. He lay back and waited for death. If only his feet weren't so cold. They still hung in the water, he realised, and he hadn't the energy to pull them out.

It seemed impossible but Adenauer came back. He pulled Jackson onto his shoulders and disappeared again into the glare of the car lights.

Kidnap? Hostage? He didn't think so.

Adenauer came back and pulled at his good arm. 'You drive?'

'To hell if I have to.' The farm gate had better be open. Anything less and he'd take the pillar with him.

Adenauer helped him to his feet and across to the shooting-brake. His feet squelched water. Swore he'd never forgive Jackson for making him get his feet wet. At the shooting-brake he checked Jackson. The young officer lay face down on the backseat, his head hanging over the footwell in case he vomited again.

Adenauer tried to move off; Barlow gripped his arm. 'Give yourself up.'

Adenauer grabbed Barlow's hand and twisted it until he had to turn or else risk the bone breaking. The wound on his upper arm caught the edge of the open door. White pain exploded in Barlow's eyes and he screamed. He found himself on his knees, vomiting repeatedly until nothing but bile appeared. When he finally managed to lift his head, Adenauer was gone, running out of the lights and downstream again.

CHAPTER 52

BARLOW CRAWLED INTO THE DRIVER'S seat and fought to stay conscious. His eyes stung with cold sweat. Eventually, he felt fit enough to start the car. Drove quietly out of the field. Jackson had sustained enough injuries without being bounced around the back seat as well. At the River Road he hesitated. Should he head for town and the hospital or back to the farm?

He headed for the Frau's farm. It seemed funny passing Alexandra's laneway and not turning in. The porch light glimmered through the hedgerow, so she was still up. He ached to be in her bed. To wake up in the night and find her stretched out alongside him. To feel her hand snuggle into his in the dark.

The cars on the side of the road stretched back a respectable distance. That number of people visiting had to be a comfort to the Frau in her grief. He was too tired to appreciate the difference in the reaction of the neighbours to Peter's death, which was in sharp contrast to their reaction to Stoop's death. Beeped the horn to move pedestrians out of the way, and at long last he got to the gate. A group of weary policemen stood under arc lights. They all held cups of tea. He hoped somebody had given them a share of the food going into the house.

Harvey stood in the centre of the men, giving orders. 'Make my bloody day,' muttered Barlow. He put his hand on the horn and kept it there.

Gillespie strutted over. 'Who do you think…?' Recognition dawned. 'Bloody hell, Sarge, are you trying to kill yourself?'

Barlow closed his eyes and let his head flop against the seat. He thumbed backwards. Gillespie flung the back door open and yelled for a first-aid kit. Other doors opened. The car bumped and swayed as officers climbed in to see to Jackson. Gentle hands eased him out onto a stretcher.

A voice said, 'Barlow, report.'

He managed to get his eyes open. It was Harvey. He sat in the front passenger seat. Other policemen hung in the passenger door and rear doorways. He wished they'd close the doors. His feet were freezing. Gillespie tucked a grey blanket around him and touched his legs. 'You're wet from the knees down,' he said, and sounded amused.

He told his tale and began to wonder if they thought he was hallucinating. A desperate chase that ended with this mad gunman saving Jackson's life? He said Adenauer had unloaded Jackson's revolver and thrown the bullets into the river. Was too tired to shake his head in disgust. Jackson, armed only with an unloaded revolver, pursuing a dangerous fugitive. No need to get the young officer into official trouble. Any bollocking, he'd do himself.

Harvey puzzled him. Even in the poor lighting he could see colour in Harvey's cheeks. The ever-immaculate uniform creased and splattered with mud. The sympathy expressed by Harvey was zero, but his questions were to the point. He only queried one answer. 'Are you sure Kurt Adenauer is unarmed?'

'Sir, his shirt was stuck to his back. Anyway, I did a body search when he helped me to the car. He has no gun, pistol or otherwise. I'm sure of it.'

That was the least he could do for Adenauer. Make the listening policemen realise that he might be a fugitive, but he was neither armed nor dangerous. At least, not dangerous in the way they thought. Adenauer had a great tension in him that threatened to explode.

Still sitting in the car, Harvey gave his orders for search parties, checkpoints and lines of communication. The man sounded like he knew what he was doing, especially when men who knew the area well made suggestions and were listened to. Eventually, Harvey told him. 'Gillespie will run you home.' Even then with the search parties forming up, Harvey sat on, staring through the window. The words came out with effort. 'Good job, Barlow.'

Barlow kept it casual. He touched his injured arm. 'There are things I can do to help, but I need Gillespie to drive.'

'Do it,' said Harvey. He levered himself out of the car and waved for the search parties to follow him.

Barlow watched them go. They had a hard slog coming through the darkness. It seemed impossible, but Harvey looked like he was enjoying himself.

CHAPTER 53

GILLESPIE HAD THE CAR PURRING up the main road before he said to Barlow, 'I should be back there helping.'

'What about your flat feet?'

Gillespie didn't even blush.

Now he could relax into sleep. Instead he found himself fuzzily awake. Watched the lights pick out the hedgerows and the moths splatter the windscreen. A car of his own would be nice. Without Maggie's hospital bills he could afford one. And a house? He liked the thought of a new start. Of him and Vera living in a brand new house. The memories in a new house would be what they made of things.

They were on the run down into the town.

It could be the waste of Peter's young life, but he was lonely that night and ached to be held and loved. Maybe others felt the same? He said to Gillespie, 'Go around by Curles Bridge, see if Edward's in.'

'You're for home.'

'Curles.'

'You'll die on me.'

'Think of the beers you'll save.'

Gillespie said, 'I'm thinking of becoming an inspector. Then I can bully you for a change.'

The area around Curles Bridge was in darkness. They drove down the slope to the water's edge. Candlelight flickered under Edward's door.

The car lights caught the vague reflection of another car. It sat parked on the other side of the bridge, in the far corner of the land flanking the river.

Gillespie said, 'We know that car, don't we?'

'Just ask Edward has he sourced an army contact for me, and where we meet them and when?'

'Sure,' said Gillespie, 'But I hope he knows what I'm talking about. I sure as hell don't.'

Barlow put the torch in his pocket and forced his weary legs to walk past Edward's hut and on over a surface of hard-packed stone to the parked car. He walked in near darkness with just the distant glow of town lights to guide his step.

At the car, he switched on the torch and shone it into the interior. A couple swiftly separated. The woman was naked. She twisted away from him and hid her face. Her spine showed clearly and her flesh glistened with youth. The man's shirt and vest lay on the back seat. He tried to pull up his trousers and underpants. They snagged on the seat and remained trapped at his knees. The material refused to tear free. He cupped his hands over his erection.

Barlow opened the door. 'You are aware, sir, that there are laws concerning public indecency? You also appear to be engaged in a gross breach of public order.'

He didn't like the man. He was a salesman, and as smarmy as they come. She obviously saw something desirable in him. What exactly that was had him mystified.

'Sir, I must ask you and the young lady to accompany me to the police station.'

'Please, officer … you see … I mean …'

The woman had a fuzz of hair at the nape of her neck. He wanted to reach out and stroke it. Thank God he wasn't fit to do more than wish.

'Are you trying to tell me, sir, that this is your first time and you'd like me to be considerate?

'Yes. Yes. Oh please, yes.'

He could see the man ache to take a hand away from his groin and reach for his wallet. If that bastard offers me a bribe, *I'll swing for him.* He wanted to bring the torch down where it would do the most good.

'A special occasion perhaps? Maybe you asked the young lady a certain question?'

'That's what it was. Yes.'

Like fuck.

The woman almost turned her head towards him. Her body pleaded for help. Begged him to go away.

'And of course the young lady said yes. You set a date and then you both got – shall we say – carried away in anticipation of the event?'

'I'm afraid so,' said the man, much calmer now. He met Barlow's gaze. Barlow nodded. A deal could be done here.

'And the date, sir?'

'July.'

'This year?'

'Of course.'

The woman started to cry.

The man didn't appear annoyed at the way things had gone. His manhood had shrunk and he could risk a comforting hand on the woman's back.

Barlow liked that thoughtful gesture. Maybe the bastard had something going for him after all? Somebody had to be a salesman.

'Goodnight,' he said and walked away. If only he could solve his own problems that easily.

Gillespie waited for him beside the shooting-brake. He almost danced a jig of annoyance. 'What were you up to?'

'WPC Day's got a dimple in the funniest place.'

CHAPTER 54

Vera kept Barlow in bed all day Saturday. She threatened to handcuff him to the headboard if he even thought of getting up.

'Shouldn't you be at work?' he asked when she brought up lunch.

'What, me head off to Woolworths, and trust you to stay in bed? No way.'

He enjoyed being bullied and spoiled. It helped in those times when he couldn't sleep. Peter was dead. His best hadn't been good enough, and that hurt.

What if Adenauer had access to other guns? That M1 had to be stashed somewhere. What would happen when the police caught up with him? Would he surrender or start a firefight? A combat veteran well armed and dug in against Harvey and his inexperience? He ached to be out there with his men.

On Sunday morning his legs wobbled under him and he held grimly onto the banisters as he made his way downstairs. He remembered gripping his mother's hand that tightly the first time he saw the sea rattle over the stones in Carnlough Bay.

'Great,' he lied to Vera when she questioned the advisability of the proposed trip. 'I could do handstands if I wanted to.'

The wound in his arm was healing. It took effort not to scratch holes in both wounds to cure the itch. Instead, he took his arm out of the sling and let it flop on his knees. Sat at the table and read the Sunday papers. Adenauer was still at large. There were pictures of him and Jackson on the front pages. Jackson's rescue by Adenauer lost nothing in the telling.

Jackson, the paper reported, had mild concussion from the fall. He was being kept in hospital for observation. Barlow hoped they gave the boy padding for his backside. That's where his toe was heading, first chance.

He's young, Da,' said Vera with all the wisdom of a granny.

She ran in and out of the scullery, making a late breakfast. Gillespie had arranged to pick them up at eleven. Barlow planned to first see Edward's contact in Cushendun, then treat everyone to high tea in the Londonderry Arms in Carnlough, on the way home.

Mrs Gillespie was going as well. She deserved something for taking care of Vera while he was in hospital. Kenny, Vera's boyfriend, too. *About time I got to know this young man.* And Edward, of course, who had set up the contact.

Gillespie arrived and they climbed into the car. Barlow sat in front; the other four in the back. He pretended not to notice when Vera and Kenny crushed together. To give the others plenty of room, they said. *Were my hormones ever that energetic?* He didn't think so. *And yet...* He allowed himself a few pleasant memories as the drive took them out of town and through fields onto the plateau where more purple heather than grass was growing. They opened the windows and let in the scented air. After a time, Mrs Gillespie complained politely of being "chill", and they closed them again.

The road wound between high rocks. He grunted when the shooting-brake lurched and his bad arm caught the door. Gillespie stopped at the top of the rise. The rest got out to admire the dry greenness of the glen that stretched before them. Barlow beeped the horn impatiently and they all got in again.

He nodded off half way down the glen, only rousing himself when they pulled up on a remote quay built into a small headland. He hadn't been there in years, yet nothing had changed. The quay held a rambling house that doubled as a pub. Disused bollards still waited for ships that had stopped calling when steam replaced sail. The day remained overcast. A light easterly brought some heat.

An aged man sat at an outside table. He was comfortably rotund and wore a herringbone sports coat. The coat was old and battered. Even Edward raised an eye at its condition. By contrast, the man's shirt was freshly ironed. Somebody, a wife presumably, had a say on what inner clothes he wore.

The man, a former army doctor, stood up and greeted Edward. 'Major Adair, this is an honour,'

'My dear chap,' said Edward and made the introductions.

The barman appeared. Barlow insisted it was his shout. Mrs Gillespie wanted a cup of tea. The last person to order tea in that pub, the doctor told her, got thrown off the quay. The Gillespies took the hint and headed off to the village on the far side of the bay. Vera and Kenny made excuses about needing to stretch their legs and disappeared. Which left Barlow, Edward and the doctor.

Barlow ordered a pint of Guinness for the iron. He sipped to get the taste – good to excellent – and put the glass down carefully. The table was made out of ships' timbers and the curves didn't exactly line up. The central leg had been part of a mast. The wood smelled faintly of tar.

Edward ordered water. It might as well have been arsenic given the grimace he made. Edward could stay dry whenever an old comrade needed his help; Barlow wished Edward would do it for his own sake.

The doctor, he noted, had a pint glass holding a half measure of gin well diluted with two bottles of tonic. 'Blood pressure,' the doctor explained and turned to Edward. 'You wanted to know about Rifleman Andrew Taylor?'

'My dear chap, yes. The man was murdered, unfortunately.'

Barlow said, 'We're looking for background information about Stoop. It can be as official or as unofficial as you wish.'

'Stoop?' queried the doctor. 'The Americans called him "Twister", and that was before his jeep went over an S mine.'

The doctor didn't like Stoop, he noted, *not even after all these years*. There again, nobody did. It made him wonder how the Frau had stuck by the man for fifteen years. She must have hated him enough to kill. Especially with Adenauer there to help her. He felt he could judge people, and he liked the Frau. Couldn't see her being involved in Stoop's death. At least, not willingly.

'What can you tell us about Stoop and his injuries?'

The doctor said, 'The hospital ran out of penicillin. Stoop, as you call him, stole a batch off the Americans and tried to sell them to us. When we wouldn't deal he sold them on the black market.' His voice took on an air of satisfaction. 'We were still out of penicillin when he got hit.'

After the sleep in the car, Barlow felt fresh and alive. The Guinness was finished, he discovered to his surprise, and gestured to the barman for refills all around.

'Stoop's injuries?' he prompted the doctor when the drinks had been delivered.

'Extensive trauma resulting in kyphosis of the thoracic spine.'

'Hence the nickname "Stoop".'

'And of course the classic S mine injury. Orchidectomy.'

'That hurts even thinking of it,' said Edward. Barlow couldn't stop his knees from coming together. It was an unconscious response.

Listening to Stoop's injuries listed like that made him feel guilty. He'd never liked Stoop. The man was always an awkward bugger to deal with. *Did that bitterness only start after the war?* He couldn't remember and felt he should have done. 'Stoop must have been in constant pain.'

The doctor nodded. 'An injury like that, rheumatism or arthritis, is always a danger in later life.' He sipped on a gin and tonic as he tried to cast his mind back all those years. 'The platoon ran into an ambush on a narrow road. The lead jeep took hits from a heavy machine gun. Stoop's driver turned off the road looking for cover. They ran straight into a minefield. The Germans shot any survivors. Stoop took a bullet through his scapula.'

Barlow's drink didn't slop over the rim when he put it down. The shock he felt, it should have. *Stoop shot in the back during the war?* That sort of information he didn't want to hear. 'What sort of bullet?'

The doctor shrugged. 'From the fragments excised from his chest cavity, I'd say a pistol.'

If fragments had been dug out, others had to have been left behind. Almost certainly, the pieces of bullet found by the pathologist in the Ballymena hospital dated back to the war.

Barlow moved uneasily in his chair. Watched the small boats out in the bay snub against their mooring lines. If the doctor could be believed, the case against Adenauer was rapidly falling apart. All he knew about the doctor was gleaned from idle gossip at Regimental reunions. Gossip that said he … Barlow studied his drink trying to remember.

In the years before the Second World War the doctor had been an up-and-coming consultant, with a reputation for having a keen eye and a steady hand. After he was demobbed, he retrained as a GP and bought a practice there in Cushendun, a village buried in the Antrim Glens. *I'd like to know why a man with his reputation would give up a lucrative career and bury himself in the middle of nowhere.* It's not that Barlow was curious about the doctor's private life as such, but this was a murder inquiry and even the smallest doubt made him wonder how much he could trust the doctor's memory.

He tried to rebuild the police case. Where and when Stoop had been shot was immaterial. Adenauer arrived at the farm already armed. Guns were easily sourced in Germany after the war. Adenauer must have kept them concealed in his kitbag. *Did Leary think to check the kitbag for traces of gun oil?* He thought not.

All those weapons! Adenauer must have found a terrific hiding place for the guns in or around the farm. And maybe the Frau lied about concealing those papers on her person and had hidden them with the guns.

He ached to smash something, anything – even the recently replenished glass of Guinness. The Frau was involved in the death of Stoop and the concealment of the weapons. *Worse than that.* She was complicit in the murder of her own son.

CHAPTER 55

THE DOCTOR, BARLOW HAD HEARD, was famous for having a gimlet eye. He found himself being scrutinised by it. 'Sergeant, I notice you keep your left hand in your jacket pocket and you favour that side?'

'I've still got stitches in.' He indicated his arm near the join with the shoulder.

'Any inflammation or infection?'

'No.'

'Well, don't take any chances.'

Barlow asked. 'Why did you give up your consultancy work?'

'After the war, I wanted more time with my wife and family.'

The answer came too glib, too well practised. While he waited for the doctor to expand on his answer he stared out across the bay. Saw how whitecaps topped the swell and how the curve in the bay compressed the incoming tide into respectable waves before crunching the gritty sand at the mouth of the River Dun.

The doctor could have been speaking to himself when he said, 'Do you know what it's like to operate day after day on butchered boys?'

No reply expected, Barlow thought.

The doctor continued. 'After the war I found I couldn't cope with that kind of stress anymore and I retrained as a GP.'

Barlow waited a moment before speaking, hoping to urge the doctor on. 'And Stoop's widow?'

'Kirstin,' said the doctor. 'Kirstin Reinhardt?' Partly, he was talking to himself.

Barlow searched out an imaginary Mint Imperial and had a good chew. There was tenderness in that memory of Kirstin, the way it came out. A doctor, a long way from home and the comforts of his wife's bed. A willing nurse. *What could be more natural?*

'She worked with you then?'

The doctor stiffened in his chair and glanced anxiously over his shoulder. Barlow recognised that look. Wives had a habit of appearing at exactly the wrong moment.

The doctor tried to sound casual. 'We took over a military hospital outside Lengerich in Westphalia. Kirstin was one of the theatre sisters. She was brilliant. Had the instrument in your hand almost before you could ask for it.'

'Married, single, child?' Barlow interrupted, not giving the doctor the opportunity to change the subject.

'Widow.' The tone was defensive. 'Her husband's regiment, the 88th, were ordered to dig in just east of Berlin. There were no survivors.'

He decided to wing a question. 'What did she do with the baby when she was working?'

'The baby was born just before we shipped Stoop home.'

Not only was the answer evasive, there was also a hesitation there before the doctor replied. In Barlow's experience, most hesitations were caused by people making up a story as they went along.

Edward had a pained expression on his face. Two almost-full glasses of water sat on the table in front of him. He emerged from his reverie and said, 'Doctor, if I recollect correctly, you were a full colonel. That entitled you to your own living quarters.'

Barlow now remembered this detail. Full colonels, he recalled, were allocated a four-bedroom house. The house came with an orderly and domestic staff. Which made assignations and accommodation for live-in lovers simple.

He said, 'Doctor, I've had one hell of a week.' His glass was empty, but he didn't want a refill. He felt weak again and bed seemed a tantalising prospect. 'I don't care about past sins or transgressions. We've got a gunman out there. How can I bring him to justice if I don't know everything there is to know about him? What makes him tick?'

The doctor pushed away the remains of his drink and stood up. 'I've told you everything I remember. After fifteen years… ?'

Barlow said, 'Put a gun in Adenauer's hand and he's totally out of control.' As the doctor began to walk off Barlow shouted after him. 'Where did the Frau spend the war, other than in your bed?'

People were sitting too far away to make out the words. But they had heard the shout and were looking over in Barlow's direction. The doctor turned back. 'For God's sake, I've got a wife and daughters.'

'And I've got a fugitive killing people.'

'Sorry, no. I can't help you.'

The doctor looked scared. His cheeks reddened as his blood pressure rose.

Barlow knew he should telephone Harvey and ask him to have a word with the District Inspector of Larne District. Have the doctor arrested and hauled in for questioning. Or maybe say "please", but that word wasn't in his nature.

'It's simple, Doc. You can go back to your nice comfortable life. Dole out placebos to nervous old ladies. Or… ' he let the word hang in the air.

The doctor slumped back into his chair. 'There's always a price to be paid, isn't there?'

'Good or bad, Doc, nothing comes free.'

They sat for a while, listening to the waves slap against the stone quay. He started with a simple question. 'Where did the Frau,' he corrected himself, 'your Kirstin, serve during the war?'

'Metz.'

Was the doctor still being evasive or did he really not know?

'Doc, Metz, for all its German-sounding name, is in France. I know because the Royal Ulster Rifles were there during the war. The Frau doesn't have any French.'

Somewhere he must have missed a point because the doctor suddenly looked confident. Like he'd put one over on Barlow.

'Sergeant, don't you know your history?'

Edward dug himself out of his apparent reverie. 'When Barlow went to school they hadn't invented history.'

Barlow hated himself for being caught out like this. He'd left school at twelve with the three Rs. A young lady, long gone from Ballymena, had coached him through the police entrance exams. There had to be more to life than police manuals and the goings-on around Ballymena. He'd never taken the time to find out any more than he needed to know to do his job.

Edward said, 'Sergeant Major, for your edification and knowledge. Metz is situated in the Lorraine area of France.'

'So they speak French.' Barlow knew he was being stubborn.

The doctor said, 'Look at it this way. The Germans didn't occupy Alsace-Lorraine in 1940. They merely recovered homelands lost in the First World War. The military sent in weren't "occupying forces". They were "garrison troops".'

'Aye,' said Barlow. He knew the answer now; even before the doctor spelled it out.

'From their point of view, Metz was part of Germany, and Germans speak German. Even though Kirstin was stationed in a historically French-speaking region she didn't have to learn French to make herself understood. Any local caught using French was deemed to be subversive.' The doctor simulated a hanging.

Barlow kept his face expressionless. Another brick in his case against Adenauer had just crumbled.

CHAPTER 56

THE BARMAN CAME TO CLEAR away the empties and wipe down the table. Edward seemed glad to see the water being removed and he kept his back firmly turned against the sea so that he could avoid having to look at an infinity of water. Barlow enjoyed his discomfort.

The doctor glanced pointedly at his watch. 'We eat early on a Sunday.'

Barlow held up a warning finger indicating to the doctor to remain seated. 'I've seen young Peter's birth certificate. He was delivered in your hospital on August 15th 1945. By you?

The doctor's eyes narrowed. 'Yes?'

'You're a liar.'

'Really, my dear chap,' Edward admonished Barlow.

Barlow nudged Edward. He did it with his sore arm, and had to suck in air in order to cope with the pain. 'You ask him then.'

They both looked at the doctor who sat mesmerised. Barlow pushed the remains of the gin and tonic towards him. 'Relax Doc, this is all off the record. I only want the truth.'

He got a nod in reply and wished he'd thought to order another round. His throat felt dry from tension. 'Look Doc, I'll tell you what I think, and you stop me wherever I go wrong.'

He got another nod.

'Stoop's in hospital, partly crippled and castrated. If news of the castration bit gets out he'll be the laughing stock of the countryside. But what if he arrives home with a wife and a ready-made family? Nobody is going to question his manhood then.' Barlow raised an eyebrow. 'Am I right so far?'

'Yes,' said the doctor. He looked more relaxed.

Barlow said, 'Now let's look, not at the Frau, but at her husband. He belonged to the 88th Regiment. You say the 88th was wiped out in the defence of Berlin.' Barlow had been caught out once on history and geography, due to his lack of formal education. Most of what he knew was derived from reading newspapers or listening to the radio. He felt he risked making a fool of himself for a second time.

'After Stalingrad, the Russians stopped slaughtering German prisoners. They needed them to rebuild the USSR after the war. Except for members of the SS and the Waffen-SS. They shot them out of hand.' He paused. 'How am I doing, Doc?'

'Yes,' said the doctor. 'The 88th Regiment was part of the Waffen-SS Polizei Division.'

The signs of tension in the doctor had eased further. He leaned forwards, hands out as if holding an offering.

Barlow felt like a priest, encouraging a penitent to confess. Getting the secrets of a lifetime off his chest. He spoke slowly because the bits and pieces were still coming together in his mind. 'Kirstin Reinhardt was the wife of a Waffen-SS soldier. That made her unemployable by the Allied Forces. An outcast among her own people who had come to hate the excesses of people like the Gestapo and the SS.' He looked at the doctor as if over a pair of glasses. 'Unless of course she already had a job and nobody found out.'

'I didn't know for a long time.' The doctor sounded defensive.

'It doesn't matter how it happened, Doc, but you two got together. You wanted contact with living, healthy flesh. She needed someone to protect her. You came with a house, and staff to babysit while she was on duty.'

The doctor said, 'You make it sound–'

'Like it was: a done deal, but after the war you had a wife and family to come home to.' He knew the truth spoken that way sounded brutal, and tried to ease the hurt. 'What you and Kirstin felt for each other at that time had to be well above affection. Why else would you have hidden her past? Or forged a birth certificate to prove the baby was Stoop's?'

The Gillespies, he saw, were on their way back along the shore. Behind them came Vera and Kenny, their joined hands swinging in unison.

He wanted the full truth about the doctor and the Frau. The sight of his own daughter, so obviously happy, made him ask gently. 'Stoop didn't meet the Frau at Metz in 1944, did he?'

'No,' said the doctor. 'I did.' He started to cry for his doubly-lost son.

CHAPTER 57

IT MAY HAVE BEEN THE Guinness or the Londonderry Arms mixed grill, with its mound of chips, but Barlow felt strength pour into his system. Vera went spare with indignation when he mentioned going back to work that evening.

Barlow turned to Kenny. 'You can't say you weren't warned about her temper.'

That shut Vera up and made Kenny blush. Gillespie did a circuit of the town. First, dropping off a dehydrated Edward at the Bridge Bar, then Kenny at his home. Kenny's house was double-fronted and set in its own grounds. Barlow didn't like the look of the garden: not a vegetable in sight.

He leaned out the window. 'This weekend thing in Portrush. Who else is going?'

Kenny became nervous and backed against the garden wall. 'Some of our school friends, sir, and my mother to do the cooking.'

Barlow had a chew on his sweet. No matter what Kenny said, Mrs Cameron was there to do more than the cooking. He looked back at Vera. She'd gone all red and hopeful.

He said, 'Portrush or Ballymena, you'll only get into the trouble you want to.'

She half strangled him with a hug. They drove on. At the Gillespies' house Barlow took over the wheel for the drive to the police station. It had to be the effect of the sea air, but his arm felt more flexible.

'Be careful of the shooting-brake,' said Gillespie, as anxious as if it was his own. 'And keep it out of cowpats, this time.'

'You just be ready in the morning. I'll pick you up.'

He drove on to the police station, where he found Jackson draped over the counter. Jackson looked like death warmed up.

'What the bloody hell are you doing here?'

'Well I ... I ... I was doing nothing ... and ... and everybody else is busy looking for Adenauer ... and ... '

'And you've earned the right to call me Sarge.'

Jackson beamed. 'Because I nearly drowned?'

'Because of the incident reports you wrote up about Geordie. They were more than fair. In spite of Harvey trying to get him hung.'

'Thanks Sergeant ... Sarge.'

The young officer should have been at home, being fussed over by his parents. Barlow touched his bad arm. Not that he was in a position to criticise. All the same, if Jackson was there he might as well hang around with a purpose. He told Jackson to dig out the reports for the day Stoop was killed. A checkpoint had been set up on the main road into town. Who had been stopped and questioned, and were any of them gun owners?

'That was done at the time,' said Jackson. 'I know, I helped.'

Barlow nodded. *So that fat heap Leary isn't entirely useless.* He liked being unfair to Detective Sergeant Leary. It kept both of them on their toes, one trying to outdo the other.

'Do it again,' he said, and checked his in-tray. A letter had arrived from the Ballymena hospital's pathology department. He put it in his pocket, unopened, to read later in private. Dug the Tillage Book out of his shelf and headed for the separate squad room where the WPCs hung out.

The WPCs' squad room was no longer homely. Harvey had ordered their chintz curtains and the Elvis print to be taken down. 'Against regulations,' he said. As yet, he'd done nothing about their pastel-painted walls. That would cost money.

The girls were all in, even those officially off duty, and all were feeling resentful. None of the male officers wanted them out with the search parties. Their job was to coordinate with the other divisions and prepare cups of tea.

He bulled in the door. WPC Day was holding up her left hand into a shaft of evening sunlight. A diamond ring glistened on her engagement finger. WPC Day went bright red. Her eyes pleaded for someone else to find out what Barlow was looking for. The other girls pretended to be busy.

Without meeting his eye she said, 'Can I help you, Sergeant?'

'Aye.'

He pulled up a chair in front of her desk and helped himself to a sheet of paper. He wrote out a list of names and below them the charges. 'All these people, all the same charges. You'll get the addresses and details you need in the Register.'

WPC Day looked at the list. 'Oh my God, you can't.'

'I can, you know.' It was nice to know she was concerned for him.

'Mr Harvey will go spare if you summons these people.'

He smiled. 'You might call this my Dunkirk.'

'Sarge, for heaven's sake.'

He jabbed a finger at the rest of the WPCs. 'You lot, put away your nail polish and mascara, and give WPC Day a hand. I need this stuff within the hour.'

He left. Denton was right. Time to find a country station and catch up on his fishing. *And Maggie?* He hadn't gone to see her yet. Maybe tomorrow after Vera got out of school. They could go together. He couldn't bear to visit on his own. Not the first time at least. Not trying to make conversation with a drugged-out zombie.

In their new house he'd make sure Maggie had a bedroom of her own. She'd want that. He found himself standing in the corridor, being sad.

WPC Day had followed him out of the room. She held him in a long hug. 'You're a big Papa Bear. Thank you.'

'It did the trick then?'

'July the tenth. You'll get the first invitation.'

He walked off singing *Baby's cheek or baby's chin. Seems to me it'll be a sin if it's always covered with a safety pin. Where will the dimple...*

'I hate you,' she hissed after him.

Leary sat at his desk in the detectives' room, which had developed another haphazard mess of files. Even the dust was back.

Leary raised his head out of his hands when Barlow walked in. 'You're better then?'

'Aye.'

The other desks were empty. Barlow sat across from Leary. 'I'd like another look at the papers Mr Comberton sent in.'

Leary heaved himself off the chair and went across to a shelf piled high with files. Unerringly, his hand pulled out the right one. 'You can have my pension too if you can catch that murdering bastard.'

Barlow went through the file. He started first with the army correspondence. The birth of Peter and the Frau's marriage were well documented. The police report made no mention of any Adenauers in her background. Barlow sucked on a sweet for a bit. Mostly to avoid looking at the rest of the papers supplied by Comberton. Even the thought of what he might find there frightened him.

WPC Day brought him a cup of tea and fetched one for Leary as well. Leary opened his bottom drawer and pulled out a packet of digestive biscuits. He held them up as an enticement. 'Are you on to something?'

Barlow said, 'When things don't add up, recast your sums.'

'That's a great help.'

The other papers concerned Stoop's financial dealings and legal documents. Comberton's attached note said that, for safety reasons, he'd taken all private papers from Stoop's house on the day of his death. One envelope contained the will of Stoop's mother. Now Barlow finally understood why Stoop had become bitter.

Stoop thought he'd fooled everyone with his instant family. But he hadn't fooled his mother. In her will she left all her land to Alexandra's husband, William. He got fifty acres immediately. Stoop had only a life interest in his twenty acres. When he died title would pass to William and his successors.

The Frau had become legally homeless on the death of her husband Stoop.

The insult to Stoop and his German son was to be found in the old woman's attached explanation. Not only did she want the land to remain in the family name of Taylor. It had to go to Taylor blood.

Barlow couldn't understand why Harvey and Leary hadn't picked up on that clause. Maybe they didn't understand it? Maybe they thought it irrelevant? He had to admit to himself that it only made sense to him because he had already talked to the old army doctor.

He flicked through the rest of the papers. Stoop, apparently, had disputed the will. He dropped the case when his own solicitor demanded one hundred guineas to defray costs. *Tight to the end.*

School photographs of Peter lay in the file. Barlow looked at one for a long time. Kept his head down so that Leary wouldn't see the tears in his eyes. Eventually, he slipped the photograph into his pocket. He thought the old army doctor might like it.

CHAPTER 58

FOXWOOD ARRIVED INTO THE POLICE station, his already long face stretched and grey. He was bedraggled and muddy as a result of ploughing through the bogs looking for Adenauer. Barlow felt almost sorry for the man as he dragged himself down the corridor.

Barlow scooped up the forms left in his in-tray by the junior sergeant, shuffled in the summonses prepared by WPC Day, and followed Foxwood into his office.

Foxwood sat slumped over the desk, head in his arms. Barlow sat across from him and waited. It gave him time to study the poster on the back wall. It warned of the danger of eelworm on root crops. The poster was new; the city inspector was beginning to learn something about farming. Barlow hoped to teach him another sharp lesson.

Eventually, Foxwood lifted his head. His eyes were red-rimmed with exhaustion and he needed a shave.

'When were you last home, sir?'

Foxwood levered himself upright in the chair. 'I don't know if I've got a home to go back to. The wife … '

Barlow nodded in sympathy and put the bundle of forms on the desk. 'These need to be signed.'

The Inspector's head sank back into his hands. 'You've got to be kidding.'

He kept nodding, still apparently sympathetic. 'I went through them myself, personal like. Maybe a skim read?'

'Give them to me,' said Foxwood and he pushed them over.

The top form had a big pencilled "X", making plain where the inspector had to sign. By the time he got to the third form he only looked for the "X".

The signings finished, Barlow scooped the papers into his hands and stood up. 'I'll get WPC Day to rustle you up a cup of tea.' He left before Foxwood had second thoughts about what he'd signed. He headed straight for the shooting-brake.

Taking the Curles Bridge Road was a detour, but he felt he had to do it. This was the end of his life in Ballymena. After tomorrow, he'd be posted to a two-man station in the bog-end of nowhere. At the back entrance to the Adair estate he pulled in and stopped. Just inside the gate stood the wreck of an old gamekeeper's cottage. He'd lived there after running away from the workhouse. Nobody knew he was there, or so he thought at the time. But Edward knew and so did his sister Grace. They never said a word and they made sure no one ever bothered him.

The old cottage could be made habitable again. Edward refused to consider it, and he could understand why. Edward couldn't bear to live as a tramp in what had been his home. The mansion and grounds now belonged to the Department of Agriculture.

He sighed and drove on. The Curles Bridge Road had another use. He could avoid Alexandra's farm on the way to Denton's house.

Denton's wife opened the door to him. Darkness had fallen, taking away the heat of the day. The subdued lighting and the heat coming off the radiators made him think longingly of his own bed.

'John, you're looking a lot better.'

'I'm nearly myself again, Missis.'

She ushered him through the hallway and down a narrow corridor to the library. 'Charles is expecting you.'

The room had a banked-up fire smouldering in the grate and a block-wood floor that gleamed under the artificial lighting. Spring-clip files and stacks of papers had taken the place of the old, often unread books that had once graced the walls. 'You should be on sick leave,' said Denton.

'I am.'

He put an envelope on Denton's desk. Denton tore it open. He began to read, then frowned and started to flick through the documents. 'Are you serious?'

'Yes, sir.'

'These people?'

'Aye.'

He waited while Denton read more and started to sweat. 'Bloody hell! I mean … this is dynamite. It'll be in all the papers.'

'I can't help that, sir, it's what I saw.'

'Harvey will have a fit.' Denton didn't sound particularly concerned.

Barlow intoned. '"No crime too small, no failure too insignificant". It's him that said it.'

'But for ragweed?'

'It's poisonous and the law requires it to be pulled.'

Denton snorted. 'I've never met a cow fool enough to eat it.' His finger hovered over the top page. 'These are leading businessmen, town councillors … '

'I don't know of a separate law for the nobs. Do you?'

'You're a trouble-making bastard.'

'They said the same thing about me in the workhouse.'

'Sorry, I didn't mean it that way.' He looked up. 'As you bloody well know.' Barlow looked back blandly while Denton went back to frowning over the signature on the documents. 'And Foxwood approved these without question?'

'Inspector Foxwood signs a lot of things.'

'With you, I learned to read the postage stamps.' He started to go through the documents in detail. One got crumpled and thrown at the fire.

'Sir, that is a legal document.'

The glare he got back could have cut glass. 'I'm not summonsing myself, is that understood?'

'Of course, Sir.' A lifetime's practice kept Barlow's smile hidden.

'When it comes to the hanging, it'll be the roughest hemp,' muttered Denton, and went back to his reading.

Barlow made himself sit back and relax. This could go either way. At long last, Denton unscrewed the top of his Parker pen and signed the first form.

He said, 'I don't know if we're right doing this.'

When he got to the last one he jerked in surprise. 'Him too! I don't know if I've the nerve to sign that one.' The pen dithered over the form for a few seconds before he shrugged and scrawled his signature at the pencilled X.

Without looking up he added, 'The roughest of hemp with barbed wire embedded. And he'll do it personally.'

Barlow wanted to take the road home by Curles Bridge, but the shooting-brake turned the other way. He passed the Frau's house. Peter's body was to be released on Tuesday and the burial to take place the next day. The house lay in darkness. He was glad of that because the Frau needed her sleep; the coming days would be stressful for her.

At the bottom of Alexandra's lane the car stopped.

The outside light was still on. Through the wavering hedgerow he could see the front windows. The kitchen light glimmered behind drawn blinds. With the car window wound down, he could hear the faint strains of music on the still air.

He got out of the shooting-brake. The dog came out of the chicken house and snarled. He bent down and patted it. The dog retreated in shock. He followed the dog into the chicken house and sat beside it on one of the laying boxes. The dog quivered, but didn't move away. It attempted a half-hearted growl.

He kept an image of Maggie before his eyes. Reminded himself of his duties and obligations to her. His heart was up that lane and in the door.

He only left when the lights went out and the door bolted against him.

CHAPTER 59

THE RADIATORS PUMPED HEAT. IN spite of that, dankness from damp coats hung heavy in the courtroom. Every bench was filled. Barlow timed his arrival to a few moments before the court sat. Settled himself into a bench among other police officers. The smell of stale drink wafted around his face. A finger prodded deep into his injured arm. He twisted round. Geordie sat right behind him, his lips curled in fury.

The prodding finger became a fist. 'See you, Barlow, see you.'

'You're a dickhead letting Moncrief represent you.'

'He's coming cheap,' said Geordie.

'You of all people can't trust him.' It didn't hurt to probe a little. 'Even if our mayor is picking up the bill.'

'Now why would he do that?' asked Geordie.

'Piss off,' said Barlow as, sharp to the hour, Judge Donaldson took his seat.

Donaldson glared round the courtroom. All whispered conversations ceased. Cupped hands concealed anxious looks. The judge was in a bad mood.

Minor cases were called and dealt with viciously. A drunken brawl? Six months. No lights and driving without due care and attention? Twenty pounds and a two-year ban. A matrimonial dispute? He gave the husband a month for common affray and told the wife "next time use the rolling-pin".

With the small cases summarily dealt with, the court got down to the real work of the day. The first case called was Regina versus Simon Arthur Whithead. The youth accused of stealing a pencil rubber from the newsagents.

At that point the mayor, Ezekiel Fetherton, stepped into the courtroom. So promptly he could have been standing outside, waiting to make an entrance. A place was made for him and he sat with a smirk on his face. His eyes never left Whithead Senior. There has to be a history between the two men, Barlow thought, *something pretty good*. He'd have to talk to Whithead Senior sometime. Remembered he would be posted somewhere else and instead settled himself to watch Harvey's 'No Second Chance' policy destroy a decent family.

Simon Whithead entered the dock and stood white-faced, but firm. The prosecution and defence counsels formally introduced themselves to the court. The clerk read out the charges against Simon: that he'd stolen a pencil rubber from Fetherton's newsagents.

Before the clerk could ask "How do you plead?" Donaldson stopped him. 'I want the charges against Mr Whithead read out again.'

This was an unusual breach of custom, unheard of, in fact. A murmur started among the lawyers and the police. Donaldson silenced the court with a look.

The clerk repeated. 'Simon Arthur Whithead, you are charged that on ... ' He finished reading out the charges and then asked. 'How do you plead?'

Donaldson interrupted. 'No, read them again.'

The clerk did so. This time he couldn't keep the surprise out of his voice.

Donaldson addressed the prosecuting counsel. 'This case concerns the inadvertent misappropriation of an item of stationery. An item retailing at two pence. A loss the proprietor only discovered when the defendant ran back to pay.' He leaned forward, the full majesty of the law threatening to overwhelm counsel. 'Why did you bring this case before the court?'

Counsel stuttered. 'Your honour–'

'Who in the Public Prosecution Service authorised this case to proceed without first querying it with the police? '

'I can't see what relevance–'

'The name,' snapped Donaldson.

Counsel hunted through his papers for the authorising name and supplied it. Donaldson wrote it down, and then said: 'I want that gentleman in court – now.'

'But he's in the city today, the Law Courts.' The prosecuting counsel even looked to the defence counsel for support.

Donaldson checked his watch against the court clock. 'If he is not here before two this afternoon I shall jail him for contempt.'

A buzz of astonishment whipped around the courtroom. Donaldson allowed it to continue while he consulted the papers before him. Barlow refused to meet anybody's eye or speculate with his close neighbours as to what had got into the judge. Donaldson looked up. Silence was instantaneous.

'Constable Jackson, step forward.'

Jackson edged out of the phalanx of policemen and approached the bench. Barlow felt sorry for him. He looked like he was going to his own execution.

'Your honour?'

'You are the arresting officer in this case?'

'Yes, sir... your honour. I took the initial statement from Mr James Wilson. Mr Wilson is the manager of Fetherton's newsagents in Market Street.

'Then what? Donaldson thundered. 'I want the absolute truth.'

Jackson's mouth opened and closed. He didn't know what to say next.

Barlow stood up and walked into the main body of the court. No way would he allow Jackson to take any bollocking that was rightfully due to Pierson, Foxwood or Harvey. Especially Harvey.

'Your honour,' he said, without prompting. 'Constable Jackson asked me how he should proceed with this case.'

Jackson gaped at him. Barlow frowned in return, wanting him to take the look of surprise off his face.

He continued. 'On my advice, Constable Jackson recommended that no action be taken. The file was then given to Acting Station Sergeant Pierson.'

Jackson's head nodded firmly at the mention of Pierson's name.

'Then sit down again.' Donaldson sounded reluctant to let Barlow go.

Barlow remained standing. 'Sergeant Pierson is off ill. With your honour's permission, I will stay with my constable.'

Inspector Foxwood was called. Why, Donaldson asked, had he authorised the prosecution? A question Barlow knew Foxwood found impossible to answer honestly. He could hardly say Harvey had allowed himself to be influenced by outside parties. He fell back on the "No crime too small, no failure too insignificant" policy.

'"No crime too small",' roared Donaldson. 'You and your stupid "no failure too insignificant".' The magistrates' courts are choked with cases. So much so that I find myself, a county court judge–' He slammed a fist down on the bench in fury. 'A county court judge, obliged to spend days dealing with minor infractions.'

'District Inspector Harvey … ' began Foxwood.

'It's your name that I see on the documents, not Harvey's. Have you no opinion of your own? No sense of proportion?'

Donaldson started a rant about wasting the court's time. About the police hounding honest citizens over stupid things – like ragweed not being pulled.'

The torrent of outrage continued until Donaldson gasped for air between gritted teeth. When he got his breath back he stabbed a finger at counsel for the prosecution. 'The Whithead case?'

Counsel said, hastily, 'The Crown will be presenting no evidence, your honour.'

Donaldson said, 'The case against Simon Arthur Whithead is therefore dismissed.' He stood up. 'Court is adjourned for half an hour.' A finger pointed at Foxwood. 'The next case I hear better have some real meat to it.'

He stormed out before the Clerk of the Court could call, 'All rise.'

A ripple of air washed around the courtroom as held breaths were exhaled.

'Shit,' said Foxwood. He looked at Barlow. 'You tried to warn me about this, didn't you?'

'You're a good man, sir. I'd hate to see your career blighted.' Kept two fingers crossed behind his back against the lie.

Counsel raced over, robes flapping behind him. He shook with panic. 'I don't know who put a burr up Donaldson's backside. But we're in trouble. We've got to come up with something good.'

Barlow said, 'There's always Geordie.'

'That eejit.'

The three of them began to hunt through case files, looking for anything Donaldson could get his teeth into, keep him busy for the rest of the day. Nothing caught their attention. Counsel and Foxwood started to panic.

Foxwood kept looking at his watch. 'Harvey should be here by now. I don't know where he's got to.'

Barlow produced a file and showed it to Counsel.

'We couldn't,' said Counsel.

'The man's in court, and his solicitor. The summons was duly served but not yet acted on.'

'All rise,' said the Clerk of the Court.

Their half hour was up.

CHAPTER 60

COUNSEL BOWED DONALDSON INTO THE chair then ran to give the clerk his instructions.

The clerk intoned. 'Regina versus Ezekiel Fetherton.'

Counsel said, 'Your honour, this is a very serious case of theft and deception. Not only that, but by watering down milk with tap water, Fetherton put at risk the lives and good health of countless children.'

Solicitor Moncrief bounced out of his seat. He didn't know his client was expected in court that day. No one had informed him. Barlow had to listen intently to pick up the words when Moncrief dropped his voice. 'Your honour,' said Moncrief, in an all-old-boys-together tone of voice. 'My client is an honoured and respected member of this community. Even if some water did get into the milk. Surely a minor infraction … ?

Donaldson asked, 'Of less significance than a tuppenny pencil rubber?'

Barlow sat back and stretched his legs in comfort, all the more to enjoy the sight of the Mayor standing in the dock while Moncrief and counsel ding-donged case law and Rules of Procedure at each other. Donaldson beamed as he decided on the relevance or otherwise of case law quoted by both sides. He decided, reluctantly, to adjourn the case for one week.

'A week?' spluttered Moncrief.

'You've already had a year to prepare,' said Donaldson, and that was that.

Fetherton stumbled from the dock and slunk out of court. Moncrief followed. As he passed Moncrief muttered to Barlow, 'I see your hand in all of this.'

Barlow looked innocent. Continued sitting while Donaldson took another short break. Watched Foxwood call all the waiting policemen together, ordering most of them to go about their business. Their cases wouldn't be called that day. Mightn't be called at all.

The clerk announced the next case. 'Regina versus George Aloysius Dunlop.'

Geordie stalked into the dock. He kept his angry stare fixed on Barlow. Moncrief had come back into the court and stood to represent Geordie. The charges of assault were read out.

Geordie glanced at Moncrief who nodded encouragement. Geordie said, 'Guilty.'

Donaldson said to Moncrief. 'Before I sentence your client, do you wish to bring to the attention of the Court any mitigating facts?'

'No, your honour,' said Moncrief. He looked at Barlow as if to say "two of us can play dirty".

Barlow found himself on his feet and shouting. 'Geordie defused a bomb in a hospital cellar.' His finger pointed at Moncrief. 'And you know it, you bastard, you know it.'

Donaldson's paperweight thundered against the bench. 'Silence in court.'

He kept shouting. 'A cellar, with half a hospital of patients above him and not one able to move.'

Donaldson's paperweight thundered again. 'Silence at once, or I will hold you in contempt of court.'

'Don't worry, your honour, I've contempt enough for the two of us.'

He slumped into his seat knowing that Donaldson had the right to jail him for contempt. He also guessed the judge would hold fire on his sentencing. There was a personal element to Donaldson's anger that day. Anger which could be easily exploited in a claim for mistrial. Any punishment, therefore, must appear to be a considered response.

'Sergeant Barlow, I'll see you in my chambers when court recesses this afternoon.'

He nodded. He'd better things to do that day than worry about Donaldson.

Donaldson turned to Moncrief. 'Your client served gallantly during the war and was awarded the Military Medal. Surely the number of lives he saved that day deserves mention as a plea in mitigation of sentence?'

Moncrief tried to keep the smirk out of his voice. 'If I may remind your honour. Your late revered father gave Dunlop the choice of the army or jail.'

A silence hung in the court. Barlow bit down the urge to go and wring Moncrief's neck.

Donaldson nodded as if Moncrief had made a good point, then he said, 'If I may remind you, Mr Moncrief. My father said that Geordie Dunlop never started a fight, but he always finished it. That he was just the sort of man we needed to defeat Hitler.'

'Hear. Hear,' said a voice from the body of the court and there was a ripple of applause.

'Also,' said Donaldson, 'I am of the opinion that it was incumbent on you to remind the court of what actually happened.' He looked at the charge sheet to check his facts. 'Mr Dunlop bumped into Constable Jackson in passing. Constable Jackson admits partial responsibility for the fall. He was off balance at the time. In addition, Mr Dunlop assisted Constable Jackson to his feet and apologised handsomely for the inadvertent mishap.'

Moncrief blustered. 'Your honour, all that is in the police statements, which of course your honour has read.'

Donaldson grunted. 'What is not in the statements is that two of Mr Dunlop's grandsons were in hospital, both of them having suffered severe injuries during the course of their arrest.'

His eyes fixed on Barlow. 'Mr Dunlop threatened the arresting officer, who happened to be Sergeant Barlow, and challenged him to a fight. He twice grabbed the police officer by the collar, but didn't actually take him by the throat.'

He sounded regretful, as if Geordie had somehow failed him.

Barlow leaned forward, listening intently as Donaldson made a play of hesitating over the sentence. *Let it work.* Could Donaldson, just for once, see Geordie on the side of the angels?

'George Aloysius Dunlop, I have examined your criminal record in detail. Much of what you did was foolish and thoughtless. If you were fifty years younger, I'd drag you home by the ear and tell your father to take his belt to you.' He glared down at Foxwood. 'Not clog up the courts with technical offences.'

He took time to check through the papers before him. 'Dunlop, I fine you five pounds for common assault, with two pounds costs.'

Geordie and Barlow both nodded.

Somebody tapped Barlow on the shoulder. On his good side this time. He turned to find Edward sitting behind him. Edward wore his good suit, a crisp white shirt and regimental tie.

'Where did you come from?' asked Barlow.

'His former Company Commander is here to speak on behalf of Rifleman Dunlop, if so required.' Edward gave a knowing smile. 'One senses that your interfering offices have again been put to good use.'

'If you mean, did I summons the judge for ragweed growing in his fields? Aye, I did, and half the members of the Masonic Hall besides.'

'Properly signed and attested by our good quartermaster?'

'You use fewer big words when you're drunk.' He pulled out his wallet and gave Edward his last pound note and the change in his pockets. 'Take Geordie to the Bridge Bar and keep him there until I arrive. It could be an hour or two.'

Donaldson looked their way and glared. *Glare all you want,* Barlow thought, confident that Donaldson wouldn't dare do anything against Edward. Edward had connections Donaldson could only dream of.

Even so, he lowered his voice. 'Tell Geordie two things. The grandsons are to get a new solicitor for their appeal; otherwise Moncrief will let them hang. And tell him to keep his fool temper in check. I'll give him the fight he's looking for.'

CHAPTER 61

BARLOW SHOULD HAVE ENJOYED HIS walk back to the police station. A warm breeze greeted him on the street corners and the sun fought its way through the clouds. Cloudy-bright, or so the camera buffs among the young constables called it.

Harvey would cancel the summonses for the un-pulled ragweed. No way would he allow members of the Masonic Hall be embarrassed when he was up for membership. But Harvey wouldn't be there forever. Nor would Barlow, not after today.

The ragweed was unimportant. What was important was people like his Vera. They were being educated. Education taught them to think for themselves. Gave them the confidence to speak out. Maggie had never tongued him the way Vera sometimes did. He wished she had.

Rough times lay ahead before the people took control of their lives. The bosses would fight to the last privilege. And Vera would be in the thick of it. The thought of Vera banging stubborn heads together brought a reluctant smile to his lips.

The closer he got to the police station the slower his step became. The front door had swung shut in the breeze. He reached to push it open. Jackson came bursting out. Barlow jumped out of the way of the young constable's battering-ram run. Jackson looked surprised and stepped backwards.

Barlow watched as bullets cut an arc over his head. Found himself counting the sound of distant gunshots: *two, three, four, five*. Splintering stonework sparked into his face. Jackson hit the back wall and slid down into a foetal position. Coins gleamed in the air and rolled noisily across the stone steps.

The shooting stopped before Barlow thought to duck. Five shots. *That M1 again.* He saw the shock on Jackson's face turn to pain, and the blood.

Lots of it.

'Sarge.'

The blood poured through a hole in Jackson's uniform. High up, on the left of his chest. Barlow pressed his hand down hard on the hole. 'You're okay, son. Take it easy.' He back-heeled with his foot, slamming the outer door shut.

The inner door lay open. People remained hunkered down. He yelled for someone to bring a compress pad. No shots came through the closed outer door. People got braver, stood straighter. WPC Day came running with a first aid kit.

Band-Aids scattered as she scooped out the compress pad. They couldn't tie it around Jackson's chest without moving him. Barlow placed the pad over the wound and held it down with his hand. It quickly turned red. The blood seeped through his fingers.

He forced himself to look into Jackson's panicked eyes. 'This will earn you a month's sick leave.'

'I'm going to be all right?'

'Hardly more than a scratch.'

Jackson coughed. Blood stained his lips and teeth.

'I'm going ... I feel ... dying.'

'You young boys. I've got worse from Geordie, and thumped the bugger back.' People stood behind him. 'Where's that bloody ambulance?'

'On its way.'

Jackson slid into unconsciousness. Barlow looked gratefully at WPC Day. She knelt in a pool of blood, her hand on his, pressing with him. Her engagement ring stood on her finger like a glob of gore.

She asked, 'Why Jackson? What's he got against Jackson?'

'It was me. Jackson just got in the way.'

"Just". He hated that word. A young boy's life's blood pumping out of him "just because."

He used his free hand to push against a pain in his own chest. A heart attack or his heart breaking, he wasn't sure which. He hoped heart attack, that way he wouldn't have to live.

Gillespie forced his way to the front of the gawkers. Barlow told him. 'Ask for a car from the nearest station. They might get the parents here in time.'

Gillespie nodded and disappeared.

At least Foxwood had started to organise the rest of the men. He wanted checkpoints set up on every road out of town. District Inspector Harvey was to be called back in. All the police already out beating the thickets for Adenauer were to swamp the roads. Stop and search every man and every car.

The ambulance came, its bell ding-a-linging. The ambulance men looked at the blood, their lips went grim. Barlow helped them lift Jackson onto the stretcher and got into the ambulance with him. Held Jackson's hand and tried to put some heat into it.

Somebody had told him once – a doctor, he thought – that hearing was the last thing to go. He kept telling Jackson what a smart kid he was. Heading for the top. Might even make Chief Constable. 'Then you'll have no time for old station sergeants.'

The ambulance pulled up at the Emergency entrance. He stayed back as the professionals took over. The surgeon waiting did a quick examination of the wound and rushed Jackson indoors, shouting, 'Theatre number two. Now!'

The doors closed behind them. Barlow remained in the ambulance. Blood dripped off the seat and pooled the floor at his feet. He tried to remember the words of David's lament for his son Absalom.

Big boys don't cry.

Eventually, an ambulance man came back and asked him to move. The ambulance needed to be cleaned. It had to be got ready for the next emergency.

He climbed out and shivered in the once-warm wind. His uniform was saturated with blood. He couldn't walk back to the police station, and Gillespie wouldn't let him anywhere near the squad car, looking like that. Maybe they'd send the police van? A nurse appeared and guided him into a shower room. Took his uniform away while he showered. His tears ran with the blood.

The nurse returned with the uniform while he was still in the shower. She entered without knocking. 'Do you mind?' he said and covered up with his hands.

His nakedness didn't seem to bother her. She wasn't much older than Vera. She came closer. 'Time those stitches were out.' She twisted his arm for a better look. 'I'll get Sister.'

She left again. He jumped out of the shower and dried himself down at speed. Nurses had no sense of decency. That young lady was likely to come back with a committee of helpers. He slipped into his combinations and trousers and laced up his boots. The trousers were damp from the sponging down. Someone had used an iron to speed up the drying process and put the creases back in.

The nurse and Sister came in. The Sister was his old adversary from his previous stay in the hospital. She pulled out the stitches with a good tweak, made no attempt to be gentle. He flexed his arm. It felt much freer. The inner stitches still pulled at his skin. They, Sister informed him, would dissolve of their

279

own accord. She had little information about Jackson. He was still in theatre. The hospital had sent urgently to The Royal Victoria Hospital in Belfast, thirty miles away, for more blood of his type.

They showed Barlow into a waiting room. It had chairs set against the sage green walls. A coffee table in the centre of the room held well-thumbed copies of *Woman* and *Woman's Own*. Harvey had got there before him, waiting for Jackson's parents to arrive. *They should be here by now*, he thought, but the father was at work and the squad car had to make a detour in order to pick him up.

He nodded at Harvey, who was staring at the floor and didn't seem to notice his arrival. Sat down. Cups of tea arrived. It gave his hands something to do. Days out in the fresh air hunting for Adenauer had put colour in Harvey's cheeks. Barlow thought he looked the better for it.

Anxious to know what was going on, Barlow left the room. Everything in the hospital sounded normal. He could hear laughter. It seemed wrong somehow. He bullied his way into a clerk's office and rang the police station.

WPC Day answered, she sounded subdued. 'Is he… ?'

'They're still operating.'

They talked a little. Everyone else was on duty. It would be selfish of her to go home. She kept repeating, 'I'm okay,' when she clearly wasn't.

He wanted to tell her to grab her fiancé and start growing babies. That life was incredibly short. Instead he said, 'I asked Jackson to dig out some reports for me. They're to do with the checkpoints set up that first day.'

'Sarge, how can you think… ?' A bit of her old impatience was back. That would make her feel better.

'Do you know where they are?'

She searched and found the reports and Jackson's summary in his in-tray. Read out the report for him. Only two of the people who had gone through the checkpoint on the first day were also registered gun owners. Both men were farmers, holding a shotgun licence for vermin. One had been at the mart, the other was in town to buy calf meal. Both had witnesses for the time in question.

Barlow got WPC Day to read out the names of every other person stopped. It ran to a page and a half of foolscap.

'Jackson's report, does it give the names of the officers manning the checkpoint?'

'Yes.' She was over her temper now and intrigued.

'Tell Gillespie to round them up. I don't care where they are or what they're doing. I want them here at the hospital, ASAP.'

He hung up before she could ask questions. He went back to the waiting room.

Harvey raised his head as he came in the door. 'Barlow.'

'Sir?'

'I gave money to Jackson to get me cigarillos. How can I tell the parents that?'

Barlow stared at his boots. They had blood on them as well. They were old boots. Maybe he'd just throw them out.

'Barlow.'

He looked up. Harvey stared back out of eyes red-rimmed with exhaustion.

'Sir?'

'Get him. Get that murdering bastard. Any way you like, no questions asked.'

Barlow said, 'This one we do by the book.'

CHAPTER 62

A NURSE BROUGHT BARLOW AND Harvey a second cup of tea. Some sandwiches as well because they'd missed lunch. She set them on top of the magazines on the coffee table. Harvey didn't seem to notice her coming or going.

Barlow helped himself to a sandwich and pushed one into Harvey's hand. 'You've got to eat, sir. You need the energy.'

Harvey nibbled the edges of his sandwich. Barlow could hardly get his own down, even with the tea. They didn't talk so he looked out the window at the Council houses over the hedge. They had been the first of the post-war housing developments. They had indoor toilets. The backyards were real gardens with grass and a long clothesline and a wooden shed to store things in. Wherever he ended up, he wanted all that.

Every now and again, footsteps clipped down the corridor. They tensed and waited for the door to open. The footsteps continued on. At long last he heard a step he recognised.

Gillespie's head appeared round the door. 'Sergeant, could I see you for a minute?'

He joined him in the corridor, closing the door against Harvey's listening ears.

Gillespie said, 'I told them to wait in the car.'

'It took you long enough.'

'You don't have to thank me for missing my lunch,' said Gillespie. He nodded in the direction of the operating theatre. 'Any news yet?'

'Not yet.'

They headed out. The corridor carried the faint sound of someone somewhere crying. *So long as it's not for Jackson.*

Two constables, Mitchell and Clarke, waited for him at the front door. They'd got out of the car to smoke and chat up passing nurses.

Mitchell and Clarke were two long-serving officers, both dependable, but set in their ways. Content to mooch about town and clip ears when necessary. If one missed a piece of gossip, the other picked it up.

He started by asking them to think back to the checkpoint on that first day: their orders, the length of time on duty. The weather. Anything he could think of to jog their memories. Then he asked them whom they'd stopped.

'We made a list,' said Mitchell.

'You did.'

'Of every man we talked to,' said Clarke.

'Did you now?' He let that question hang in the air.

The two men eyed each other. Clarke said, 'Sergeant, people come along you know couldn't be involved.'

That's exactly what he expected to hear. But could they give him a name? Rather than ask, he stood silent, let their anxiety work for him.

Clarke said, 'There were those soldiers, a truckload of them.'

He looked at Barlow, expecting him to say something. Barlow said nothing though he ached to shake the information out of them.

'And Mr Moncrief, of course,' said Mitchell.

'That's right,' said Clarke. 'He was picking up his son at a friend's house.'

A little bell dinged in Barlow's head. These two seemed well informed about Moncrief's movements. 'Friendly was he?'

'Couldn't have been nicer,' said Clarke.

Normally, Moncrief wouldn't wipe his boots on a police uniform. Yet, here he was being friendly. Barlow closed his eyes and visualised a map. The River Road led to the main road and the main road led into town. Where? Which friend?

He was on to something and he didn't want these two old women spreading the word. Bloody Moncrief! *What was he up to?*

He said, 'In future, I don't care if it's a battalion of soldiers, I want every name.'

He told Gillespie to run Mitchell and Clarke back to the station and then come back to collect him. He'd find some excuse to slip away from Harvey.

He got back to the waiting room just as Jackson's parents appeared from another direction. A doctor walked with them. Harvey must have been told they were coming because he was at the door.

The father and mother were middle-aged and quietly dressed. They stood a head shorter than Jackson. That surprised Barlow. He'd always thought of Jackson as coming from a tall family. The father, he knew, worked at Stormont, in Finance. The mother doted on Jackson, her baby. Harvey introduced himself and Barlow.

Mrs Jackson's eyes lit up.

She said, 'Mr Barlow, he thinks the world of you.'

'He's a credit to your rearing,' said Barlow, stunned at Jackson's opinion of him.

'What happened?' asked the father.

Harvey's mouth opened and closed. Nothing came out.

Barlow said, 'He insisted on working even though he should have been on sick leave. We kept inventing reasons to get him out into the fresh air.'

Over the parents' shoulders he could see the surgeon approach. The surgeon wore fresh scrubs and was walking slowly. He saw Barlow looking at him and shook his head.

CHAPTER 63

BARLOW GOT INTO THE CAR beside Gillespie. Gillespie started the engine and they drove off. Down the road he asked. 'Where are we going?'

'Damned if I know.'

Gillespie pulled in.

It seemed a lifetime since Jackson had chased Adenauer in Denton's field. A handful of days, and now this. He knew he had to get his head around things. First sighting, Adenauer was a dead man. He didn't want that to happen.

They sat parked on a quiet residential road.

Gillespie asked, 'How are the parents taking it?'

'Hard.'

'If it was one of mine, I think I'd go mad.'

Barlow chewed on an imaginary sweet. He said, 'Could you see Moncrief shooting cattle in the bum?'

They eyed each other. Gillespie said, 'Are you thinking, the son?'

'He's fat, he's indolent, he's spoiled.'

'And he's a bastarding Moncrief,' finished Gillespie.

Barlow did a bit more chewing. Traffic increased, the in-bound cars giving way around the squad car. Nobody dared beep their horn in irritation.

He said, 'Denholm Moncrief is shooting at the cattle when he spots me watching. He tears off on his racing bike. Gets to somewhere that has a telephone, and rings Daddy to come save him.'

'Where?' asked Gillespie.

'Have they any relations out that direction?'

'Or school friends,' said Gillespie. 'My boys would know.'

'You know where to head then,' said Barlow and settled back to do some more chewing.

He was surprised at the direction they took until he checked his watch. Four o'clock already. The boys would be home from school.

That reminded him. He'd arranged with Vera to visit Maggie. *I've too much on.* The relief at not having to go made him feel guilty. Doubly guilty because Jackson's death would have Vera upset. *What comes first: Vera or the job?*

At the next junction he pointed to the left, in the direction of the police station. 'I'll take the shooting-brake and go and see Maggie. You have a word with the boys. Get a bite of lunch while you're at it.' He checked his watch again. Wasn't he supposed to be up before Donaldson about now? *Bugger him, he can wait.* 'I'll see you back at the station at five o'clock.'

It had to be an architect with grandiose ideas and a tight budget, mused Barlow as he stood outside the institution for the mentally infirm. The front could double as a Scottish hunting lodge, but the wood panelling and plaster mouldings only lasted one room back. From there on, narrow corridors led to sparse rooms. Everything was painted a sickly yellow.

Vera clung to Barlow as they went in the door. He appreciated the warmth of her hand in his. Maggie had been an inmate before. This time they'd put her in the Secure Unit, with all the other homicidal maniacs.

He worried for Vera. *Is she tough enough for this?* Her eyes were red from crying over Jackson.

According to the parents, Jackson had thought him "good". Jackson had wanted to be just like him. Barlow knew the boy had been learning when to turn a blind eye, and when to clip ears. In exchange, he'd ached for Jackson's belief in the goodness of people and his innocence. Something he never had.

A nurse escorted them through a maze of corridors and up stairs. Doors were unlocked to let them through, and then re-locked behind them. He realised he hadn't spoken to Vera since they'd arrived at the front door. 'I'm sure she's fine,' he said, and Vera clung that bit tighter.

At least they hadn't given Maggie the electric shock treatment. She wasn't strong enough, her heart might give out. "She's having a good day," was all the nurse would say.

'Does she know we're coming?'

'We didn't tell her.'

'Aye, why spoil her day.'

They found Maggie in a small sitting room with plastic chairs and high windows. Barlow glanced out and could only see clouds.

Maggie wore a dressing gown and slippers. The clothes clung to the bones on her shoulders and her breasts had shrivelled. She allowed Vera a hug, but only fluttered fingers at him.

Vera cried. He ached to cry as well. After a minute or two, Maggie's attention faded. He wanted to hold her hand, but found himself frozen in the seat. Vera filled the silence with talk about school and homework. Little details she never told him. Especially the odd criminal activity some of her friends got up to.

A nurse came and said that the psychiatrist wanted to see him, that she'd stay with Vera and Maggie. The nurse didn't have to say it. They had Maggie on suicide alert.

The psychiatrist's office was down the corridor. The office was small and cramped, little larger than a double ward. The psychiatrist and Barlow had got to know each other over the years. The only new thing about Maggie's condition this time was the violence.

The psychiatrist asked for more details and listened to Barlow, nodding sympathetically now and again. 'It happens. Schizophrenics have two or more personalities. Hate and love are at opposite ends of the spectrum, and right now, Sergeant, Maggie has unfortunately set her mind against you.'

'Will it improve, Doctor? Will she get better?'

'We'll do our best.'

"Do their best?" *They've been doing that for half a lifetime.*

Alexandra came to mind: sharing cigarettes, lying in the warmth of her arms, listening to the dawn chorus outside the window. He bowed his face in his hands. It was wrong to pray to God for an immoral love, yet he couldn't bring himself to pray for Maggie. All he could ask was for help to get through that day.

The psychiatrist said, 'I'm so sorry about that young policeman. I feel responsible.'

Barlow looked up, puzzled. He hadn't noticed before, but the psychiatrist had been crying. Was crying now.

The psychiatrist wiped his tears and blew his nose. 'Sorry, sorry. You have your own problems.'

'Doc, what do you mean "responsible"?'

'I gave Adenauer unaccompanied ground parole.'

Barlow frowned. 'What does that mean?'

'I let him walk in our grounds unescorted.' He held up a thick file as if in justification. Adenauer's name was on the front. 'He responded well to treatment. I was starting to think in terms of a release date.'

The psychiatrist's words speeded up as he tried to get them out before tears choked him. 'He fooled me, and now that young fellow is dead.' He started to cry again.

Barlow said, 'Could Adenauer and the Frau – Mrs Taylor – have arranged his escape during one of her visits?' He waited for the tears to ease, then asked, 'Well, Doc?'

The psychiatrist said, 'She came once, but we had to turn her away. There's a court order banning her from seeing him. She may be a material witness.'

Barlow got out one of his imaginary sweets and had a good chew. 'I thought it might be something like that.'

CHAPTER 64

GILLESPIE WAS WAITING WITH THE squad car engine running when Barlow arrived into the station yard in the shooting-brake. Barlow swung himself into the passenger seat and they set off.

'Tensley's farm,' said Gillespie without any preamble. 'Over the tin bridge. Out the Belfast Road, then turn onto the Raven-hill Road.'

'Why?'

'Denholm Moncrief runs about with a group of equal-ly-minded young thugs. Timothy Tensley is the only one who lives near River Road.'

'Right,' said Barlow and sank into his own misery. Maggie dying would cause as many complications as Maggie alive. *My God, suicide watch*! He ignored Gillespie's anxious glances. *Some things you keep to yourself.*

Tensley's farm, he recalled, trying to distract himself from his woes, was the talk of the countryside. One thousand rolling acres of quality farmland in an area where forty acres would rear a family in comfort. One hundred milk cows, whereas the ordinary farmer made do with half a dozen. The Tensleys sent their eldest sons to Trinity College, Dublin and the youngest son became a Church of Ireland minister. The current owner of the Tensley lands, Robert William Tensley, had served in the army during the Second World War. *The Hussars, of course, nothing as common as the Royal Ulster Rifles.* He liked to be addressed as Captain Tensley. Strictly, only majors and above had the authority to retain their army titles.

Captain Tensley was driving the last of the Friesian milkers into the byre when Barlow and Gillespie pulled into the yard.

He saw them approach. Turned his back on them and walked into the milking parlour.

'Bastard,' said Gillespie.

Barlow got out of the car and stalked into the milking parlour. Tensley, he noted, stood watching as a stockman chivvied the cows into their individual stalls. Another man placed the restraining chain around their necks. Tensley was in shirtsleeves and had a deep tan in the V of his neck.

'Captain, I'd like a word.'

'Can't you see I'm busy?' He didn't even have the manners to look around as he spoke.

'Sir, this is urgent.'

'Try again tomorrow.'

Barlow rammed the captain past the surprised stockmen and pinned him against the hayrack. The cows on either side moved nervously. Their horns swept the air terrifyingly close to Barlow's face. 'Now.' And added as an afterthought. 'Please.'

He wondered if he'd gone too far. But Harvey had said "any means", and he was in no mood for people who mucked him around.

'I'll have your pension for this,' spluttered Tensley.

His men abandoned tending the cattle and came to help their boss. Gillespie's bulk filled the doorway. 'Now, boys, go about your business.' Without a leader to take the initiative, they backed off.

Barlow eased his grip on Tensley. The captain straightened and brushed himself down. 'The estate office,' he said and stalked across the yard to a range of lean-to buildings. Boughs of venerable fruit trees overhung the sloping roof. An old Victorian dining table served as a desk. The chairs were made of a functional white wood, darkened by use and by age. The room was dull. The back wall backed onto the orchard and had no window. The front wall window featured just four small panes of glass, set in a heavy wooden frame.

Tensley clicked on the light and picked up the phone. He dialled zero. 'Operator, put me through to the Ballymena police station.'

Gillespie came hard on Barlow's heels. He whispered. 'Go easy. We're only guessing here.'

Barlow said, 'Sir, I'd like to ask you a few questions about the day Stoop Taylor died.'

He let Tensley make his call to the police station. No, District Inspector Harvey was not available. Nor Inspector Foxwood either. Tensley left a message for them to contact him at the earliest opportunity. He hung up and started to dial another number.

Barlow moved closer. 'Sir, may I ask who you are calling now.'

He got a look down a haughty nose. 'My solicitor, Mr Moncrief.'

That supercilious attitude infuriated Barlow even more. Any class the Tensley's could lay claim to, they had married into. Captain Tensley's great-grandfather, Barlow knew for definite, had been an itinerant cattle drover.

He drew his truncheon and smashed it down on the telephone. Bits of Bakelite scattered across the room.

'Gawd,' muttered Gillespie and took a half-step towards the door.

'Sir, I repeat, I am here about the death of Stoop Taylor.' He gave the phone another thump to make sure it stayed out of action. 'If you contact Mr Moncrief's office I will place you under arrest. The charge will be "attempting to pervert the course of justice".'

He breathed hard into Tensley's face. 'Do I make myself understood?'

Tensley sat down and folded his arms. 'Sergeant, I have no intention of speaking to you without a solicitor present.' He looked pleased with himself, like he had time on his side.

Barlow nodded. Not only had the great-grandfather been an itinerant drover, he'd made his money by stealing cattle. More than a drop of Dunlop blood coursed in the Tensley veins – and the Dunlop bloody-mindedness.

He made himself comfortable on the edge of the desk, with his leg almost touching Tensley's arm. 'Sir,' he said in his most reasonable voice. 'Policemen don't like colleagues being shot. When that happens, they expect full cooperation from the public. When people fail to cooperate, it's not forgotten. Either by the police themselves.' He paused for effect. 'Or by their families.'

Gillespie said, 'You do have sons, sir?' He pulled out his notebook and flicked through the pages. 'Now, last week, your youngest boy – Timothy, isn't it?'

Barlow said, 'You get the picture, sir.'

Uncertainty flickered in Tensley's face. 'But Denholm didn't do anything.'

Barlow put his hand behind his back and gave Gillespie a thumbs-up. 'Perhaps you would care to tell us what he did do?' From here on there would be no "sirs", even sarcastic ones.

Now, Tensley was anxious to talk. First, he qualified his statement with "don't knows … I'm sure it's only a coincidence … Not a boy of that breeding."

Around lunchtime on the day Stoop died, Denholm cycled into the yard, looking for Tensley's son, Timothy. Timothy was away for the day. Denholm had a rifle slung over his back.

Gillespie asked, 'What sort of rifle?'

Tensley became vague. 'I never really looked at it.'

Gillespie persisted. 'An M1 carbine?'

'I don't really know. Something small anyway.'

That pleased Barlow, if indeed anything could please him that day. Loyalty in the Masons only went so far. There had to be a way of turning that crack into a rift. Break up the bosses' comfortable monopoly.

Tensley continued with his statement. Denholm had asked to use the phone to ring his father. They talked for a long time. Denholm cried on the phone, Tensley was sure of that. Moncrief came and picked his son up in the car. Denholm collected his bike the next weekend.

'What sort of bike?'

'A Raleigh Rapide.'

Barlow nodded at Gillespie who was writing out the statement. 'Put that down as well. A Raleigh Rapide racing bike.'

They finished the statement. Tensley read it over carefully and then signed it.

Barlow picked up his cap. His hands were shaking from a combination of both anger and fatigue. It made him wonder if he'd ever get over the stabbing by Maggie. Tensley sat at the desk, no longer a confident man.

Barlow leaned close enough for Tensley to pull back a bit. 'Sir, forget about charges of conspiracy and perversion of justice. You contact anybody. You get anybody to contact anybody. Anybody contacts anybody, and I'll break your bloody neck.

CHAPTER 65

'You took one hell of a risk,' said Gillespie when they were back in the car.

'So did you, pretending you had something on the son.'

Gillespie laughed. 'I'd soon get something on him if I had to.' He put on the siren.

'We're not in that big a hurry,' Barlow said, needing time to think through his next move.

'Indulge me, Sarge.'

The car surged forward. Gillespie flicked it round the bends. Once on the main road, he put the boot to the floor.

Barlow looked across at Gillespie. The years and marriage had been good to him. The first time they met, Gillespie had a jumper-full of apples progged from an orchard. The cheeky bugger had offered to sell him one.

Barlow said, 'Remember the time your Richard took a knife to school and threatened to cut someone?'

The car wobbled into the path of an oncoming beer lorry. Gillespie hauled it back onto their side of the road. The lorry driver shook his fist at them as they flew past. In a way, Barlow wouldn't have minded an impact. He was dreading the prospect of everything else he had to do that day.

'Don't even go down that road,' said Gillespie, when he had the car straightened. 'I still get nightmares thinking about it.'

Barlow persisted. 'Not just any knife, but a Gurkha kukri. He had it honed to needlepoint sharpness.'

'You should have seen his backside after I'd finished with it.'

'Aye, but what did you do with the knife?'

Gillespie got impatient, as Barlow knew he would, hating to be prodded into conversations he didn't want to get involved in. 'I dropped it overboard the next time I went fishing.'

'And before that?'

'I kept it in my locker at the station.'

The annoyed look disappeared from Gillespie's face. He looked over. 'That's what you're thinking – the rifle. Moncrief wouldn't trust Denholm again. He'd keep the rifle in the office where Denholm couldn't get at it.'

Barlow checked his watch, 5.50pm. Moncrief's office would be closing soon, if it wasn't already closed. He leaned forward and gave the siren another blast. 'Can't you go any faster?'

They made it with a minute to spare. Gillespie parked across from the office. Lights still burned in most of the front rooms, although the front door was shut. The door would take more than a shoulder to burst it open. It was wood-panelled and set in stone.

Gillespie said, 'Sarge, we need a search warrant.'

Barlow pointed to a darkened window. 'Moncrief's gone for the day. He'll be at the Masonic Hall by now.'

'So what, it's just round the corner?'

'With this Adenauer hunt going on, would you by any chance have a Lee Enfield in the boot?'

'Bloody right. I'm not going up against that man with anything less.'

Barlow pointed at the telephone wires running across the wall of the offices. 'I don't fancy anyone contacting Moncrief while we're there, do you?'

Gillespie rested his head on the steering wheel. 'I'm not hearing this.' He slapped Barlow's hand away when he stretched for the ignition key. 'If I'm going to lose my pension, I'll do it myself, thank you.'

They got out of the car. The street was quiet with businesses locked up for the day. Gillespie unlocked the boot and pulled out a Lee Enfield. Pushed in a clip of bullets and worked a round into the breech.

People hung around Fetherton's newsagents at the far corner. Barlow moved to block their view while Gillespie used the roof of the car to steady his aim. The shot thundered in the street, echoed in its silence. Moncrief's telephone line whipped into the air.

'Policing was a nice cushy job,' said Gillespie regretfully.

'You could make Inspector yet, if you shifted yourself,' said Barlow as Moncrief's front door opened and a young secretary appeared holding a bundle of letters for the last post. He charged across the street and carried her back into the hallway. Found himself breathless with excitement as he blocked the secretary from slipping away. 'Where's the vault?'

The secretary had gone white. Letters slipped from her hands to the floor. She pointed to an inner door.

'Show me, love.' He made the "love" deliberate. The young girl had to know she personally wasn't in any trouble. He helped her pick up the dropped letters. She almost dared to say "thank you". They went through the inner door into a wide hallway. Gillespie came hard on their heels.

The vault was right in front of them, the door still open. Shelves of files lined the walls. Boxes and trunks were stashed in every corner: such and such a trust, the estate of the honourable someone or other.

Barlow hesitated. He'd assumed a room full of papers and the rifle stuck behind the door. This vault would take forever to search. He probably had two minutes, five at the most.

He smiled down at the secretary. 'Where's the gun kept, love?'

She pointed to a high shelf. The files on that shelf were stacked upright. On all the other shelves they lay on their sides, spines sticking out. *Should have seen that for myself.* He jumped onto a wooden trunk with a curved lid and reached up. The lid cracked under his boots.

A male voice said, 'What do you think you're doing?'

He glanced back. A young solicitor with slicked-back hair and the early gloss of Moncrief's grooming stood in the doorway. Barlow shrugged and slid a hand between the files. He could feel something, leather definitely.

'Get out!' said the young solicitor.

He searched along the leather, *there has to be a handle.* Files fell from the shelf, their papers scattered across the vault floor. He found the handle and hauled. The weight of files coming down around him made him duck. The edge of one caught his wound and he shuddered a breath through clenched teeth.

The young solicitor asked, 'What are you looking for? Where's your search warrant?'

'In the morgue.'

Gillespie looked like he was praying.

Other people gathered in the hallway. An older woman tried to swing the vault door shut, trapping them inside. Gillespie put his foot in the doorway and blocked it open.

The leather case was the length and thickness of a gun case. Barlow dumped it on the trunk and clicked back the catches.

'I'm warning you,' said the young solicitor.

A woman came out of an office. 'I can't get through. There's no dial tone.'

'Run then,' said the young solicitor and she disappeared. Barlow noted that she went to get her coat first.

He opened the case. A .22 rifle lay recessed in a shaped bed of green baize. Other recesses held boxes of ammunition and cleaning rods.

He held up the case for the young solicitor to see. 'Did you know about this?'

'Ye ... No.'

He thought the young man would do well in court. He was a quick thinker. *Pity it's all the wrong training.*

He said, 'That's a good thing, or I'd have you up in court. An unlicensed rifle, and an automatic at that. Someone's going to get six months.'

Bloody Moncrief was going down. *Serve him right for Jackson.*

CHAPTER 66

THE MASONIC HALL TOOK UP the middle floor of a mid-terrace Georgian building. The front door opened to Barlow's push. The woman from Moncrief's office sent to fetch her boss could be seen struggling up the hill behind them. Gillespie beeped the horn and drove off. Barlow ran up the stairs two at a time.

At the top he stopped and listened. The clack of billiard balls came from the front of the building. He turned in that direction. An appalled silence filled the Billiards Room when he walked in; he took careful note of who was there. Moncrief stood warming his hands at the fire. Other members sat around with their drinks. Mayor Fetherton and Captain Denton sat at separate tables, he noted, which might be important for his enquiries.

He placed the gun case on the billiards table, scattering a rack of red balls in the process. He clicked the case open. For a moment, the only movement in the room was the swirl of cigarette smoke under the centre light.

Mayor Fetherton choked on his drink. 'This is outrageous.'

Barlow said, 'Mr Moncrief, would you care to identify your own rifle?'

'How dare you burst in here?' said Moncrief.

Denton sat deep in a leather chair: a glass of brandy in one hand, a cigar in the other. He asked in a casual tone, 'Moncrief, is it yours?'

Everyone else backed off a little. Barlow thought it showed a crack in their joint resolve. If he got to stay on in Ballymena, let alone in the RUC, he'd make a point of breaking up their self-serving cartel.

Moncrief walked over to the billiards table. 'I have to look at it first.'

His speed nearly caught Barlow off guard. He had to slam the case shut, almost nipping Moncrief's fingers. 'Now, sir, you don't want to get your fingerprints on it, accidental like.' He raised an eyebrow. 'Not until we identify the ones that got there deliberately. If you see what I mean.'

Moncrief reddened with fury. 'If you dared seize that rifle without a search warrant … '

'Sir, as I told the young man in your office, my search warrant is lying in the morgue.' That caused a stir among the listeners.

Just then, the woman tapped on the door and came into the room. She pointed at Barlow. 'Mr Moncrief, he took the gun.'

Barlow could have kissed her. She'd identified Moncrief as being in possession of the gun, if not the actual owner. And in front of witnesses.

Moncrief's face went mottled red. 'Get out,' he screamed at her. She fled.

'Mr Moncrief, you are under arrest for possession of an illegal firearm, namely a .22 automatic rifle. For being an accessory before and after the fact. For conspiracy to pervert the course of justice. For withholding information vital to the solving of three murders.' He blamed his light head on hunger. He hadn't eaten since breakfast. But he needed to get the last dig in. 'And for being a supercilious, dyed-in-the-wool pain-in-the-ass.'

He pulled out his handcuffs. 'Please turn around and put your hands behind your back.'

Fetherton stood and pointed at Denton. 'Charles, do something. This is outrageous. How dare he arrest a man of Moncrief's standing.'

Denton stood up as well. 'Fetherton, before you get so righteous over Moncrief, could you explain something to me? You've a contract with the army to provide a fixed amount of beef every month. Yet, the number of beasts bought by you from dealers varies month by month.'

Both men were too heavily built to go toe-to-toe. Denton pushed his stomach against Fetherton's, nudging him backwards. 'The difference is always the number of cattle stolen by the Dunlops in that month.' He nudged again as a gasp went around the room.

'I lost six prime bullocks,' said a voice.

'I lost four,' said another.

Denton turned away from Fetherton and toasted Barlow with a sip of his brandy. Barlow wished he could return the compliment. Fetherton might somehow avoid the charges of watering down milk, but he'd never survive being caught stealing from fellow club members. The Fetherton empire was finished, the schoolchildren's milk safe until the next contractor figured out he could cut corners.

Meanwhile, Moncrief had slipped around the billiards table, and was heading for the door.

Barlow cursed himself for taking his eye off the man. He called out. 'Moncrief, you're under arrest.'

'An illegal arrest after an illegal search,' said Moncrief, grandstanding for his friends. It also, Barlow realised, set up his defence for refusing to be handcuffed.

He knew that if he chased Moncrief there would be a struggle. Moncrief would claim police brutality. Well, two could grandstand.

He drew his revolver. 'Last warning,' he said.

Moncrief laughed. 'You wouldn't dare.' He pulled the door open.

Barlow fired. The door slammed shut. Moncrief screamed and fell to the ground. The smell of gunpowder hung rancid in the air.

Barlow wondered if he could resign and save his pension before Harvey had him prosecuted.

'You shot him,' said Fetherton and fainted. The wooden floor flexed under his crushing weight. Glasses in the bar clinked together. Denton's cigar dropped to the floor and was recovered with a curse. Nobody else spoke or moved. Barlow faced them, smoking revolver in hand.

He holstered his revolver and walked around the table. Moncrief lay nursing his wrist. A sliver of wood had caught his cheek. He hadn't yet noticed the blood.

In a way, Barlow couldn't believe the man he'd now become. Up until a few weeks ago, he had kept the weapon unloaded. Now every chamber was filled.

He examined the door. The bullet had ripped out a splinter of wood. *Hopefully, it stopped in the far wall,* hadn't gone through far enough to annoy the neighbours.

'My wrist is broken,' said Moncrief.

Barlow wrinkled his nose as if smelling something offensive. 'And you've wet your pants.'

'I have not.'

'Whatever you say, sir.' He looked at the other club members and raised his eyes as if to say, "Why argue?" Moncrief might deny wetting himself, on a stack of Bibles. But he'd be sniggered at for the rest of his life.

He rolled Moncrief onto his face and handcuffed him. Moncrief refused to get to his feet unaided. Barlow grabbed him by the collar and heaved, which further added to his indignity.

Barlow picked up the gun case and advised the prisoner. 'You can either walk like a Christian, or be dragged. The choice is yours.'

Denton opened the door for them. Moncrief went quietly, his back stiff with wounded pride. Behind them, the room burst into indignant talk. Fetherton came in for a lot of abuse.

Barlow allowed himself to feel pleased. In a way, they weren't a bad bunch. Arrogant perhaps, but they'd done a lot for the town, kept people in work through bad times. Now they'd been warned. Maybe in future they'd go for the icing instead of taking the cream and cherry on top.

He nodded in approval when they reached the street because constables Clarke and Mitchell were already waiting there with the second squad car. Their mouths opened when they saw Moncrief.

Barlow held up the gun case. 'If you two had done your job properly in the first place, Jackson might still be alive.'

He wanted them to share some of the guilt. He couldn't bear to admit the truth to himself. *If only I'd acted sooner.* Jackson's death, he bitterly acknowledged to himself, was his fault and nobody else's.

CHAPTER 67

CLARKE AND MITCHELL MIGHT HAVE fouled up on the checkpoint issue, but they knew how to take their revenge without being told. They didn't slip Moncrief in through the rear yard. Barlow stood and watched as they parked the car at the front door and made a fuss of getting Moncrief out of the back seat. A crowd had gathered before they'd finished. The two constables addressed their prisoner by name several times so that no one would be in any doubt as to whom they'd arrested.

The cut on Moncrief's face was little more than a nick. Barlow said loudly, 'Moncrief wants a doctor to check that. He thinks it might need a stitch.'

The look Moncrief gave him, he should have dropped dead on the spot. In a way, he wouldn't have minded. He'd teased Jackson mercilessly and Jackson had still been grateful for his mentoring. If only he could make a full report to Harvey and go shut himself safely inside his own house while events took their turn.

Three people lay dead. Stoop's death he couldn't have prevented. Young Peter's, maybe, but Jackson certainly should still be alive. Whatever had to be done he had to do himself. No more innocent people must be put at risk. He came to that decision as they escorted Moncrief into the Enquiry Office room and called for the fingerprint kit. Leary came running with it.

He explained to Leary about the rifle and where it had been found. Leary lifted the gun case reverently into his arms. He would personally check it for fingerprints. Barlow reckoned he was good for a couple of biscuits the next time he took tea in the detectives' room.

Other officers came into the Enquiry Office: people either on regular duties or resting up between searches for Adenauer. They stood in a sour half-circle around Moncrief.

Barlow frowned, but said nothing as he took off the handcuffs and opened the fingerprint kit. Moncrief refused to hold out his left hand. 'It's broken,' he complained.

'At least you're still alive to feel it,' somebody said.

'Maybe not much longer,' somebody else added.

'That's enough, boys.'

Moncrief's attempt to dominate the situation faded. 'I'm entitled to a solicitor of my choice being present,' he said.

'As a prisoner, you're also entitled to slop out the toilets, so shut up.'

'And I need a doctor.'

WPC Day asked, 'Do you really want the police doctor?'

That raised a laugh. Barlow managed a smile at the thought of the local police doctor examining Moncrief's hand. The man was rough and ready with his treatment. Any injury was bound to be sore after he'd finished.

Moncrief looked at the men closing in around him and allowed himself to be fingerprinted. Conscious of pending complaints of brutality, Barlow thought it best to do the fingerprinting himself. He let Moncrief hold the damaged hand steady while he rolled the card round the whorls on each fingertip.

Nothing more could be done until Harvey arrived back from the search for Adenauer. Moncrief made his permitted phone call. One of his junior partners agreed to represent him.

Barlow read him his rights and then personally escorted him to a cell. He didn't want Moncrief being tripped up on the stairs. After that, he sat in the kitchen and drank cups of tea while WPC Day fussed around making a three-egg omelette and worrying about him.

He was finishing up the omelette when Gillespie drove into the yard with Harvey in the back seat. Harvey stormed off into his office. Gillespie wandered into the kitchen. He had dried blood on his face.

Barlow said, 'Are you telling me that Denholm Moncrief, a schoolboy, managed to head-butt you?'

'Resisting arrest, wasn't he?' said Gillespie, and smirked.

Barlow pushed the remains of the omelette in his direction. 'You're as bad as me, in your own sweet way.'

Harvey sent for Leary instead of Barlow. A few minutes later, Moncrief followed Leary into Harvey's office.

Barlow loosened his belt and tried to relax. He would give Harvey half an hour; after that he had things to do that couldn't wait.

CHAPTER 68

AT THE END OF THE half hour, Barlow creaked to his feet intending to take the shooting-brake and head out. Sergeant Pierson was back on duty. He intercepted Barlow as he was trying to stretch the many aches and pains out of his abused body.

'Harvey wants to see you immediately.' Pierson said, putting great emphasis on the "immediately".

Barlow found Harvey sitting poised behind his desk. The District Inspector had changed into a fresh uniform. His muddy wellingtons stood in a corner. Both Moncrief and his junior partner were also there, looking pleased, which didn't bode well for Barlow. WPC Day sat in a corner, pencil poised over a notebook, ready to take notes.

Barlow snapped to attention, honouring the Queen and not the District Inspector. He'd riled Harvey often enough to recognise the symptoms of a man burning with fury.

'Barlow, Mr Moncrief has made a list of complaints against you. The least of which is an allegation of police brutality.'

He said nothing, cautious in case a simple yes could be deemed an admission.

'In addition, Mr Moncrief has detailed several charges. Charges that you levelled against him in public and in a manner designed to reduce his standing in the community. He is threatening to sue the police force for defamation of character.'

'Indeed, sir.'

'He also alleges that you tried to murder him.'

Barlow chewed on an imaginary sweet for a moment. He decided he could safely say, 'If I'd wanted him dead, he'd be dead.'

'He further alleges that you discharged a police-issue revolver in the Masonic Hall.' Harvey's voice rose in pitch at the insult to a revered institution. 'In the Billiards Room.'

'Those old Webleys make one hell of a racket, sir.'

Harvey closed his eyes. 'Barlow, don't try to rile me. I've got enough problems.' He opened his eyes again. 'Final point.' His finger tapped a scribbled note on the page in front of him. 'You made an illegal search of Mr Moncrief's offices.'

'Sir, obtaining a search warrant takes time. I didn't want the evidence to disappear.'

Harvey frowned. He hadn't forgotten his own excuse for searching Stoop's house without a warrant. Nor had Mr Comberton apparently. He harped on about it at every opportunity.

To Barlow's surprise, Harvey didn't claim that this was a different case and different circumstances. Instead he turned to Moncrief. 'As I understand it, Barlow failed to present a properly executed search warrant. A search warrant, which he'd neither requested nor obtained.' Harvey kept going down his list of notes. 'He also forced his way into your offices, invaded your vault without permission, sent important files scattering and removed items without the permission of the solicitor present.'

Moncrief glowed with pleasure. 'And he was rude to my staff.'

'So he did all these things?' asked Harvey.

'Yes,' said Moncrief. 'Yes.'

'No,' said the junior partner. 'No.'

'And this shooting,' said Harvey, rushing his pen down the list. 'Why did he try to shoot you?'

Barlow kept an eye on the portrait of the Queen. For a penny he'd damn them all to Hell and leave. He had things to do, and the longer he delayed the harder it got.

Moncrief hesitated between changing his "yes" to a "no", and hanging Barlow properly in the process. He went for the hanging. 'In my opinion the arrest was an illegal act. I had no intention of letting Barlow handcuff me – '

'Sir,' said the junior partner half way between panic and a warning.

'– let alone accompany him to the police station,' finished Moncrief.

'Mr Moncrief, you've already been formally charged,' the junior partner interjected, 'anything you say... ' He collapsed his head into his hands.

The certainty left Moncrief. 'Of course when I said ... And the rifle ... I meant I had no prior knowledge.'

'Of course,' said Harvey smoothly, and buzzed for Leary to come in.

Barlow chewed hard on his sweet and wondered what the hell was going on. Especially when Harvey pointed to a chair beside WPC Day and said, 'Sit down, Barlow, you're supposed to be on sick leave.'

Barlow sat down beside WPC Day. His arms moved restlessly. He folded them to still his nervousness. What Harvey was up to was beyond him.

He looked over at the notebook on WPC Day's lap. The page was covered in shorthand hieroglyphics. 'Did you get all that?'

She gave his knee a friendly bump with hers. 'Not the bit about you being on sick leave.'

Harvey asked him, 'What was the distance between you and Mr Moncrief when you discharged your weapon?'

He felt that a safe question to answer. Unlike Moncrief, he hadn't been charged yet. 'The breadth of the table.'

'And you hit?'

'The door.'

Harvey turned to Moncrief. 'So how did your wrist get hurt?'

'Don't answer that,' said the junior partner.

'He was opening the door with the intention of evading arrest,' volunteered Barlow.

Out of the corner of his eye he saw WPC Day furiously scribble that down.

He added. 'The force of the bullet knocked the door out of Moncrief's hand. That's what caused the alleged injury.'

'It's broken,' snapped Moncrief.

'Rubbish!' said Barlow.

Leary knocked and entered. 'Report,' said Harvey.

Leary looked like a man who had dropped a penny and found a gold sovereign. 'Sir, the rifle recovered by Sergeant Barlow is a Ruger 10/22 semi-automatic rifle.'

Barlow got the impression that Leary actually winked at him before continuing.

'This rifle is unlicensed. In fact, the late District Inspector refused to license semi-automatics under any circumstances. Unfortunately,' added Leary in a "so what" tone, 'the rifle is a rimfire. Accordingly, we cannot tie it in with the empty shells found in Stoop Taylor's manure pit.'

'However,' he paused and licked his lips as if savouring a celebratory pint after work, 'I am confident that ballistics will be able to match a bullet from this rifle with the one recovered from the back end of the bullock.'

He stopped to draw breath. He looked pleased with himself.

'Fingerprints?' asked Harvey.

'Nothing,' said Leary and paused again.

Barlow allowed himself a suck on the imaginary sweet. This question-and-answer routine sounded like something prearranged between the two men. What was he being set up for? Maybe that wink had been a warning? Especially as Moncrief had started to look confident again.

'Nothing?' queried Harvey.

'Nothing on the green baize, but on the stock and barrel of the rifle, plenty.'

Barlow breathed easier. Someone had handled that rifle. Not himself. He wasn't that stupid or that careless, but Moncrief had been. He could see it in the lengthening of his jowls.

'Mr Moncrief's fingerprints are all over the rifle,' said Leary. 'Beautifully clear prints that would stand up in any court.'

Moncrief made a choking sound that passed for a cough. 'Mr Harvey, if we could have a word in private?'

The fix was on. The old boys' network was alive and well. Barlow spat the imaginary sweet out of his mouth in disgust.

Harvey heard the spitting sound and frowned. It appeared to distract him from Moncrief's request. 'Anything else?' he asked Leary.

'We also found Denholm Moncrief's fingerprints. Especially on the trigger and around the firing mechanism.'

Moncrief jumped to his feet, white-faced. 'You're bluffing.'

Right now, he wasn't a solicitor. He was a father suffering for his child. Barlow felt almost sorry for him. *What if it was Vera?* he asked himself as he said with a gentleness that surprised him. 'Denholm is currently under arrest. He assaulted an officer in the lawful execution of his duty.'

Leary added. 'Constable Gillespie is currently in hospital having facial injuries treated.'

Moncrief said to Harvey. 'Perhaps if we could … ' He made a gesture as if to banish everyone else from the room.

Harvey made to stand up, then seemed to realise that he hadn't the height to intimidate Moncrief. 'Mr Moncrief, the time for private conversations is long past. I have three deaths on my hands and a dangerous fugitive on the loose. Thanks to you, we have wasted hundreds of police hours trying to trace a gunman who may or may not have vital information about the recent killings.'

Moncrief's hands joined in supplication. 'He's my son.'

'And I, as District Inspector, have to draw a line somewhere. You Mr Moncrief are well over it.'

Barlow gulped in surprise. This was a Harvey that he thought didn't exist.

Harvey turned to Leary, 'Take Moncrief away. The charges against him are: possession of an illegal weapon, prior knowledge, knowledge after the fact and conspiracy. Write up the charges and I'll endorse them.'

Heavens. Something he'd dreamed of for years: Moncrief in prison.

WPC Day was scribbling furiously to catch up. 'And the son?' she asked.

'Possibly murder.'

'No,' said Barlow.

CHAPTER 69

Everyone froze at Barlow's "no". He was as surprised as the rest of them.

'No,' he repeated and tried to unscramble his thoughts. He got to his feet and moved about the room, restlessly. 'This thing finishes today.'

He stayed well back from the rest of the people in the room as if distancing himself from his own words. 'First, District Inspector Harvey, bearing in mind what you said earlier in the year, I must first declare a personal element.' He paused to get the tone of his voice right. He didn't want it to sound bitter. 'Moncrief and I are first cousins.'

Surprise rippled through everyone in the room.

'First cousins,' he repeated. 'Moncrief's uncle seduced my mother with promises of marriage and then abandoned her.'

Harvey's eyes went from Barlow to Moncrief. Moncrief nodded.

Harvey pointed a finger at first Leary and then WPC Day. 'This stays in this room. I don't want to hear it repeated around the station.'

'Thank you,' said Moncrief.

'Bloody right,' said Barlow.

That declaration was the easy bit. For what he had to do next he wanted to punch a wall. Maybe a broken hand would take away the pain he felt.

'Denholm had a rifle on the day of the shooting. He was in the vicinity of River Road. And he was seen to be distressed and upset.' He looked over at Moncrief. 'Captain Tensley made a written statement to that effect.'

Tension made him pace an area confined by the feet of others. 'If we charge the Moncriefs, all we'll ever get is evasions, half-truths and lies.' He thumped his chest with his fist. 'I have to know the facts. I have to know for sure.' Kept pacing as the words formed themselves in his head. 'Denholm is in the byre. There's nothing to steal and no birds to shoot at because the rain has kept them grounded. He sees the cattle and, being a Moncrief, Denholm cannot leave things alone, cannot help but do damage.'

He stopped in front of Harvey. 'Sir, give him his deal. All those charges dropped against him and his son. But only if I'm satisfied that we've been told the whole truth.'

Harvey looked shocked, Moncrief hopeful. Leary scowled at Barlow who shrugged back. The conviction of a solicitor would make the London papers and bring fame to the arresting officer. He had just scuppered Leary's certain promotion.

The junior partner acted outraged. 'I cannot agree to that. You are offering us a one-sided deal. How can we be sure you'll keep your word?'

Barlow said, 'I might be a bastard, but unlike you lot I'm a straight bastard.'

'Has my son been formally cautioned yet?' Moncrief asked.

'I made sure he wasn't.'

'So anything he says cannot be held against him?'

'That is correct.'

Harvey said, 'I don't like this arrangement. They're getting off too easy.' He looked at Barlow, puzzled. 'When you say, "finishes today" do you mean Adenauer back in custody?'

'I think so, sir.'

Harvey's eyes glazed over. He seemed to be dreaming of a full night's sleep with no nightmares.

Barlow reminded him. 'You said, "Any means, any way, no questions asked".'

'Did I?' His eyes focused again. 'I'll never understand you, Barlow.'

'We'll be forever fighting,' said Barlow.

Harvey nodded. At the prospect of them constantly fighting, or agreeing the deal, Barlow wasn't sure which. He pushed for the deal by sending Leary to bring Denholm into Harvey's office.

Meanwhile, he went and sat beside WPC Day. He needed to listen to Denholm's replies and judge their truthfulness. Not get caught up in the questioning.

'They're getting away scot-free,' WPC Day hissed.

He whispered back. 'Nobody mentioned the cattle. This station is full of tittle-tattling old women. The cruelty people are bound to hear soon enough.'

She smiled. 'Sarge, if we don't prosecute, the USPCA might do it themselves.'

'Aye,' he said and chewed nervously while he waited for Leary to bring in Denholm.

Denholm's face was blotchy from crying. His forehead had a livid mark where he'd butted Gillespie's nose. Gillespie wouldn't be pleased. He'd sacrificed an egg cupful of blood and now the culprit was going to get off. It would take more than a beer to calm him down.

Moncrief told his son what they'd agreed. With a wary eye on Barlow, he ordered him to tell the full truth. Leary and Harvey carried out the interrogation.

Denholm had gone shooting on his own because Tensley's son was at a rugby match. He claimed he'd slipped into the hayloft on the Denton Demesne to shelter from the rain.

Not that Barlow believed that, at least not entirely, but at least the boy was talking.

Yes, Denholm had shot at the cattle. No he hadn't noticed Mr Taylor's body lying in the gateway. But he had seen somebody at the far hedge. When asked for a description, he said he had a vague recollection of a tall man, but couldn't really be more precise. The noise the panicked cattle made frightened him. He was afraid someone would come to investigate. He'd immediately left the Denton Demesne and gone straight to Tensley's farm, and from there to home.

The Moncriefs and the junior partner watched Barlow nervously for his reaction. Barlow creaked his bones off the chair and borrowed a sheet of paper and a pencil from Harvey. He drew a rough sketch of the River Road. Marked in the farms along the road, and the hayloft.

He held the pencil out to Denholm. 'Show me where you saw the man.'

The pencil dithered across the page a few times before Denholm made an X. 'There I think.'

Barlow passed the page to Harvey. 'I've got everything I want.'

He walked out.

The Moncriefs tried to leave as well, but Harvey ordered them to stay. From the voice that followed Barlow down the corridor it sounded like the Moncriefs, father and son, were getting a good bollocking.

He collected his cap and drove the shooting-brake out of the station yard on his own, glad that Gillespie was still at the hospital. He didn't mind risking Gillespie's pension, but had no wish to risk the man's life. Gillespie had a young family who needed him.

He stopped at the Bridge Bar. It was full of men on their way home from work. Edward had Geordie trapped in a far corner. Their table held a medley of empty glasses, all of them on Geordie's side.

Geordie saw Barlow first and shook his fist. 'There's that bastarding Sergeant Major.'

'Really, Rifleman Dunlop.' Edward sounded reasonably sober.

Barlow joined them. Geordie's latest pint was only half drunk. He finished it for him.

Barlow said, 'If it's a fight you want, I'm your man.'

CHAPTER 70

Barlow drove, with Edward in the passenger seat. Geordie sat in the back, leaning forward between the two men. Barlow kept his window down. The stench from Geordie's belches would have knocked an elephant unconscious.

'Great car this. I wouldn't mind driving her,' said Geordie.

'You don't have a licence.'

'I've been doing a bit of lorry work recently.' Geordie gave another belch.

'Shut up,' said Barlow, trying not to breathe until the worst of the belch had passed. 'Did you really think Moncrief had forgotten all about you busting his jaw?'

Geordie's laugh sent more beer fumes his direction. 'Serve the bugger right. He got two of my mates sent to jail while we were at Catterick Camp.'

'They deserved it.'

'But not the dishonourable discharge that bastard pushed for. They were never the same men afterwards.'

Barlow thought that some day he would admit to Geordie that he knew the real story behind Moncrief's broken jaw. Geordie had thumped Moncrief for spreading lies about Barlow's mother. That blow had cost Geordie six months in an army prison. A prison that made the Crumlin Road Prison look like a holiday camp. Some day Barlow should say thank you properly, and buy the man a drink. *But not today.* And maybe not ever. Keeping Geordie out of jail was the best thank you he ever could give the man.

Edward enquired. 'May one ask why one wishes to avail of one's services?'

'You may,' Barlow said, but he was too busy with his thoughts to actually answer the question.

He turned off the main road onto River Road. Kept his eyes fixed ahead of him as they drove past Alexandra's entrance. He turned into Stoop's yard and came to a stop in the gateway.

'I could have knocked your block off nearer home,' said Geordie.

Barlow took off his gun belt and handed it to Edward. 'Stay with the car until I get back.'

For once, *thank God*, Stoop's house was clear of visitors. The old tractor sat parked near the front door. He took the keys out of the ignition and threw them to Geordie to hold.

Somebody had tidied all the odd bits of machinery into a corner. A shower of rain had left the cobbles gleaming in the dull sunlight. A lick of paint on the outhouses and the place would start to look half decent.

The front door was closed and the curtains drawn. He had to knock several times before the Frau answered.

'I sleep.' Her face was grey. She looked exhausted.

'Sorry for disturbing you, Missis. Would you give Herr Adenauer my compliments? I'd like to see him.'

The grey turned to white. 'I not understand. No man here.'

'Missis, when a man loves a woman, he's only happy when they're together. That's why Kurt Adenauer escaped, to be with you. Not logical, maybe, but then he was in a mental institution.' He ached to call on Alexandra and offer his soul in exchange for her love. Instead, he raised his voice. 'Kurt, Kurt Adenauer, it's John Barlow. I'd like a word.'

'Please, no man here.' She tried to push him off the doorstep.

'Adenauer,' called Barlow again.

He heard footsteps. Adenauer came charging down the stairs. Barlow stepped to the side as Adenauer ran straight at him. Adenauer brushed through the Frau's restraining hands and burst into the yard. Geordie and Edward and the shooting-brake blocked his escape. Geordie held up the tractor keys to show it wasn't available either. Adenauer almost pawed the ground in his frustration.

'Guten Abend, Herr Adenauer,' said Edward.

Adenauer turned on Barlow, eyes blazing, hands ready to take him by the throat. Barlow put his back comfortably against the wall. Folded his arms to show he was no threat. 'You're not ready yet to cope with Joe Public.'

The Frau pleaded. 'Nein, nein, nein.'

Adenauer spun around to check on the other two men. Geordie advanced towards him, fists raised. 'Come on, you Kraut. I've beat harder men than you.'

Adenauer gave a roar of rage and charged at Geordie. The two men crunched together in a fierce hug and fought to put the other down for a kicking. The Frau looked like she'd collapse with worry.

Barlow patted her on the shoulder. 'Go and put the kettle on, Missis. We'll be ready for a cuppa after this.' She burst into tears. 'Oh God,' said Barlow.

Adenauer and Geordie broke apart. Adenauer swung a fist. Geordie blocked the blow and punched back. Adenauer stumbled against the tractor. Geordie waited until he'd found his balance, then hit him again. Adenauer thumped Geordie in return.

The fight followed the slope of the yard, down among the machinery. The two men traded blows with the minimum attempt at defence. Stood close and battered ribs and stomach. A grunt of effort accompanied every swing.

Barlow needed Geordie to win. He didn't know what he'd do if he lost. A carload of policemen parked up the road would've been handy for back-up. *Maybe I could send in Edward?* Edward was like a spider. He'd still keep trying, even if all his arms and legs were snapped off.

Geordie backed into the handle of a plough and ricocheted off. 'Bastarding thing.'

The two men stopped and drew breath.

Geordie gave the plough a kick. 'The old bugger only gave me a couple of quid for it.'

Barlow called out. 'When did you ever have a plough to sell?'

'Don't ask,' said Geordie and took another swing at Adenauer.

Adenauer thumped back, but they were both running out of steam. Geordie was ageing and overweight. Adenauer had been ill and unable to exercise properly for weeks.

Barlow linked the Frau's arm in his and made her walk down the yard with him. The next time the two men stopped for a breather Barlow and the Frau got between them.

'Enough,' Barlow told Geordie.

'Is sufficient unto the day,' said Edward who had followed them down.

The Frau just gripped Adenauer's fists and cried. The fists became gentle arms hugging her to him.

'We could all do with a cup of tea,' said Barlow.

CHAPTER 71

To Barlow the small living room seemed empty without young Peter – and Jackson. The Frau, he noticed, had resurrected some old ornaments and vases and put them on display. They gave the house a sense of purpose, of being a home. Peter's photograph had pride of place on the mantelpiece, with a black ribbon draped over it.

He and Geordie took seats between Adenauer and the door. The Frau used hot water and Dettol on raw knuckles and scraped ribs.

With their shirts off, Adenauer was all rib and bone, while Geordie's stomach rolled over his waistband. One time, way back, it had been all muscle. Barlow felt sad at seeing an old comrade age. There again, if it came to another fight between the two of them, a dig under the ribs would do Geordie a lot of damage.

The Frau clucked away at both men in German. Edward didn't have to translate. They all knew she was marvelling at the stupidity of people who felt compelled to fight. Every time she looked at Barlow he saw hope in her eyes. He'd never seen that in them before.

Edward came in with a tray of tea and a plate piled high with sandwiches.

'Frau Taylor says the neighbours have been very generous.' Edward smiled over at Adenauer. 'Deniable of course, but she says Herr Adenauer hid in the attic any time visitors called.

Barlow glared at the Frau. 'You mean, of course, Herr Reinhardt of the Waffen-SS Polizei Division.'

Geordie wrinkled his nose. 'And a bloody officer too. I can smell them.'

Edward said, 'One hopes one is not being personal.'

The Frau looked frightened. The man who had once been her husband took her hand and put it to his lips. Barlow could only marvel at Adenauer. Hardly ten minutes before he had been in a murderous rage. Now he was the tender lover.

Barlow spoke slowly while the Frau translated for him. He wanted Adenauer to understand that he knew, or guessed, part of his story. 'The Waffen-SS Polizei were formed from the ranks of the ordinary police forces of pre-war Germany. When Jackson fell into the river the old police instinct to help a comrade in trouble surfaced.'

Adenauer spoke in German. Edward translated. 'He's heard of the death of Constable Jackson and expresses his condolences.'

Adenauer said something else, his voice more intense. 'He assures me he killed neither Jackson nor young Peter,' Edward added.

At the mention of Peter's name the Frau began to cry. Adenauer soothed her.

'I know he didn't kill Peter or Jackson,' Barlow said quietly.

An old burn mark disfigured Adenauer's arm just below the shoulder. Leary had mentioned it way back, when they first arrested Adenauer. He pointed to the scar. 'That was self-inflicted to destroy your SS tattoo.' It felt odd, talking to an old enemy about the war.

Adenauer nodded. With the Frau and Edward stumbling a translation, he told his story.

'My real name is Ernst Reinhardt. I was a member of the Waffen-SS Polizei division. You must understand, from 1943 onwards, people were ordered to join the Waffen-SS. They did not necessarily volunteer.

'I started as an ordinary policeman in the city of Münster in Westphalia. I was transferred into the Waffen SS in November 1944.' He hesitated before adding: 'And before you ask, yes I did see people in my unit do dreadful things to the civilian population.'

He stopped, waiting for his listeners' reaction. The Frau looked worried, Edward frowned. Barlow withheld judgment. He'd heard of one German soldier who refused to act as a guard in the concentration camps. Against all the odds, the man had not been punished, let alone shot. Perhaps Adenauer had been like that? No, he thought, not likely.

He nodded at Adenauer to continue, and took another sup of tea. Edward made a good brew.

'I took part in the retreat of the army from Poland. On the outskirts of Berlin, orders came for us to dig in and hold back the Russians as long as possible.' He shrugged. 'The Colonel ordered me to take a supply lorry to Division Headquarters to collect more ammunition. We found ourselves cut off by the advancing Russians and had to hide in a forest.'

Adenauer's voice softened. His mind, Barlow guessed, was back with his comrades in eastern Germany. 'First, came the sound of the battle: small-arms fire, mortars, heavy artillery. The shelling was so fierce the earth seemed to hang in the sky. Then the Russian Petlyakovs flew over, dropping incendiaries, and the forest burst into flames.

'We imagined the smoke held the smell of our friends burning to death. Perhaps it did.' His voice strengthened again as he fought back the memories. 'The big sounds stopped. For a long time after we heard single shots. The Russians didn't take prisoners among the SS.'

'So I heard,' said Barlow, and looked out the window. The near sky hung dull with leaden clouds. Sunset wasn't that far away and things needed speeding up. 'So, you found the body of a Kurt Adenauer and swapped your uniform and identity with him.' He pointed to Adenauer's arm. 'That's when you mutilated your arm to burn off your SS tattoo?'

Adenauer said, 'Yes,' and continued to speak through Edward. 'The real Adenauer was an Obergefreiter in the Luftwaffe. The shockwave from a bomb killed him so his uniform was intact.' Adenauer grimaced and rubbed at the burn on his leg. 'I was a bit too free with the petrol.'

He became serious again. 'The Russians captured me soon afterwards and I spent many years in the Gulags. I was one of the last prisoners to be released.'

He had simplified a big part of his wartime experiences, Barlow reckoned, *maybe not as innocent as he tries to make out?* Even so, several years in the Gulags, and more than fifteen years separated from the woman he loved, seemed punishment enough for any man.

He pushed on with his questioning, not wanting to lose remaining daylight. 'How and when did you get here?'

Adenauer seemed to sense Barlow's growing impatience to be finished with the rest of the story, and spoke quickly. 'The real Adenauer came from near Dresden, so the Russians repatriated me to the German Democratic Republic. There, everyone is paranoid about spies. I didn't dare admit to using a false name.

'For the same reason, I couldn't go looking for Kirstin.' He squeezed the Frau's hand in apology. 'The GDR is building a lot of ships and they are short of seamen. The Russians made me work on barges on the Volga. So now I am a sailor. At every German port we call into I look for old friends. Eventually, I met someone who knew of Kirstin and I came.' His hand waved vaguely around the room.

Barlow needed to keep Adenauer talking. 'Okay, you're in London. You jump ship and catch the boat train and the Liverpool ferry. What then?'

'I was lucky. I saw a lorry with Ballymena Brewery Company on the side.' He made a rubbing sign between finger and thumb. 'Some money exchanged hands and I got a lift to Ballymena. On the way into town I saw a sign for River Road. The lorry man let me off and went on.'

Recollection of the embarrassment of that day made the Frau move away from Adenauer. She fussed around the fireplace, tidying things while she gave her side of the story. 'When Ernst… Kurt,' she used that name deliberately; it was obvious she'd been training herself to think of him as that – 'walk in the farmyard that afternoon, I nearly die.' She put a hand to her chest. 'Of happiness.'

'The day Peter was killed, where did you go after you left the asylum?' Barlow asked.

Adenauer gave a bitter laugh. Edward translated. 'I didn't realise that there are two bridges in the town. I went in all sorts of directions. If I'd been here … perhaps … '

The Frau managed a smile through her heartbreak.

After fifteen years of living with Stoop? Barlow shook his head at the miserable life the Frau must have experienced. The return of Adenauer must have seemed like an apparition from Heaven. Stoop, or so the Frau recounted, was almost as happy as she was. She wanted luxuries like meat. Not just on Sundays, but during the week as well. She also demanded a new dress every year. Stoop said she could go with Adenauer and good luck to her, but the boy had to stay. In any event, Peter wanted to remain on the farm. He loved farming and the animals.

'It break my heart,' she said.

'What happened the next morning?'

'We talk all night, Kurt and me. We agree a house in town, there I see Peter often.' She looked at the picture with the black ribbon.

'And then?' asked Barlow, wanting the truth as he saw it, confirmed. Not tears.

'At breakfast we all talk. Peter say they need more land to make farm... ' She struggled for the right word.

'Viable?' suggested Edward.

'Yes, make money. My husband.'

She was referring to Stoop. Kurt scowled and she quickly rephrased it. 'Mr Taylor, he tell Peter to go school, that he will get him land.' She looked puzzled. 'Always he talk about rights and land.'

'And?' asked Barlow.

'He leave, he do not come back. Then police come.'

Anxious to be gone now, Barlow pushed hard with the questions. He wanted to know what Kurt had done that day. Her answer was always the same, stubborn. 'Kurt stay with me, all time.'

'So what were the two of you doing across the road in the hayloft?'

The Frau went bright red and rushed into the kitchen. She rattled plates to make herself busy. Adenauer looked nearly as uncomfortable. Edward seemed more to guess the answer than translate. 'After fifteen years, Kirstin and I ... ' Adenauer's hand pointed to the ceiling. 'Not here. Not for both of us.'

Maybe not for the Frau at all, Barlow reckoned. Even now, Adenauer was not a man to cross. So, they waited for the workers on the Denton Demesne to take their lunch break and then went up into the hayloft for sex.

JOHN MCALLISTER

'Dirty enough,' muttered Geordie. Edward frowned at him to be silent.

Adenauer said, 'The gunman. I can give you a description.'

As a former policeman, Adenauer's description would be perfect, but Barlow needed a quick change of subject. 'We know who it is.'

He leaned forward, wishing he could punch a hole in Adenauer's story and uncover a tissue of lies. 'Why did you take the shell cases with you?'

He watched the man's eyes for any sign of evasion as he replied in German.

Edward translated, 'I heard the cattle roaring in pain. I knew something bad had happened. People might see us leave and blame us for the shooting. I took the shell cases and threw them into the manure.'

He found it a scary thought, of being in that hayloft with a maniac, as Adenauer was at that time. If he'd come across the couple, Adenauer would have attacked, forcing him to shoot. *And if I had missed?* He decided not to dwell on that point.

Adenauer said, 'You were very professional. There was never a chance of catching you unawares.'

Buttering up is buttering up and Barlow didn't let it distract him from his chain of thought. Still, it was a compliment coming from an expert. He couldn't but feel pleased about that.

'You and the Frau that morning, did anyone see you? Have you any witnesses? Is there any evidence that you're telling the truth?'

The Frau appeared back in the doorway. She cupped her hands under her lower stomach. 'One,' she whispered.

Barlow was disgusted at himself for noticing that she'd put on weight, but not what sort.

Geordie leaned forward and said to Adenauer: 'If you fixed up that machinery down the yard, we could get a good price for it.'

The Frau translated and Adenauer nodded. Both looked pleased at having a new friend.

Geordie added. 'Maybe sell it back to the people I stole it from in the first place.'

The Frau went from being pleased to totally outraged. Her finger wagged. Adenauer must not have anything to do with this terrible man.

Barlow slipped out of the house while the other men were still laughing.

CHAPTER 72

OUT IN THE YARD THE dullness of the day had gone. Pink cotton-wool clouds stretched across the sky. The sun was a ball of hazy red, resting on the far horizon.

If only it were dawn instead of sunset, Barlow wished, because then it would be over.

His body wanted to stop and delay; his feet kept him moving. He got into the shooting-brake and reversed it out of the yard without looking. Maybe a lorry would come along and sideswipe him, then it would be someone else's job.

Nothing hit him so he drove down the River Road. At the entrance to Alexandra's farm, the dog came out of the chicken house. *Useless mongrel.* It followed the car up the laneway into the yard. He stepped out of the car holding the envelope from the pathologist giving the results of the blood tests. The dog stood beside him with its tail down. 'Go on, you cur,' he said and got a brief tail-wag in reply.

Alexandra appeared out of the open shed, carrying a billhook. She wore wellingtons, he noted, a stockman's coat and a knotted scarf protecting her clothes. There was something fresh and clean about them all. The pony trotted to the edge of the straw and whickered a greeting.

She said, 'You parked down the lane the other night and didn't come in.'

'I did.'

He took her by the hand and led her back into the shed. There was too much cheerful light outside for what had to be said. The sweet smell of the farm came off her. He breathed it in.

'Are you okay?' she asked.

'Aye, I'm fine now I've done my thinking.'

'It's none of my business.'

A grindstone and an oily cloth lay on the seat of the cart. She'd been sharpening the billhook. He slipped it out of her hand and balanced it on a nail high on the wall. 'It has to be.'

She gave an uncertain smile and touched a hand to his chest. His heart pulsed harder under her fingers as he took in the sheen of nylon between boot and coat and the fact that she'd taken time to put on lipstick. Her smile slipped as he eased the stockman's coat from her shoulders. Let it fall to the ground and ran his hands over her hips. She was wearing her best frock: green silk. The hem he thought daringly high for a woman of her age.

He said, 'If things had gone right I was hoping to renegotiate.'

She undid the buttons of his uniform jacket.

He hung it over the billhook. 'Way back then we promised no complications.'

'We did,' she agreed, almost in a whisper, and didn't even nod her head first.

He unknotted the scarf and lifted it gently off her head. Admired the fresh perm and the way her lips curled in a smile. With the heightened colour in her face, she looked almost pretty.

'I'm thinking of retiring from the force when Vera is settled in a job.'

She led the way behind the cart to the few bales of hay kept handy for the pony. She loosened her clothes for him. Her underwear was new and freshly ironed. He was careful with her nylons, not wanting them to ladder.

'Any pension coming would always go to Maggie.'

'I'd expect no less of you,' she said.

He dropped his trousers, glancing self-consciously at the laneway. This was no time for Edward or Geordie to appear.

'I was willing to work for my keep.'

She settled herself on the straw bales. 'The milk cheque runs the farm. The money I get from the calves and pigs keeps the house.'

She wriggled around, making sure the sharp ends of the hay wouldn't snag her skin. Just watching her did funny things to his tummy. *Nice things,* making him ache to hold her and protect her.

Ready for him she said, 'With permanent help I could milk another cow or two. That would've given you some beer money.'

They coupled gently. He was in no rush. It was obvious that Alexandra had been thinking things out as well. They'd both come to the same conclusion.

They dressed again without speaking.

He buttoned his uniform jacket and put on his cap. 'Tell me why you did it.'

'It's my land.' She looked at him sadly.

'The will says different.' Her lipstick had smeared slightly. *Is there any on my face?* He rubbed at his lips to be sure there wasn't. 'Once I knew, the signs became obvious.'

She burst out. 'I was married off to an old man to bring the land into my family. I've given my life for it. Nobody will take it from me. Nobody! Not even you.'

If this was what land did, he didn't want a house and garden of his own.

He asked. 'Not even Jackson or young Peter?' and moved to block her from the billhook.

She paced nervously up and down the shed. 'I thought if Peter was dead the land would be mine and she'd move away. Then it wouldn't matter anymore.'

He stopped her with his hands on both her shoulders and looked into her eyes. Realised that what he'd always taken for loneliness was something beyond sin and guilt. It was almost a relief to know that they'd lock her away forever. The very thought of a rope round that bony neck choked him. He kissed her. Hated not getting a response.

When they moved apart, she said, 'The will was made to spite Stoop. I brought the old woman into the main house. If I hadn't, she'd have died of pneumonia years before she did.'

'Maybe, but what if Stoop proved your son was by a lover and not by your husband … '

'He kept threatening to. When he came around that morning, he said this time he was going to law.' She became heated. 'He forced his way into the house and took my son's identity tags as evidence. They show his blood group as Type A.'

'Stoop said that his blood group was O so his brother's had to be O. Somehow he'd discovered that mine is O as well. He said William had to be the son of another man.'

Barlow nodded sadly. 'Some man with the blood grouping of A or AB.' He produced the pathologist's envelope from his pocket and opened it. 'The pathologist's secretary wasn't sure which Mr and Mrs Taylor of River Road her boss meant.' He thought back to his interview with the pathologist. 'Or maybe she was told to be unsure, so she gave me both.' He pulled out a card and held it up for her to see. 'Stoop was wrong on one point. Brothers don't always have the same blood type. It depends on their parents' blood mix.'

He pointed to the relevant line on the card. Her husband's blood group was AB. 'So when you ran after Stoop and hit him with … ?'

'The shovel,' she said and walked past him out of the shed.

He called after her. 'You didn't need to kill Stoop. No one would ever have known the truth.'

The dog was lying in the doorway. It scampered out from under her feet.

Barlow and the dog followed her towards the house. 'Where are you going?'

Without turning she said, 'I need a bath first.'

'Before you slash your wrists with the billhook?'

She wouldn't let him take her hand. He put an arm out to block her from going in the front door.

He said, 'There are worse things than hospital.'

'Please don't stop me.'

CHAPTER 73

BARLOW DIDN'T WANT TO ARGUE with Alexandra; he needed to keep her calm while he summoned help. Even so, he hesitated. Entering the house seemed some sort of final step. Thought it best to comply with her wishes as long as he could.

They went into the house. She remained standing in the small hallway. He went ahead and stationed himself at the cutlery drawer. *God alone knows what cutthroats she has in the bathroom.* He would tackle her on the stairs if necessary.

'I'll call to see you at least once a week,' he said. 'And I'll keep things right on the farm until they say you're better.'

The lie came easy. The Controller in the Court Funds Office would sell everything. Put the proceeds in government stocks. There would be no farm for her to return to. *If they ever let her out.*

'I'll phone now,' he said and stepped towards the phone. Drawer or stairs, he could be at either before her.

He had to look away to see exactly where the phone was. The phone clicked as he lifted the receiver to his ear. There was a second click. Alexandra had produced an M1 carbine from behind the hall-stand. She held it under her arm, pointing it straight at him.

'It's too late for that,' he said.

But it wasn't. He'd come on his own and he hadn't told anyone his suspicions. He needed to wipe at the moisture gathering on his lips, but didn't dare. She'd recognise it as a sign of nervousness.

Her eyes burned. He had to keep her talking. 'So the Americans gave you more than a few groceries?'

'It was surprising what they'd do for a bite of home cooking.'

So what did she intend to do? Kill him and pretend he'd come to kill her and she'd fought back? They'd just had sex. Maybe she'd claim rape? Maybe that had been her plan out there in the shed? And there was always the possibility that she'd get away with it. She was mad enough to try. Especially as he'd left his revolver with Edward. Not that he fancied his chances. Her aim was steady, no uncertainty there.

'I'll ring the ambulance service. They'll take you straight to the hospital,' he said, trying to keep the tightness in his chest out of his voice. He started to dial the police station's number. Hopefully, someone with brains would answer. The Bakelite telephone shattered, the receiver whipped out of his hand. Smoke curled out of the rifle barrel, his ears hurt from the noise. *Bloody hell!*

She brought the M1 up to her shoulder. 'The Americans said I was a good pupil.'

The slightest squeeze of the trigger and he'd be gone. *Would Vera cope?* He supposed there were prayers he should say. He had to keep her talking. 'You made two mistakes on that first day. If I didn't know you so well I wouldn't have noticed.'

'Only the pony,' she said. 'I used him to get Stoop's body back onto his land. When that young fool started to shoot the cattle, I panicked and ran.'

'Leaving the pony in the field was one,' he said. 'The pony roared like a bull because you left him out in the rain. I heard him when I was on the River Road.'

She didn't say anything about rushing back to the house and putting on fresh clothes, though he waited for her to say it. Or of making herself busy baking in case the police came. Which they had done. Nothing was out on the cooling racks when he arrived. That meant she'd only started to bake and hadn't been at it all afternoon, as she'd tried to imply. Which was why she hadn't offered him anything to eat. Not noticing something as obvious as that was bad. *Made a man think of retiring*, if he got the chance.

The table was between them. To tackle her he'd need a clear run. He moved around the table, talking at the same time to try and distract her. 'That cut barbed wire was also a mistake. Stoop wouldn't have worried where he cut just so long as his cattle got through. You cut it where, with a bit of straining, you could re-staple it to the post.

He was around the other side of the table now, her aim still centred on his head. The dog lay in the doorway, muzzle buried between its paws. *Good,* he thought, relieved. There was always the danger that the brute would take her part. Savage him if he tried to disarm Alexandra.

She said, 'Don't you see, I have to kill you? It's the only way I can hold on to the farm.'

'I thought you were going to kill yourself?'

'I don't have to now that you're here.'

If only he'd waited another five minutes before coming. Now, he'd be blamed for the killings. Rape at least. What would Vera think?

His body tightened in anticipation of a bullet smashing into his chest. He needed a distraction to give himself a chance of tackling her. Or worse, a sign that she was about to fire. Then he'd have nothing to lose.

He heard a tractor roaring down the road at full throttle and glanced out the window. Over the hedge he saw Geordie driving and Edward and Adenauer standing on the back axle. They'd recognised the sound of an M1, and were riding to the rescue.

Alexandra heard them as well. She looked out the doorway. The tractor tyres screeched as it turned into the laneway. Barlow took his chance and dived for her knees. She fired. The bullet burred past his neck setting up a shockwave of heat. His damaged arm caught the door jam. He found himself lying on the floor, the good arm trapped under his chest, the bad arm hanging useless.

He felt too much pain to worry about death. *Had she ever loved him?* That seemed really important.

She pointed the M1 at him, stepped back to get a better angle and tripped over the dog as she fired. His whole body kicked. At least his good arm was now free. He struggled back onto his feet. His left leg wouldn't work. There was a tear in his trousers. Blood seeped along the floor. From the leg, he thought, not the arm. That was a relief, not bleeding to death while he waited for her to kill him.

Instead of shooting, she stepped into the yard, the M1 swinging between him and the men on the tractor. The tractor engine died to a quiet idle. Barlow hung onto the half door for balance. The three men had taken cover behind the tractor wheels. Three of them, two shots left out of a five-shot load. He had to give at least two of them a chance of life.

He made the left leg support him for one step out into the yard. Pressed down on the knee to stop it from buckling. The rifle swung his way. He took a second step and stopped with the muzzle boring into his chest, right above his heart. 'Shoot. My heart's broken anyway.'

She looked so calm, the lines around her mouth deepened into a gentle smile. Whatever she was going to do, she was going to do, and there was no way he could stop her. He didn't know if he wanted to, the farm was too important to her to want to live without it. 'Please don't do anything stupid.' He felt hot tears on his cheeks. 'Please.'

'I didn't want to love you,' she said, the M1 still steady in her hands.

She eased the M1 away from his chest and backed across the yard. He watched her as she left the yard and went through the gate and slowly walked up the field towards the fairy thorn. Her path took her into the rays of the setting sun, a black figure moving into a great brightness. Did she turn once and look back at him? *Couldn't be sure.* Hoped so as he dragged himself back into the kitchen and sat in the armchair. The dog jumped into his lap. It was shivering.

He tried not to hear that final shot.

CHAPTER 74

IT WAS LATE WHEN GILLESPIE dropped Barlow off at his house. He had to help him out of the car and hold him up while he found his balance on the pavement.

Did he hear Gillespie mutter, "Fat, useless fool"? Thought he had because Gillespie was still narked. He'd risked a broken nose for nothing. Denholm Moncrief and his father had walked, free of all charges.

WPC Day, *bless her*, had kept him up to date on the gossip. Harvey had withdrawn his application to join the Masonic Hall rather than risk being blackballed by half the members. Was there a chance he might force the Masonic Hall to hold their next AGM in Crumlin Road Prison? A nice thought to hold on to.

Edward and Geordie had left as soon as the ambulance arrived. They were supposed to run Adenauer back to the asylum. They would, eventually, but they had to pass the Bridge Bar on the way. *About now*, closing time, he reckoned.

Heavy painkillers kept his head floating above most of the pain. "Barely more than a flesh wound," the hospital told him. He refused to stay and they didn't want to keep him.

At least he could use a cane to help himself along. The bullet wound was on the same side as the stabbed arm. Two painful steps took him to his front door. Flickering light showed through the window – Vera had the television on. All the other houses were in darkness; *work comes early*.

He pushed the door open. Kenny sat in his chair. Vera was sitting on Kenny's lap, curled into his neck. Both were fast asleep. It seemed a million years since he and Maggie had been like that.

Kenny's hand was under Vera's skirt. Not too far above the knee, *but far enough.*

He cleared his throat and the young couple startled awake. They shot apart.

Vera smoothed down her skirt and ran to him. 'Da, I was so worried.'

Her hug nearly knocked him off his feet. The wall saved him. He couldn't hold back the gasp as pain sizzled up and down his leg.

'Oh, Da. Sorry, Da.'

She helped him to his chair. He kept his arm around her, holding her to him. Tears had dried on her cheeks and on the tips of hair tumbling over her face. 'That old bitch, she could have killed you.'

What can I say to defend Alexandra? Vera would always believe that she'd led him on. That pretending to love him was only a ploy on her part.

Finally, Vera noticed the dog. It had slipped out of the car and into the house. It lay curled in under his legs. 'Where did that come from?'

He said, 'You should have heard them in the hospital. It won't leave me.'

She bent down and patted it. He thought it might snap. It licked her hand.

'What's its name?' she asked.

'Dog,' he said.

'Toby,' she called to it and it flicked its tail.

Kenny kept well back from Toby. He straightened his clothes self-consciously. 'I'd better be going now.'

Barlow said, 'I'll not make the stairs for a couple of days. Would you give Vera a hand to bring down the single mattress?'

He gave Vera's arm a squeeze. 'You don't mind sleeping in the double bed?'

'Of course not.'

She and Kenny disappeared up the stairs. The words "mattress" and "double" seemed to float before them.

He sat back in the chair and worked his leg into a more comfortable position. It meant pushing the dog across the linoleum, out of the way. It gave a soft growl, *dare you,* and rested its head on the arch of his foot.

From above came the creak of floorboards, and grunts of effort from Kenny as he struggled with the mattress. The sounds stopped for a moment, followed by a "don't, he'll hear" from Vera, then a nervous giggle. *Maybe WPC Day would talk to her about precautions.* Vera made life, with all its bumps and bangs, worthwhile. Gave a man a sense of belonging, of achievement.

The day and its happenings filled his head in a confusion of thoughts. It would never have worked for him and Alexandra. Not long term. The hurt in Vera's eyes would have drawn him back and he had promised to stick by Maggie through good and bad.

Impatient taps sounded on the door, then the window, then the door again. *Fecking hell!* If somebody had killed Harvey he'd go back and prove justifiable homicide, *other than that …*

He heaved himself to his feet, dragged his bad leg to the door and opened it. Edward stood there. Even in the poor lighting he could see that Edward was white-faced and shaking.

Edward grasped the wall. It seemed to give him comfort. 'Grace is coming.'

'Have you got the DTs again?'

Edward held up an envelope. Barlow snatched it out of the air as he dropped it.

'Grace is coming,' repeated Edward.

'So's salvation,' he said, having a good look at the envelope. It had an Australian stamp.

Edward continued to grasp the wall. 'She's talking about coming home for a visit.'

'What, your sister? Hoity-toity Lady Muck, too-good-for-the-likes-of-you, Grace?'

Edward's nose compressed in indignation. 'The Honourable Grace Alexandra Elizabeth Montmercy, née Adair.'

'And how does she think you've been living?'

'Directorships, the family trust.'

'She's going to kill you,' said Barlow.

He made his sigh one of real bother. Hauled Edward into the house and dumped him in a chair before the range. Shouted at Vera to put the kettle on.

ACKNOWLEDGEMENTS

THE JOHN BARLOW IN MY book is based on a real-life policeman of the same name. In my youth, story after story about the "doings" of Barlow were whispered around my home town of Ballymena. He was sly, he was cute, he was sleekit and, according to rumour, had blackmailed the District Inspector to get staying on in Ballymena when the man wanted him posted. Mention Barlow to one of my brothers-in-law, and his blood pressure shoots up. Yet an old friend, Harry McLarnon, says, 'John Barlow, now there was a great man.'

Five "Barlow" stories were written as part of my submission for an M.Phil. in Creative Writing from Trinity College, Dublin. One friend, Kevin Hart, who shapes a cross with his fingers to ward off evil if I even mention the RUC, kept nagging at me for another Barlow story. A minor theme in the new story suddenly gripped me and *The Station Sergeant* was born.

I kept John Barlow's real name in my stories and book, to celebrate and keep alive the memory of a man who strode Ballymena like a colossus. In real life, John Barlow was a mere constable but I have accorded him the long-delayed accolade of Station Sergeant.

In those days, every town had their own Barlow and I have used the inspiration of the lives and careers of some of these men: Sergeant Mick Campbell of Ballymoney, Sergeant Harry McBride of Armagh, Constable Bob Corrigan of Keady and Sergeant Joe Campbell of Cushendall (killed in the line of duty).

Before Ballymena people start to shout 'Foul!', the Ballymena I depict is the Ballymena I remember as a child, with a lot of changes to suit the story. Mill Row, which ran up the side of McCann's pub on the Galgorm Road, is now somewhere around Mount Street. Curles Bridge on the Broughshane Road replaces the Penny Bridge. The original Adair Castle Demesne is now located somewhere to the west of the new Municipal Cemetery and River Road exists under another name. However, Ballymena never had a dedicated psychiatric unit. That was in Antrim town. We thought the people there had more need for it.

Also, for the sake of clarity for the younger readers, I have given the modern equivalents of policing terms that were current then: Police Station for Police Barracks; Enquiry Office for Barracks Room; Chief Constable for Inspector General, and so on ...

I would like to thank Kevin Hart for his nagging, and the following people who played a part in bringing the book to completion: Novelist Sam Millar who critiqued my first draft and put me on the right road; Dr Stella Hughes for willingly giving of her expertise in medical knowledge; the Writers-in-Residence and the members of the Wednesday Group at the Seamus Heaney Centre, Queen's University, Belfast, for their 'friendly fire' critiques; and Neil of the PSNI Museum for willingly answering my questions; Glenn Meade, Bill McGinn, Dr S and Mrs C Day, Bob Corrigan, Callum Gibson, Emily DeDakis, and Sammy Gillespie (letter of indemnity for the use of your name lodged with solicitor); Andrew Mangan and Arlene Hunt of Portnoy Publishing for their professionalism and support, and Brenda O'Hanlon for doing such a fantastic job of editing my book.

Finally, a big thanks to my understanding and supportive family and, in particular, to my wife, Patricia, and our children,

Lucie and Daniel. And a special mention of my 'mate', our late pug, Barnaby. Sometimes he lay on my feet to keep them warm. Sometimes, I had to sit with my legs cramped under the chair, my arms at full stretch to reach the keyboard.